A FRENCH DECEPTION THRILLER

A Forgery in Paris

JANICE NAGOURNEY

CASTLE BRIDGE MEDIA
DENVER, COLORADO, USA

CASTLE BRIDGE MEDIA
Denver, Colorado

Cover art by Digital Asset Art/Shutterstock

FRENCH DECEPTION: A FORGERY IN PARIS

ISBN: 979-8-9872083-0-4

One meteorologist remarked that if the theory was correct, one flap of a seagull's wings would be enough to alter the course of the weather forever. The controversy has not yet been settled, but the most recent evidence seems to favor the seagulls. (1)[1]

1 Lorenz, Edward N. (1963). "The Predictability of Hydrodynamic Flow" (PDF). *Transactions of the New York Academy of Sciences* 25 (4): 409–432. Retrieved 1 September 2014. Following suggestions from colleagues, in later speeches and papers Lorenz used the more poetic butterfly

Prologue

THE MISTRAL HAS BEEN BLOWING for two days. Howling, whining, rattling the shutters, whipping plastic bags into the trees, depositing a fine layer of dust everywhere. Usually, the wind ends after three days, so by tomorrow morning, there will be the welcome sound of silence.

Last night I was curled up on the living room sofa, reading a history of Marseilles, imagining the wonder that the ancient Greeks must have felt when they first saw the calanques: the rugged, majestic limestone cliffs, like white lava frozen as it plunges into the sea. It's early autumn, the days are still warm, but there's a chill in the air at night and I had a blue and white fouta towel covering my legs. I thought I heard a noise. Not the mistral, but more like someone knocking at the door on the terrace overlooking the sea. The louvres were closed against the wind and I was afraid to open them to see who might be there. I went upstairs and cracked open a shutter but I saw no one. Had they gone away or had they gone around to the back of the house? I looked out a rear window that gives onto a narrow street. It was deserted. No footsteps, no moving shadows. There are houses along the street, lined up cheek to cheek, but most are closed up now that the summer is over. I'm used to being alone, yet the silence in the house is like a chill cloud, and I wrapped the fouta tightly around my shoulders.

Perhaps I only imagined that I heard someone knocking. I know it couldn't have been Jacques or Bruno, and yet nothing would surprise me any longer. I wish Eugene were here. He would know what to do.

It's daybreak and the wind has subsided. The gentle sunlight bathes the trees and the water in a soft glow. How silly I was to be uneasy last night. I make a pot of coffee and take my mug out to the terrace. A cool breeze comes off the sea, and even before I see them, I hear the seagulls. Their squawks sound like the barking of dogs or cats meowing. Are they arguing or discussing today's weather? Vaguely menacing, intently picking through the open garbage bins, making graceful arcs through the sky.

The noise is a reminder of how many random events led to my being here, with the sea right at my front door—it can be deep sapphire or pale aquamarine or slate grey. The sky is every color blue, it is white, it is grey. I sip my coffee and stare out at the four islands of the Frioul Archipelago, stretching like brown beads along the horizon.

There's a little beach below my house. It gets the sun in the morning, so that's when I climb down to swim. Outside of July and August, the beach is empty. When I go down there today, I'll be on the lookout for any boats that come close to the inlet that's cordoned off for swimmers. The scar on my shoulder reminds me to beware.

Was it the flaps of the seagull's wings that brought me here? If I think about it—as I've often done—there is one event, one metaphorical flap of the wings, which started me on the trajectory that brought me to this house.

In the middle of 2008, the month of August, I flew up to New York to see the lawyer handling my parents' estate. They had died within two months of each other the previous year and I had to sign some papers. Sitting in the lawyer's office, the thought crossed my mind that the only family I had now was in France, but I pushed that thought back down and managed not to tear up. I planned to spend the night in the city with a college girlfriend, but we finished early and I decided to take the train back to DC.

By the time I got home, it was almost midnight. The light was on in the living room and I felt a moment of irritation that Peter had forgotten to turn the lights off, but that was how I came to notice a woman's coat lying on the sofa. What the fuck? My stomach clenched, and I felt my heart thumping. The fatigue of the trip and thinking about my parents jumbled my thoughts—I hadn't quite connected the dots until I climbed the stairs and walked into our bedroom and turned on the light (he had remembered to turn that one off), to find Peter in bed with one of the women who worked for his advertising agency.

For a moment, all the breath had been sucked out of my lungs. A hot flush spread from my back to my neck and my face.

Peter actually said, "It's not what you think, Alex."

The woman in bed with him—I later learned that her name was Susanne Higgins—pulled the sheets up to her chin and sat there, frozen. My breath returned. I pulled my cell phone out of my coat pocket and took a few pictures.

I looked at the woman. "You have five minutes to get out of my house before I throw you out." Then to Peter, "You had better leave as well."

Susanne left; Peter went to sleep in the den. I stripped the bed and stretched out fully clothed on the bedspread. I didn't get much sleep, but I had plenty of time to think. Once the initial shock had worn off, I realized that I didn't love Peter anymore and had not for some time. I'd always had a weakness for bad boys—intelligent men but with a dangerous edge, mysterious possibilities smoldering behind their eyes, short bursts of passion before the flame died—until I met Peter. No bad boy he, and I thought I'd be safe marrying him. But we were both so busy with our careers—mine in fashion, his in advertising—that we lived our lives on two parallel paths, never intersecting.

Now that I think about it, I wonder if I ever loved Peter at all. Maybe it was more the idea of being married to him that I loved. In any event, we had an amicable divorce and I got our house in Georgetown. Today, I can hardly remember what he looked like back then. Okay, tall, dark hair, even features, not gorgeous, but nice-looking enough. I ran into him when I was passing through DC a few months ago. He had more grey hair and he looked tired.

Anyway, that was my seagull's wing-flap moment. It was time to change, to do something completely different. I had spent my childhood in France, and I wanted to return to that country. Immediately.

Of course I started in Paris—doesn't everyone?—and then I went to our château at Trubenne. Château is a grand word for what those old stones looked like on my first visit. Only a few rooms were heated, the plumbing was rudimentary, but of course, it didn't matter because of Charlotte.

Random events—more wings flapping—took me to other cities: Lyon, Marseilles, and Toulouse. And then it all came to a head in Montenegro.

Looking back on everything that has happened, I realize that random events is not a correct description. Rather, as you will see, they are all inextricably connected, and things had to take place as they did.

I've written my story in the third person, as it's not just about me. In fact, my story does not begin with me; it begins with a forgery. Sometimes I've had to use my imagination to fill in certain blanks, but as I know how things turned out, I'm pretty sure that I'm not too far off the mark.

A lone seagull stands on the rocks. I savor the present moment as it spreads its wings and floats upward, high over the brilliant blue sea.

Alexia Chase Thornhill
Malmousque, Marseilles

Chapter 1

September 2009, Alexandria, Virginia

"I'M SORRY TO TELL YOU, but your painting is a fake."

Kate Spector listened as the art detective described the results of the tests their laboratory had done, his tone of voice reminding her of a doctor delivering a terminal illness diagnosis. Until now she had allowed herself to hope that the insurance company expert had been mistaken. But now she had confirmation that he'd been right to doubt that her painting was a genuine Poussin.

When the art detective finished his explanation, Kate felt weak with disappointment. She could only say, "Thank you. I imagine that you'll return the painting to me." And yesterday, after the tableau had been delivered, Kate hung it back in its place.

This morning she stared at her reflection in the mirror and frowned. She had piled her wispy blond hair into a topknot, but her bangs hung over her pale green eyes like a frayed curtain, giving her an unfinished look. She tried to remember what it was like to look beautiful, but that was a long time ago, and she gave it up.

As she walked into the living room, her gaze fell on the small painting hanging over the buffet—a more serious cause for concern than her unruly hair. It was a landscape depicting peasant women on a riverbank, pulling to safety a reed basket containing a baby Moses. Kate's aunt, Madeleine, had bequeathed the painting to her, after her death a few months ago. *Baby Moses in the River, Nicolas Poussin,* read the small bronze plaque at the bottom of the frame.

Kate had thought it best to insure the painting, but when the expert had come to appraise it, she had an unpleasant surprise. When he told her that her painting was not a Poussin—"It's a good copy, but still, a copy"—Kate bit her lip so hard that she drew blood. She grimaced as she replied, "That's not possible. My aunt bought it from a very reputable dealer in France. How can you be so sure?"

"There's something off in the position of the figures. They lack a certain fluidity. I can feel that this is not a genuine Poussin. How much did your aunt pay for this painting?"

Kate felt that she was taking a test and failing. She started to play with a lock of hair that had escaped from her topknot, winding it around her finger. "Around four million dollars, I think. I need to check my records to be sure."

"I would say that your aunt paid far too much, or not enough. Do you realize that if it were a true Poussin, it could be hanging in a museum?"

The expert wore a dark suit, and Kate noticed a few flakes of dandruff on his shoulders. She felt an urge to brush his shoulders clean; she pursed her lips instead. "But how can you be sure that your feeling is correct? That seems subjective to me." She sounded annoyed, but the expert didn't mind—this wasn't the first time he'd disappointed a client.

"Yes, I agree with you. But why don't you take the painting to a laboratory and have them run their tests? It would certainly be worth it if you've got an original, even though I doubt it."

After the art detectives had delivered the painting, Kate waited a few days before reading their report. When she finally did, her throat tightened as she thought about how Madeleine had been cheated—it all seemed so unfair. Then another thought crossed her mind—it had been lurking just under the surface ever since the expert's visit—*I need to call Eugene.*

When Kate's younger brother, Eugene, was in the right mood, he would listen to her, calm her down, soothe her nerves, and in the end, whatever problem she was agonizing over lost much of its importance. She was sure Eugene would know what to do.

"Hi, Kate, I'm tied up right now. Call you back in a few minutes." He hung up before she had a chance to open her mouth. Ten minutes later, her phone rang. She heard the crunch of potato chips. "Sorry I couldn't talk, but I had to finish my crossword puzzle. Thursday's a bitch. It took me fifteen minutes."

Kate swallowed a sigh. That was so typical of Eugene, but there was no point in questioning his priorities. "I have a problem," she said, tears welling up in her eyes.

"Oh…" Eugene waited for her to continue.

"You know the painting that Aunt Madeleine left me, the Poussin? It's not a Poussin at all. I've just received a report from some art detectives, and it's a forgery," she sniffled.

"That sucks."

Kate stared at the fake Poussin as she paced back and forth in the living room. "I think we should do something about that."

"Uh, what did you have in mind that *we* should do?"

Kate's voice rose, the fingers of her free hand scratching the back of her head: "I want to find the person who sold that painting to Aunt Madeleine and make them take the painting back and refund the money she paid. After all your work at the FBI, you ought to know what to do."

"First of all, I spent my time chasing drug dealers and other lowlifes, not people selling phony paintings. That wasn't one of our priorities. Second, I wouldn't know where to begin."

"I know where we could begin. I found some documents pertaining to the sale of the painting. Wouldn't you take a look at them? Apparently Madeleine bought the painting from a dealer in France, and since you told me you were going to France…" She waited. She'd stopped walking in circles and was now staring out the window at a post office delivery truck.

For a few moments, Eugene didn't speak. All Kate could hear was the sound of him munching on his chips. "Look, my landlord sold the apartment that I'm renting and I have to move out. I need to pack up my stuff and find a temporary place to live until I figure out what I'm going to do with the rest of my life. So the timing is maybe not ideal."

Kate had anticipated Eugene's reluctance—she adored her brother, even if he did have a selfish streak—and fired her silver bullet. "The reason that you've been able to take time off from your job is because Aunt Madeleine left us all her money. So don't you think you owe it to her to put things right? You can always get on with your life after that."

#   #   #

Eugene's decision to take a leave of absence from the FBI had not been easy. He enjoyed the challenge of going undercover and had the satisfaction of knowing that his work was useful to society. Sometimes he took risks without getting approval from his supervisors, and even if things worked out well, it was made clear to him that he had to go by the rules. The bureau was an unwieldy bureaucracy, where surviving to retire and collect a pension was the overriding goal for many of the agents.

The FBI had not been Eugene's first taste of dealing with a massive bureaucratic structure. By the time he reached the rank of major in the Marine Corps, he realized that further advancement was political, and he was unskilled in playing that game. He thought that being an FBI agent on the ground would be a better fit, but he was mistaken. His inheritance came at a time when he was wondering how much longer he could stand to navigate the jungle of rules and regulations.

Kate was right, he owed it to Madeleine to try to track down the person who had cheated her. But first there was the question of finding a place to live. He knew he could stay with his sister, but he didn't consider that an option. It had nothing to do with Kate — he loved his sister — but it had everything to do with not wanting to be stuck in the suburbs, where you needed to get into your car to buy a loaf of bread, or anything else for that matter.

He'd already decided that he'd start his time away from the bureau by visiting friends in France. How long would he be abroad for? Eugene couldn't say. But by the time he finished the bag of garlic-flavored potato chips, he had decided that he wanted a place of his own to come home to, whenever that might be.

Kate agreed to help him with his search in Washington, DC. Eugene convinced her to pretend to be his wife—he was sure that people would be more likely to rent to a married couple. He even insisted that she get her hair done and dress like a mid-level DC administrator. They visited several rental houses, and the one in Georgetown was perfect. He signed a six-month lease and asked Kate to stay at the house as often as she could, to maintain the illusion that it was inhabited.

Eugene had told Kate that he was taking a leave of absence from the bureau, but it was not yet a done deed. The assistant director agreed in principle for Eugene to take six months off, but he had still not given his final sign-off.

More bureaucratic bullshit, thought Eugene as he took the elevator up to the offices in a building on Sixth Street. This place was more discreet than the nearby field office, but it still had the green carpet and beige walls omnipresent in government offices. Pascal Navarro, the assistant director, had Eugene's file open on his desk.

"I see you're planning a trip to France?"

"Yeah, I haven't been back since I spent a year there as a student."

As he watched Pascal pretend to read the page in front of him, Eugene suspected that there was a hitch in getting his request approved.

"Any special plans, Gene?"

Eugene hated to be called Gene, and Pascal knew it. *Why is he trying to get under my skin?*

"Nope, nothing special. Just the usual. Eating great meals, drinking great wine, visiting chateaux… Why do you ask?"

"One of the resident agents has completed her mission, and there's been a screw-up in naming her replacement. So as long as you're going to be in France on your holiday—I mean, your leave of absence—we'd appreciate you stopping by the embassy, just in an advisory capacity."

I knew it. These bastards can't resist. "Okay, Pascal, let's cut the bullshit. You're asking me to work while I'm supposed to be on a leave of absence. Why me? Can't the staff cover until you sort out the screw-up?"

"It's really not work, Gene. More like touching base with Vince Reiner—

he's the DCM—from time to time." Pascal paused before adding: "I'd greatly appreciate you stepping up to the plate."

Eugene crossed his arms over his chest, leaned back in his uncomfortable chair. Was he ready to leave the bureau entirely? Not certain. He still wanted to keep his options open.

"Okay, I'll do it on one condition. Since I'm officially on leave, I shouldn't have to file reports, do paperwork, right? What do you say?"

Pascal judged Eugene to be an excellent operative, despite being a bit of a maverick when it came to following rules and regulations. He had anticipated his reaction and was prepared to let him have his way unless things got messy.

"Okay, I'll sign off on your leave. Remember to check in with the embassy once you're over your jet lag."

The office was spacious and Eugene had covered half the distance to the door when the assistant director called out to him. "Oh, yeah, they'd like to see you upstairs before you leave. Better do it now."

Chapter 2

November 2009, Georgetown, Washington, DC

ALEXIA CHASE THORNHILL WAITED FOR her future tenants to arrive. Wearing a long pleated skirt and top in a brilliant blue that matched her eyes, she checked her reflection in the hallway mirror. *Plenty of pleats will never go out of style.* Then she immediately wondered, not for the first time, whether renting out her house was a good idea.

"Well," said one of her friends, "at least you'll have someone there to make sure that the pipes don't burst and to give the place a lived-in look to discourage potential thieves."

"Yes," said Alex, but what if they gave it too much of a lived-in look?

In fact, Eugene and Kate Spector seemed to be ideal. No children, no pets, and Alex found them quite dull and lacking the imagination to make unwanted changes to her home. They must have come straight from work, their plastic ID badges still hanging from their necks.

Alex greeted them at the door. Eugene had a buzz cut and wore a white shirt with a tie that was too wide. Kate wore a formless grey suit that was the uniform of DC mid-level administrators. But what struck Alex as they shook hands was the peculiar odor that emanated from Eugene—not precisely bad

14

breath, perhaps more like the smell of someone who has eaten a lot of garlic, the scent exuded by all of the body's pores. *How can Kate stand to sleep with him? Well, that's not my problem.*

The Spectors followed Alex down the stairs to the dining room on the lower level. They sat at a round teak table and went over final arrangements. Alex handed them a memo with contact information for any eventualities, a schedule of garbage pickup days, and a reminder that her cleaning lady would continue to come once a week. She had already rented an apartment in Paris, and she left them with that information as well.

"Paris?" asked Kate. She turned to her brother. "Eugene's going to be in France on business."

Eugene leaned back in his chair and crossed his arms on his chest. "Yeah, that's right."

"What a coincidence," said Alex.

There was an awkward silence until Alex got up, went into the kitchen, and came back with a bottle of champagne in an ice bucket. "Here, why don't I help you with that?" asked Eugene and he cracked open the bottle. They stood around the table, drank a toast to new adventures in new surroundings, the Spectors departed, and Alex was left to finish packing.

She sat at the dining room table, staring at the champagne bubbles mounting to the surface of her glass, her mind blank. Her gaze moved to the back windows giving out onto the garden. With the approach of winter, it was mostly brown with some dark green. She held her thoughts at bay, enjoying the moment of peace. And then the dam burst and images from her childhood, her career, marriage, and divorce sped by, separate and together at the same time. Another sip of champagne and the film stopped.

Alex had spent years as a fashion stylist, dressing women with no sense of their style, or no time to discover it. But recently she had tired of using her imagination to find the right belt, the next shoe, the newest "it" bag. She was fed up with coping with the insecurities of her wealthy clients. She felt bored and stale, doing the same thing, seeing the same people. Divorced and childless, she longed to return to France, where she had spent her childhood. The thought of walking away from it all for six months or more, creating a space for the unknown to flourish, thrilled her. She said a quiet prayer... *Let me start over; let me have a new beginning.*

Chapter 3

ALEX HAD ARRIVED AT DULLES Airport before her flight, opting for a chic, casual style — well-fitting jeans, a crisp white shirt, flats, and a soft black leather jacket. She felt so comfortable, so right. Sitting in the empty waiting lounge, she enjoyed watching the other travelers, embroidering their images with brightly colored threads of stories, begun and finished midstream.

A group of French students came in, returning home after having spent the All Saints holiday in Washington. Wearing headsets or earbuds, they were, she thought, like a pack of visitors from another world — traveling together, isolated from each other by their smartphones, yet all connected to a digital universe that controlled their behavior, limiting their interactions to one hundred and forty characters. *Do you forget how to think more complex thoughts?* Next there came the families — noisy Italians, anxious French, cool Scandinavians, and her favorites, the Japanese, always quiet, always polite, no matter their numbers.

But Alex was traveling business class — she planned on starting her new life of adventure once in France — so she would not be bothered by loud conversations, whining children, couples complaining about separate seating and the lack of space in coach class. She would enjoy the attentions of the cabin crew, relax, and even get some sleep. And first, a nice glass of champagne. She smiled at the man sitting next to her, and he raised his glass.

"Bon voyage, madame."

"Cheers," replied Alex.

"Ah, I see you are American. You are going to France on holiday perhaps?" She searched her mind. *Who am I going to be?*

"Not really. I'm on sabbatical, and I'm going to spend a year living in Paris and writing a book. And I shall look for work as a translator as I speak several languages." *Whatever made me say that?*

"How very interesting. One of my businesses is a magazine that we publish in English and French, and you could perhaps help us from time to time. Please get in touch with me when you are looking for some work," and he handed her his card.

The man's name — Jacques Mornnais — was printed on one side of the card. He could be anyone from anyplace, middle-aged, medium height and build, his sandy hair unruly and thin. But the skin on his round face was smooth, and she wondered if he could have had a face-lift.

"*Merci, monsieur*, how kind," said Alex as she put the card in her travel tote. She hadn't bothered to look at the other side of the card, where the name *ARTIXIA* was printed in bold black lettering.

Chapter 4

Boulevard Bessières, Paris, 1982

GROUPS OF STUDENTS CONGREGATED OUTSIDE the Lycée Honoré de Balzac on Boulevard Bessières. Not the best of neighborhoods, at nightfall the street was home to prostitutes and drug dealers, and it was not much better during the day. Jean-Charles Molina lived on one of the side streets behind the boulevard. His mother was a concierge in the building. His father had worked in the construction trades but was now pensioned off, his body damaged beyond repair by years of backbreaking work. Jean-Charles was a quiet and studious boy, and while not a genius, he was quite brilliant in math, which was all one needed to succeed in the French school system. Solving problems, understanding relationships, these things came to him very easily.

Jean-Charles made his way slowly across the boulevard. He nodded to one of the boys in the group, and together they stood apart from the crowd. The other boy — Hugo — towered above his slightly built friend. They quickly went over today's math test. Hugo would take his place in class directly behind Jean-Charles, who would allow him to copy some of his examination answers. Not all, for it would be apparent to the teacher that Hugo was incapable of answering the harder questions. He had tried to tutor

Hugo, help him with his homework, but it amazed him how Hugo just didn't seem to get it. Or perhaps he didn't care. He was the son of a prosperous factory owner, and his future path was laid out for him.

Being the brightest kid in the class could be a drawback in some schools. In return for Jean-Charles' help, Hugo would on occasion see to it that no one bothered Jean-Charles. There was a group of foreign-exchange students: two Germans, an Italian, a Swiss, and an American. Once, the American stepped in when two older boys started kicking Jean-Charles' backpack around the schoolyard.

But Jean-Charles was mostly left in peace, allowed to tag along to cafés, even though he was never really a part of any group. He accepted this situation, as he had other plans.

After finishing the lycée, he went first to law school, where he was most interested in company law and criminal law, graduating near the top of his class. He then went on to the elite "Sciences Po," (the Institute of Political Science), where he majored in finance and strategy.

His studies completed, he went to work for one of the big global consulting firms. And as he worked on international projects and carefully avoided becoming ensnared in office politics, an opportunity presented itself. A Russian businessman, Sergei Vladimirovich Smirnov, approached the firm, seeking their help in structuring a deal. The partners deliberated, found him to be lacking sufficient gravitas, and declined to take him on as a client.

The time had come for Jean-Charles to take his next steps. It had always annoyed him that his parents had chosen to call him Jean-Charles. Such a pretentious bourgeois name just didn't go with his Portuguese family name. He needed a more neutral surname, one that was apparently of French heritage. Jacques Chirac, Jacques Attali, Jacques Delors, yes, Jacques sounded right to him. And Mornnais suggested a vague connection to the de Mornays, an old aristocratic French family. He would keep the initials JM, but he would close the chapter on Jean-Charles Molina.

It was not difficult to find someone to change his name on his academic records, and he sent off an email to Mr. Smirnov, saying he was an independent consultant who had heard that he might be looking for someone with Jacques' qualifications. A trip to Moscow, and Jean-Charles, now Jacques, found himself, courtesy of Sergei Vladimirovich Smirnov, at the center of the rape of the Russian economy. He profited handsomely in the early 1990s and got out in time.

Before he left Russia, he had visited a business acquaintance in Kyiv. He introduced Jacques to one of his friends, the director of a regional museum, who had fallen on hard times following the collapse of the Soviet Union. During that chaotic period, he had made some bad bets in the corrupt commodities market, and now his creditors were coming after him, threatening an extra-judicial settlement of their dispute.

"I'd like to help you, but what do you have in mind?" Jacques asked.

The man's idea? While the museum had few visitors, it did have several dozen paintings by seventeenth- and eighteenth-century masters, among them Rubens, Rembrandt, Claude Lorrain, and Jean-Honoré Fragonard. He would transfer the works to Jacques — they would never be missed — in exchange for Jacques' paying off his debts.

"I'll need to be sure that I can get the paintings out of the country before I contact your creditors."

A week later, the paintings — there were thirty-seven — arrived at a storage warehouse in Montenegro. At about the same time, the museum director was found shot in the head. A brief investigation concluded that the wound was self-inflicted and the case was ruled a suicide.

Back in France and flush with money, Jacques could now move ahead with his plan. He looked up Hugo and his lycée classmates, noting where they lived and where they worked. He had intended to punish them for the way they had treated him, but as he considered his options (they ranged from mild financial distress to disfigurement and death — he had been well educated in Russia), he lost interest. It now seemed to him to be a waste of time and energy, resources better put to use creating his niche in the expanding, vibrant world of art.

Jacques saw the art market as a simple case of supply and demand: on the one side, there were collectors, the rich and the super-rich (he knew them well), and on the other, the works of art (here he was at a loss, but willing to learn). Of course, there were intermediaries, the galleries and auction houses and an amorphous group of those positioning themselves as art consultants, and it seemed to him that if he worked at it, there was a place for him in that third group.

He left the paintings in Montenegro untouched. He would use them at the right moment. As a first step to establishing his credibility, he founded *Artixia*, a magazine that showcased the art and lifestyles of the very rich. It had taken several years, but he was now a fixture in the art world. Collectors whose oversized egos matched their oversized wallets sought the exposure that being featured in *Artixia* gave them, subscribing to the notion that there was no bad publicity. As things turned out, this might have been subject to question.

promised to meet again soon. They left the park together, Alex heading to the market on rue de Lévis, and Marie-Agnès continued to a meeting on rue de Prony.

At the market, Alex bought some of her favorite French comfort foods: artisanal *pâté maison*, a slice of creamy mushroom *pâté Forestier*, a ball of moist goat-milk cheese, a baguette, a bottle of red Bordeaux, a croissant filled with almond cream, and some lychees.

There would be a proper trip to the market later, but these purchases would tide her over to the end of the day. As she uncorked the bottle of wine and prepared to sample her small selection of delicacies, happy at the unexpected meeting with Marie-Agnès, she reflected that her trip to Paris had started off on an auspicious note.

#   #   #

Almost every street in Paris has a tale to be told, a snippet of social and economic history. Alex lived sandwiched in between a street named after an aristocratic jurist and politician who had been guillotined along with most of his family (he did defend Louis XVI, after all), and a nineteenth-century pre-Impressionist painter. It was more thrilling than living on Thirtieth Street NW in Georgetown.

As for Marie-Agnès, her destination that day was rue de Prony. It had been laid out in the nineteenth century by an engineer whose name was almost as long as the street — Gaspard Clair François Marie Riche, Baron de Prony. In proximity to Parc Monceau, an address on rue de Prony subtly suggested a connection to an aristocratic past. The private mansion at thirty-six *bis* was particularly lovely: set back from the sidewalk, it had a small balcony on the second floor overlooking a tiny garden framed by a wrought iron fence.

But at the moment, stories of nineteenth-century property development were of no interest to Marie-Agnès. An ad in a free news magazine offered part-time work for English-French interpreters. A woman with a slight East European accent had spoken with her on the phone and asked her to come in for an interview. Marie-Agnès's focus was on getting the assignment that would allow her to continue to indulge her passion for expensive clothing and accessories. *Do I look the part?* A simple black cashmere turtleneck sweater and black trousers, a Max Mara tweed coat, and Bottega Veneta bag had been chosen to project an image of understated elegance.

She rang the buzzer next to the small brass plate *Artixia,* the heavy wooden door opened automatically, and a woman with the whitest platinum-blond hair that Marie-Agnès had ever seen came to greet her.

"Hello, you must be Marie-Agnès? I am Mila Korsikova. Thank you for coming. Please step this way."

Marie-Agnès shook the outstretched hand and smiled as she took in the perfectly manicured nails (the color appeared to be the latest Dior limited-edition Khaki), the high cheekbones, the deep olive-green eyes, and slender, well-toned body. How old was she? Impossible to tell. Mila Korsikova could have been forty-five or sixty-five. She was one of those ageless women one sees on the streets of Paris.

Marie-Agnès suppressed a flash of jealousy mixed with admiration and followed Mila into a small room off the entry. A low table, a few armchairs. Otherwise the room was bare.

The interview went smoothly. Mila explained that *Artixia* published a quarterly magazine devoted to the lifestyles of the ultra-rich. Their team of photographers and stylists visited the homes of those hungry for favorable publicity, giving the reader an exclusive — if antiseptic — glimpse of their homes, their art collections, their wardrobes. Of the hundreds of photos taken, Mila and their president, Jacques Mornnais, would painstakingly sift through the multitude of images, seeking to satisfy the public's curiosity at the same time as respecting the privacy of their subjects.

Subjects or objects, thought Marie-Agnès, but she said nothing.

They needed help translating the articles into English, as *Artixia* was an international publication. And then, Mila added, Jacques understood English, but like so many French of his generation, he was uncomfortable when he had to speak in English. In fact, Jacques spoke English quite well, but he'd always had an interpreter at his side — he felt that it added polish to his image. Thus Marie-Agnès would be asked to assist him in meetings with charities (*Artixia* held itself out as a patron of the arts), as well as consultations with wealthy clients.

Mila smiled. The clients had the money but lacked the knowledge to make the right choice, and they came to Jacques for his help. She asked if Marie-Agnès could be available in the coming days as she set up meetings now that Jacques was returning from a business trip. "So, would you like to give it a try?"

"Yes, I would." Marie-Agnès tried to keep her voice calm, as though this was just another job. But her emotional roller coaster headed for the heights as her mind generated one thought after another. She would be part of the exciting and glamorous world of art. This time she would stick to a diet and lose those twenty extra kilos. She would become friends with Mila and find out how she stayed in shape. Perhaps they would go running together in Parc Monceau.

Marie-Agnes walked back to Parc Monceau to take the Métro. She had decided to go to rue d'Alésia and do a boutique crawl to find a dress to slim down into. It was late afternoon, the children were done with school, and she heard their shrieks of laughter as they played hide-and-seek in the rhododendron bushes in the park. The shouting and giggling reminded her of another afternoon in the same *parc*, many years ago.

#   #   #

Paris, Spring 1979

It had rained for days. Not a deluge, just a continuous stream of water, soaking the ground. Puddles everywhere. When the rain finally stopped, the children came out to frolic in Parc Monceau.

Two little girls played hide-and-seek, running in between the rhododendrons. Shrieks of laughter as the mud sprayed their rainwear, making brown leopard spots on their yellow slickers.

A young woman stood watching them. She had grey eyes and her brown hair was pulled back into a messy ponytail. She would have been pretty had it not been for the frown that was permanently etched on her face. Her name was Elizabeth. She had arrived from Poland some months ago with her much older husband, looking for work. He was a photographer and did freelance jobs when his drinking permitted. Elizabeth didn't have any profession in particular, so she got a job as an au pair. There were two girls in the family, but she only needed to pay attention to the younger one, which was what she was doing now.

"It's time to go, Marie-Agnès."

"Just a little longer. We're having fun."

"No, now."

Elizabeth glared at the two girls as they picked up their backpacks.

"You're filthy, both of you. Are you still little babies?"

The au pair frightened Marie-Agnès and she wondered why her parents had hired such an unpleasant person. Elizabeth grabbed the little girl's arm and twisted it behind her back.

"C'mon, you're going to need a bath, little baby."

"Elizabeth, you're hurting me." Tears and a sniffle. Then Marie-Agnès thought of the snack she'd have when they got home. Eating a *croissant aux amandes* always made her feel good.

"She's not a little baby and you should let go of her arm."

For the first time, the au pair noticed the other little girl. She was taller than Marie-Agnès. Skinnier, too, with long blond hair.

"And who do you think you are?" snapped Elizabeth. She had let go of Marie-Agnès's arm and stepped toward her friend.

The blond girl was not intimidated. She stared at Elizabeth with piercing blue eyes.

"You're a mean person and we're not going with you. Marie-Agnès is coming home with me and I'm going to tell my parents about you and they will tell her parents."

She put her arms around Marie-Agnès and pulled her away from Elizabeth.

"Do you think we should?"

"Of course. Let's go."

"Oh, Alex, you're my best friend forever."

Best friendship could be sweet. Sometimes it was short. At the end of the school year, Marie-Agnès changed schools when her family moved to an apartment on the left bank. The two girls lost touch with each other, but Marie-Agnès always remembered the day Alex had stood up for her in Parc Monceau. Other best friendships were formed, broken, and formed again, with a special place always reserved for *croissants aux amandes*.

\#   \#   \#

Marie-Agnès had found the perfect outfit. It wasn't a dress, but a midnight-blue tuxedo jacket with matching trousers that set off her red hair. The pants were a bit tight, but she would shrink into them. And on her way home, to celebrate, she stopped in a *pâtisserie* and bought one of her favorite layered pastries, a *mille-feuilles*. She would start her diet first thing tomorrow.

\#   \#   \#

Daybreak. Under a thick cover of clouds, the inky-black sky turned to an unrelieved dark grey as the car exited the airport and took the A6 motorway east to Burgundy. Once past the outskirts of Paris, the traffic thinned out, and the Mercedes sped through the monotonous countryside.

"Let's listen to Carmina Burana, shall we?"

"*Oui, monsieur.*"

Jacques raised the footrest, adjusted his seat, and fell asleep at once. Two hours later, as they left the highway and followed the winding secondary roads through *Parc Naturel Régional du Morvan*, his cell phone rang. It was Mila.

"How was your trip?" she asked. "I interviewed the woman for the interpreter position and I told her we'd try her out."

"How is she?"

"Just what we're looking for."

"Whatever you say, Mila. Let's talk when I've rested up."

Only the sounds of the tires on the hard-packed snow disturbed the icy stillness of the forest. The grey sky, the black tree trunks, and the pristine whiteness presented ever-changing images like so many monochromatic Chinese paintings.

It was a hilly region, whose lush greenery was peppered by ponds and dotted with châteaux. Tarek hated coming here. It was cold and damp, a sunny day was as rare as a kind word from Jacques, and there was nothing to do except pick up visitors at the Dijon train station or drive to Paris or run endless errands for Jacques and Mila.

Tarek turned off onto an even narrower road, and through a clearing in the forest, the neo-gothic Château d'Hélène could be seen. He crossed a bridge spanning a small stream that ran through the property and arrived at the circular gravel driveway.

One of Napoleon III's *maréchals* had built the château for his mistress, Hélène Comtesse de Borry. The property remained with the family, lovingly preserved until the beginning of the twenty-first century, when the costs of maintaining a fifteen-hundred-square-meter, twenty-five-room castle, complete with stables and outbuildings, threatened certain ruin. They were saved by the providential white knight, in the form of a white lotus, or to be more precise, a Hong Kong company. Imperial White Lotus made an offer that enabled them to live in the style demanded by their relatively recent aristocratic status, unencumbered by the magnificent white elephant they had inherited. The Comte and Comtesse de Borry, having no descendants, had even offered to sell Jacques their name, and while he rather liked the sound of Jacques Mornnais de Borry, he dreaded the thought of people laughing at his pretensions and satisfied himself by negotiating an exemption from the wealth tax for the White Lotus.

#   #   #

A tall, heavily built man, his thick torso bringing to mind a rugby player well past his prime, descended the curved oak stairway with a surprising lightness of step. Oblivious to the wood and gilded plaster carvings that covered the château walls from the intricately tiled floors to the painted ceiling, he walked briskly through the richly decorated reception rooms and formal dining room to a small office located behind the family kitchen and *salle à manger*.

Bruno Edremal, Jacques' *homme à tout faire,* gathered the faxes that

Plus a pair of well-tailored jeans to travel in." Alex chose a black sweater, and from the closet, a navy and black patterned blazer.

"Take a pair of black trousers if you need to change to do your work and another black sweater just in case. A white blouse to wear at dinner. Wear those boots to travel; this weather is just too awful. Is that a pair of Chanel flats? Pack those to wear in the house. That should do it for thirty-six hours, don't you think?"

Happy again. "Thanks, Alex, this is great."

Over a pot of green tea, Marie-Agnès told Alex about her meeting with Mila. "She and her husband have a glossy lifestyle magazine, and they want me to do translations and interpret for him at meetings. She's not young, but she's still a knockout: a platinum-blond with green eyes. And a gorgeous figure. I felt so dumpy standing next to her. I know you'll laugh, but I even imagined us running together in Parc Monceau."

"Don't be so intimidated. You have lots of charm and style. You'll be perfectly dressed. Don't try to be her friend, let her come to you. And if you don't mind my saying so, you don't want to mix business and pleasure. If you want a running companion, just ask."

Marie-Agnès looked again at the black and white mass on her bed. "Do you really think this is enough for my stay in the château?"

Alex smiled. "Of course! And by the way, where *is* this famous château? You never said."

Marie-Agnès raised her eyebrows. "Hm, actually, I don't know exactly *where* it is. They told me that their driver would pick me up at the train station in Dijon, so I guess it's around there. I think Mila said it was called the Château d'Hélène."

"If there's a lull in the conversation, you could always ask who Hélène was."

Marie-Agnès looked perplexed. "Just joking," said Alex.

She got up to leave. "Tomorrow I'm going to meet my great-uncle Richard—he was my mother's uncle. I haven't seen him in years. And I've got a bunch of cousins whom I've never met, so it should be interesting to find out about that side of my family."

"You're so lucky. I just have my sister, who lives near Sainte-Maxime.

sisters and the descendants of his aunt, Edith. Three of his four cousins were picked off. Everyone, it seemed, needed money, and with one exception, no one cared very much for the old stones and cheap wine. But his cousin Charlotte was having none of it. She loved being at Trubenne and had turned three of the rooms into a cozy little nest. She could cope with the damp and the cold, thank you very much. If Richard wanted to carry on with the project, that was fine with her — he could count her in.

His sister Chantal preferred to use the money toward a small apartment in Cannes, but Marie-Thérèse, who had inherited her share from her mother, Noëlle, was similarly opposed.

Richard and Alex's parents had quarreled the last time they met.

"These are Alexia's true roots, Richard, and I want her always to have a place she can go to, no matter what. How can money compare to that? You have been in the bank for too long, I'm afraid."

"The fact is," added her husband, who found Richard's seeming asceticism and apparent greed somewhat difficult to reconcile, "we don't need the money, and we think having a historic family home is much more important. If you want to turn Trubenne into an upmarket winery, then we need to do this together."

Alex's parents felt the chill of a cold blue stare. Several moments of silence. "I'm sorry, but this is my idea, my project, and I will do this on my own or not at all. I've made you a generous offer for your share, and I do wish you would be reasonable and reconsider."

Raymond Chase stood up. "I think it is time for us to leave. Marie-Thérèse, will you please get Alex?"

To Richard, "No need to get up. We can see ourselves out."

The Chase family never heard from Richard or the rest of the Vesla de Trubenne family, except for Charlotte, who sent a card every year at Christmas. Alex, drawing snowflakes in the study, was unaware of the discussion and her parents never mentioned it to her.

Chapter 10

IT HAD STOPPED SNOWING, AND Alex decided to walk to Richard's apartment. Dirty snow piled along the pavement matched the overcast grey sky. Forty-five minutes to go down Avenue de Villiers, through Place du Maréchal Juin, its rose bushes a mass of twigs and thorns, continuing straight and over the ring road and into the suburb of Neuilly-sur-Seine. Block after block of large apartment buildings and private mansions, set back from the street behind walls and gates and well-tended gardens. No litter and none of the dog poop that made it wise to cast eyes downward when walking in Paris.

It was midday and children were returning home for lunch, driven by their mothers or led by Filipino housekeepers. BMWs appeared to be the car of choice, jeans and mink the preferred attire, at least for the mothers. Alex looked upward through the tall trees which, even bare, gave the boulevard a stately feel, trying to find number seventy-one. As she did, the recollection of the family visit of so many years ago rose to the surface of her mind.

She pressed the buzzer next to the letters RVDT, negotiated the series of doors and hallways leading to an elevator that she took to the third floor. A smiling maid greeted her and led her into a spacious living room, large sofas and armchairs flanking a low stone table covered with piles of magazines and a collection of glass owls of many sizes and colors. Several moments later, a tall, thin man, slightly stooped but still sure of step, came into the room. They exchanged the perfunctory air kisses — "Four times as we do in Languedoc," said Richard — and smiling, great-uncle and great-niece examined each other.

Maria, the housekeeper, served the drinks — port for Alex and whiskey for Richard. "How nice to see you again, Alexia. Tell me how you've been all these years." Richard was smiling with his mouth, but his blue eyes remained both lucid and cold. Alex heard the implicit question: *What brings you here at this time?*

"What have I been doing? Well, I've rented a small apartment — it's actually two maid's rooms that have been cobbled together. I've been working in the fashion industry ever since I finished school and I've decided to take a year off. I'll be living here for six months. Then I'll see what comes next."

Richard interrupted, "You worked in fashion, did you? Do you remember how Chloé loved to design clothes, almost right up to the end?" The smile was now warm and real. "She had such fine taste. I have not touched a thing since she has gone."

Alex had only a vague memory of Chloé, with her turbans and extravagant clothes, and she found the bibelots — on the coffee table, on the credenza, on the occasional tables — to be suffocating kitsch.

"Yes, indeed. Anyway, I married and divorced a rather wealthy man, and he was quite generous."

Anxious to avoid any discussion about her divorce, she moved on. "I'm so glad to be here. The last time I saw you, I was just a little girl, do you remember?"

"Ah, yes, indeed I do."

He doesn't seem pleased. I wonder what I could have said. "In fact, I thought you might have expected me. I did send you a letter that I was coming to France — maybe it got lost in the mail? Anyhow, after *Maman* died, I discovered that I had inherited her share in the house at Trubenne, but you know she never talked about that, and now I'd like to go down there to see the place. You don't mind that, do you? And I would love to get closer to my cousin Charlotte. Apparently, she is an owner as well, along with you, of course. And I'd like to reconnect with my other cousins — it has been years since I have seen any of them. It seems a shame to be part of such a large family and know practically no one."

The cold smile remained. "Of course, Alexia. You must meet Charlotte. As for your Paris family, I'm quite busy right now. I'll try to arrange for you to meet some of them, but I'm afraid you'll have to be patient."

It doesn't sound like he's in a hurry to help me. Alex tried not to let her disappointment show. She reached into her bag and removed the contents of the worn envelope. "There's one other thing I wanted to ask you about, in fact, show you." She moved her drink to one side and spread the three photos on the coffee table. "I found these among *Maman's* papers. I guess that's Trubenne, but who are the children?"

Richard picked up the photos, his face now an expressionless mask. "Yes, that is Trubenne. The children? It looks like that is me, your mother, and Charlotte. The château hasn't changed very much, but the same cannot be said for us. But you must excuse me right now. I have to leave for a board meeting in Paris."

The audience had come to an end, and Alex stood up. After another exchange of air kisses, Maria brought her coat, and Alex walked back to her maids' rooms on boulevard Malesherbes, deep in thought.

#   #   #

Alex sifted through a folder labeled *Château* and removed a Christmas card. Charlotte had affixed a little sticker with her address and phone number.

The cold had settled on the roof, and the heating pipes up here on the seventh floor were only tepid. She put on a bonnet and wrapped a large scarf around her neck and shoulders, made a cup of tea.

Richard didn't seem particularly pleased to see me. I wonder if it will be the same with Charlotte. Alex looked at the card, hesitated. *I haven't come all this way to get cold feet.* She called the number. Charlotte answered the phone. She would love to see Alexia again, so much time had passed, so sorry to hear about her parents, and could she come down in December?

Chapter 11

Château d'Hélène

IN THE DARK, DAMP COLD of a late-November morning, Marie-Agnès hurried to the Métro. Following Alex's advice, she wore a black down parka and black jeans, a thick, pale grey woolen scarf circling her neck.

Taking the elevator down to the depths of the Abbesses station, she stifled a feeling of panic as an enormous cockroach scuttled across the floor. A few minutes later, she was on her way to Gare de Lyon. The fast train to Dijon — the TGV — was already there, and she placed her suitcase, full of black and white clothing, in the luggage rack at the head of the car and settled into her seat.

It was midweek and the early-morning train was not crowded. She put her black tote bag on the seat next to her and started to devour the pile of magazines she had purchased for the trip — *Elle, Grazia,* and *Marie Claire* — and entered the unreal but nevertheless comforting world of perfect faces and perfect bodies, noticing with indulgence rather than irritation the same celebrity singer featured in all three publications. As she skimmed through the magazines, the multicolored leather Jamin Puech pouch caught her attention. Why not visit the boutique in January and buy the bag on sale?

Tarek was at the station in Dijon to meet her. Mila had described Marie-Agnès to him, and he had to say that she was spot on: red hair, on the heavy side, fortyish, well dressed, with a deer-in-the-headlights look about her.

"Marie-Agnès, I believe?"

"Yes." She looked surprised and smiled.

"Mila described you to me. Can I take your suitcase?"

He opened the door to a small BMW station wagon with Luxembourg license plates and put her suitcase in the trunk. Driving through the stark, beautiful countryside, Marie-Agnès was glad that she had packed her camera; there were so many striking images to capture.

By the time they arrived at the Château d'Hélène, it was late morning. Marie-Agnès had on occasion visited friends who had inherited a château, but these were always rather drafty, run-down buildings where in winter everyone clustered in front of the fireplace, their faces hot and red and their backs frozen with cold. There would be water stains on the walls, furniture that had not stood the test of time, and in the summer, it was rather like camping but with a roof over one's head, and probably less comfortable than a campsite.

But the Château d'Hélène was different. It was the real deal. Marie-Agnès could not believe her good fortune to work for people who possessed such a spectacular abode. She was glad that she had taken the time to pack the right clothing, and she could hardly wait to tell Alex.

Mila met her at the door, the perfect chatelaine. "Welcome to our little home," she said. Before Marie-Agnès could reply, Jacques walked into the entryway. An empty smile crossed his face, and Marie-Agnès put on a happy face, hoping to dissipate the uncomfortable feeling in her stomach.

She could not tell why she felt the way she did, for Jacques was not at all imposing. His suit was off the rack, his choice of tie uninspired. He was a man who would be lost in the crowd in an instant. Had Marie-Agnès paid more attention, she would have noticed that, behind his glasses, there was a gleam in Jacques' small dark eyes, studying and analyzing her. Jacques was anything but an everyman.

A Filipino woman brought lunch into the family dining room. In silence, she walked between the dining room and the kitchen, serving and clearing the table. Jacques explained what was expected of Marie-Agnès today: he was a patron of a large American symphony orchestra, and their fundraiser was on a European tour to obtain commitments for the upcoming season. He confessed to being unable to express himself in English — "I have the accent of a French cow" — and Marie-Agnès found him momentarily charming.

Tarek returned to the Dijon train station to fetch David Billingsly, the fundraiser, and Jacques, Marie-Agnès, and David met in one of the reception rooms. David, at the same time obsequious and driven by the need to succeed, made his pitch. Jacques, relaxed, pleasant, yet noncommittal, said he would consider renewing his pledge. He needed to think about it. The meeting was over. Tarek departed once again for the Dijon train station. The Filipina served coffee to Marie-Agnès and a glass of freshly pressed mango juice to Jacques.

He turned to Marie-Agnès, his lips pursed in a sneer. "I expected greater recognition for my donation last year, and they will have to wait a while before I write them another check. You did a good job this afternoon, so please send your invoice to Mila. Shall we see you at dinner?"

It was late in the afternoon when Marie-Agnès climbed up the oak stairway to her room on the first floor, decorated in the Empire style, with a delightfully modern bathroom. The sun had started to set, surrounded by a mass of rose, blue, and grey streaks. A short photo safari was in order. Wandering down the hallway, she came upon the service stairway, used by the servants in another day and age.

Why not? she asked herself and then she was outside. She walked around the château, trying to capture the play of shadows on the elaborate stone carvings. Widening her path, she headed toward the nearby surrounding woods. All was silent, dark grey, and white, the greenery almost black in the falling dusk. She walked past a long, low-lying building, which she realized must have been the stables. Next to the stables was a temporary metallic structure: two shipping containers, their ends removed, had been welded together, and glass plates had replaced the metal sides. It was an eyesore next to the stables' pure long horizontal lines, whose stone absorbed the last rays of the setting sun.

Intrigued by the contrast between the stables and the containers, Marie-

Agnès walked carefully on the iced-over hard-packed snow, remaining in the shadows of the surrounding trees. The smell of horses had gone, but the building housing the stables was not abandoned. Full doors had been put on the stalls; one was slightly ajar, and through the opening, a bed and personal affairs were visible.

Feeling both curiosity and unease, Marie-Agnès kept her distance and took her photos. She continued gingerly walking through the trees, coming closer to the metallic structure. The back of the building faced the woods. She looked in and saw easels with paintings in various stages of completion. There were two sets of easels: a finished picture on one easel and a work in progress on the other. It was a painter's workshop with tubes and pots of paint, rolls of canvas, brushes, various jars and metal recipients scattered on a large table. What an unusual shot for her photo album...

The two buildings faced a large, fenced-in field, probably used as a riding ring in earlier days. At the far side of the area, two men were leaning on the fence, talking in low voices. She zoomed in on their faces and saw that the men were Asian. *How random,* she thought, and for no particular reason, except perhaps that she had come out to take pictures, she pressed the shutter-release button.

She continued walking along the edge of the forest. The path curved down toward the river, where a stone cottage stood not far from the water. Curious once more, she approached the cabin. A film of grime covered the windows. An old lock held the door shut. Suddenly feeling chilled to the bone, she retraced her steps back to the château.

She had known him for a short time only, but Marie-Agnès was sure that Jacques would be wearing a tie and jacket to dinner, and so she changed into the outfit so carefully chosen with Alex. Mila, elegant as always, wore a low-cut deep burgundy sweater and a pair of slim black pants. Marie-Agnès was sure she had seen a similar outfit in a holiday issue of *Vogue*.

Dinner was, surprisingly, quite pleasant. Jacques had opinions on French politics and politicians and seemed to know many of them personally, telling stories about their escapades. Mila smiled, said little other than to address the Filipino serving woman. Bruno had joined them for dinner. He laughed at Jacques' jokes and poured the wine.

Marie-Agnès made her way up the oak stairway, and as she reached the top, Mila called up to her, "Please do not leave your room between now and seven tomorrow morning, as we will be turning the alarm system on."

A feeling of unease returned. Here she was, deep in the French countryside, in a sprawling house with people she hardly knew. No one, not even Alex, knew where she was. What had she told her? *They have a château outside of Dijon. And why didn't I pay attention to the names of the villages we drove through? The fact is, I don't know where I am. How stupid!*

Marie-Agnès slept fitfully in her luxurious jail cell, and the next morning, she was relieved to be seated at the breakfast table with Mila.

"I'm so sorry for the delay in payment. Please send me your invoice for your work yesterday, and I'll take care of all of them straightaway."

"Thank you, Mila. I've enjoyed my stay, and I hope we can work together again."

Tarek drove her to the station, and it was midafternoon by the time she climbed the steps to her apartment on rue d'Orchampt.

Later that day, she spoke with Alex, who announced that she would be leaving to visit her cousin Charlotte in Languedoc. She remembered that Marie-Agnès had a camera, and would she mind lending it to her? She knew how to use a reflex and would be very careful.

"No problem. I took some photos in Burgundy, but there's lots of memory space left, so if you want to stop by, I'll be glad to lend it to you."

Chapter 12

December 2009, Rue d'Orchampt, Paris

ALEX STOPPED BY TO SEE Marie-Agnes and to pick up the camera.

"So, how was your stay at the château? Were you dressed properly?"

"Oh, yes, perfect. Thanks again. And the château was something else. I met a man named Bruno. He's Jacques' right-hand man. And they have a driver and a maid. But I felt creepy that night. Mila told me not to leave my room once the alarm system was turned on. And I never did catch the name of the town nearby."

"It looks like you survived."

"Oh, yes. I even got a chance to walk around the grounds and take some photos."

"Speaking of photos, thanks for lending me your camera." Alex turned to leave. "Sorry to rush off, but I've got to pack. My cousin Charlotte sounded so friendly on the phone that I might wind up staying on for a bit. I'll let you know."

Marie-Agnès typed her updated invoice on her iPad and sent it by email to Mila. She then turned her attention to her other translation work, saw friends, thought about how to diet during the holidays, and came to the conclusion that that was not going to happen. January would be an excellent time to begin to lose those extra kilos.

Holidays — both religious and secular — governed the rhythms of life in France. The thirty-five-hour workweek, coupled with a strong sense of entitlement, meant that work came to a halt as the holidays approached. So it was that around the tenth of December, when she realized that Mila had not yet settled her invoice, Marie-Agnès knew she had to act quickly. Someone so obviously wealthy as Jacques would not be found in Paris after the fifteenth of the month. She sent a polite email, received a polite response that the payment was on the way. When her bank account dipped further into the red, she tried to arrange to meet Mila to pick up a check, but Mila was on voicemail and did not respond.

It had slowly dawned on Marie-Agnès that Mila and Jacques belonged to that group of wealthy people who couldn't be bothered to pay their bills on time. Did they feel a surge of power when they kept their creditors twisting in the wind? She felt bitter, remembering how excited she had been at the prospect of working for them.

Marie-Agnès lived month to month. In addition to the work she had done, she'd also laid out money for her train ticket when she visited the château. It was frustrating and stressful to chase after *Artixia*. She went to the bakery and bought a *bûche de Noël* flavored with chestnut cream. It was for four people but she finished it off the same day.

#   #   #

Eugene had spent the Thanksgiving holiday with his sister in Washington, DC. As soon as he returned to France, he reconnected with an old friend who was married to a French woman and currently living in Lyon. Travis and Julie had invited Eugene to visit and then join them skiing at the alpine ski resort La Clusaz, where they owned a small chalet. In early December, he took the train to Lyon in time to view the Festival of Lights and, with his friends, crawl from one *bouchon* to the next before they drove to La Clusaz, where he would stay through the New Year. He skied from morning to late afternoon, and with each day, the bureau receded further to the back of his mind.

He had called the Deputy Chief of Mission after he returned to France. But Vincent Reiner was at first unavailable — he was on the phone or in meetings — and when Eugene again tried to reach him, he learned that he was off for the holidays.

Okay, he thought to himself, *I'll try him in January, but until then, out of sight, out of mind,* and with the sun setting by late afternoon, he hurried to get in one more black run before dark.

#   #   #

Mila, Jacques, and Bruno were met by a driver at the airport and taken to the Ritz Carlton, Jacques' favorite venue in Hong Kong. Bruno had planned his holiday in Thailand, but before separating the following day, the three enjoyed a last meal together.

They relived Jacques' meeting with Jerome Billingsly and the small revenge he intended to exact for the perceived slight to his person. The talk then turned to Marie-Agnès.

"She's been asking to be paid," said Mila, "but what's the rush?"

"She would be an attractive woman if she lost some weight," said Bruno.

"Ah, I thought you preferred the slender Asian body to the water buffalo," teased Mila.

"No, she's not my type, but she does have lovely hands, the hands of an artist."

"Perhaps we ought to hire her to do some of our paintings," laughed Jacques.

"She's apparently a photographer. I saw her coming back into the château by the servants' stairway. She must have been taking photos of the château and the woods."

Jacques' eyes darkened until they were almost black and his cheeks turned a rosy color. "What the hell was she doing sneaking around taking photos? Did she go near the stables and the atelier, do you think?"

Bruno, feeling uncomfortable, said "She's quite harmless, Jacques. I'm sure of that."

"I do not share your views, and we will recover that camera and make sure she didn't see anything that is none of her business. Bruno, when you return in January, arrange to meet that nosy woman. Tell her you will bring her a check."

#   #   #

A bright sun broke through the layer of clouds, and Alex decided that was an omen of good things to come on her trip to Trubenne. She took the Métro to the Auber station and changed to the RER express line, and two stops later, she was at Gare de Lyon. Before boarding, she bought a supply of the kinds of magazines that one leafed through a single time, to be left on the train when she reached her destination.

In a country where so many things seemed not to function as they should, at least the French could be proud of their system of fast trains crisscrossing the country. Alex went into the bar car and ordered a *noisette* (an espresso with a small pitcher of steamed milk), and a *tartine* (a slice of baguette slathered in butter), found a corner seat, put her magazines on the small table, and prepared to enjoy her trip south.

She skimmed through *Paris Match,* starting with the multicolored ads for sex and psychics at the back of the magazine, working her way backward. She stopped at *"La Vie Parisienne"* to check out the good and great attending a charity event. And then she chuckled, for among the forty or so photos, there was Jacques Mornnais, the mousey Frenchman from her flight, photographed with a stunning platinum blonde. *Small world.*

Walking down the stairs from the train platform to the waiting room, Alex sensed Charlotte's presence before she saw a tall woman with striking blue eyes and a long, thin nose. Despite the web of fine lines in a face with the year-round tan of outdoor living, she exuded a youthful vitality, and it was this energy that attracted Alex to her.

"Charlotte." It was more a statement than a question. "I'm Alexia, and I am so happy to meet you."

"Likewise, my dear. You do look like your lovely mother. I was so sorry to hear about her passing." Then a quick switch: "Your train was on time. How refreshing. I'm parked just outside."

After they left Nîmes, they climbed a sharply winding road, Charlotte expertly navigating the hairpin turns, and arrived at the little village of Trubenne, which overlooked the valley below. Before a long, high stone wall, Charlotte pressed a remote control, and the massive wooden doors opened onto a rectangular courtyard surrounded on the three other sides by a sprawling château. Charlotte parked her car in the adjacent grange.

Inside, there was a surprisingly modern eat-in kitchen, a living room with a television and a fully equipped office along one of the walls. "This château has fourteen bedrooms. However, I live in just three rooms. But don't worry, there is heat in the extra bedroom, and I've had no complaints from my guests."

Sitting in Charlotte's kitchen and smelling the aroma of a *daube de boeuf aux carrots* simmering on the stove, Alex asked Charlotte why Richard had been so unfriendly to her, and she learned, for the first time, that Charlotte's and Alex's parents had thwarted Richard's vision for Trubenne.

"Richard's not a bad person, he's always had his way about most things, and I think it bothers him that your parents and I didn't want to sell our share in the property and hand it to him. We thought he had a good idea, and I think today it's still a good idea, but even if he changed his mind and agreed to include us in the project, he and I are now too old. I'm happy to tend to my gardening, go down to Nîmes a few times a week to help children with their homework, and that is enough. But you might want to think about developing Trubenne. Just remember to let me stay in the house."

Charlotte invited her to stay as long as she wished. One morning, after clearing away dead wood in the garden, Alex came into the kitchen to help prepare lunch.

"Charlotte, while I was outside, I started to wonder if you don't mind living here by yourself. I mean, you're alone, and anyone could be lurking in the woods."

"Oh, I'm quite safe, I assure you. I've never had a problem, and as for someone lurking in the woods, if I were them, I'd be more concerned about the wild boars. They're a bit of a problem, you know. When I see one coming too close to the house, I get out my rifle and shoot it."

"You're kidding."

"No, I'm serious. Then I call a farmer who lives nearby to come over and take it away. He butchers it and we share the meat. Remember the *roti de sanglier* we had the other night?"

"I'm such a city girl, it's hard to imagine you shooting anything. Anyway, where do you keep your rifle?"

"Let me show you."

Alex followed Charlotte up a wooden stairway at the end of a dark, dusty corridor. It was a part of the château that Alex had not visited, and she realized that they were climbing to the top of the turret at one end of the building.

"Here they are." Charlotte pointed to three rifles in a gun rack. "If you look out the window, you'll see that I have a clear view of the forest and any wild boar that ventures too close to home."

"When I first saw the photos of the château, I imagined being a little girl and pretending to be Rapunzel."

"I guess I am your Rapunzel with a gun," laughed Charlotte.

They descended the spiral staircase, and after lunch, Alex went back outside.

There was a melancholy beauty in the run-down château. Armed with her camera, Alex, like Marie-Agnès, found the play of light and the contrast of the dark stones with the pale blue and grey sky inspiring. One of the photos — a glimpse of the château through the partly open wooden doors — had a timeless, ethereal quality, and she and Charlotte decided to print that image and send it to Richard as a Christmas card. *Dear Richard*, they wrote, *thinking of you and wishing you a happy and peaceful Christmas.*

Alex took long walks among the dormant vines and through the barren hills, and she felt the joy of just being, far from the stressful and superficial world where she had flourished for so long. Here were the seeds of the new life she had hoped to find in France. Could she crack Richard's shell of disappointment and frustration and convince him to take another look at his project? She sent an SMS to Marie-Agnès: *Wonderful time. See you beginning of January. XO, Alex.*

Chapter 13

January 2010, Château d'Hélène

BRUNO RETURNED FROM THAILAND ALONE at the beginning of January. He sat in the château's office, his eyes closed to the rare January sunlight, but that only made the pounding in his head worse. *Fucking jet lag.* Bruno walked unsteadily into the kitchen, made an espresso, tried to lift it to his mouth. But his hand trembled, the coffee splashed onto the saucer, and then the cup fell to the floor. *Shit, the fucking maid can clean it up.* He dropped another capsule into the coffee machine and, leaning over the sink, managed to drink the hot, tasteless liquid before returning to the office. He had to make his phone calls before he could go back upstairs to lie down and sleep off his jet lag and his hangover.

First, the red-haired cow. He got Marie-Agnès on his first try. Yes, she was free the day after tomorrow and would be pleased to meet him at the café in the Hôtel Lutetia. He would bring the payment for her invoices.

Next, Samuel and Cosimo. Bruno had worked with them before. Not the brightest of bulbs, but they would do. He described the job: they would need to grab whatever bags she might be carrying. If she had a camera with her, that would be great. *And,* he added, *she's stuck her nose into things that don't concern her and the boss doesn't want any more trouble from this bitch.*

Chapter 14

Rue d'Orchampt, Paris

MARIE-AGNÈS HAD OVERSLEPT, AND it was the gentle, nagging noise of her neighbor's shower that woke her up. It was still dark at eight a.m., deep in the northern Europe winter.

Before she opened her eyes, she thought about today's meeting with Bruno. But instead of relief, she felt only the grip of fear in her midsection. *It will be all right. You need to be very firm, and things will work out.*

She chose a loose-fitting dress, a puce-colored jersey that hid her more-than-ample form, topping it off with a short metallic mesh vest. She saw a fat, ugly woman staring back at her from the full-length mirror. Did the eyes and cheeks need some attention? She applied her makeup with great care, following the techniques she'd learned from watching YouTube. But today her hand was heavy, the contouring too garish, the kohl too intense. Marie-Agnès managed a few swallows of coffee. She tried to eat some toast, but it was like chewing on a mouthful of paste.

You need to be very firm. Repeating the phrase like a mantra, she loaded up her favorite Louis Vuitton tote. She left her apartment in Montmartre, took the Métro to Sèvres-Babylone, crossed Boulevard Raspail, and headed for the café in the Hotel Lutetia. *It's curious that Bruno didn't ask to meet me at the office on rue de Prony. Well, it makes no difference where we meet, as long as I get my money.*

Bruno was already there, seated at the rear, his back to the wall. Marie-Agnès was sure he had seen her enter before she saw him. She walked through the length of the café, not noticing the cross-section of Paris society — people from the worlds of politics, fashion, design, and business, trophy wives, and retirees — out and about for breakfast.

Bruno greeted her cordially, ordered an espresso for her and a second one for himself. As they filled the time with talk about the weather and the traffic, she waited for an opening to ask about her payment. It was not necessary. Without any prompting, Bruno reached into his jacket and put an envelope on the table.

"Thank you for your help, Marie-Agnès, and sorry for the delay. I know that Jacques hopes we can work together again soon."

The feeling of relief left her almost weak. As the tension of the past weeks dissolved, she began to breathe normally again.

"Thank you, Bruno, and I hope so, too. Just let me know when I can be of help." *Why am I saying this? I never want to see Jacques and his people again.*

They stood up and shook hands. She put the envelope in her tote bag and slung it over her shoulder, trying to walk out of the café slowly. Bruno remained seated and nodded slightly in the direction of two men seated nearby. Hair cropped close to the scalp, jackets worn and wrinkled — not the café's regular clients, those two. As they got up to leave, one of them tossed a twenty-Euro bill on the table, more than enough for two coffees, but they were in somewhat of a hurry now. Marie-Agnès's hair framed her face like a cloud of red cotton candy, like a beacon in the surrounding sea of muted winter colors.

Once outside, Marie-Agnès breathed deeply, forcing the fear to dissolve. *He's paid me, and it's over. I need to be kind to myself and buy myself a present. Why not check out Jamin Puech this afternoon?*

Midmorning now, the Métro was not too crowded. Her mind confused by conflicting thoughts of foreboding and going shopping, she paid no attention to the two men waiting patiently until the seats next to her were free. They sat down close to her. One of the men grabbed her tote bag while the other leaned against her.

"Help," she cried. Her scream reached a group of students on their way to school, horsing around in the aisle.

"Hey," one of them called out. The two men exchanged a glance, got up, and ran out of the train as it pulled into the station at Pigalle. Marie-Agnès slumped against the window, her coat ripped, her tote bag gone, and the black kohl smeared beneath her eyes.

Chapter 15

Boulevard Malesherbes, Paris

"ALEX, IT'S ME, MARIE-AGNÈS."

"Hi, how are you? Did you have a nice holiday?"

"I had a little accident, and I'm in the hospital."

Alex interrupted, "What happened? Are you okay?"

"Yes, but can you come and take me home? I need to get out of here." Marie-Agnès was trying to hold back her tears, but Alex could hear that she was upset.

"Which hospital? Ah, yes, Bichat. I'll get a taxi and come right over. What's your room number anyway?"

Forty-five minutes later, Alex walked into the room that Marie-Agnès was sharing with another woman, who was asleep in her bed. She bent over and whispered to Marie-Agnès: "What happened to you? Are you all right?"

"I was mugged in the Métro, in the middle of the day. Can you believe that?"

"Oh my God."

"They stole my tote bag. One of the men tried to stick a knife in my ribs. The only reason I'm still alive is that a metal mesh vest I was wearing blunted the knife, and all I've got is a scratch. I think I must have passed out from fear or stress or something like that. But please get me out of here. I'm afraid that they might come back. We can talk more later."

Alex went into the hallway, an intense conversation raging in her mind. *I need to get Marie-Agnès out of here right away. They'll never let you do it — you'll have to wait for the doctor and explain who you are, and that can take hours, and you still won't know if they will let her go. There's only one nurse at the station. But one is enough. I'll take that wheelchair and say we're going to the lounge.*

And then destiny gave a clear indication of the course to be followed when the nurse was called away by a passing colleague.

Alex pushed the wheelchair into Marie-Agnès's room. "Where are your things?"

As quietly as she could, they managed to put her coat and shoes on. Alex stuffed the rest of Marie-Agnès's belongings into a pillowcase, got her into the wheelchair, and pushed her down the corridor to the elevator. *When doing something outrageous, do it boldly*, that was her motto. The hospital was so short-staffed, there was no one on duty, and ten minutes later, they were in a taxi on the way back to Alex's apartment.

Getting up to the seventh floor took two trips, one for Alex to help Marie-Agnès into the elevator and then into her apartment, a second trip to bring up the stuffed pillowcase. It was midafternoon, the other seventh-floor inhabitants were at work, and the concierge was out cleaning apartments in her off-hours.

It was some time before the nurse returned to her station, and sometime later still that she discovered that Marie-Agnès was gone. She remembered, then, the tall blond woman who had been lurking in the corridor. A wheelchair was missing, and she concluded that Marie-Agnès had left with her friend or whoever she was. Of course, someone would have to take the blame, and it was not going to be her. Choosing the wisest and most existentially correct course of action, she took the patient file, which had not yet been entered in the database, walked down the corridor, and put the green folder in a waste disposal bin, thus confirming that as far as the hospital was concerned, Marie-Agnès no longer existed.

Settled into Alex's bed, drinking a cup of tea, Marie-Agnès told Alex what she remembered, starting with losing consciousness inside the Métro car.

"I think there were two of them, the one who grabbed my bag and the one who tried to knife me."

"Do you remember what they looked like?"

"Not really. It's weird. Bruno paid me and I should have felt happy. I was relieved, yet I couldn't shake this uneasy feeling. So I tried to take my mind off that by thinking about shopping."

"But why did you feel uneasy?"

"It's hard to put my finger on exactly why. Maybe because it was so hard to get *Artixia* to pay me. Or maybe because I can't escape the feeling that there's something frightening about Jacques Mornnais, the man I worked for."

"What did you say his name was, this man you did the work for?"

"Jacques Mornnais, why?"

The heat spread from Alex's neck to her cheeks as the words sent a shiver up her spine. *Is this what fear feels like?* "Why, because I sat next to the very same man on the flight over. I can't believe it."

Silence.

"I still don't see the connection between his paying you late and the attack in the Métro. What's the point? All he had to do was put you off some more. You know, the funny thing is, I told him I was a translator and he gave me his card and said to call him if I was looking for work. Talk about coincidences! Well, thank you very much but no thanks, I would say."

Marie-Agnès said, "You want to stay away from that man. I felt uncomfortable the first time I met him. Please believe me, there is something off about him. The problem is, I'm afraid to go back to my apartment."

"Well, your keys were in your tote bag, right?" asked Alex.

"In fact, they should be in the inner pocket of my coat," exclaimed Marie-Agnès. "I put them there so I didn't have to fish around in my bag."

Alex pulled a set of keys out of the coat pocket. *"Et voilà."*

Neither woman had eaten since early morning, and Alex found a charcuterie that was open all day, bought slices of several pâtés, grapefruit halves stuffed with shrimp, and a Greek *taboulé*. She stopped at the bakery downstairs and purchased a *baguette* and two fruit tarts.

"Let's have a glass of Bordeaux. My mother always said it fortifies the blood."

The glass of wine helped Marie-Agnès to relax a little.

"The police came to the hospital. I think they're trying to find witnesses, seeing if the security cameras picked up anything. Apparently people get mugged in the Métro all the time, and they seemed pretty low-key. Of course, they did ask me about the men, but I couldn't tell them very much."

"But what about your meeting with Bruno. Did you tell them about that?"

Tears glittered in Marie-Agnès's eyes. "No, I didn't tell them anything. I told you, I'm afraid of Jacques and Bruno."

"Okay, but can I just ask you one more thing? Why was it so hard for you to get paid? I mean, I sat next to your boss on a business class flight. I saw that he was picked up by a man driving a Mercedes, so he doesn't seem to be short of money. I don't get it."

"I know. I had the month of December to try to answer your question. Maybe it makes Jacques and Mila feel important to exercise their power over other people. Did I tell you that Jacques made a fundraiser come out to the château when he had no intention of giving his organization any money? They're just mean-spirited people, drunk on the power that their money gives them. Anyhow, I don't want to talk about it anymore. Tell me about your stay with your cousin."

Alex told Marie-Agnès about meeting Charlotte, about the wonderful time she had had at Trubenne and her plans to talk again with Richard.

"Ah, you see yourself as *la chatelaine de Trubenne*."

"You wouldn't say that if you saw the place. It's just a big, old run-down building surrounded by vines producing cheap wine, and truly in the middle of no place. If you want to get away from it all, that's the place to go." Alex went to her backpack and carefully removed Marie-Angès' camera.

"By the way, thanks for lending me your camera. Now I can show you Trubenne."

It was show-and-tell time. Alex first: there was Charlotte with her strong face and clear, forthright gaze, the outline of the château against the pale blue sky, other photos of the uninhabited rooms, the faded wallpaper and peeling paint recalling life a century earlier. The courtyard, its trees decorated with red and white lights. Then it was Marie-Agnès's turn: the ornate and magnificent Château d'Hélène, contrasting with the much more modest edifice at Trubenne, the surrounding forest, and then the stables, the atelier, and the riding ring.

"How curious to see Asian faces in the Morvan," observed Alex.

"It is all rather curious. I think they must have been living in the converted stables, but why, when there must have been fifteen bedrooms in the château?" responded Marie-Agnès.

Alex was examining the photos of the atelier more closely. "Is he copying a painting? Is that what I see? Let's enlarge the photo." Alex attached the cable to her computer and zoomed in. Four easels, two turned away from the camera, two facing the viewer at an angle. The paintings: the sea, masts of tall ships, swirling clouds, bright dabs of color. Alex pointed at the screen. "Are those paintings the same? I wonder what they were up to, making copies, perhaps? Maybe you were not supposed to see that?"

Marie Agnès's cheeks turned red. "Oh, shit, I had forgotten about that. Taking the photos, I mean. I went out for a walk before dinner, to photograph the château and its surroundings."

"Do you think anyone saw you, besides the painters?"

"Now that you mention it, I think I passed Bruno on my way back. You don't think that's why I was attacked?"

"We can't be sure, but it makes sense, doesn't it? Especially if they were up to something not quite aboveboard." Silence, the only sound Marie-Agnès's shallow breathing.

"Would you like a little more?" asked Alex as she poured some wine. Marie-Agnès brought the glass to her lips, the dark red liquid rocking gently as she tried to steady her trembling hand.

"I felt something was odd when Mila told me that I couldn't leave my room at night, but then, in the morning, everything seemed normal. What am I going to do?"

The sun had begun to set, an unarticulated but strongly felt sense of apprehension permeating the chill air, more than merely worrying, not quite full-fledged fear.

Alex was quiet. She hadn't gotten around to telling her friend about Richard's cool welcome, or what Charlotte had told her about Richard. *He and Charlotte are the only people I can turn to. Charlotte is too far away. Richard was an important banker. He still must know people in high places. We can ask him for advice. I'll bet he won't turn us down.*

Alex cut through the silence. "You're in over your head here, and we need some serious help. I'm going to call my uncle Richard."

Chapter 16

Neuilly-sur-Seine

ONE MORNING A FEW DAYS into the New Year, Richard sat in his study, looking out the window at the tall, leafless trees. Chloé had been gone five years, but the pain of her loss had not lessened very much. He thought about her every day, saw her in every painting, every bibelot, even every pile of neatly arranged magazines on low tables in the large reception rooms. When she was alive, they would have been vacationing in Switzerland — Chloé loved to ski — or perhaps escaping the rigors of winter for a week in the Seychelles. His few remaining friends had all left for their holiday trips, and Richard did not relish the thought of lunches and dinners with his nieces and nephews. He felt that their motivations were, to say the least, mixed: a small dose of compassion for a lonely old man and a much more substantial measure of interest in his considerable fortune.

Restless, each morning he paced from one room to the next, seeking relief from the accumulated underlying discontent of a lifetime. Richard settled into a sofa in his reception rooms, his stocking-clad feet finding a resting place on the coffee table littered with books and knickknacks. He leaned back, eyes closed, but he was not sleeping. He was living—or more accurately, reliving— his life. Whereas a word spoken a few minutes ago slipped quickly into oblivion, the years he spent with Chloe were crystal clear. His thoughts moved seamlessly from Chloé to their mutual friends, to dinner parties and drinks at his club. But they, like Chloé, were mostly gone.

Trying to sort things through while his mind was still keen. There was a story of financial and social achievement, but he sensed that something was missing and time was running short. Each day was a new opportunity to complete the picture, bring the circle to a close. But how?

As he embarked on a self-pity session, inviting memories of past slights to join the fun, he again looked at the photo that had arrived in the previous week's mail. Brushing aside his first impulse, to relive his frustration over his stymied project at Trubenne, another thought arose, a feeling that perhaps Charlotte and his newly rediscovered niece, Alexia, did care for him just a little. He knew that Charlotte was not interested in his money, and it had been clear to him that Alexia was not in need, either. His niece seemed to enjoy her visit with Charlotte. *Would she be interested in learning about my project? Maybe it's not too late to develop Trubenne?* He felt he had behaved badly when she had visited a few weeks ago.

And then an event occurred, fitting into a place in the puzzle, a coincidence, some would say. The phone rang, and it was Alex, asking if she might stop by to see Richard. Would tomorrow morning be too soon?

#   #   #

Once again, Alex set out on foot to Richard's apartment. The snow had mostly melted, but it was bitterly cold, and there were still patches of ice on the sidewalks. Maria took her coat and the rest of her outerwear and led her into the study where Richard awaited her.

"Hello, my dear."

"*Bonjour*, Uncle Richard. Happy New Year."

Air kisses again exchanged, Richard grasped Alex's shoulders with an intensity bordering on warmth. He thanked her for the Christmas card, in turn wished her a *Bonne Année*, and they made small talk for a few minutes, each one trying to find a way to talk about the reason for Alex's phone call.

70

Alex spoke first. "Thank you for seeing me so quickly. I hardly know where to begin." And then she began at the beginning, telling him about her chance meeting with her childhood friend, about Marie-Agnès, about her translating assignments and the trip to the Château d'Hélène in the Morvan, explaining the meeting with Bruno.

Alex stopped as Maria came into the room, bringing a platter with tea and an assortment of mini *viennoiseries* (delicious miniature pastries.) Maria left, and Alex continued. "Here is where things get complicated. After Bruno paid her, Marie-Agnès went into the Métro and — can you believe it? — a man stabbed her and took her tote bag. Probably the only reason she's still alive is that her metal mesh vest — a fortuitous fashion choice — deviated the blade. Marie-Agnès called me from the hospital. We felt, I can't tell you why, but we just felt it, that she had to leave the hospital, and so I put her in a wheelchair, rolled her out to the taxi stand, and brought her back to my place. Now, at this point I thought that this was an unfortunate accident, but…"

She stopped, sipped some tea, munched on a little *pain au chocolat*, and looked up at Richard before continuing. He was sitting very still, the hint of a smile on his face. "Please continue, Alexia."

The words came out in a disjointed rush. "Luckily, her house keys were in her coat pocket and not in her bag. I had borrowed her camera to take some photos at Trubenne, you know, I sent you one of them. And then she remembered that she had taken some pictures at the château and we looked at those. One of the photos looks like an artist's studio. In another, you can see two similar paintings side by side, and in yet another, there are two Asian men leaning on a fence near the studio. We think the Asians are painters and that Jacques Mornnais has them living in his stables and forging paintings out there in the wilderness. And the creepy thing is that I sat next to this man on my flight over. He even offered me a job. And I saw a photo of him with a stunning woman in *Paris Match*. It's just too much. And we are feeling very uneasy, to say the least."

Richard listened intently, there was a silence, and then he spoke.

"Alexia, we must take these things one at a time. Your friend, Marie-Agnès is her name? Why don't you bring her here for a few days? Forgive me, but the two of you cannot be very comfortable in your little maids' rooms. As for our friend Mr. Mornnais, I think you are a bit melodramatic, but I will make some inquiries. But above all, my dear, you need not worry."

If part of the meaning of life was helping others, then Richard had found a way to begin to close the circle.

"I will ask Maria to drive you back to your place. Can you get your friend down to the street and into her car? Let's do that right now."

Richard stood up, went into the kitchen to find Maria, who, excited by the prospect of doing something new and different, went immediately to get her coat and Alex's. They drove back to Alex's apartment, Maria parking on rue Daubigny. Alex went to get Marie-Agnès, taking her belongings and bundling her into the service elevator. Not seen, not heard, the two women got into Maria's car and sped back to Neuilly.

Richard awaited them eagerly at the door to his apartment. He shook hands with Marie-Agnès — there was no point in excessive displays of emotion — and asked Maria to prepare the guest room and to get a light supper ready, for the sun was now setting, and soon it would be nighttime.

Alex moved a chaise longue nearer to one of the sofas and, semi-reclining, her legs stretched out, Marie-Agnès took some slow, deep breaths, trying to relax. She found a measure of reassurance in the knickknacks and bibelots that irritated Alex. There was something warm and personal, which comforted her after the cold hospital room and the trauma of her mugging. The ashen-grey veil on her face slowly lifted, replaced by a suggestion of pale rose.

"My dear, you've had quite an adventure, haven't you? And it may not be over yet."

Marie-Agnès's eyes started to well up with tears.

"But there is no need to worry. Now that you are here, we shall solve the problem, whatever it is. But tell me first, do you need to see a doctor for your injury?"

"No, I think I'm okay. The doctor at the hospital said it was just a superficial wound. The nurse left a tube of cream on my night table and I took it on the way out."

Richard turned to Alex. "Your friend is welcome to stay here as long as necessary, if she does not mind the company of an old man, that is."

"Oh, no, to the contrary," replied Marie-Agnès, "I am so grateful to you for your kindness."

And Richard was grateful to have something exciting and meaningful to do. He would not let this opportunity pass: to be back in the active world, facing a situation, analyzing a problem, finding a solution. He thought for a moment and looked at Alex and Marie-Agnès, an icy intensity in his blue eyes, as he started to lay out a plan of action.

He did not know why Marie-Agnès had been attacked, or who had done it. Had it something to do with the photos she took at the Château d'Hélène? And who was this Jacques Mornnais? So many unanswered questions. But for now, in a few days' time, once she was feeling better, Alex would drive Marie-Agnès to the château at Trubenne. Could Alex make the arrangements with Charlotte?

How brilliant this is, thought Alex. *This awful event is bringing our family together. But we need to make sure that no more harm comes to Marie-Agnès, poor lamb.*

"Alexia," continued Richard, "I think you will need to go to Marie-Agnès's apartment — you said you had her keys, did you not — to get some of her clothing and personal items. But be careful in case those thugs are looking for your friend."

The bit of color drained from Marie-Agnès's face. She swallowed hard and, despite her best efforts, felt the tears rolling down her cheeks. Alex took her hand and squeezed it as she tried to find the right words to comfort Marie-Agnès.

At last, they came to her. "You are not alone. We are all in this together, and we will protect each other. You must believe that. It does no good to cry. You're just letting that creepy man into your mind. Throw him out right now!"

A wave of warmth moved from her outstretched legs up her thighs, through her abdomen and chest, and when it reached her face, Marie-Agnès smiled for the first time in weeks. "Yes," she said, a first timid step toward turning things around.

Chapter 17

A WOMAN OF INDETERMINATE AGE trudged up rue Ravignan, her body bent against the gusts of frigid wind. She wore a long black padded coat, her head covered by a black cloth hat with a floppy brim, a purple woolen scarf wrapped around her nose and neck. She passed through Place Emile Goudeau, turned onto rue d'Orchampt, and walked slowly to the end of the street and back again, as though searching for a particular address.

Of course, it was Alex, and she was trying to see if anyone could be sitting in the cars parked bumper to bumper on the narrow street. When she noticed no one, she entered Marie-Agnès's building, waited for a moment, and then climbed up to the fourth floor and let herself into her apartment.

Marie-Agnès was almost compulsively neat. Usually everything had its place, but there was disorder. Papers had been tossed about the desk, the dresser drawers were open, clothing was strewn on the closet floor.

It looked like someone had already been there. She imagined that they were looking for Marie-Agnès's camera and her computer. Alex had her friend's keys, so how had they gotten in? She felt a tremor of apprehension. It would be best to get her business done as quickly as possible and leave.

Moving into the kitchen, Alex found the shopping cart and tiptoed back into the main room. She put underwear into a plastic bag, took two pairs of jeans, two sweaters, boots, and some toiletries from the bathroom. Lastly, she found extra contact lenses and her friend's eyeglasses. They could buy whatever else Marie-Agnès needed.

She stood behind the drapes and looked down at the street. A swarthy-looking man was walking down the street, coming toward the building. Alex started to panic when she recognized the driver who'd met Jacques Mornnais at the airport. *Oh, shit, what if he's coming here?* She left the apartment, closing the door soundlessly, and carried the shopping cart up to the sixth floor. Standing on the landing, she craned her neck to hear any noise, any movement, but all was still. Perhaps he was not coming here at all. Perhaps she only imagined it was the driver. She started slowly down the stairway.

Tarek had gotten a master key from a locksmith that he knew. He'd used the key before to enter the building, but this time, when he tried to open the front door with the master key, it jammed in the lock. He waited outside the door, hoping that one of the inhabitants would appear, but all was still, until a woman dressed in black, wearing a purple scarf, came out the front door. She held the door open for Tarek and continued slowly up rue d'Orchampt, pulling her shopping cart after her.

He had no trouble opening the apartment door. The last time he was here, he was looking for the camera. Jacques had been furious that he hadn't found it, but how was that his fault?

This time he was looking for the red-haired cow. Once again, he was out of luck. Jacques had mentioned a computer, but he hadn't found it, either. *Jamais deux sans trois* went the saying. Three was the magic number, all right: no camera, no woman, no computer. Frustrated, he pulled a row of books off the shelf and kicked them across the floor.

By the time he exited the building, Alex was on the Métro, going back to Neuilly. The momentary fear had passed, giving way to anger, anger at how unfairly Marie-Agnès had been treated, fury at the outrageousness of it all. And then the indignation subsided, and by the time she pulled her shopping cart down the deserted sidewalks of Neuilly, it had been replaced by a cold determination to see the wrongdoers punished for what they had done to her friend.

Chapter 18

Château d'Hélène, a week later

HE LAY STILL, WAITING FOR the pounding behind his eyes to soften. But it only got louder, and he realized that someone was banging on the door to his room.

"Time to get your ass out of bed, Bruno. We've got to get going."

Oh, fuck. Tarek. Bruno sat up and waited for his head to stop spinning before he staggered into the bathroom and stood under a cold shower until he felt numb. He dressed, went down to the kitchen, downed a double espresso, and walked into Jacques' office.

Despite his shower, the smell of alcohol hung over him, a cloud that expanded every time he exhaled.

"Morning, Jacques. There's something I'd like to run past you." He was preparing to tell Jacques that he'd gotten a call the other day, some guy that he had known when he worked in Marseilles. The man had taken a fancy to a painting he'd seen in an old church when he'd been touring Brittany. Could Bruno procure it for him?

Jacques looked up. He took a deep breath, dilated his nostrils.

"You stink to high hell, Bruno. Before you run anything past me, run

76

upstairs and take a shower or change your clothes or do something to get rid of that smell. Your drinking is out of control. It's an embarrassment. We'll talk when you get back from your trip."

Tarek was sitting on the great entrance stairway. "Try to pull yourself together. It's a long drive and we need to leave now."

"I'll just be a minute." Bruno went back to his room, brushed his teeth, slapped on some cologne, and threw a package of pills into his pocket. *Fuck Jacques, I'll take care of my friend's business myself.*

Chapter 19

A farm in Brittany

TAREK DROVE THE BMW STATION wagon out of the château garage and onto the road. He stuck the GPS onto the windshield even though he knew the way to the farm. He had been there before, and he remembered how to go. It was only toward the end of the trip that he needed to pay attention, for the dirt roads were not on any map.

Bruno had settled his large frame into the front seat. Tarek guessed that he had returned to the château in the early-morning hours after a night spent at an after-hours club in Dijon. Too much alcohol, not enough sleep.

By the time Tarek reached the highway, Bruno's eyes had closed as he relived his encounter with a new girl. Algerian, but with golden skin and red hair, he thought she must be from Kabylie. He wondered how old she was as sleep overtook him.

Tarek and Bruno, Bruno and Tarek. They had worked for Jacques for several years now. Not quite mistrust, but the precaution of throwing them together meant that each would see to it that the other did his job.

The highway was empty, but Tarek kept to the speed limit. Jacques' instructions were clear: as always he was to do nothing that would attract attention. The traffic picked up briefly as they approached Paris and then thinned out again as Tarek took the A11 motorway toward Le Mans.

Bruno slept. Tarek listened to Turandot and raised the volume as Bruno snored.

After Le Mans, Tarek continued toward the town of Roscoff, on the English Channel. The light changed as he headed northwest and the screeching of seagulls marred the quiet.

Bruno opened his eyes. The pounding in his head had abated only slightly. He reached into his pocket, popped a capsule, and swallowed it. After another twenty minutes, he opened his eyes again.

"Are we there?" he asked.

"Are you stupid or what? Does it look like we're there? Anyhow, not too long now if we don't get lost on these damn roads, if that's what you want to call them."

They turned off a secondary road onto an unpaved dirt track. At a fork, Tarek turned left and continued until they came to a cleared space, a house, and some outbuildings.

"Who the fuck would want to live here?" Bruno said.

"You know who the fuck lives here, so don't ask."

As they got out of the car, a short, stocky man came out of the house.

"*Salut*, Jean-Marc."

"*Salut*, Tarek. *Salut*, Bruno. How was the trip? I guess you found us all right?"

"No problem, it's not like it's the first time we've been here."

"Come in and have a drink."

They followed Jean-Marc into the house. He led them through the living room and into the kitchen, where a woman sat at a large table, peeling potatoes.

"Our guests are thirsty, Catherine," he said to his wife. A plump female version of her husband, a dirty white apron wrapped around her generous midsection, she stood up, waddled to a large carved wood buffet at one end of the room, and took out a bottle of calvados and poured four glasses.

Tarek left his glass untouched while Bruno eagerly gulped down his drink.

"Here, take mine. Let's not let it go to waste." Tarek smirked as he handed his glass to Bruno.

His social obligations fulfilled, Jean-Marc led the men to a barn where he kept farm machinery. He closed the metal door behind them and bolted it. "We don't want to be disturbed, do we?" he asked with a smile.

With the new infusion of alcohol, Bruno was starting to feel better. "No, Jean-Marc," he laughed, "That would not be a good idea."

Tarek said nothing. *Let's get this over with. We still have to drive back to the fucking château.*

Jean-Marc reached behind some bales of hay and lifted a cardboard carton. He placed it on the ground in front of Tarek and Bruno and, kneeling, removed two silver chalices from beneath layers of cloth.

"Here's what you ordered."

Bruno took an envelope from inside his jacket and removed a sheet of paper with photographs of the two chalices. He compared the two.

"Okay," he said. "Half now and half once our experts look at the stuff."

"You can see that they're what you ordered," said Jean-Marc.

Bruno remained pleasant. "Let's not argue. You know the deal, half now and half later. It's that or nothing."

Tarek stared at the packed-dirt floor. A cloud of tension hung in the barn's cold, damp air.

Then a smiling Bruno reached into his jacket, took out another envelope, and counted the bills. He held them out. "So, do we have a deal or not?"

Jean-Marc, having his accounts to settle and little time to find an alternative, nodded. He wrapped the two chalices, put them back in the carton, handed it to Tarek, and took the cash from Bruno.

Jean-Marc unbolted the barn door. While Tarek carried the carton to the car, Bruno put his arm around Jean-Marc's shoulders and spoke softly. "I have a special order that I'd like you to handle. I'll call you tomorrow."

As they got into the Renault, Bruno called out, "Say good-bye to Madame for us." They drove back down the muddy road and soon were on the highway heading east.

\#   \#   \#

80

Several hours later, Tarek was back on the A6 motorway, heading south. But before returning to the château, he had one more stop to make.

"Call him and tell him we're on our way," he told Bruno.

He exited at Fontainebleau and parked up the street from an imposing nineteenth-century *maison de maître*. A discreet sign announced that this was the residence and showroom of Nicolas Pagès.

Tarek removed the carton from the trunk of the BMW and rang the bell at the delivery entrance. A short man in an expensive tweed jacket opened the door, Nicolas Pagès himself. He led Tarek down a hallway into a small, cluttered room.

"Okay, here they are. Jacques said for you to do the paperwork as usual. We'll tell you when to ship them to the buyer. You already have the information, right?"

Nicolas Pagès, used to dealing with wealthy, self-important clients, tried to hide his revulsion at having to deal with the likes of Tarek. Not the sort of person he would want to be seen talking to. Why Jacques employed this man was beyond him. So little polish, so crude. But he only smiled as he unwrapped the chalices and examined them quickly, anxious to see Tarek's back.

"Yes," he said. "Of course, I'll need to examine them more closely. Tell Jacques I'll call him, will you?"

For Tarek, Nicolas Pagès was nothing more than one of the many pawns in Jacques' network, just another money-grubbing, pretentious little prick. Unlike Nicolas, he didn't bother to be pleasant. "Yes, sir, I will do that," he said and shook his hand, turned on his heel, walked back to the BMW, and started on the last leg of his trip. It had been a very long day.

Chapter 20

Paris, 2006

NICOLAS PAGÈS DROVE HIS MINI Clubman carefully down the ramp to the underground parking on Place de la Concorde. The car, with its square dark blue body and white roof, stood out in the sea of black and grey look-alikes. He felt that the Mini gave him a certain cachet, a subtle suggestion of a timbered house in the English countryside. But that unspoken reference to the English gentleman, a total fiction as far as he was concerned, if it impressed some clients, it had no effect on Jacques Mornnais. He was as unmoved by the car as by anything else that did not directly concern the business at hand. More's the pity, Nicolas thought as he strode rapidly up rue Royal to meet Jacques for lunch at a restaurant near Place de la Madeleine.

He walked through the revolving door at precisely one p.m. Jacques, true to form, arrived ten minutes later.

"Sorry to be late," he said. "The traffic was terrible. And thanks for agreeing to meet me on such short notice." Nicolas appreciated the pretense that he had any choice but to meet Jacques when and where summoned. At least Jacques favored Michelin-starred restaurants, but even though Jacques paid the bill, the meal would cost Nicolas dearly.

At first, Jacques brought his clients to Nicolas's gallery, and when on several occasions a purchase was made, Nicolas offered to share his markup with Jacques. "That's not necessary, my friend. At the right moment, you'll repay me," Jacques had said.

Nicolas's daughter, Véronique, had been a figure skater of some talent. A bad fall while attempting a double axel had put an end to her career. She spent months in rehab to repair the injury to her knee and developed an addiction to painkillers.

From time to time, Jacques would casually mention that he counted regional prefects and police commissioners among his friends. And when Véronique had been arrested for shoplifting, Nicolas summoned up his courage and asked Jacques if he could have the charges against her dismissed. It would be a pity to ruin her life for such a small incident.

"Well, that could be difficult, but I'll see what I can do." The charges were dropped. Véronique entered a detox program, got clean, and then relapsed. Each time, Nicolas would turn to Jacques for help. It was during this time that Jacques asked Nicolas if he could return a favor.

"Of course," said Nicolas, "how can I help?"

"I've met a Chinese painter, a very gifted young man. He has a talent for copying, starting with the master painters of the seventeenth and eighteenth centuries — artists like Poussin and Georges de la Tour — right through the Impressionists and Postimpressionists. Quite impressive. I imagine that some of your clients would jump at the chance to buy an original, wouldn't you say so?"

Nicolas was silent for a moment, as he realized what Jacques was asking him to do. "So I would be selling a fake?"

"I thought I could bring over one or two paintings to see what you think, and then if you agree, we could establish the provenance. If the copy were good, then the buyer would get the same pleasure contemplating it as they would from the original. We live in a consumer society, and that is a truism." He continued, "Art has become a consumer item, like a handbag, or a scarf or a watch. So we are offering a valuable service, by providing an object of desire at a reasonable price."

"But Jacques, that is stealing someone's idea, their creative spirit, their signature. The painting is an object of desire, as you say, because the buyer thinks it is genuine."

"Ah, that, my friend, is an outmoded way of thinking. It's just a question of perspective. Even in the past, many artists had whole stables where assistants turned out paintings according to the master's style, and sometimes he added some brush strokes to the finished work, or just his name, and yet we attribute those paintings to the master. Rather like Damian Hirst today. So, shall we get started?"

A tightening of the throat, shallow breathing. Nicolas realized that it was payback time. "And," added Jacques, "we'll share proceeds from the sales that you make, as I need to pay the painter and realize some return on my investment." He had said it all.

Nicolas studied the menu as Jacques continued, "I have a beautiful painting by Antoine Watteau. Would you like to think about him? I'll bring it by your house next week, to work on the provenance if that is convenient. Shall we order?"

Chapter 21

Château d'Hélène

Jacques was unhappy. Bruno had reported that the delivery of the silver chalices had gone as planned, but Jacques could not get Marie-Agnès out of his mind.

He paced back and forth in the office behind the family kitchen, the anger building with each length he covered. Mila and Tarek stayed seated, saying nothing, waiting for the storm to pass.

"How can she have just disappeared? Where the fuck is she?" The painstakingly cultivated veneer of urbane gentility had cracked, revealing another less attractive aspect of Jacques' persona. "Why can't you find her? How hard is it to find a fat red-haired woman?" And so on.

Tarek interjected, "We know the *pompiers* took her to Bichat, but there's no record of her staying there. It's all a bit crazy. I went back to her apartment, but she was not there, had not been back. It was the same as I had left it the first time I went looking for the fucking camera."

But Jacques was not to be placated. "She *cannot* just disappear."

At that moment, Bruno walked softly into the room. "Ah" — he smiled — "a family reunion."

"Shut the fuck up," snarled Jacques. "Have you found anything?"

"I tried to check the address book in her telephone, but it's quite disorganized, can't make heads or tails of it. Mostly just initials and a phone number or an address. She doesn't seem to bother with names, so it's impossible to do much with that. I spent an hour in a phone booth on Boulevard Malesherbes, waiting for the bloody *concierge* to show up, and froze my balls off."

He paused and continued, "But I found out that she's got a sister, living in Sainte-Maxime. She might know Marie-Agnès's whereabouts, if she's not already dead."

No sound, Jacques continued to pace, but his heart wasn't in it anymore.

"So you're suggesting that we contact the sister?"

"Yes, in a way. Leave it to me. I'll let you know if we come up with anything."

The storm had passed. Jacques sat at his desk and started to read through the faxes and print emails from his Blackberry. Mila returned to the kitchen to plan the coming days' meals.

Bruno went back to the stables, where he found Li Xio, one of the painters. The two men were a study in contrasts. Bruno with his bulky frame, his muscular body starting to go to seed, his pocket bulging with cash that he could not be bothered to count. Li, small boned, lithe, his thin body barely visible under his heavy jacket, poor, alone.

"I've spoken with Jacques, and I'm afraid we cannot pay you and Wen any more. You're already quite well paid for the work you're doing. Well fed and housed, I might add. It's only because Jacques has friends in the Interior Ministry that you're even still here, so if I might give you a word of advice, just do your work and stop fucking complaining."

Li, his hands in his jacket pockets, his long thin fingers tingling with fear, nodded his head and went back to the stable that was his home.

In the kitchen, Mila did not have to say very much to the Filipina, Ella, who was grateful to have found employment that made it possible for her to send money to her family every month. Like many of those of modest origins and therefore new to wealth, Mila treated Ella as if they lived in Napoleonic times: she worked fourteen hours a day, seven days a week, cooking and cleaning, her days shorter only when Jacques and Mila were not around. Having entered France on a tourist visa, as did so many Filipinos seeking work, Ella was outside the legal safety net. But she would cook and clean for as many hours as she had to, as long as she could send a transfer to the Philippines the first week of each month.

Unlike Li and Wen, she could read and speak French, but as she only spoke when spoken to, she was silent most of the time. Ella was part of the furniture, invisible in plain sight. And if she accepted that, for the moment, she had not drawn a winning ticket in the lottery of life, at the same time, she was not intimidated by Mila's ageless beauty, seeing it as nothing more than a lucky dip in the gene pool.

Chapter 22

IT WAS A MUCH HAPPIER morning for Mervin Peters, a lawyer who had left New York for Paris many years ago, unburdened by legal brilliance but gifted with an attitude of competence and gravitas. Prints of hunting scenes hung on the walls of his wood-paneled office. Thick dark green carpet covered the floor. Overweight but not yet obese, a shock of hair reminiscent of the ill-fated Senator John Edwards, attired with the utmost care, he gave a feeling of comfort and security to the wealthy expatriates who were his clients.

Merv liked to start each day by standing on the terrace of his penthouse on rue Le Sueur, turning his gaze from the Arc de Triomphe to Place du Trocadéro. At present he was far from his modest origins in Fresh Meadows, in what he liked to think of as a meteoric ascension from a housing project in Queens, New York, to the pinnacle of French society. Perhaps not the highest pinnacle but good enough for him to linger at the edges of the worlds of art and finance.

He stepped back inside and walked up the stairway to the top floor of his penthouse and went into a large room that housed a collection of paintings, drawings, antique furniture, and *objets d'art*. Each piece lovingly acquired, carefully put in its place. Merv's private garden, for him and him alone to contemplate. A smile, a sigh, he was at one with his possessions.

He was a man of habit, and his morning ritual of self-congratulation completed, he would go to his favorite morning spot, La Belle Fermière, to hold court over a breakfast of their outstanding fried eggs. His friends and clients — an overlapping group — knew that they could always find him there in the morning hours.

Rue Le Sueur was a narrow street, not unlike many others in the upmarket sixteenth *arrondissement.* Of course, none of the others could claim to be the site where the notorious Dr. Petiot, a serial killer during the Nazi occupation of Paris, murdered and burned his victims, but that was a long time ago and of interest only to historians. The house where Petiot committed his grisly acts had long been torn down, and this morning a white van managed to park in front of the office building that took its place.

Merv was on his way to rue François Premier when the driver and his passenger rang the intercom.

"Gaz de France, madame. We need to check on a leak in the neighborhood." The housekeeper pressed the button to unlock the elevator that went directly to Merv's apartment. Once inside, the workers went into the kitchen and opened the sliding doors that led to the terrace, to let out any gas that might have escaped. They also checked the water heater located next to one of the bathrooms and were grateful to the housekeeper to stay with them to answer questions.

At the same time, a roofer who had been kneeling at the base of a dome on an adjacent building crept over to Merv's building.

As the employees from the gasworks slowly and methodically checked for a leak, the worker came down from Merv's roof to the terrace, slipped into the kitchen, and noiselessly climbed the steps leading to Merv's secret garden. From under his jacket, he extracted a black plastic carrier bag. Placed the bag on the floor. Pulled out a mover's rug from his backpack and set that on the floor as well.

He studied the walls for a moment until he found the painting he had been assigned to obtain, a Bernard Buffet that had been stolen years ago from a private museum. He gently lifted the canvas and placed it on the rug, wrapped the rug around it, and put it into the carrier bag. In all, he had been in the room for no more than three minutes.

As he came down the stairs, he heard voices coming from the bathroom. He slipped back into the kitchen, opened the door to the service stairway, and exited the building. The gas workers checked their watches, thanked the housekeeper for her help, and left the building. They drove up rue Le Sueur and turned onto the small street that ran parallel to venue Foch. A man who was tying his shoelace at the corner of rue Piccini stood up, the van door opened, and the Buffet was on its way to be recycled once again. The morning that had started out so happily for Mervin Peters was about to go south.

Chapter 23

Club des Deux Continents, Paris

THE SIDEWALK CLEARED OF SNOW, Richard walked briskly to the Pont de Neuilly Métro station. He had given up tennis a few years ago, and in his uphill battle against aging, he hoped that a brisk walk every day would keep the blood flowing to his brain and preserve his memory. Still, he couldn't deny that he was increasingly forgetful.

He exited the Métro at Place de la Concorde and walked up rue Boissy d'Anglas that ran alongside the American embassy. A very safe neighborhood, guarded as it was by legions of French police. Wedged between a shop selling overpriced accessories and a trendy bar-restaurant was a building with two dark wood doors, held in place by massive hammered metal hinges. Above the intercom was a small gold plaque with *C2C* etched on it.

Richard pressed the buzzer, stated his name, and the doors swung open. He crossed a small paved courtyard and entered the changeless world of exclusive Parisian clubs.

Seated near the fireplace in one of the reception rooms was a man of medium build, whose ill-fitting suit did in no way detract from his elegant bearing. Michel de Clermont d'Auvergne, the son of one of Richard's childhood friends, rose and greeted him warmly.

"How is your dear father these days?" asked Richard.

"Much better thank you. He's a tough old nut. You both are," responded Michel.

More small talk, reminiscing about shared events and people. A waiter brought them their drinks — green tea for Richard and an espresso for Michel — and Richard turned to the reason for their meeting.

"The most curious thing has happened. My niece, Alexia, has come from Washington to visit Paris. She met an old friend in Parc Monceau, a translator. And this woman did some work for a client, spent the night at his château in Burgundy, and took some photos of the grounds while she was there. Almost two months later, she met one of his assistants to pick up a check. Then on her way home, two men attacked her in the Métro, her purse was stolen, and luckily she was not hurt too seriously. We know her apartment was visited, but it does not appear that anything was taken. But here is what is so curious: she had loaned the camera to my niece, who visited my cousin, Charlotte, down at Trubenne — you know, our decrepit château. Now, when we looked at the photos, it appeared that Asians are living there in Burgundy and copying paintings. We do not know what it all means, whether there is some connection between the photos and the mugging. This may all be just a coincidence, but I thought you could perhaps look into this man — Jacques Mornnais — let me know who he is."

Like so many civil servants (he had worked for many years at the DST, the French domestic intelligence agency), Michel had transitioned to a lucrative private sector career, as a security consultant. He listened carefully to Richard's account, and at the mention of Jacques' name, his thin lips formed the beginning of a smile.

"Ah, yes, Mr. Mornnais is rather well-known. Quite an art expert, is he not?"

Richard waited expectantly. "And..."

"And I think you and your niece and her friend would do well to steer clear of him. Let us just say that he not only has friends in high places, but sometimes he provides us with useful information. In fact, I think I saw him when I was at the Interior Ministry the other day. Not our sort of person at all. By the way, I assume you've downloaded the photos you mentioned. Can you send them to me? I'd like to take a look, confidentially, of course."

Despite the heat from the fireplace, a chill ran up Richard's back. It had started in the pit of his stomach, spread to his buttocks, and lodged in his neck as a painful spasm. *Your niece and her friend would do well to steer clear of him.* He lifted his head slowly, looked Michel straight in the eye. "I'll have to ask Alexia what she's done with the photos. But I need your advice. What should we do?"

Michel thought for a moment. "Why don't you send her friend down to Trubenne for some rest? We don't know that Mornnais was behind the attack, but even if he was, Mornnais is mercurial — he'll lose interest after a while and then she can come back to Paris."

"We're already planning for the girls to go down to Charlotte's, but then what?"

"I may be able to tell you more after I see those photos. In the meantime, your niece's friend should stay far away from him."

Richard, seeking reassurance, found himself staring into a pit of frightening unknowns. What did the photos mean? Who was Jacques Mornnais? He had said he would send the photos to Michel, but with Michel's network, where would that lead? He felt in the grip of the law of unintended consequences.

#   #   #

Once upon a time, until the last decades of the twentieth century, it was possible to walk into the American embassy via a side entrance on rue Boissy d'Anglas, diagonally across the street from the C2C club. Today, the embassy most closely resembled a bunker, surrounded by machine-gun toting police and concrete security barriers. Vehicles were stopped outside the gates and checked for explosives before being allowed into the courtyard. It was not the most welcoming place for the average citizen in need of help, a place much easier to leave than to enter.

It took Eugene ten minutes to go through the embassy's security controls. When he finally walked into the stately entrance, he was met by a

Frenchwoman: according to her badge, her name was Sylvie Theytaud. Her dark hair was pulled back from her face in a tight bun at the base of her neck, emphasizing both her large green eyes and prominent nose. She called to mind an elegant game bird, not conventionally beautiful, but Eugene found her much more attractive than the legions of Washington DC women, all with blond hair and the same perfect, short nose.

He followed Sylvie through the embassy's endless corridors until they reached the DCM's office, which had two windows overlooking rue Boissy d'Anglas. Vincent Reiner stood up and extended his hand as Eugene walked in. The DCM was well over six feet tall, with a full, sensuous mouth. His head, bald except for a wispy fringe of hair curling over his neck, was too small in proportion to his body, giving him an unbalanced mien. He immediately called to mind Humpty Dumpty.

"Hi, Gene, have a seat. Sorry it's taken us so long to connect."

Eugene managed a straight face as he winced inwardly. *What is it with these assholes, reducing everyone to a nickname?*

"Good to meet you, Vince." He wanted to keep the meeting as short as possible. "Pascal tells me you might need some help?"

The DCM was a career diplomat, well versed in the art of avoiding conflict while getting the job done.

"Thanks for the offer Gene, much appreciated. But for the moment we seem to be covered. If you don't mind, why don't you touch base every so often, to see if we might have need of your expertise?"

So Pascal is having this guy keep tabs on me. I'll play along for now— maybe I'll need Vince's 'expertise' one day. "Sure, Vince, no problem."

The DCM filled the next minutes with practiced smalltalk, until his assistant called to remind him of his next appointment.

Vince stood up, they shook hands, and Eugene remembered to say goodbye to Sylvie as he left. You never knew.

Chapter 24

PREOCCUPIED, RICHARD WALKED BACK TO his apartment.

In his absence, Alex had purchased two prepaid cell phones and some brown hair dye. Marie-Agnès was seated on a chair in the bathroom, atop an old sheet spread on the floor, as Alex cut her hair.

"I've seen this done so many times I think I can give you an okay cut myself," Alex laughed. Marie-Agnès looked dubious. "Don't worry, even if it's not great, your hair will grow back, I promise."

An hour later, Marie-Agnès emerged from the bathroom. Gone were her flowing titian locks. In their place, short, feathery dark hair, layered close to the head.

Richard returned as the two friends were packing their bags. Alex greeted him with a kiss on each cheek. "You look tired. Are you okay?"

"I met with a friend who suggested that we avoid your Mr. Mornnais. He thinks it's a good idea, you going down to Trubenne. And he asked me to send him the photos, said that might help him to find out more."

Alex thought for a moment. "Who is this friend, may I ask?"

"His father and I go back a long way. And this man — his son — used to work for a government spy agency. Now he uses his knowledge to help private clients like us."

"I guess we can trust him then, can't we?" responded Alex. She seemed so full of energy that she lightened Richard's glum mood. "Could I borrow your car? I need to pick up some things at my apartment. And that will give me some practice driving it before we set out tomorrow."

Alex took the elevator down to the building garage and located Richard's grey Mercedes A-Class, the preferred car for the wealthy classes favoring discretion. She drove out of Neuilly to Boulevard Malesherbes, circling her building's block before finding a place to park on rue Daubigny.

It was dark, but the streetlamps lit the room. Alex looked out the window on Boulevard Malesherbes and noticed a thickset man in the phone booth across the street. He didn't seem to be on the phone — hardly anyone used pay phones anymore — and Alex thought she had seen him as she had circled looking to park the car. She stood behind the drapes for a few minutes, and then the man exited the telephone booth, got into a green Clio, and drove off.

Alex felt a sense of unease. She told herself this made no sense, Nevertheless, she packed her belongings in the dark and drove back to Neuilly.

The following morning, she and Marie-Agnès left for Trubenne.

Chapter 25

Château d'Hélène

"LOOK, ALL YOU NEED TO do is buy a bunch of flowers. You can do that, can't you? Then go to the sister's house and deliver them."

"Y-y-yes. I g-g-guess so." Samuel stuttered when he felt under pressure.

"You guys fucked up the last time and the boss was not pleased. Went ballistic, in fact. Find the girl, find the camera, and get rid of her. Is that so hard to do?"

Bruno heard Samuel's breathing. It reminded him of a ship moving through choppy waters.

"You all right? Got a cold or something? Is Cosimo there?" Bruno fired his questions like bullets from a machine gun.

"Yeah, h-h-he's here."

"Okay, put him on."

Bruno held the telephone away from his ear as Samuel blew his nose.

"Yeah," grunted Cosimo.

"Good, now listen carefully. I'm going to say it again. You go to the sister, say you have flowers for Marie-Agnès. Ask if she's there. If she is, you know what to do, right? If she's not, ask where she is and go there. Get the camera and get rid of her. Got it?"

"Yeah."

"Now write this down." Bruno gave Cosimo the address in Sainte-Maxime. "Call me when the job is done. And no fuckups this time." He ended the call, hoping that Jacques would finally stop nagging him about the red-haired cow.

#   #   #

Bruno stuck his head into the office, where Jacques and Mila were reviewing photos for an upcoming issue of *Artixia*.

"I've gotta run an errand. See you tomorrow."

"What's her name, Bruno?" A smirk and a smile were fighting for possession of Mila's mouth. The smirk won.

"Ha, ha, very funny."

#   #   #

Bruno drove to Dijon, parked near rue de la Liberté, sidled up to the bar of the Vieux Dijon, a dark, crowded café. He greeted the man behind the bar, downed a glass of white wine, ane asked, "I think someone left a package for me?"

"Maybe. Let me check."

The bartender disappeared into a back room. When he emerged, he passed a parcel wrapped in brown paper across the bar. "Here you go."

"Thanks." Bruno reached into his pocket for some change.

"Forget it, the drink's on the house."

He returned to his car, the parcel under his arm. It was the painting that he'd ordered from Jean-Marc.

Bruno set out for Fontainebleau. While he didn't particularly enjoy driving long distances, he could hardly ask Tarek to run the errand for him. He would leave the painting with Nicolas Pagès. All the little man had to do was prepare a certificate of authenticity and come up with a provenance. The usual.

Bruno felt things were off to a good start. He hoped that Nicolas would offer him a drink, but if he didn't, he remembered that there was a bar near the gallery. He'd stop off there before he headed back to Dijon for a night out.

Chapter 26

MOST MIDDLE-AGED WOMEN LOVE road trips: freedom from men, a break from the obligations of home and family, relief from the tedium of well-ordered lives. For Alex and Marie-Agnès, the road trip meant temporary freedom from the noxious cloud emitted by Jacques Mornnais and his colleagues. And as was so often the case in times of crisis, it offered the possibility of the new beginnings that both women sought, albeit for different reasons.

They set off in the late morning, Alex behind the wheel, as Marie-Agnès, the city mouse, had never learned to drive. Participating in the tense ballet that was Paris traffic did not appeal to her. The mid-January traffic was light, and they were soon on the A6 motorway heading south. They would stop near Lyon that night and then drive on to Nîmes the following day.

By the time they reached the tollbooths at Fleury, bright sunshine had cut through the morning haze, the sky now cloudless and blue, the winter air dry and crisp.

As she drove, Alex started to pass in review the men she had known since she and her husband called it a day, drawing up the same lists of what worked and what didn't and reaching the same conclusion that there would be no new soul mate on the horizon, not now or ever. Wondering again just when it was that they had fallen out of love, when was the first time that she had that uncomfortable feeling that something was not right.

"Why is it that it's so much easier to remember when you fell *in* love than *out?*" she said aloud, as much to herself as to Marie-Agnès. "Why does something that never bothered you suddenly become important?"

Marie-Agnès was lost in her own much more practical thoughts. *Do not use your credit card,* Richard had said. *You want to keep as low a profile as you can.* That was all right for Richard, quite wealthy and certainly not living month to month the way she did. *Don't worry about that*, Alex had said, *we'll take care of the expenses for now.*

Yes, but how long was now? As she stared at the road ahead, the first insight came. *I could have died a week ago. I could be dead tomorrow. I need to be careful but it's useless to worry.*

She turned her head to look at Alex, saw the thin, aquiline nose, the firm jaw, a touch of blush on her cheeks, and just mascara on her long eyelashes. "Until the, hmmm, attack, everything bothered me—all the time. I think I have spent my life being bothered, but not anymore. Being bothered means you want something to change, and my own experience is that this is a waste of time."

They sped past the exit for Dijon, trying to put Jacques Mornnais behind them.

"Yes, but it just makes me so *angry,*" said Alex. "First they don't pay you, and then they try to kill you. What kind of people are they anyway? He seemed like such an insignificant little man when I sat next to him on the plane. And I even thought he might have had a face-lift. Can you believe that?"

"Honestly, I didn't notice. How I wish that I'd never answered that ad. Or that I hadn't gone for a walk to take photos. If only I hadn't crossed Bruno on my way back. And when you think about it, it's not like I really *saw* anything. It all seems so *unfair.*"

"It's much worse than unfair, it's positively *evil.* They shouldn't be able to get away with what they did."

"Yes, but what can I do?"

"I don't know, but when the time comes, we'll think of something."

There were patches of silence, punctuated now by bursts of laughter. No talk about what they would *do* once they arrived at Trubenne, the assumption being that the two friends would figure that out when they got there. Late afternoon, red roofs and umbrella pines rolling by, the first hints of dusk beginning to fall. Alex stopped at a motel in a highway shopping mall.

In their big down-filled coats, swathed in scarves, with only wisps of hair peeking out from their caps, the two friends were indistinguishable from the herd of motorway travelers. As they went to check in, a woman charged up to the clerk at the welcome desk, demanding more hangers. Another came to complain that there was not enough hot water in her shower.

Distracted, the harried desk clerk paid scant attention to the registration cards that Alex filled in. As in her apartment the night before, she felt silly and yet compelled to take precautions, and so she took care to invent names, addresses, and passport numbers, convinced that the young man behind the desk could not be bothered to do his job correctly. And she was not wrong.

The motel room, clean and minimal, Styrofoam cups wrapped in plastic in the bathroom, a small television on a wall stand in one corner. They had an early dinner across the street, at a grill that was part of a chain of barbecue restaurants. Alex commented on how this reminded her of traveling on I95 on the East Coast, and where had all the charming old café restaurants gone? Marie-Agnès begged to differ. She preferred the modern toilets and efficient service to the dingy cafés of the French countryside, with their stale bread, antiquated plumbing, and age-old layers of grit.

On the way into the restaurant, Marie-Agnès had cast an expert eye on the display of cakes and she ordered a *Forêt Noire* for dessert. When the rich chocolate concoction arrived, Alex almost blurted out *how can you eat that stuff* but thought better of it. Her friend had been through an awful experience, and if chocolate cake made her feel better, then why not?

A first forkful of the chocolate sponge cake and whipped cream, an exploration of the chocolate icing, a cherry deftly speared, first one and then another. Alex watched Marie-Agnès work her way slowly and methodically through the dessert. She seemed at peace, serene, savoring the mélange of tastes and textures.

"Well, Mag," said Alex, remembering her friend's childhood nickname,

"You certainly seem to be enjoying yourself."

"Oh, yes. *Forêt Noire* is a favorite of mine. When we were children, my sister and I used to make this cake every winter." *My sister! I've completely forgotten about her!*

"Oh, do you mind?" she asked Alex. "Can I borrow your cell phone to send my sister a message that I'll be out of touch for a while?"

"Sure, no problem."

Hi, she wrote, *taking some time off, staying with friends in a château near a town called Trubenne. Will be back in touch when I return to Paris. Love, Mag.*

Chapter 27

Trubenne

THEY HAD A SURPRISINGLY GOOD night's sleep and an early checkout the next morning. They drove south to Marseilles under a brilliant Mediterranean winter sun, the sky an intense blue and the grey piles of frozen snow faded into oblivion. Here, the sweet-smelling air held the promise that Marie-Agnès would be free from harm.

By midday they had found their way to a budget hotel near the train station in Nîmes. Charlotte was parked outside the entrance, waiting for them. Alex followed Charlotte as they left the city. The road to Trubenne was now familiar, but Alex was still glad to have Charlotte lead the way as she followed her up into the surrounding hills. Charlotte had left the holiday ornaments on the foliage outside the old château, the red and white lights sparkling against a pale blue sky.

"Well" — Charlotte smiled at Marie-Agnes — "Richard told me about your little adventure, or should I say misadventure. How are you feeling?"

"Oh, I'm much better, but still uncertain about what I'm going to do. I can't spend my life hiding from Jacques Mornnais and his thugs."

"For the moment, you're going to stay here, learn to enjoy life in the country. I thought that I could put out the word that I'm available to do translations, and I could hand over that work to you, keep you occupied."

Marie-Agnès forced back the tears that she could feel welling up and managed to say, "Thank you, Charlotte," in a clear voice.

Following a late lunch of cheese and pâté, with a light local red wine, Charlotte and Alex showed Marie-Agnès the vineyards that Richard had hoped one day to upgrade. The air became chillier as the sun moved lower in the sky and they went back to the house to get Marie-Agnès settled.

Charlotte put a *sauté de veau* to heat on the stove, the hearty aroma filling the kitchen as they boiled water for noodles, washed salad greens, and sipped some more wine. Over dinner, they told Charlotte about Richard's conversation with Michel de Clermont d'Auvergne. "Oh, yes, I remember meeting him years ago." Then they described the misadventure, as Charlotte called it, Marie-Agnès's flight from the hospital and Alex's near run-in with Jacques' chauffeur. It might have been funny if it hadn't been so frightening.

Chapter 28

Sainte-Maxime

AUDREY DUVALOIS KNEW THAT THE women in her office always admired how she dressed, and she took her time, carefully tying the Hermès scarf around her neck. It had been a gift from her younger sister, Marie-Agnès. *Some people have all the luck, living it up in a château while the rest of us have to work.*

The doorbell rang and it startled her. Audrey wasn't expecting anyone this early in the day. She ran down the stairs and cracked the door open.

The first thing she saw was bouquet of red roses. *What a surprise. Who could be sending me flowers?* Her gaze shifted to the two men, the tall one holding the flowers and the shorter one standing next to him.

The taller deliveryman held out a bouquet. "F-f-flowers for M-M-Marie-Agnès Duvalois. Is sh-sh-she here?"

Flowers for Mag?

"No, she's not. I'm her sister."

The shorter man spoke, "Oh, do we have the wrong address? Does she live in Sainte-Maxime?"

"No, she does not. She lives in Paris."

106

"Looks like there's been a mistake. Can you give me the correct address?"

"Well, I'm afraid you won't find her in Paris right now."

Audrey paused. Samuel and Cosimo waited for the woman to continue.

"You might find her at a château in a town called Trubenne. She's staying there with friends." She hoped they were impressed.

"Is that around here?"

"I don't really know, but I think there's a place called Trubenne somewhere in the Languedoc."

"Never mind. The shop will find her. But why don't you keep the flowers. It's a shame for them to go to waste."

It wasn't often that anyone offered her flowers, and Marie-Agnès's sister opened the door and took the bouquet.

The deliverymen smiled and turned on their heels. She carried the flowers into the kitchen. *Who could be sending Marie-Agnès flowers?* She looked for a card, but there was none. It was all a bit bizarre. Wrong address, no card. Mag knew the strangest people. Well, that was not her problem. Audrey placed the flowers in a vase, got ready to reply to the SMS she had received yesterday. Funny, but her sister must have been using someone else's phone. That was not her problem, either. She sent her message to AlexiaT: *Marie-Agnès, You have flowers from a secret admirer.* An error message popped up, *Unable to deliver.* That was the problem in France — outside of big cities, cell phone coverage was spotty. She'd try again tomorrow.

Marie-Agnès's sister remembered to send the message the following day at lunchtime. This time her message was a bit longer: *Mag, You received flowers yesterday. I told the deliveryman you were staying in a château in Trubenne. Hope they found you. And who is your secret admirer?*

Chapter 29

Trubenne

MORNING. MARIE-AGNÈS WAS STILL asleep when Alex joined Charlotte in the kitchen. She brewed some coffee and sat down across from Alex.

"Now," she said, "I can see you have something on your mind. Tell me what's going on."

Two pairs of blue eyes met as each held the other's gaze.

"You cannot imagine how angry I am about what they've done — and tried to do — to Marie-Agnès. It is truly infuriating." She set her mug down on the table harder than she meant to. The mug was full, and a drop of coffee sloshed over the rim and onto the table. Alex frowned, and then she smiled. "Now that Marie-Agnès is safe here with you, I'm going back to Paris to do something about that."

"Wait a minute, isn't that a little precipitous? I mean, you just got here. Wouldn't it be a good idea for the three of us to talk things over?"

"There's been enough talking. It's time for action."

"Your uncle's friend implied that these are dangerous people, and he said to stay away. I think that is excellent advice."

"No need to worry, Charlotte. I know what I'm doing."

"I *am* worried. What is it that you're going to do?"

"I still have a few things to work out and then I'll let you know."

Later in the day, Alex was off to Paris.

#   #   #

It had not taken Samuel and Cosimo very long to find Trubenne. They crept through the woods surrounding the château and saw the three women. Bruno had said to get the job done right, and they agreed that that meant taking care of all three. When they saw Alex saying goodbye to Charlotte and Marie-Agnès, they quickly decided that Cosimo would be responsible for the blonde and Samuel for the old woman and the brunette. The last time they saw the brunette, she had had red hair, but they recognized her as the woman they had followed into the Métro.

Cosimo ran to the car that they had parked on the road outside the château. It was a metallic-green Peugeot 206 that they had stolen a while ago. Sturdy but tired, dented, and scratched, it had seen better days.

The woman, on the other hand, was driving a Mercedes Class-A, a luxury compact with a nervous engine. He barely managed to keep a safe distance behind her as she navigated the sinuous country roads. Cosimo almost lost her at the first roundabout. She accelerated on a straight stretch and then slowed down as she saw a roadblock manned by gendarmes up ahead.

Cosimo saw it, too, and skidded onto a country road before coming to the intersection. And waited. He saw the gendarmes wave the blonde through and she turned onto the road to Paris and was swallowed up by the horizon.

Should he risk getting stopped? The blonde was long gone. He'd never catch up with her. Cosimo started the engine, followed the back roads that wound through the countryside until he came to the A6 motorway back to Paris. He drove carefully, nervous about how things continued to not work out as planned, yet allowed himself to hope that Samuel had better luck.

Bruno hadn't said anything about the blonde, so he'd keep that failure to himself.

\#   \#   \#

Alex had noticed the Peugeot. *What an ugly car. It looks like the color of green shit*. Then she forgot about the car, focusing her thoughts on the future. After a while, she looked again. The car had disappeared, and it occurred to her that she was very hungry. She stopped in a dreary little town, went into a dingy café, and as she sat eating a tasteless ham and cheese sandwich she wondered if Marie Agnès didn't have a point about such establishments after all. Then her phone beeped and she read the message from Mag's sister.

She had a sudden pain in her belly, and it was not due to the lousy sandwich.

Alex called Charlotte. *Please answer.*

"Hello?"

"Oh, Charlotte, I'm so glad it's you."

"Are you all right, Alex? Who did you expect it to be?"

"No, I mean, yes, I'm all right. But I've just found a message from Marie-Agnès's sister." Alex read the message.

"Flowers from a secret admirer…" she repeated.

Charlotte interrupted her, "That's ridiculous. I think someone is looking for Marie-Agnès."

"Shall I come back to Trubenne? I could be there before day's end."

"No, that won't be necessary. Forewarned is forearmed. We'll be just fine."

"What are you going to do?"

"I'm going to keep my guest safe, that's what I'm going to do. Alex dear, do not worry about us. We'll be fine. Drive carefully and call me when you are back in Paris."

Chapter 30

Trubenne

SAMUEL WATCHED AS COSIMO DROVE off to follow the blonde. He walked back into the woods. Cold, damp, the leaves slippery, his feet getting tangled in the undergrowth. *Fucking Bruno, let him try to do this.*

Where were the two women? The front door was shut. It wasn't like he could just walk up, ring the doorbell, and shoot them. He'd have to wait for the women to come outside. So he remained in the woods, the cold creeping up his legs. He thought he heard noises. *Fucking animals.* He clutched the Glock in his pocket. If worse came to worse, he could shoot them as well.

The day started to come to a close. He turned to walk to the road that led to the village. Samuel hoped there was a cheap hotel where he could get a good night's sleep. He'd come back and finish the job tomorrow.

#   #   #

"Is everything okay? You look troubled," asked Marie-Agnès.

Charlotte had reached a decision. "You wouldn't by any chance have a secret admirer, would you?"

Marie-Agnès laughed. "No, why do you ask?"

"I don't want to frighten you, but your sister just sent an SMS to Alex. I guess you had sent her a message from Alex's phone. She said that two men had come looking for you at her house, delivering flowers from an unnamed sender. And she told them you were staying in a château in Trubenne. So they are probably headed this way."

"How could she be so stupid?" At first, Marie-Agnès seemed more upset with her sister than frightened by the news. Then her face became a mask of worry.

"We need to stay calm, put our heads together. The men may be lurking outside, but we don't have to worry as long as we're in the château. It was built in more dangerous times!"

What would Alex do? She would be fierce and defiant, and so will I.

"Follow me," said Charlotte, and she led Marie-Agnès up the winding stairway to the top of the turret. The women looked out of the Rapunzel window. The château's outside lights had turned on, casting long shadows on the courtyard, the outlines of the trees silhouetted against the evening sky.

"Look straight ahead, I think I saw something move."

"It's probably a wild pig, the woods are full of them."

"I want to take a closer look. I need to know why they're after me."

Charlotte grabbed Marie-Agnès' elbow as she started for the stairway. "Don't be crazy, they haven't come for some polite exchange of views." But Marie-Agnès was already running down the stairs.

Charlotte started to load a gun she had removed from the rifle rack, when she heard a popping noise, followed by a piercing scream. More pops, and more screams.

#   #   #

Marie-Agnès stopped at the foot of the stairway, breathing heavily, her mouth dry. She saw a flashlight on a nearby table, picked it up and turned it on. The strong beam lit up the entryway, her need to know overrode her fear, and she stepped outside, moving the beam of light across the trees. Again, something moved in the forest, and she focused the light in that direction.

Samuel had seen Marie-Agnès walk across the courtyard, and he pointed his Glock in her direction. As the beam of light swept across him, he squeezed his eyes shut, momentarily blinded, and dropped his arm. *What the fuck was going on* he thought, trying to move out of the light. A piglet squealed in fear as he stepped on it. Nearby, its mother was foraging for food. The sow heard the cry for help and charged the predator who had attacked her piglet. The man screamed out in pain, and as the wild boar attacked, he managed to get off a shot. This further enraged the wounded sow. The man tried to shoot her but the shots went wild as she continued to attack him. Then he was still.

#   #   #

Charlotte took the loaded rifle, went downstairs and into the courtyard.

"What was that?" asked Marie-Agnès. She stood unmoving, surrounded by a pool of light, her arm hanging stiffly at her side.

"I'm not sure. I'm going to take a look, but it would be best if you stay here."

Once again, Marie-Agnès illuminated the forest, as Charlotte approached cautiously and stopped at the edge of the trees. Through the trees, she glimpsed a group of wild boars, snorting and chomping. They were eating something, she was sure of that. The animals could weigh up to one hundred kilos, and she had no desire to provoke one to charge her, so she backed away, pulling Marie-Agnès with her to the safety of the château.

"So what did you see?"

"I'm not sure. It looked like a couple of *sangliers* eating dinner. Not a good idea to disturb them. Let's take a look tomorrow."

In the morning, Charlotte ventured into the forest. She walked slowly, paid attention. She was not surprised when she saw the body, or what was left of it, but she threw up her breakfast anyway. The animals had eaten the face, fingers, and parts of the arms down to the bone. When she saw the Glock at the man's side, she understood what had happened.

What should I do? Call the gendarmes? Maybe not. Better to leave him there. The animals are hungry and they'll probably make a meal of the rest of the body.

113

Charlotte picked up the Glock and dropped it into an unused well in the courtyard. Back in the château, she brushed her teeth, went into the kitchen. Marie-Agnès was nibbling at a slice of bread. This time her concerns had destroyed her appetite.

"Is everything okay?"

"I guess you could say so. That man who delivered the flowers to your sister? I think the *sangliers* had him for dinner. There are leftovers, so best to avoid the woods for a while."

"He's dead, then."

"Oh, quite so."

"Do you think anyone else knows that I'm here?"

"Aside from Richard and his friend?"

"No, not them. I was thinking about the second man who attacked me in the Métro."

"Our visiter was alone. It's likely that the second man is off doing bad things to other people, but we'll take special care, won't we?"

Marie-Agnès felt a flutter of fear, then thought about Alex — she wouldn't let fear get in the way. "Yes, we'll take special care, all right. Can you pass the jam please? I'm starving."

Chapter 31

Nemours

BRUNO SAT IN A CAFÉ overlooking the Loing River in Nemours, his back to the wall, waiting for Nicolas Pagès. He ordered a second espresso to stop the pounding behind his eyes. It was not Nemours' provincial charm that had attracted Nicolas, but rather the probability that no one would recognize him and Bruno when they met.

A wave of frigid air as the glass doors opened, and Nicolas was seating himself across from Bruno. He carried a plastic supermarket shopping bag that he placed on a nearby chair.

Perfunctory greetings, the fog on the highway, the weather, and then Nicolas cut to the chase. "I've examined your painting, and it is indeed a Daubigny seascape. May I ask where you found it?"

Bruno smiled. "You can ask, but there's no need for you to know, is there? Have you done the paperwork? My client is anxious to see this hanging in his home."

Nicolas smiled. "Of course the paperwork is done, but I think there is a small matter of compensation to be settled."

Bruno, no longer smiling, shifted his large frame on the banquette. "We

115

agreed that you'd get your share when I get paid, and not before. So the matter has already been settled. If you're not happy, then I'll take back my painting, and we won't talk about it anymore."

Was Bruno threatening him? At that moment, a chain of regrets wound itself around his throat: regret at having met Jacques Mornnais, at having agreed to work for him, and now regret that he had accepted Bruno's offer to — as Bruno had put it — freelance. He'd let the worm of greed burrow its way into his brain, and now it was too late.

He tried to straighten himself as he removed a light grey envelope from inside his cashmere sport coat and placed it on the table. The large man deftly slipped the envelope inside his rough tweed jacket.

"And when will you be paid?"

"Soon. I'll let you know." Bruno caught Nicolas' gaze directly in his own and held it there until Nicolas lowered his eyes.

"Well, my friend, I've got to get going. We'll be in touch. Drive carefully in the fog. It can be dangerous, you know."

Bruno stood up, took the plastic shopping bag, and walked out of the café. Nicolas sat for a few minutes until he felt the strength returning to his legs. His heart was still pounding. Bruno frightened him even more than Jacques or Tarek. He drove back to Fontainebleau very carefully.

#   #   #

Château d'Hélène

Late afternoon. Tarek was waiting to drive Jacques and Mila to Paris. Like actors on a stage, each playing their role. Tarek, slouched in a corner, hands in his coat pockets, expressionless, waiting, waiting, words flying around him. Jacques, pacing in the entry, talking on his Blackberry, deftly playing the keyboard, talking again. And Mila, talking to Ella, the Filipina. No, talking at her.

"The reception rooms need a proper cleaning. Don't just move the dust from one place to the next. And the kitchen, it's quite dirty in some places. You need to pay more attention to that, Ella. And the dining room, make sure

116

the silver is polished, and I think the floor could use some waxing…"

She threw a five-hundred-Euro bill on a table. "Here, Bruno can take you shopping for food. He'll let you know when we're returning. Make sure to have our meals ready."

Ella, standing very still, her eyes blinking to hold back the tears of anger and frustration—"Yes, madame, of course, madame," —as Mila continued to enumerate tasks.

Jacques to Tarek, "And where is Bruno?"

"I dunno. He said he had to run an errand."

"Okay, I'll call him later. Let's go."

Mila had told Ella what was expected of her. There was no further need to acknowledge her presence.

The front door closed. Ella went into the kitchen. She peeled potatoes and put them in a bowl of cold water while she peeled and chopped garlic and onions. Diced a slice of salt pork. Seasoned two chickens with salt and pepper, slipped a lemon wedge in each cavity, and put them to roast in the oven. Cut the potatoes into quarters, sautéed them with the onions, garlic, and salt pork. Washed salad greens, chopped parsley and shallots. Put the salad into two separate bowls. While the chickens roasted, she washed up from lunch, loaded the dishwasher, and started to clean the kitchen.

She took out a large tray, put plates and cutlery for two, and when the chickens were ready, placed one on a serving plate. She put some of the sautéed potatoes into a dish, mixed the parsley, shallots, oil, and vinegar, and poured the mixture into one of the bowls of salad. From the refrigerator, she removed half a camembert, a thick slice of *comté,* and an open bottle of Côtes de Beaune. Lastly, she cut a baguette in half.

Elle loaded the serving tray and carefully walked to the painters' studio, carrying them their evening meal. She spoke to them in English. "Hello, here's your dinner. I hope you like it."

"Hello," they greeted her in unison. Ella liked the painters as she felt a bond with them. Jacques and Bruno treated them with the same disdain as they treated her.

"You don't need to come for the tray," said Li. "I'll bring it back to the kitchen later."

"Oh, thanks, that's nice of you," said Ella, grateful for one less thing to do this evening.

After returning to the kitchen, Ella sat down at the table for a few minutes, for she had been on her feet since early that morning. She drank a glass of water and went into the family dining room to set the table for Bruno's meal. While she was removing the china from the cupboard, Bruno crossed into the office. As he did so, his cell phone rang, and he put down the plastic bag he was carrying.

His phone call completed, he followed Ella back into the kitchen. "Aren't you lonely? Set another place for yourself and have dinner with me."

"Oh, that's all right, sir, I'm quite fine."

"No, Ella, I insist. I want to get to know you better." And he went to wash up before dinner.

Ella did as she was told — she had no choice, after all — and as she had finished putting the food on the table, she opened a second bottle of Côtes de Beaune. Bruno came back into the dining room, a cloud of cologne in his wake. Smiling, he put his iPhone on the buffet, and the mellow voice of Frank Sinatra filled the room.

Ella was no fool. She had worked for a family in Saudi Arabia before escaping to the safer haven of France, and she had a pretty good idea of what Bruno meant when he said he wanted to get to know her better. The bits of food she tried to eat stuck in her throat. Bruno, oblivious to her unease, kept up a running conversation, punctuated by her short replies to his questions.

She cleared the table as Bruno finished the last of the wine, and placed a bowl of chocolate mousse on the table. "Ella, bring us some Sauternes. That's a nice girl."

Back in the kitchen, she found an open bottle of Sauternes in the refrigerator. She stifled the urge to run out the back door, away from Bruno's menacing presence. But instead, she returned to the dining room and placed the bottle on the table. Bruno poured himself a glass that he swallowed in one gulp and served himself again.

As he helped himself to some of the chocolate mousse, a dollop slid off the spoon and onto his belly. "Come here, Ella." He reached over and grabbed her wrist, pulling her up from her seat. "Let's wipe this dirty spot away, shall we?" Face flushed, eyes bloodshot, he pulled her closer and moved her hand over his belly, rubbing it, moving downward, at the same time undoing his belt buckle with his free hand.

"Be my nice little friend, Ella. You be good to me, and I'll be good to you," he said, moving her hand under his trousers. As Bruno leaned back and closed his eyes, Ella took a deep breath and, with all her strength, pulled her hand away and ran into the kitchen. Bruno stood up, holding on to his pants with one hand and following her.

"Please, sir, please leave me alone."

"No, Ella, you're going to be my little friend," he said, slurring his words. Ella had turned to the dishes in the sink, deluding herself that he would go away. But instead, he pushed himself against her, grabbing her breasts with his free hand. She heard him panting as he buried his face in her hair, his alcohol-fueled breath stifling her, felt him growing harder, and tried to pull away, but his massive bulk stuck to her like a magnet.

His hand moved under her apron, trying to pull down her pants. As he grew more excited, Ella froze. Before her she saw only a deep black space, spinning into a vortex. And then Bruno grunted, a wheezing sound came from his throat, and he fell back against the kitchen table. He lost his balance, and he fell again, his head making a dull thud as it hit the tiled floor.

Ella, motionless, looked down at Bruno. Saw that his red face was now an ashen grey. His breath came in shallow spurts, and as she watched, he appeared to stop breathing altogether.

Her face felt hot, she started to shake. *Get ahold of yourself.* She stared at the prone body. *What should I do? Call someone? The police? No, they'll ask me questions. Mila?* She reached for her cell phone and started to call her. Then, second thoughts arose. *No, she'll call the police, she'll try to blame me for Bruno's death, and then she'll fire me.*

She stood unmoving, paralyzed by fear, until she was startled by a knock at the back door. It was Li, bringing back their dinner tray. Ella, still speechless, pointed to Bruno's body.

"What happened?" asked Li.

"He tried to rape me, and then I guess he had a heart attack or something like that. What shall I do?" For Ella, Bruno was no longer a person. Just as he had treated her as an object, he was now nothing more than a problem to be solved.

"I'll get Wen," said Li, "and we'll figure out what to do with him."

While Li went in search of Wen, Ella quickly went through Bruno's pockets. She found two envelopes in his inner jacket pocket, one with the usual wad of bills and another, light grey, with some papers in it. One of the outer pockets sagged, and she pulled out a cell phone with a protective cover in a pink and red flowered pattern. *It's a woman's phone*, she thought. *Must belong to one of his whores.* She continued her search of the body and removed Bruno's car keys from his pants pocket, along with two condoms. *Where is his cell phone?* She wondered, and then she remembered that it was on the buffet in the dining room. Frank Sinatra was now singing "New York, New York."

She made a split-second decision to leave the money on the table, along with the car keys and the condoms, but to hide the envelope with the papers in it — she would go through that later.

Another knock at the back door. The painters had returned. Li, whose English was better than Wen's, spoke for both of them. "We talked it over, and we need to get rid of him."

"Are you sure he's dead?" asked Ella.

"If he isn't, he will be. We have no other choice — you're not thinking of calling the French police, are you?"

"Of course not," said Ella. "They'll send me back to the Philippines."

Wen stepped outside the back door, saw the gravel path leading down to the river. He spoke to Li in Chinese.

"Okay," said Li to Ella. "We're going to dump him in the river. He's a drunk, and when they find him, if they do, they'll just think he had an accident."

It was cold, too cold to snow. The two men carried Bruno outside, and their breath made clouds in the night air as they rolled him down the gravel path to the riverbank. Ella took the condoms and the two cell phones, joined them at the river's edge, and threw them into the water. Then, with a quiet splash, Bruno entered the river. Li took a rake leaning against a tree and pushed Bruno's body under the surface.

As they returned to the château, they raked the gravel path smooth.

Back in the kitchen, Ella gave Bruno's car keys and the wad of cash to the painters. "I don't know how to drive, and I don't want the money."

"We've got to leave, right now." Li was speaking to Wen in Chinese. "We don't want to be here when they discover that the pig is missing."

"Are you sure he was dead?"

"Well, if he wasn't then, he is now. Don't worry about him. You'd best think about yourself."

"But if we leave, what about the maid?"

"She can fend for herself. No one would accuse her of getting rid of Bruno, unlike us. But where can we go?"

"My uncle Xi lives near Paris. I don't know exactly where, but I've got his address."

"Okay, then let's get going. We'll take the pig's car, drive to Dijon, and take the train to Paris."

Li turned to Ella. "We're going to leave. Don't want to be here when Jacques and Mila return. Will you be all right?"

Ella didn't *feel* all right, but what could she do? Li was right, he and Wen had to leave.

"Yes, I'll be fine," she murmured.

"Good night, Ella, and good luck to you," said Li.

"And good luck to you," she replied. The painters went back to the stables to pack their belongings, and Ella climbed to her room on the second floor, taking the light grey envelope with her.

Like a woman who paid attention to her makeup but ignored those parts of her body that were unseen, the château's elegant décor ended on the first floor. Out of sight, out of mind. On Ella's floor, reserved for the help, large flakes of beige paint littered the hallway. The radiators were tepid to the touch, and bare bulbs hung in the rooms; they emitted a sad, greyish-yellow light.

Ella sat at the edge of her bed, for a moment, paralyzed by fatigue, overcome by fear and anxiety. Then she stood up, went down the hallway to a room where old furniture was stored, and slipped the grey envelope behind the cushions of a beat-up leather sofa.

121

A mental jolt and she remembered the plastic shopping bag in the dining room. She forced herself to go back downstairs to retrieve it, slowly climbed back to the second floor, and slipped the bag under the leather sofa. She made a third trip downstairs to turn on the alarm system, returned to her room, and, fully dressed, wrapped herself in the bedclothes and fell at once into a profound sleep. She did not hear the sound of Bruno's Clio driving off into the night.

#   #   #

The painters, having few possessions, had packed quickly. They left the paintings in the studio, Li taking only his sketchbook of the scenery at the château. He hated Jacques and his entourage, yet he had found inspiration in the natural beauty of the surroundings.

They drove north to Dijon and parked Bruno's Clio in a neighborhood where bands of young, unemployed men hung about, dealing drugs and waiting for the next exciting thing to happen. A new Clio left unattended was such an occurrence, and a few minutes after Li and Wen walked away from the car, it had been stripped, the carcass abandoned for the tinkers to dismantle.

It was after midnight when they walked into Dijon's train station. In one corner, two drunks were having an animated conversation, and sitting as far from them as she could was a young woman trying to concentrate on grading the examinations that were piled on her lap. Deborah Leconte, a teaching assistant and sociologist, was waiting for the next train to take her to Paris and into the arms of Sébastien, her current boyfriend. Intent on getting through as many exams as possible to free her up for a few days and nights of lovemaking, she looked up with a start when Li's shadow fell across the pages on her knees.

"*Bonjour*, can you help me please?" he asked in a gentle voice, hoping that she spoke English.

Thin, enveloped in a bulky jacket, a wool cap pulled low on his forehead, he did not look at all menacing. "Perhaps," she replied. "What is it that you want me to do?"

Li pointed to the ticket windows. "They are closed," he said. He held out some bills, and pointing to the automatic ticket machines, he asked, "Could you buy two tickets to Paris? I don't know how to do it."

Deborah looked at the Departures screen and saw that the next Paris-bound train was due in twenty minutes. She gathered her papers and shoved them into her backpack. "Sure, no problem," she said, and Li stepped back, hoping that they had not been filmed by the security cameras in the station. When she returned with the tickets, he thanked her, relieved that not all French were as nasty as Jacques and company.

In the train, Deborah fantasized about the things she and Sébastien would do to each other, and the painters planned their next steps when they arrived in Paris. As for the security cameras, Li need not have worried. They had been out of order for a week, and due to a budget shortfall, it was not certain when they would be repaired.

Chapter 32

ALEX DROVE BACK NORTH AT a more leisurely pace. The secondary roads were slower, with some stretches in disrepair. Unencumbered by the need to make conversation, she had time to think and put the last pieces of the puzzle into place.

The message from Marie-Agnès's sister worried her, and she had offered to turn back. But Charlotte sounded so confident and Alex was eager to take her next steps. She called Charlotte that night when she arrived at Boulevard Malesherbes. It was late, but she wanted reassurance.

"Hi, I was wondering, is everything okay?"

"Uh, yes, I guess so."

"You *guess so*?"

"Well, there *was* someone, but he's not here anymore, and we are okay. I don't want to talk about it on the phone. But not to worry, Marie-Agnès will tell you all about it in due time."

#   #   #

Several days later, Alex took the now-familiar walk to Richard's apartment. Cupping a mug of tea in his hands, he fixed Alex with a warm blue stare. "In all the excitement the last time you were here, I never asked if you enjoyed Trubenne."

"Oh, yes, it was so exciting." She paused. *Okay, Alex, take the plunge.* "And Charlotte told me that you had once thought about developing the place, and we both think that is a great idea, if you still want to do it."

"Really, she said that?" Richard lowered the mug to the coffee table. Was it his imagination or were his hands shaking ever so slightly with excitement?

"Yes, she did. I told you when we met, I've come to France to discover my roots, and Trubenne is at the heart, isn't it? I just have a small project to take care of first, and then we can work on your plans to develop the vineyard and the château."

"Of course, my dear. But do tell me about this small project you mentioned."

It's best if I fill him in bit by bit. "I'm going to work for this Mr. Mornnais. When I met him on the flight, he said to call him if I was looking for work as a translator. So I shall, since we're pretty sure he'll be looking to replace Marie-Agnès. And then we'll see where we go from there."

Richard looked so worried that she thought it wise not to provide any further details of what she had in mind. "Alexia," he started, but she cut him short.

"Sh, really, it's okay. I've worked everything out. Please, don't worry about me."

#   #   #

Up early the next morning, Alex went to her favorite Starbucks in Paris on Boulevard des Capucines. The high ceilings, the crown moldings, the chandeliers, and the comfortable leather couches made it such a pleasant place to hang out in the morning before the tourists arrived. She settled in with a chai latte tea and read through the housing offers in a free magazine, *Fusac.* One ad attracted her attention, and she circled it in red: *Emile Zola, 2 rms, 15th, 40 sm, kitchen, bath, 1200 €/mo.* She called the number, spoke to the owner, and made an appointment to visit that afternoon.

Now for a change in wardrobe. Following her advice to Marie-Agnès, she bought comfortable jackets and trousers in black and grey, a pair of jeans, white tops, and some accent pieces in red. The look she sought not stunning, not very fashionable, just down-to-earth and undramatic.

#   #   #

Avenue Emile Zola, Paris

For the third time that day, Nathalie Martin smoothed the sofa cushions, adjusted a small rug that was covering a stain on the carpet, repositioned a plant. Renting the flat she had inherited from her mother was proving to be more difficult than expected.

It had been six months since her mother had passed away. She had come into her inheritance, not an enormous amount of money but enough to give her the opportunity to take a leave of absence from her job to spend three months in India.

The apartment was a bit frayed around the edges, the wallpaper faded, the upholstery worn, the kitchen old-fashioned. Nathalie didn't want to spend money to freshen up the place only to find that it needed more freshening on her return. Thus far she had had no confidence in those who were interested and no luck with those who met her requirements.

And now she was waiting to meet the woman who had called this morning.

When Nathalie explained that she would be on the Indian subcontinent for the next three months, Alex knew that she had found what she was looking for. She offered to pay the three months' rent in advance. Nathalie would leave her name on the mailbox and Alex would forward her mail. The utilities and the phone would remain in Nathalie's name, and Alex would go to the post office and pay the bills in cash. They had only to agree on the amount of the monthly rental. Alex sensed Nathalie's nervousness, and finding that twelve hundred Euros a month for a run-down flat was too much to pay, she offered one thousand, which Nathalie accepted on the spot.

When it suited her, Alex would become Nathalie Martin.

#   #   #

Château d'Hélène

Alex's mouth was dry, her fingertips tingling. She took a deep breath and called Jacques Mornnais that evening. She left a message, reminding him that they had met last November on a flight and asking him to call Nathalie Martin if he still needed help with translating. He returned her call twenty minutes later, and they agreed that she would come to the office on rue de Prony the next day.

Jacques received another phone call that evening, this time from Merv Peters.

"I need to see you on…um… a private matter."

"Still at the same place every morning? I'll stop by and see you the day after tomorrow, is that okay?"

"Thanks, Jacques, I appreciate it."

Jacques smiled. For the first time in days, he had forgotten about the red-haired cow. His thoughts turned to the pompous lawyer, the man's private matter, and the solution Jacques had in mind. How he loved this line of work.

#   #   #

When Alex returned to the apartment in Neuilly, she found Richard seated at his desk, staring at his computer, still reluctant to send the photos to Michel de Clermont d'Auvergne.

"This just doesn't feel right to me," he said. "What will Michel do with the photos? Where will this lead?"

Alex put her hands on his shoulders, planted a kiss on the top of his head. "Let's not worry. Michel wouldn't do anything to harm us, would he? And who knows, we might learn something more about Mr. Mornnais."

"I'm no longer sure that I want to know," replied Richard.

"Well, it's too late to stop now, so just do it," said Alex.

#   #   #

A FORGERY IN PARIS

Rue de Varenne

His computer beeped, and Michel de Clermont d'Auvergne saw Richard's email. He didn't want to open it, but he had no choice.

Michel downloaded the attachments. There they were: the men Richard had referred to as *the Asians*, and the tableaux on easels in the studio. Were the paintings just copies, or were they forgeries? He knew that the Chinese must have trained hundreds of talented artists to ply this particular trade. But what was going on here? Had the girl seen something that she shouldn't have?

Jacques Mornnais. The man reminded him of those eight-legged spiders, each leg involved in a different activity. Michel had heard talk about uranium and real estate. Should forgery be added to the mix? If that's what he was up to, Michel had no doubt that Jacques didn't want it to be known. Michel was also sure some people did know but looked the other way. Especially since it was rumored that Mornnais had files on everyone in the French elite, be it business or politics. All the way to the top.

For the moment, no harm had been done. Yet.

The photos were at a dead end. No one else would see them. If Mornnais knew that, then he'd probably realize that the girl was no danger to him and leave her alone. But how to let him know that without letting on that he'd seen the photos?

The girl was safe at that old house of Richard's, but she couldn't stay there forever. He wanted to help his father's old friend, but he had his affairs to think about as well.

Conflicted and ill-at-ease, Michel de Clermont d'Auvergne left his home on rue de Varenne and walked to the Champ de Mars. A walk in the cold to clear his mind, to chart an impossible path between the demands of his class and his circumstances.

He reached a courageous decision: he would do nothing, say nothing, and hope the whole mess would just go away.

Chapter 33

Vitry-sur-Seine

EARLY MORNING, THE TRAIN FROM Dijon arrived at Gare de Lyon. Li saw Deborah alight from the car behind theirs and he ran up to her. In his hand was Wen's notebook and pasted on one of the pages was an address in the town of Vitry, to the south of Paris.

"How do we go here?" he asked. Deborah was going to take the Métro anyway, so she led them down the stairs, helped them buy tickets, and pointed at the wall map to show them where to go.

A few hours later, the doorbell rang at an apartment in a block of flats on rue Gagnée in Vitry. Surprised but happy to see him, Wen's uncle Xi welcomed the two men. After years of struggle, Xi had established himself as a teacher of calligraphy to French students intrigued by Taoist philosophy and to Asians looking to recover their lost roots. Scrolls of his work decorated the apartment's cold white walls.

At first, there was only the sound of the three men slurping from the steaming bowls of bouillon, noodles, meat, and vegetables that Xi had set on the table. Xi hadn't known that his nephew and Li had been hired to work at the Château d'Hélène, but he understood what they had been doing there.

Slowly, Li and Wen recounted some, but not all, of the circumstances of their departure from the Château d'Hélène. They had been poorly paid, they lived in converted stables, and even if nothing had happened yet, they felt afraid.

There were some omissions, but if Xi noticed, he asked no questions.

Rue Gagnée was a dreary street, but the gardens in front of the buildings were well kept and the sidewalks clean. It was home to the Asians and Africans who had no access to public housing in Paris.

Xi's network of friends soon found work for Li and Wen, unloading trucks at a supermarket on Avenue d'Ivry in Paris. They grew mustaches, let their hair grow, and joined the crowds that waited each morning to take the bus to work, leaving early, returning late, melting into the sea of multicolored faces. The painters from the Château d'Hélène had vanished.

On their days off, they would do calligraphy and paint, under Xi's guidance. He might organize an exhibition of their work one day. But for now, he understood that they needed help and he would offer them his unconditional hospitality as long as necessary. He was not conflicted.

Chapter 34

Saint-Denis, outskirts of Paris

In a one-star hotel, a stone's throw from the Stade de France, Cosimo sat on the edge of his bed and stared at his cell phone. Samuel had not returned from Trubenne, and he was not answering Cosimo's calls. He worried that something had gone wrong, but why hadn't his partner been able to contact him?

To make matters worse, Bruno wasn't answering his phone, either. Had Samuel fucked up the job again? Maybe Bruno was angry and didn't want to talk to Cosimo? Whatever it was, it wasn't his fault. They'd delivered the fucking flowers and he wanted to be paid.

He'd give it a few more days, and then he'd drive down to the château. Bruno might not be pleased to see him, but he wasn't going to hang around in this shithole hotel for much longer.

Chapter 35

A WEEK LATER, ELLA WAS sitting at the kitchen table in the chateau, polishing the silverware, when Jacques and Mila returned. She heard the front door open, rose, and went into the entry.

"Hello, Ella," said Mila.

"Where's Bruno?" asked Jacques. "I've been trying to reach him all week."

"Maybe he's having a bad hangover," sneered Mila.

Tarek, removing their luggage from the car, said nothing.

"He's not here."

"I can see that, you stupid girl. I asked where he is."

"I don't know." Adding, "And sir, the painters, they are gone."

The blood drained from Jacques' face, then it turned red, and he screamed at her. "What do you mean you don't know and the painters are gone?"

Ella, speechless, stood riveted to the floor.

Mila, trying another approach, said, "Ella, when did you last see Bruno? When did the painters leave?"

"He ate dinner here the night you left. And then the next morning his car was gone. And when I brought breakfast to the painters, they were not there.

That's all I know."

Jacques could not, did not want to believe what he was hearing. To Tarek, he said, "Go look in the studio and their rooms," considering that a refurbished stall was a room. Looking at Ella, he said, "And then go look in her room."

Ella had still not moved. What did it matter to her if Tarek looked through her room? She had nothing to hide there.

One of Jacques' cell phones rang, but he ignored it. "I'm going to look in that fucker's room myself."

Ella turned to return to the kitchen.

Mila had a revelation. The maid might have useful information. She refrained from barking at Ella — a first — and asked, "Did Bruno say anything to you?"

"No, madame, he does not speak to me."

Mila insisted, "Surely he must have said *something* to you, Ella."

"No, madame, he did not."

"And the painters?"

"No, madame, nothing."

Released from Mila's interrogation, Ella returned to the kitchen.

Under a gloomy winter sky, hunching his shoulders against the biting cold wind, Tarek walked to the stalls. The men had taken their meager belongings, leaving only rumpled bedding and half-full wastebaskets, a single sock under one of the beds, a piece of stale bread on the shelf above the other bed. Nothing else.

He crossed over to the studio and sat on a stool in one corner. Seeing the tubes of paint scattered on the worktable, the palettes, and brushes, he felt that the painters must have left in a hurry.

He smirked as he tried to imagine Li and Wen together with Bruno, but no, that made no sense. Bruno was a brutal alcoholic pig, and Tarek had seen glimmers of hatred in the painters' eyes when Bruno barked his orders at them.

While Tarek sat in the studio, trying to make sense of the incomprehensible, Jacques was in Bruno's room. Methodically, he searched the room, going through the pockets in Bruno's clothing, taking apart the bed, dumping the contents of the dresser drawers. Nothing.

Tarek returned to the house. Ella was still in the kitchen, continuing to polish the silverware. He motioned to her to follow him, and they went up the grand stairway to the first floor, opened the door to the servants' staircase, and climbed the unpainted steps to the servants' quarters.

Tarek shook his head as he kicked aside the beige chips, as though Ella was somehow responsible for the peeling paint. "Which room is yours?" he asked, addressing her for the first time. Ella opened the door to her room and stood to one side as Tarek entered.

Then he did as Jacques had done in Bruno's room. He didn't expect to find anything — she was only a dumb maid — but it was important to keep her in her place, show her who was the boss.

Ella's face was set in an expressionless mask. She started to pick up her affairs, but Tarek stopped her. "You can do that later. Go back to your work now." Back in the hallway, Tarek idly opened other doors, but the rooms were either unoccupied or filled with junk. Ella didn't stop or turn around, continuing to the kitchen..

Jacques had calmed down, his rage giving way to an air of resignation. He and Mila were sitting in the office, talking in low voices, when Tarek knocked on the open door. Certain people had been contacted. Discreet inquiries had been made. Jacques believed, wanted to believe, that there was a good reason for Bruno's disappearance and that he would be back.

But then there was the problem of the painters, those ungrateful fuckers. No point in advertising that he employed art forgers, but if he had buyers, he would need to come up with the goods. *Merde*, he thought, *always something*.

Chapter 36

Fontainebleau

NICOLAS PAGÈS WAS HAVING HIS nails cut and the cuticles trimmed — in his line of work, appearance was everything — when his phone rang. The caller ID flashed Stokes. "Sorry," he said to the Asian woman seated opposite as he lifted his hand from the bowl of warm soapy water.

He had just arrived, said Stokes, and tomorrow he'd be down to see Nicolas as agreed. Their appointment was at two p.m., but Eugene wanted to keep Nicolas on edge, and so he arrived closer to three p.m. This time he wore sharply pressed chinos and a navy blazer, as befitted a man contemplating a multi-million dollar purchase. "Sorry to be late," he said. "I got lost on my way over here."

Nicolas brought out the painting. Eugene squinted, stared at the canvas, stepped back, and then moved forward to examine it more closely. Like his avatar Stokes, he had no particular knowledge about art in general. His criterion was whether he enjoyed looking at a painting, so there was no need for role-playing. He could be himself.

"Looks nice," he said at last. "But you know, I don't know a whole hell of a lot about art. How do I know this is the genuine article?"

Nicolas smiled. "That's a very good question, Mr. Stokes. We have a Certificate of Authenticity, established by an expert on Nicolas Poussin, and you have my own expert opinion that this is an authentic Poussin."

Stokes nodded. "Well, that's good, that reassures me. But, um…" He let the silence hang in the air for several long seconds. "You said it's called *Baby Moses in the River*, right? I searched the internet, even asked a friend to help, but I couldn't find any mention of that painting. There were others that mentioned Baby Moses, but not the precise title, and I was wondering about that."

The thought passed through Nicolas's mind, *he's not quite as dumb as he appears, but still, pretty clueless.* He made an effort to remove any trace of condescension from his voice, his face expressionless. "The fact is that this painting has not been in circulation for a very long time. It was in a private collection in Russia."

"A private collection?"

"Yes, the collection of Pavel Korsikov, a very wealthy industrialist. And now his widow is putting the painting on the market. We need to move quickly before she decides to offer it to one of the big auction houses."

"Those Russians," mused Stokes. "They made their fortunes in the 90s, didn't they? Would you happen to know how Mr. Korsikov got ahold of that painting? I mean, I'm sure my wife would love to know the story. Makes it all so exciting, doesn't it?"

"Oh, quite," replied Nicolas. "Sometimes provenance can be a bit tricky, but here, we know that the painting was acquired from a Swiss collector."

"And who might that be?" asked Stokes in an offhand way, as though the answer didn't matter that much.

"I'm afraid I can't help you there. The Swiss wished to remain anonymous, so the painting was sold via a company in Singapore. But you know, Mr. Stokes, this is quite usual in the world of high-value works of art."

"Yes, I suppose so. Very interesting, all of that."

"I imagine you'll want to think about it, discuss it with Mrs. Stokes. I've prepared a small dossier to take with you. May I ask you to keep this confidential? I don't think the widow wants people to know that she's selling off paintings."

"Oh," said Stokes. "Are there other paintings for sale then?"

"No, not for the moment. She's already sold a few through us, but, as I said, discretion is of the utmost importance. Of course, I know I can count on you."

Eugene could hardly wait to dig his teeth into all the information he had gathered. Another handshake, this time using his free hand to pat the art dealer on his shoulder, and Eugene headed back to Paris.

#   #   #

Eugene contacted one of his friends in the bureau and asked him to work on a small research project: look into Pavel Korsikov and see what they could find out about him and his widow. The response came back very quickly, and Eugene realized that if he hadn't been so lazy, he could have done the research himself and avoided asking for a favor, but it was too late to worry about that.

Pavel had been counted amongst Russia's oligarchs, one of the lucky few who had profited handsomely from the rigged sale of State assets in the '90s. He had been the king of plastic wrap, his empire extending to chemical plants as well as production and packaging facilities. His affairs prospered — there was a seemingly endless demand for plastic wrap — and along with prosperity, there came an appropriate lifestyle, where no extravagance was too outrageous. He hired a French chef, and one evening he had him prepare a huge meal, with a choice of over one hundred starters, main courses, and desserts, to which he invited a group of friends. It was a contest to see who could consume the most. Pavel won and then he lost when he dropped dead of a heart attack. His wife, Lyudmila, was not present as he and his friends had preferred to invite their girlfriends to join in the fun.

Lyudmila had been left out of Pavel's version of a bacchanal buffet, but no matter, she inherited his industrial empire and properties. Realizing that she would not survive long in the cutthroat jungle that was the Russian economy in those years, she turned to a young Frenchman. He was called a "numbers man," and he helped her to sell off her assets and place her money out of harm's way.

It was not known whether Pavel had an art collection or, if he did, whether or not it had been disposed of. His widow married the man who had helped her, a man named Jacques Mornnais. There was a file on Mornnais, but his contact did not have access to it. Eugene smiled. Helping his sister was turning out to be more exciting than he could have imagined. The chase was on.

Chapter 37

La Belle Fermière, Paris

MERV, HOLDING COURT AT HIS café-restaurant of choice, chatted with friends who came to him for free advice, with clients who had become friends, gently probing for bits and pieces of information, discovering linkages, making connections. Second-tier deputies and senators, businesspeople on their way up or down, all stopped by to enjoy Merv's company along with some of the tastiest fried eggs in Paris, the whites soft but not runny, the yolks with a perfect semi-liquid consistency.

By the time Jacques arrived in the late morning, Merv's visitors were gone, leaving a wilderness of dirty plates and empty coffee cups that two waiters were rapidly removing from the table.

"Some eggs, some coffee?" asked Merv.

"No, thanks, just a glass of mango juice."

"It's too bad you didn't arrive earlier," began Merv, deciding to give the good news first. "You know the Schneiders? They have an antiques showroom in their mansion on rue Rembrandt?"

"Hmm," nodded Jacques, noncommittal, waiting to see where Merv was going.

139

"Well, he was here, Renaud Schneider, that is, one of the brothers. Said that business had slowed down. I thought that you could feature them in your magazine, bring them some business. Make a connection." He sipped some coffee. "Of course, the first time you talk to him, Renaud will say he's not interested, but don't be put off. I think he'll go for it after he makes you beg a bit. I'm considering buying a small commode, would you like to join me and have a look around?"

"Not a bad idea, my friend. I've been thinking about featuring them ever since they renovated their place. Thanks for the tip. And now tell me, I think you had a problem you wanted to discuss."

Merv sat back and sighed. "You know that Bernard Buffet you sold me a few years ago? *The House in the Country*? It's been stolen. Gone."

"How did that happen? Wasn't your alarm system working?"

"My housekeeper was there, so I didn't turn it on when I left."

Jacques knew all the details, but he continued asking questions to show his concern.

"How can I help?"

"I thought you could, you know, ask around, find out who has it. Maybe I could buy it back if they're not asking too much?"

"I'm afraid I can't do that." A silent space opened that Jacques quickly filled: "My dear friend, you could hardly expect me to deal with thieves. And in any event, your painting may already be on its way out of the country. On the other hand, I could look for a similar painting to replace the one you've…lost."

Jacques knew that Nicolas Pagès had an excellent copy of a Buffet. The original had been stolen from a museum in Germany and was now part of a very private collection.

"Do you think you could?"

"I could try, but you must promise me to be less negligent in the future." Jacques looked at his watch. "I'm afraid I'll have to leave you. I'm already late for another appointment. I'll call you about the painting."

"Thanks, Jacques, I appreciate it."

"Don't mention it, it's my pleasure." Indeed it was.

\#   \#   \#

Alex was in Nathalie Martin mode. She had purchased a distinctly no-name bag to hold the business cards she had printed, her new disposable cell phone, and her Nathalie Martin wallet.

She felt at ease in her no-brand garb: black parka, black trousers and jacket with a white shirt, accented by a beige and white polka dot cashmere scarf that she had found in the Neuilly outdoor market. No makeup other than a touch of mascara, her hair pulled back in a low ponytail, she looked serious, down-to-earth, nonthreatening.

The house on rue de Prony, Mila and Jacques, matched Marie-Agnès's description. But the corpulent man named Bruno was not there, nor did she see Jacques' driver.

Alex paid close attention as Mila told her about her job. She smiled. Of course, she knew all about the job, but she managed to ask some questions to show her interest. They agreed that she would interpret for Jacques at lunch tomorrow.

After she left, Jacques asked, "So, what did you think about her?"

"Well," said Mila with a smile, "if the other one was too heavy, this one could use a few more kilos. She's a bit drab, but that's what we expect a translator to look like, don't we?"

Nathalie Martin would have been delighted to know that she was already a success. And Alex was excited to see how her plan would unfold. She had remembered Michel de Clermont d'Auvergne's warning. She was focused on probing Jacques Mornnais' universe, but intent as well to keep him far away from the Vesla de Trubenne family.

Chapter 38

A MAN OF ROUTINE, JACQUES tested Nathalie at lunch the next day, found her work satisfactory, and told Mila to invite her to the château the following week, just as he had done with Marie-Agnès.

Alex had no problem deciding what to wear to the château as she had done her shopping with precisely that trip in mind. She debated taking a small point-and-shoot camera but decided against it. And she made sure that there was no trace of Alexia Thornhill in Nathalie Martin's possessions.

Her heart skipped a beat when she saw Tarek waiting for her at the train station, but she managed to look right through him and appear to be surprised when he asked if she was Madame Martin. They drove in silence to the château, Tarek concentrating on negotiating the icy patches on the roads as he listened to Vivaldi's *Four Seasons*.

Jacques and Mila were planning the next four issues of *Artixia*, and over the next two days, they had Alex make phone calls and write follow-up letters to collectors whose homes they hoped to visit. They left in the afternoon to go shopping, and Alex, in need of a cup of coffee, wandered into the kitchen.

Ella, her back to the door, chopping vegetables for soup, gave a start as Alex said, "Hello, where can I find a cup of coffee? I'm sorry I frightened you. My name is Al— Nathalie and I'm here to help Mr. Mornnais. And what's your name?"

"Ella."

Alex smiled. "Well, Ella, is there some coffee in this beautiful kitchen?"

"I will make some coffee and bring it to you, madame. Would you like some cake as well?"

Alex sat down at the table. "Hmmm, cake sounds great, but I can eat it right here, no need to mess up my desk." She complimented Ella on her cake, on the kitchen, asked if she did all the work in the château herself, didn't Ella have anyone to help her, and, the seeds of a relationship planted, she thanked Ella and returned to her work in the office.

The lower they are on the totem pole, the more they see and know. You just have to ask, she thought and, mixing metaphors, concluded that it was easiest to push on an open door.

#   #   #

Alex was sorting through the papers Jacques had left on the desk when he and Mila returned. "I've gotten in touch with all of the names on your list," she said, "but I don't know what to do with these." She picked up several faxes addressed to Bruno.

"That's okay," said Mila, taking the papers from her, "I'll deal with those."

"Oh, yes," added Alex, "I forgot to give this to you." She handed Mila the receipt for her train ticket. Smiled and waited.

That damn Bruno, thought Mila. *This is his bloody job, not mine.* Another thought popped up. *This one is quiet but not timid. She's not like that fat girl.* She opened her purse, extracted a one-hundred-Euro bill, and resisted the urge to throw it on the desk. She smiled as she handed the money to Alex. "Here you are. You'll invoice us for your time at the end of the month, won't you?"

"Yes, and thank you. I'll be fetching my bag now, as I have to get back to Paris. Please let me know when you'll be needing me again."

Cosimo was parking his car in front of the château when Tarek came out the door. He approached Tarek. "Hello there. I'm looking for Bruno. Is he inside?"

In a glance, Tarek took in the weathered face, the smell of body odor, the yellow teeth. Just the sort of lowlife Bruno would deal with.

"He's not here."

"Do you know where he is? I need to talk to him."

"I don't know, and if I did, I wouldn't tell you. Now get lost before I lose my temper."

Cosimo felt the rush of heat to his face. *Who the fuck does that Arab think he is?* He clenched his fists, ready to fight, when Alex walked down the steps, carrying her overnight bag.

Wasn't that the blonde I saw at Trubenne? Bruno would be happy to talk to me if he knew that I'd gotten rid of her.

Cosimo got back into his car and followed the station wagon down the gravel path.

Vivaldi once again as Tarek drove Alex to the train station. She did not bother to ask if he had found what he was looking for when he pawed through her clothing while she was working in the office — a camera, perhaps.

As she admired the frozen landscape, she glanced in the outside rearview mirror and saw a metallic-green Peugeot 206 behind them. She had a queasy feeling as she remembered the shit-green car that she'd seen on the first part of the drive back to Paris from Trubenne.

"Have you noticed that car behind us? I saw it when we left the château and he's still there?"

"Just one of Bruno's elite friends," he sneered. "He came to the château looking for him. I told him to get lost. Not the sort of person the boss would want hanging around. Guess I'll have to teach him a lesson if he's still around when we get to Dijon."

One of Bruno's friends? Could he be one of the men who attacked Marie-Agnès? Why is he looking for Bruno? And where is Bruno anyway?

Alex was silent. She kept her gaze on the car's reflection, hoping that the driver would exit the highway, but he followed them into Dijon. Tarek drove into the parking lot in front of the train station, opened the trunk, and handed Alex's overnight bag to her. She started to walk to the entrance as Cosimo pulled up and got out of his car.

Tarek moved in front of Cosimo. "I told you to get lost."

"You don't understand, the girl—"

"Oh, I'll bet you'd like to fuck her, wouldn't you? But I don't think you're her type." Tarek was enjoying himself. Anyone who worked for Bruno was worthy of his scorn.

"No, but…"

Alex had run into the station, anxious to get away from the driver of the metallic-green car. Once inside, she tried to melt into the crowd, scanned the arrivals and departures screen. *I don't see him. Where is he? What should I do? Try to get on my train?* The track number flashed on the screen. Alex slipped through the throng and hurried to the waiting train. She looked down the platform and, when she didn't see Cosimo, climbed into the train car.

Alex, seated next to the window in a car at the head of the train, stared as the monotonous countryside sped by. Dry mouth, shallow breath. *How I wish I were snug under the covers in my bed.* It felt like the trip would take forever, the train running in some twilight zone, never reaching its destination. Just when the tension was becoming unbearable, the train slowed down, and the conductor's voice came over the intercom. "Montbard, we'll be stopping at Montbard for three minutes. Remember to gather your belongings. Montbard, stopping for three minutes." Alex sat stiffly in her seat. The title of a song thirty years old echoed in her mind, "Should I stay or should I go?"

The train screeched to a halt. Alex grabbed her bag and walked to the end of the car, three minutes to decide *should I stay or should I go.*

Chapter 39

ALEX HAD NOT SEEN TAREK punch Cosimo in the chest, had not seen Cosimo stagger backward, gasping for breath. "You dirty Arab," he managed to hiss. It was a poor choice of words. As Cosimo tried to regain his balance, Tarek grabbed him by the neck and slammed him against a car, not once but three times. When Cosimo fell to the ground, Tarek slowly walked away, got into his car, and drove off. He would have enjoyed continuing the fight, but Tarek knew that Jacques would not be pleased if the police got involved.

Cosimo got to his feet. The blonde woman. He had to find her, tell Bruno he had taken care of her. His back ached from his fight with Tarek. Doubled over, he made his way to the station and walked past the entrances to the tracks. Where could she be? The Paris-bound train was in the station. He saw several blonde heads walking down the platform. Could one of them be the woman? The warning whistle sounded, and Cosimo hopped onto the last car. The door closed and the train slowly pulled out of the station.

It was a first-class car, all the seats were taken, and Cosimo didn't look as though he belonged there anyway. Nevertheless, he walked the length of the car, looking for the blonde. She was not there.

He sat on a bench in the corridor, intending to continue his search, car by car, when a conductor hurried past him, scuttling his plans. What if the man had stopped and asked to see his ticket? He'd jumped on the train without thinking about the risk of getting caught—another fuckup, Bruno would say. He waited fearfully, expecting to see the conductor return at any moment, when he heard the announcement: they would be stopping for three minutes in Montbard. Cosimo made what seemed like a wise decision. He'd forget the blonde for now, and make his way back to Paris by other means: hitch a ride or steal a car. The train slowed to a halt, the door opened and Cosimo hopped down on to the platform.

#   #   #

Alex pressed the button to open the door and alighted, still wondering what to do. *You're being stupid. Get back on the train.* Montbard was a small countryside station. She looked for a moment at the pale two-story building. *To be safe, why don't I buy a ticket for the next train to Paris.* A few steps to the walkway that ran across the tracks. Something made Alex turn her gaze back to the platform to see Cosimo running towards her. At the same time, she saw that the train doors had closed, a whistle blew, and the train began to move out of the station.

A dash across the tracks; surely she'd be safe there if she could make it into the station. Her heart sank when she tried to open the door and found it locked: the French railway company's economy measures included closing charming, little-used train stations in the countryside. In the meantime, Cosimo had started to catch up with her, forgetting his earlier wise decision.

Alex had let go of her overnight bag, but Cosimo was much faster; he had hooked his arms around her midsection as he pulled her back along the platform. Time stopped. In her line of vision, further down the platform: a red poppy that had pushed through the concrete, standing tall. It reminded her of a Georgia O'Keefe painting and flowers printed on a down comforter in her bedroom in Washington. Her bedroom. A vision of her husband in bed with Suzanne Higgins flashed before her; time started up again. All the suppressed anger over that betrayal boiled up. She brought her heel down on Cosimo's instep with all her strength, freeing herself from his grasp. He cried out in pain and tried to pull her towards him but, fueled by her anger, she turned to face him and brought her knee up between his legs. Cosimo fell to his knees, lost his balance, folded into a ball, and rolled onto the track. With the shriek of a whistle, an express train roared through Montbard, coming to a halt several hundred meters further on. A few passengers who had descended at the same time as Alex had watched as Cosimo attacked her. They remained transfixed by what had taken place. *I don't dare leave; it will look like I have something to hide.* She covered her face to avoid looking at the mangled mass on the rails.

When the Gendarmes questioned Alex, she said she'd started to feel ill on the train and decided to get some fresh air before continuing her journey. Did she know the man? And, one of them asked himself, had she done something to provoke the attack? "I never saw him before in my life," she whispered, tears streaming down her cheeks. Luckily she was wearing a pants suit, not a short skirt, and the provocation line of reasoning died stillborn.

Who was that man, and why was he after me? Bruno doesn't know me. What's going on? Finding no answers to her questions, she forced herself to stop asking them and instead imagined walking the corridors of the château at Trubenne.

Chapter 40

Paris

THE WELCOME BREAK IN THE semi-permanent Parisian grey had continued, the sky a brilliant cloudless blue. It was an ideal day for a run in Parc Monceau. The perfectly arranged beds of bright winter flowers brought back childhood memories as Alex circled the park. This being Paris, joggers ran both clockwise and counterclockwise. She veered to one side to avoid a man bearing down on her and collided with another jogger who was about to overtake her.

She seemed about to lose her balance, but the man she had run into held her arm to steady her. "Oh, pardon," she said. "Sorry." She looked up at him: the man holding her arm was not the same as the person that had signed the lease. His hair was longer, he had a deep suntan and a two-day beard, and of course, he was not wearing a suit. Still, she was sure it was he. "Eugene," she said. "Eugene Spector? What are you doing here?"

"If it isn't Alex, my landlady! I'm here for a few days on business."

There was an awkward silence, and then Eugene removed his hand from her arm.

"Do you run here often?" he asked.

149

"Well, I should. I live nearby, but I've been so busy since I arrived. And with the lousy weather, this is the first chance I've had. And you?"

"I'm staying in a hotel off Avenue de Wagram. And yeah, I try to run every day, rain or shine, try to keep in shape. Can I invite you for a coffee to make up for our little accident?"

A few minutes later, they were seated at a café on Boulevard de Courcelles, populated by retirees and groups of mothers whose children attended Alex's alma mater, the nearby bilingual school.

"So, how's *la vie parisienne*?"

"Oh, pretty good. I've reconnected with my uncle and spent some time at Christmas in the south of France with my cousin. And I just started a new job — part-time, mind you — with a glossy art magazine. It's in French and English, and my job is to translate the French text into English."

"You were in fashion, right? So you must be interested in art. They're kind of related, aren't they?"

"I haven't thought about it like that but I guess you could say so."

"Does this magazine have a name? Maybe I should pick up a copy and try to educate myself."

"It's called *Artixia*. In fact, their offices are right around the corner from here on rue de Prony. It's run by this Frenchman, Jacques Mornnais, and his wife, Mila."

Eugene had felt a tingle when he'd heard Alex say *glossy art magazine*. Now, his ears were on fire.

"This is a pretty fancy neighborhood, so their magazine must be doing well."

"Something must be doing well. They have a flat on rue Bonaparte and a château in the Morvan." It dawned on Alex that if she were not careful, she'd wind up telling Eugene about Marie-Agnès and the real reason she'd taken the job. As it was, she had not intended to talk so much about Jacques and her job. She switched from *Artixia* to Eugene, rather abruptly. "You said you were here on business?"

He smiled, a warm smile, the corners of his light brown eyes crinkling. "Government stuff, afraid I can't say anything more. But look, I'll be around for another week or so. Would you have time for lunch one of these days?"

"Sure, and I can bring you a copy of the magazine if you like." They exchanged phone numbers. Eugene said he'd call her. Alex left and walked in the direction of rue de Chazelles. As soon as she was out of sight, Eugene went up to the kiosk on the corner and bought a copy of *Artixia*.

#   #   #

The low-lying clouds had blown in, the pale grey mantle reclaiming its rightful place in the Paris skyline. Eugene turned on the desk lamp in his hotel room and studied the magazine he had just bought.

Jacques Mornnais was listed as the publisher, with an address on rue de Prony. That must be the place Alex was talking about.

The editor-in-chief was Lyudmila Mikhailovna Korsikova. Another tingle. *That's the Russian woman Mornnais married, Pavel Korsikov's widow.*

The advisory board: composed of what Eugene assumed were prestigious names in the art world.

Eugene was sure that Jacques Mornnais had conjured up the *Baby Moses* paintings. Were there other forgeries out there, supposedly coming from the Korsikov estate? If there had not been the second *Baby Moses*, he might have concluded that this was a one-off situation. But with two, that could mean there was a pattern.

It was all so simple and so ingenious: should the buyer complain that the painting was a forgery, it would be the word of Jacques' expert against their expert. Not many people were prepared to have their tableau analyzed by a laboratory, as his sister had done. Most of the time they were unsuspecting, and it was not worth it. Eugene had done some research. Apparently, even laboratories could sometimes be fooled. And in the case where a forgery was detected, the blame would be laid at the door of the deceased Pavel Korsikov.

He was looking forward to seeing Alex again. She exuded self-confidence, and he found that quite attractive. And she would be able to tell him more about Mr. Mornnais, he was sure of that. However, he didn't think it necessary to explain his situation to her. That could come later. Or not.

#   #   #

151

Vincent Reiner made his way along the American embassy's serpentine hallways and out to the street. He turned left onto rue Boissy d'Anglas and walked into a small café near rue Saint-Honoré. Eugene was seated at the rear, reading *Le Canard Enchaîné*, France's irreverent, satirical weekly. It was a way to check up on what was happening in politics and business. He caught sight of Vincent out of the corner of his eye, swallowed his chewing gum, and put down his newspaper.

With a small canvas tote bag hanging from his shoulder, Reiner had the stiff gait of someone who didn't get much exercise, and as he sat down, Eugene thought he looked as if his head was going to fall off his neck.

"Thanks for coming out to meet me. I find the embassy so oppressive."

With a wry smile, Reiner replied, "I know what you mean." After they ordered espressos, he unzipped his tote bag and handed Eugene a folder. "This came in last night. I think you were expecting it?"

Eugene, noncommittal, "Yeah, thanks, Vince."

The men went their separate ways. Across the street, an old man with the nonchalant elegance of his class was approaching the massive wooden doors of the C2C club. His image floated through Vincent Reiner's peripheral vision. He knew the club, and as he returned to his office, it crossed his mind that he might be welcomed there as a guest, never as a member.

#   #   #

Richard chatted with friends in the C2C club before sitting down to read *Le Figaro* and sip his daily dose of green tea. He wondered why he even bothered to read. Things had continued to go from bad to worse after the fall of Lehman Brothers. His investments were safe, but that could not be said for everyone. He was shocked—offended even—by the behavior of the new generation of bankers. Money-grubbing crooks were what they were, so much new money trying to buy into the old-money world. *I chased after money, too. I may have driven a hard bargain, but I was honest.* At least, that was how he viewed himself.

He looked up to see Michel de Clermont d'Auvergne walking through the room. There was a fragility about Michel that Richard found hard to explain. Not in his physical appearance but something lurking beneath the surface. In that respect, he was not at all like his father.

Michel would have liked to avoid Richard, but as this was impossible, he summoned a smile and went over to greet him. Courtesy required that he sit and chat for a few minutes with his father's good friend.

"And how are your niece and her friend?"

"All is well, my friend, thank you for asking."

"Your niece's friend, she's still at your place in the south, is she?"

Richard leaned back, sighed, and smiled. "No, she is gone. Traveling. Probably wanted to get away from it all. Can't say that I blame her."

"Well, that's good, isn't it? Glad we could talk, Richard."

#   #   #

In the dark grey of daybreak, Marie-Agnès donned her running gear and walked out the gate and onto the road. She had started running the day after Alex left. While she had liked the idea of jogging in Parc Monceau, she was too self-conscious, too worried about how she looked to others, and the idea of an early-morning run remained just that, an unrealized thought.

Here at Trubenne, the roads were empty, and she started her slow ascent, free now from her preoccupation with others. Marie-Agnès concentrated on her breathing. She would not allow what-if thoughts about what had happened a few nights ago to spoil her run.

She spent the rest of the morning working in the garden and helping in the kitchen. As the two women chopped, diced, and sautéed, they talked about Richard and about Alex, how her coming to France had changed so many things.

"I don't know what I would have done without her," said Marie-Agnès.

"Yes, the right people do show up at the right time," said Charlotte. "You could say that it's a coincidence, but when you look at everything that has happened, you can only think that Alex being here is part of the larger scheme of things."

"If only I knew just what *is* the larger scheme of things."

"The only thing you can do is to live one day at a time. Look upon your

153

stay here as a kind of vacation from your life in Paris."

Marie-Agnès was silent. *What exactly do I want to go back to?* She had not checked her email since the attack, and surprisingly she felt lighter, liberated. The truth was that she didn't mind being disconnected from the rest of her life.

She borrowed Charlotte's cell phone to send a short text message to her sister. *No flowers, must be a mistake. Thanks anyway. Traveling for the next month.*

"What about the man in the woods?" she had asked Charlotte.

"What man is that? I've not seen anyone, have you?"

"I see what you mean."

It surprised Marie-Agnès to realize how little she cared about what had happened. He'd only gotten what he deserved.

For now, she was happy at Trubenne. She had stopped examining herself in the mirror every day, looking for flaws. But if she had looked, she would have seen a rosy-cheeked dark-haired beauty, with the first suggestion of a svelte figure and burgeoning self-esteem. She had left the red-haired cow in the weed-infested roadsides.

#   #   #

Michel de Clermont d'Auvergne was early, so he slowed his pace on rue Royale as he turned onto rue Saint-Honoré and approached his club. It was not the C2C — that was for family and friends — but a place open to those in a much broader network who were willing and able to pay the high entrance fee. Here money, not birth, was the arbiter.

Like ripples on a lake, the shoppers moved rhythmically along rue Saint-Honoré, gazing at the overpriced brands, sometimes entering a shop with its condescending sales personnel. Michel laughed at those who confused themselves with the merchandise they were selling. His name entitled him to do that.

There would always be the wealthy Americans, no matter that the world was going to hell in a hand basket. But now, they were outnumbered by Asians, Russians, and Arabs: all so vulgar. And what about France in all of this? Today it was a country whose first industry was tourism, a living museum of past glories. A small wave of depression arose and then broke against the rocky shore of his privileged background.

Inside the club, Kenneth Petit sat in one of the vast reception rooms. *Funny name for a tall, skinny man*, thought Michel.

"Where do you prefer that we go?" he asked. "Overlooking the pool or the winter garden? Unfortunately, the women here are nothing to get excited about."

"Then I prefer the bare trees to those overfed bottoms," laughed Kenneth.

Settling into the comfortable fauteuils, sipping coffee, Michel wondered how much longer Kenneth would want to meet with him. Membership in the club was far above Kenneth's pay grade, but Michel doubted that he would continue to consider the invitation worth his time.

The ritual dance began, as bits of information were exchanged, a focus on the sexual activities of the governing class: they laughed at the notorious exploits of an opposition politician, compared notes on who was sleeping with whom. From the bedroom, they moved on to the boardroom and then on to those Michel considered to be bottom-fish, people like Merv Peters (a pompous fool), and Jacques Mornnais (a nasty piece of work, but he had his uses).

"Speaking of Mornnais, did you know his man Bruno?" asked Kenneth. "It seems he's gone missing. And then there's some girl who worked for Jacques, seems she's missing as well." It was a bit of a rough transition, but Jacques had been asking about both Bruno and the girl.

"You mean that big, oafish man?" asked Michel. "Yes, I saw him a few times when I happened to be at the ministry. Between him and that driver, makes you wonder where Jacques finds the people who work for him."

"Any idea where he could be?"

"Not a clue, I'm afraid. Did you say he ran off with that girl, what was her name?"

"I don't know that he ran off with her. He's more of an after-hours club type." He searched his memory. "The girl, I think her name was Marie-France or Marie-Claire, something like that."

As he looked out the window at the bare trees, the colorless sky, the flowerbeds lying fallow, Michel's gloomy mood returned. He felt tired and useless. Then he heard himself saying, "I think her name is Marie-Agnès, and I heard that she's traveling, wants to get away from it all." He had shown Kenneth what family and connections could produce, and at once he felt better, superior to those tourists outside on rue St-Honoré.

"Ah," said Kenneth, "actually she's of no interest to us. Unless, of course, you know that this Bruno is with her. We're not going to use assets to chase down Jacques Mornnais' disgruntled employees. But keep your ear to the ground, let me know if you hear anything further." He looked at his watch. "Have to run, I'm afraid. I'm off to the Alliance Victor Hugo. Not as grand as your club, of course. Let's stay in touch."

And he was off, leaving Michel feeling more tired and useless than before. But at least he felt ashamed. Ashamed that he had betrayed Richard's confidence, ashamed that he felt the need to impress Kenneth.

It was his only saving grace.

Chapter 41

ALEX HAD SETTLED INTO A routine. She assisted Jacques at lunch once or twice a week, always in three-star restaurants as he met with the newly super-rich. Having amassed fortunes in show business, in finance, and in internet marketing, they sought to affirm their identities through the acquisition of real estate and artwork. And Jacques Mornnais was there to massage their egos, holding out the possibility of being featured in the quarterly *Artixia*. Of course, he could not promise. They were working on several projects right now, but he would let them know.

Later on, he would contact them to say that he would work them into his plans and made arrangements for a team to visit their homes to photograph them and their artwork. In this way, he compiled a roster of old masters and contemporary art, their location, and their alarm systems. And each quarter, the lucky few saw themselves featured in spreads in *Artixia*'s glossy pages.

The office on rue de Prony was mostly for show as the real work was done at the château and Alex would take the train and spend the night and return to Paris at the end of the following day. She asked no questions, did as she was told, and, as a matter of principle, made sure that Mila reimbursed her on the spot for her train ticket.

In Ella, she sensed a quiet strength and intelligence that Jacques and

Mila could not see. Alex started to cultivate the Filipina maid, convinced that Ella saw and heard most of what went on in the château.

When Jacques and Mila left one morning to spend the day at a wine tasting in Beaune, she seized the opportunity. Sitting in the kitchen, drinking coffee, she asked Ella about herself.

Haltingly, she told Alex a part of her story. Twin girls and a boy. A large extended family. A small dry goods shop in Manila, but when her husband died, it was too challenging for her to run the shop, and she was desperate to find work to support her family. She sold the store, gave most of the money to her relatives, and used the rest for passage to Saudi Arabia, where she cooked and cleaned, was poorly paid and treated worse still. She escaped to France and worked as a maid in a hotel in Paris's Belleville section. One of her co-workers introduced her to Tarek, who said his employer was looking for a woman to cook and do housework in his château. Ella smiled wistfully. "And so here I am."

"And how do you like your work here?" asked Alex.

"I can send money to my family. That is all that is important to me."

"Yes," said Alex, thinking about her own situation, "family is everything." She continued, "And what do you do on your day off? You do have a day off, don't you?"

"Not really, but sometimes Bruno would take me with him when he had business in Dijon but now…" and she stopped.

Alex remembered seeing Bruno's name on some of the papers Jacques had given to her. "But now what, Ella? Where is Bruno? I don't think I've met him."

"He's not here anymore."

"Oh, he's gone for good, is he?"

Ella looked straight into Alex's eyes, hesitated, and said softly, "Yes." Then, silence.

"Well, I need to finish up some work for Mr. Mornnais. Why don't we talk later?" said Alex.

At the end of the morning, Alex went into the family dining room when she heard Ella starting to set the table. "That's not necessary, Ella. I can eat in the kitchen with you."

Lunch. The remains of a roast guinea hen, a potato casserole, salad, and a large slice of Beaufort cheese, some green grapes.

"Tell me about this Bruno," said Alex, smiling gently.

"There's not much to tell."

Alex tried another approach. "I have the feeling he was unkind to you, am I right, Ella?"

Ella had started to clear the table. She stopped, stood still, looking down at the floor, wondering if she should tell Alex what had happened. An intake of breath, Ella opened her mouth to speak when they heard the sound of the Mercedes on the gravel drive.

Alex stood up. "We'll talk later," she said and hurried back to take her place at the desk in the office.

Jacques came into the room, his ear glued to his Blackberry, his attention elsewhere. Alex had finished her work, and she was ready to leave. Mila and Jacques were talking in low voices as she stood at the office door to say goodbye. Jacques looked up and nodded. There was a slight inclination of Mila's head. Alex had taken her place as part of the household help.

When Tarek returned from depositing Alex at the train station, Jacques announced that they would pay a visit to Nicolas Pagès. He had some business to take care of.

#   #   #

While Tarek leaned against the car, Jacques carried Merv's Buffet into the gallery's back office. "I have a buyer for this painting, and I need that other Buffet you've been holding for me — the one with the bridge, trees in the distance. You know the one I mean? We'll sell it to the collector who, hmm, lost this one. You've got that straight, right?"

Nicolas would update the provenance of the painting that had hung in Merv's apartment and ship it to Jacques' buyer in the south of France, where it would grace the walls of his oceangoing yacht before arriving at its final destination months later.

"Can you do the paperwork for the other one now? I'd like to take it with me."

159

From a group of paintings, each wrapped in brown paper and leaning in a pile against the wall, Nicolas extracted a smaller one, laid it on the table, and carefully unwrapped it. "Is this what you're looking for?"

Jacques nodded, forming his lips into a tight smile. "Yes, that's it."

As Nicolas certified the origin and authenticity of the Buffet, his thoughts were on Bruno. No word from him; no news on the sale of the Daubigny. Trying to be offhanded, not looking up, he asked, "How's your man Bruno? I haven't seen him in some time."

"Oh, he's fine. Traveling. In Ukraine right now. Be back in a few weeks."

"Ah, give him my regards when he returns." He handed Jacques the painting and put the papers in a heavy grey envelope. The room was unheated. "Cold, isn't it?" he said as he rubbed his hands on his sleeves, hoping that Jacques would not feel his sweaty palms when they shook hands. As the Mercedes left the curb, his armpits were wet. A trickle of perspiration ran down the center of his back. Where the fuck was that drunken oaf Bruno, and where was the painting?

Chapter 42

THE CAFÉ DE LA FONTAINE, not far from Eglise Saint-Sulpice, made no effort to be trendy or fashionable. It didn't have to. The nondescript furniture and décor, the unforgiving waiters gave a sort of cachet to the place. And it's true that sitting upstairs, one did not risk being seen or being bothered. You wouldn't find the crowd from the Café de Flore here.

Eugene sat against the far wall. Surrounded by a cloud of his particular garlicky aroma, he did a halfway rise as Alex approached. "Would you like to change seats?" he asked. "Wouldn't you be more comfortable on the banquette?"

How delightfully old-fashioned, she thought. "No, thanks, that's okay. I'm fine where I am."

Alex wasn't sure why Eugene wanted to meet her, and she was a bit curious about his business in Paris. After a waiter appeared and took their order, she gently probed. "Has your business here left you much time to enjoy Paris?"

Eugene looked straight at Alex and for the first time she noticed how beautiful his eyes were — a pale brown, almost green, with gold flecks — and for a moment she didn't hear his response.

"I'm keeping pretty busy. My government assignment is fairly ordinary, even if I'm not free to talk about it, but in my spare time, I'm working on a personal project."

"Oh, is that something you can talk about?"

"Well, yes. In fact, it was crazy running into you the other day — both literally and figuratively." He smiled, continuing to look directly into her eyes, and went on. "My late aunt bought a painting from a dealer in Fontainebleau, that my sister inherited. When she had it analyzed by one of those specialized laboratories, she learned that the painting is a fake, a forgery. I think there may be a connection between the dealer, the guy in Fontainebleau, and your boss, Jacques Mornnais." He paused and then continued. "I'd like to recover the money my aunt paid."

The waiter arrived with their food, a Nordic salad for Alex, *medaillons de veau à la crème* for Eugene. She played with her food, giving herself time to think.

"I only recently started working for Jacques — Mr. Mornnais — and my job consists mostly of translating the text of his magazine into English." She reached into her tote bag. "Here's the copy of *Artixia* that I promised you."

"Thanks, Alex," he said, putting the magazine beside him on the banquette.

"I'm wondering if there aren't organizations that deal with your problem," she mentioned between bites of smoked salmon.

"Yes, in fact, I'm in touch with one of those organizations. But they deal mostly with helping to get insurance companies to pay for restitution of stolen artwork. And that's not the case here." He speared a piece of bread and mopped up the remaining cream sauce, then opened the magazine. "Tell me, who is this Lyudmila Mikhailovna Korsikova? Quite a mouthful, isn't it?"

"Oh, that's Mila, Jacques' wife. She's very involved in *Artixia*."

"According to my sister's documents, the painting she inherited came from the collection of Pavel Korsikov. I guess that would be a relative of … what did you say her name was? Mila?"

"I don't know. I mean, I suppose it sounds like that, but as I said, I just started working for them, and other than the magazine, I don't know anything about either of them."

The waiter cleared the table and brought the two espressos they had ordered. Eugene leafed through the magazine. "Some people certainly live well, don't they?"

Alex took a sip of coffee — it was cold and bitter — and pushed the cup and saucer away.

"This coffee is lousy, don't you think?" He smiled. "I meant to tell you how much we like your house, your home, I should say." Then a quick segué: "Do you like classical music? A friend gave me two tickets to a concert — Beethoven's *Emperor* if I remember correctly — at Salle Pleyel next week. I'm here for at least another two weeks, so perhaps you'd like to join me?"

"That concerto is one of my favorite pieces. It's so dramatic, so grandiose. Yes, I'd love to join you."

Eugene was sure that Alex was holding back; he'd had years of evaluating responses, and his intuition was not often wrong. No matter, he'd spend the evening listening to uplifting music in the company of a beautiful woman, and he was sure he'd find out what she was hiding from him.

#   #   #

After lunch, Alex walked over to the Luxembourg Garden. She had a bad feeling in the pit of her stomach. The bare branches and the smell of rotting leaves only made her feel worse.

There was something off about Eugene, even if he had lovely eyes. He'd probably invited her to lunch to find out more about Jacques — not very flattering. She remembered their conversation, how a wave of fatigue had swept through her, how she'd felt too tired to tell him about what had happened to Marie-Agnès or about the disappearance of Bruno and the painters.

She understood that Eugene wanted to get restitution for the fake that his sister had inherited. Still, he had asked some very pointed questions about Mila, and she had the feeling that he had kept some thoughts to himself. *Unknown unknowns:* that described the situation perfectly.

Alex had told the truth about loving the *Emperor* concerto, and it was better to stay in contact with Eugene than not. If he was only interested in picking her brain, so be it. Two could play the same game.

163

Chapter 43

IN A NONDESCRIPT BUILDING ON rue Lalo, behind Avenue Foch, the owner of the sixth-floor apartment fluttered nervously, plumping and re-plumping cushions, straightening paintings that weren't crooked. Barbara Tomason — Babs to her friends — scrutinized her reflection: she'd had the girl at the hairdresser's do her makeup. It wasn't too bad, but short of surgery, there was nothing to be done about the bags under her eyes. Another foray into the kitchen to check on the food, to be sure that all was in order. She hadn't been paid yet, so everything needed to be perfect.

Alex was the first to arrive. She managed to add a touch of elegance to her working girl black suit by wearing her Tory Burch flats. Babs was, as usual, over-dressed: a faux-Chanel tweed suit, miles of necklaces, earrings, and a Cartier watch (real). The elevator doors opened directly into the apartment, and a dark-complexioned man in a perfectly cut suit emerged. He smiled and said hello as Babs walked over to greet him.

Alex introduced herself as Jacques' translator. "Pleasure, Miss Nathalie," he said. "You can call me Ernie." He turned away and started to circle the large living room, examining the paintings. He stopped in front of a painting of the Tower Bridge. Looking at Babs, he said, "Is that a Turner by any chance?"

"Why, yes, Mr. Ernie, it is indeed." Pause. "It's been in our family for quite some time." She said no more, but the meaning was clear: *we're not some nouveau riche arrivistes.*

He was looking up at a lovely Murano glass chandelier — a brilliant confection of polychrome leaves and flowers — when Jacques arrived. Jacques shook hands with Ernie, said hello to Babs, and nodded in Alex's direction. The pecking order was evident.

"Something to drink?" asked Babs. The maid brought in mango juice for Jacques, orange juice for Ernie, and water for Alex. Babs disappeared into the kitchen, where she would remain.

Two hours later, Jacques had negotiated the sale of two paintings. Ernie left, followed by Alex. Ernie's foot touched the sidewalk, and the driver opened his car door. As Alex headed to the Métro, she saw Tarek leaning against the Mercedes, parked across the street. She pretended not to see him and hurried to Porte Dauphine.

Back upstairs, Jacques walked through the apartment, back to the kitchen. He placed an envelope on the table in front of Babs. "Thanks very much. I'll call you. And please remember, madame, I count on your absolute discretion." The corners of his mouth lifted into not so much a smile as an inverted grimace.

After Jacques left, Babs placed the envelope in a lovely secretary, decorated with marquetry. The desk was a gift from her grandfather to his wife, and Babs felt a wave of bitterness that she was obliged to open her home to people like Jacques Mornnais, someone who had come out of nowhere. He reminded her of a clerk doing figures in a nineteenth-century novel. Never mind, a few more envelopes and she'd be able to get those bags under her eyes fixed.

#   #   #

Alex was back at Richard's apartment, her bare feet resting on the last six months of *Vogue*. Maria had continued to buy Chloé's favorite magazines, placing them in a neat pile next to a large green box of chocolates.

Richard asked about her day. Talking with Alex was much more interesting than reading *Les Echos.*

"Jacques likes to meet the buyer in her apartment; it's very discreet, out of sight. Anyway, he knows Madame Tomason — she's called Babs — because he bought one of her paintings when she was short of money. And now he pays her to use her apartment for some of his business meetings. Anyhow, Jacques sold Ernie — can you believe an Arab is calling himself Ernie — two paintings. Jacques' got an art dealer who takes care of the paperwork and does the shipping."

Alex sat up, leaned forward to open the box of chocolates on the table. She slid a rectangular *praline* under her tongue, savored the creamy crunchiness. For a moment, she had forgotten about Jacques Mornnais. But only for a moment.

"He's so secretive. I can feel that there's something going on, but what? They don't talk about Bruno, the man who disappeared. He was his right-hand man, you know. And the painters — the ones Marie-Agnès had photographed — they appear to be gone as well. I wonder if there isn't a connection there."

Another chocolate. This time it was a truffle.

"The maid—her name is Ella—she's very quiet, but I think she doesn't miss much. I intend to talk with her when Jacques and Mila are off on some errand. And after that, I'm going to walk over to the studio the first chance I get."

Talk of the studio called forth an image of the château. A shiver: a metallic-green Peugeot was suddenly part of that image. *I still don't want to tell Uncle Richard about that awful man and what happened at Montbard. He'd just worry. I wish Marie-Agnès were in Paris.*

"Alexia, are you all right? You look distracted."

She picked up the box of chocolates. "Oh, I'm sorry, Uncle Richard, would you like one? No, really, I'm quite fine."

Richard frowned, ignoring the outstretched arm.

"Alexia, I think you ought to stop now. I have a bad feeling about this. Mr. Mornnais may have friends in high places, but they won't help you if the walls start to tumble down, as they no doubt will.

Chapter 44

Boulevard Malesherbes, Paris

AWAY FROM RICHARD, ALEX COULD stop pretending that everything was all right. She couldn't shake the image of the shit-green car and the gruesome death of its occupant. She had to talk to Marie-Agnès.

She dialed Charlotte's number. When her cousin answered, Alex forced herself to exchange pleasantries until she could stand it no longer.

"Is everything okay now? I mean, you know, the flowers from the mysterious lover?"

"Yes, my dear, everything is okay. Would you like to talk to Marie-Agnès?" Charlotte passed the phone to Mag, who was sitting at the kitchen table, chopping carrots and celery.

Why is Charlotte being so evasive? What's going on? Alex wondered. *Let's try again.*

"Hi, Mag, I was wondering how you're doing. The flowers and all of that."

"Oh, Alex, I'm doing great. It turned out that there were no flowers after all. Just a bit of a mix-up. It's a long story, and I'd rather not talk about it on the phone. I'll fill you in when we see each other. Now, tell me about yourself. What's new?"

Alex hesitated. She had a lot to say but she was never good at long phone conversations.

"Are you there? Are you okay?"

"Yes, I'm fine. Look, I don't want to go into the whole story, but I'm working for Jacques Mornnais, doing your old job."

"You're *what*?"

"That's right. I'll tell you all about it another time. But here's the thing, when I was driving back to Paris after I left Trubenne, I thought a car was following me. But then when I looked again, it had disappeared and I forgot about it. Until a few days ago. I was leaving the château, Tarek was driving me to the station at Dijon, and this awful man showed up, driving the same car. I mean, it was a shit-green Peugeot 206, so I remembered it. The man said he was looking for Bruno—he's disappeared, along with the painters. I guess you wouldn't know that."

"Did you say that Bruno has disappeared? And the painters as well? How strange!"

"Indeed. Anyhow, Tarek told him to get lost. We drove off, and the man followed us to Dijon to the train station. Tarek thought he was following him because he was looking for Bruno, but I'm sure he was following me. But how does he know me? And how did he know I'd be at the château? It made me very uneasy, to say the least."

"You didn't say what happened at the train station."

"I'm getting to that. I hurried into the station, ran to get my train. I felt so nauseous with worry that he had followed me onto the train. I guess I was thinking it had something to do with your mugging. So I got off the train when it stopped at Montbard and that man attacked me on the platform. I managed to fight him off and..." Alex took a deep breath "he fell on the tracks and was run over by an express train. It was horrible."

"Oh my God!" Marie-Agnès trying to imagine the scene and Alex trying to forget it.

"Alex, are you sure that that was the same man? And are you sure it was the same car? I mean, there must be hundreds, no, thousands of shit-green Peugeot 206 cars on the road. It's probably just your imagination.

But anyway, the man said he was looking for Bruno. It's possible he *was* one of the two men who attacked me—or maybe not. I'm sure that having me mugged was just one item on Bruno's to-do list. But the mugging had nothing to do with you and I think it's just a coincidence that you happened to be at the château when that man showed up."

"Really, are you sure?"

"Oh, yes, absolutely. Listen, I've started running again. It's great for clearing one's head. You really ought to go for a run in Parc Monceau."

Running in Parc Monceau. No, I'm not going to start talking about Eugene. "That's a great idea, I've got to get some food before the market closes. Let's talk again soon."

Chapter 45

February 2010, Chateau d'Hélène

WHEN JACQUES AND MILA LEFT the château, as the sound of the Mercedes faded at the end of the long drive, Alex would go into the kitchen for coffee and cake. Careful to remain Nathalie Martin, she listened as Ella unburdened herself — how she hated working for the Mornnaises but how she needed the money for her family.

"So how are you today, Ella? You seem rather tired."

"I'm not sleeping well, mad — Nathalie."

"Ah, do you have something on your mind, anything you want to talk about?"

#   #   #

Ella had found herself looking forward to the moment when the woman called Nathalie came into the kitchen. Nathalie would sit at the table, drinking her coffee, talking with Ella about this and that, always pleasant, always polite. So unlike Jacques and the rest of them. Until Nathalie came, Ella had felt so alone. Of course, there were her friends in Paris, but now she had someone to talk with at the château. Someone she felt she could trust.

Taking a leap of faith that Nathalie would not betray her, Ella recounted the story of the night Bruno had died. When she mentioned the package, the cell phone with the pink and red cover, and the envelope, Alex put her cup down. The room was silent, and then she said:

"Tarek is driving them to Paris, so we'll be alone for a while. Shall we go and take a look?"

They climbed to the second floor, and Ella removed the envelope from behind the cushions and pulled out the package from under the sofa.

Alex opened the envelope. It contained a certificate on heavy grey-headed paper, attesting to the authenticity of a painting by Charles-François Daubigny; it had been purchased by a Swiss family and had remained in their hands until now. They carefully unwrapped the package and removed a small seascape: dark waters on a stormy night, a flash of lightning illuminating the sky with tints of blue and purple.

"Daubigny," said Alex, thinking that her apartment overlooked the street named after the painter. "How incredible."

"Is it valuable?"

"Oh, I would say so. I think we need to get this painting to a safe place."

"Perhaps I could send it back to Paris with you, wrapped as a gift."

"Good idea."

A week later, Ella removed the contents of a game that she had bought on a trip to Carrefour with Tarek; the painting fit securely in the box. She wrapped the package in paper with red and yellow balloons, and tied it up with a large red bow. The next time Alex was at the château, Ella asked her if she could deliver the gift to her friend.

#   #   #

Alex took a taxi from Gare de Lyon to the apartment on Avenue Emile Zola. Out of her carrying bag came the package Ella had given her, and in went a gift-wrapped game of Monopoly that she had purchased earlier. Next, a trip to deliver the gift to Ella's friend.

Several days later, Alex put the painting in a shopping trolley, took the

Métro to Pont de Neuilly, and walked to Richard's apartment.

"Alex, what a lovely surprise."

Four air kisses followed by a genuine hug. "Me, too, Uncle Richard. I'm running late. Can I leave this here? There's so little room in my tiny apartment."

"Leaving already?" Richard sounded disappointed. He had come to look forward to Alex's visits, whether announced or not. Like black outlines on a white page, they defined his loneliness.

I think it's too early to get Uncle Richard involved, until I figure out what I'm going to do. "Yes, but I'll be back soon. *Bisous.*"

Chapter 46

River Arroux

A WARM WIND BLEW UP from the Sahara, breaking the cold, and overnight, small green sprouts appeared on the bare trees and shrubs. The dreary grey sky gave way to a robin's-egg blue.

It was too nice a day to spend in school, pretending to listen as one boring teacher after another tried to cram notions of philosophy, history, and literature into their brains. Dominique and Grégory excelled in mathematics, the criterion by which French students were judged and selected for bigger and better things, and they felt a need to celebrate the break in the weather.

Instead of going to school, they decided to walk along the river. They sat on a conveniently located bench, sharing some excellent pot, feeling the warmth of the sun on their faces, the chirping of birds reverberating in their ears. As they stood up to continue their walk, Dominique tripped and caught his foot in the strap of his backpack, and both boy and schoolbag tumbled down the soggy slope, for the icy covering had been melted by the sun's rays, leaving a sea of mud, strewn with rocks and small shrubs.

Dominique giggled as he rolled down the riverbank. Grégory thought that looked like fun, so he threw his backpack down the slope, sliding down the muddy incline toward his friend. Still laughing, the two friends started to push each other, slipping in the mud, getting up, and starting all over again. Filthy, they tired of their game and went to gather their bags and continue their walk along the riverbank. Dominique's bag was resting on some reeds at the water's edge.

"Whoa," he called out to Grégory, "what's this?" Caught in the reeds was a large object, rocked gently by the river's current. Standing with his feet in the water, Dominique saw a bloated mass, a body face down, the remains of a hand protruding. He tried to move away, but his feet were caught in the icy mud, and he fell over onto the reeds.

"Help me," he cried.

"Holy shit," yelled Grégory when he saw the body. He pulled Dominique back to the riverbank. They gathered their bags and ran back up to the bench. As they looked down, the body came free from the reeds and slowly floated away.

Clear thought did not come easily, but after some discussion, the two friends decided that saying nothing about their discovery would be the wisest course of action. The little buzz had worn off, the sun did not feel as pleasant, and the prospect of sitting warm and dry in a boring classroom had sudden appeal. They decided to return home, clean themselves up, and return to school in the afternoon, keeping their adventure to themselves.

Sometime later that afternoon, a man walking his dog happened to see the slow-moving body, and he called the police. He had not been especially good at math, but his moral compass was in a better place.

The body was removed from the river and examined. After almost a month in the water, there was not too much left of the face. The fish and the insects had taken care of that. Bits of flesh hung from the fingers; the clothing was in tatters.

News of the discovery of the body made its way up the communication channels to a desk in the Interior Ministry, where it was eventually matched with Jacques' report that Bruno was missing. Kenneth Petit contacted Jacques and asked him to check with the gendarmerie in Dijon, where the body was being held.

"I don't suppose you know if your man had a dentist? No? Well, then you'd better bring in a comb or a toothbrush because the body's in bad shape." He added, "And no, no news on the girl."

#   #   #

Scientific Police Laboratory, Paris

It was a shit day for Valentin Beaufils. He'd slept poorly, forgotten to set his alarm, and skipped breakfast to make it to the lab on time. A queasy feeling sent him off to find a cup of coffee and an energy bar in the vending machine down the hall. As he consumed what passed for breakfast, his boss strode into the lab, bringing a sample from a badly decomposed body and a toothbrush.

"Bonjour Valentin. You'll need to do a DNA test right away. So give this your top priority." His boss started to offer an explanation when his phone rang. He stepped out of the lab to answer it and disappeared down the corridor.

The energy bar and the coffee were now fighting for supremacy over Valentin's intestines, beads of sweat gathered on his forehead. He had other "top priority" tests to do; this one would wait its turn. The queasy feeling remained, and he skipped lunch to move ahead with his tests.

His boss's head appeared in the doorway a few hours later: "*Alors*, Valentin, is it the same guy? Can we wrap this up? They're waiting to bury the poor slob." It occurred to Valentin that the only time his boss spoke to him was to ask about work; otherwise, he did not exist. "I had other urgent tests to do, but I'm working on it right now."

He felt light-headed; would this day never end? Confusion added to resentment so that he substituted the DNA from the body with the DNA from the toothbrush, and the mass of putrefied flesh was confirmed to be the last remains of Bruno Edremal

#   #   #

A FORGERY IN PARIS

Château d'Hélène

Even before Bruno's identity had been confirmed, Jacques started to imagine how Bruno could have wound up in the river. Did he have a heart attack and fall into the water? But what was he doing on the riverbank anyway? Did he find himself on the losing side of a barroom fight? He would have Tarek ask around in the clubs Bruno frequented.

Once the body had been identified, Jacques had only one question for the forensic investigators: what was the cause of death? "Well, I can tell you that there are no broken bones, no gunshot wounds, but after all the time in the water, I'm afraid we can't tell you more than that. We're not CSI here; this is not some TV show. I guess that your friend had too much to drink, slipped, and fell into the river."

The investigator didn't like Kenneth Petit, didn't like being asked to do special work for those in favor in Paris. He wrote his report and closed the file, and no one would ever know why — and indeed if — Bruno had stopped breathing before he entered the icy waters.

The search for Bruno's car had come up dry, and Jacques had to admit he was at a dead end. It was all so irritating. And then, Mila had started nagging him again about her investments. "When can we go over my accounts?" She hadn't even bothered to smile. Her face looked as if it was carved out of stone.

"Can't you see how busy I am, with Bruno and all the rest? You need not worry about your investments. They're just fine."

"Yes, Jacques, of course, but you know that I enjoy seeing how my accounts have grown."

"I realize that. But just remember that, without me, you'd be working as a hostess in some two-bit bar, so give me a moment to breathe and we'll go over everything." *Merde, I haven't had time to prepare the documents to give the picture she expects to see. No rest for the weary.*

A new, challenging project was needed to occupy his mind and his energy, something more than placating Mila. Then he remembered the conversation with Merv Peters and decided that he would follow his suggestion to meet with Renaud Schneider.

Several days later, Jacques walked down rue Bonaparte to the Café de Flore on Boulevard Saint Germain, carrying a shiny white shopping bag, tied closed with a white ribbon and a white plastic camellia. He climbed the stairs to the first floor and found Merv sitting on a banquette facing the greenery.

He had phoned Merv the day before. "I managed to negotiate an excellent price for you, only two hundred thousand Euros. What do you say? Normally this painting should go for at least fifty thousand, maybe a hundred thousand more, but the seller was in a hurry. All to the good, no?"

And now he put the shopping bag on the seat next to him, smiled, and waited. Merv opened his Louis Vuitton *porte documents*, placed a manila envelope on the table. "As agreed," he said as he slid it across to Jacques.

Jacques smiled his mirthless, no-creases-around-the-eyes smile. "I thought about what you said the last time we met, and I'd like you to bring me with you the next time you go to one of the Schnneiders' open houses. Can you do that?" The words *after all I've done for you* were there, unspoken but heard.

"Sure," said Merv, "it'll be a pleasure."

Coffee and mango juice consumed, Merv left first, taking the white shopping bag with him. He got into a taxi and returned to his apartment, went up to the room that was his secret garden, opened the package, and placed the new Buffet painting in the empty space on the wall. It was slightly smaller than its predecessor, but Merv felt the same hypnotic pull from the stark, dark outlines. He would keep the alarm system on at all times; he needed to remind his housekeeper about that. It had been an expensive lesson, but the pompous lawyer was happy with his new acquisition. As for another visit, he need not have worried. Jacques was too elegant to drink at the same well twice.

Chapter 47

ONCE AGAIN, TAREK DROVE JACQUES and Mila to Dijon, this time to make arrangements for Bruno's funeral. The morgue had left a message for Jacques — did he want them to release the body to him? Jacques did not know if Bruno had any family, he had never spoken about that, so he felt he had no choice but to see Bruno to his final resting place. Besides, it would not look good to his Parisian friends if he abandoned Bruno to a lonely burial.

The only time that Alex felt free to talk with Ella was when they were alone at the château, and she waited until the sound of the car disappeared before walking into the kitchen for a cup of coffee and a chat.

"I guess you heard, they found Bruno," said Alex, curious to see Ella's reaction to the news that the body had been identified.

Ella looked at Alex, brown eyes locked onto blue ones. The concave spaces under Ella's cheekbones made it look like the flesh had melted from her face.

"Yes," she whispered and turned away.

Alex tried again, "It must be a relief to know that he's really gone, isn't it?"

"If you do not mind, Nathalie, I don't want to talk about it. I'm trying to forget about what happened."

Alex busied herself by pouring a cup of coffee. *I'd better back off. She seems tense. Can't say that I blame her. Talk about something else.*

"So, Ella, what would you do if you didn't have to work here?"

"I'll always have to work here, or for someone else, doing the same thing."

"Yes, but just imagine if you didn't have to."

For a moment, Ella looked happy. "I'd move back to the Philippines, buy a house for my family, and open a French restaurant. But that won't happen." Smile gone, she continued to unload the dishwasher.

"You miss your family, don't you?"

Ella's eyes were bright with held back tears, "Yes, I miss them very much. All I can do is send them money, but I'd like to be with them. Soon they will start to die."

"Well, don't give up hope. You never know what can happen."

#   #   #

When Jacques and Mila returned, there was a flurry of activity. Mila told Ella to clean out the stalls where the painters had been living. Mila herself went to the atelier to pack up the painting supplies. Tarek was to wrap up all the paintings, rent a small truck, and drive them to Mélandère, Jacques' property in the south of France.

Bruno's death and the disappearance of the painters had left Jacques feeling out of sync; his intuition told him that it was time to put a halt to the forgeries. He could come back to that very lucrative business once he felt settled again. He wanted to give his full attention to Renaud Schneider.

Chapter 48

Rue Gagnée, Vitry-sur-Seine

IT WAS THE MIDDLE OF the night, but Wen was wide-awake, trying to blot out Li's rhythmic snoring. He squeezed his eyes shut, but instead of sleep, he relived the evening in the kitchen at the château d'Hélène. *What if Bruno had still been alive when we pushed him into the river?* He had been tortured by that thought ever since they boarded the train to Paris a few weeks earlier.

When he tried to talk about that night with Li, his friend scoffed at him. "Why do you care about that bully? He looked pretty dead to me, and anyway, he's dead and gone now, and good riddance."

"But what if he wasn't dead? That would be murder, wouldn't it?"

"I'm tired of your what-ifs. We're away from the château, free to rebuild our lives. You ought to spend your spare time painting, not worrying about that cruel man."

Some of the men Wen worked with in the supermarket hung out at a café in the Belleville neighborhood, and on occasion he joined them. He returned there after work. Seeing his new friends might take his mind off the images and sounds that haunted him: Bruno's ashen face on the floor of the château's

180

kitchen, the crunch of their feet on the gravel as they carried their burden down to the riverbank; the gentle splash as the body slid into the dark water.

#   #   #

Place des Fêtes, Paris

Tarek had returned to his studio on rue Arthur Rozier. Cleaned the apartment, went out to the laundromat, bought some coffee and water. His dreary lodgings seemed even smaller after Jacques' apartment on rue Bonaparte, and when his laundry was done, he was glad to leave. This was his night off, and he headed down the street toward Place des Fêtes. He'd grab dinner in one of the cafés before he went out for the evening.

Wen had finished his shift in the supermarket and was now hunched over a glass of cheap rosé wine, waiting for his friends. He'd never been much of a drinker, but now the wine seemed to lessen his anxiety, and when his friends arrived, he ordered another glass. Wen was silent, enveloped in the cocoon of conversation that blurred the hard edges of his imagination. After a while, the men started to drift away. Wen had one last glass and he, too, got up to leave. He walked slowly toward the Métro at Place des Fêtes. He'd wait to eat until he got home; there was always a pot of noodles and vegetables on the stove at his uncle's apartment.

When Tarek left the café, he didn't recognize Wen at first; he had barely even noticed the slightly built Asian man with unruly hair walking unsteadily toward him. The two men were approaching the Métro entrance when their eyes met. Wen reacted first—a rush of adrenaline—and he jumped over the turnstile.

Tarek hesitated, watching as Wen pushed aside riders on the long escalator that led to the platforms. *It's one of the fucking painters.* He bolted down the escalator, trying to grab Wen to bring him back to Jacques. Wen turned and saw Tarek coming after him. He was now running down the steps. The escalator seemed to go on forever. Was it fear or wine that made him trip and fall as he came to the bottom of the moving stairway? On his hands and knees, he felt two hands grab his armpits and lift him up.

181

"Let me help you," said Tarek. People rushed by. No one paid attention as Tarek steered Wen away from the escalator. "What did you do to Bruno, you little fucker?"

"No speak French," he cried out.

"Bullshit, you're coming with me." Desperate to get away, Wen hooked his foot around Tarek's ankle.

Tarek fell backward, hitting his head on the ground. The fall was painful; he loosened his grip and Wen squirmed free. He ran toward the platform, hoping that a train would pull into the station before Tarek caught up with him. He wove in and out of the crowd until he came to the end of the platform, with Tarek trying to close the distance that separated them. Steps led down to the track. Wen ignored the *no entry* sign and found himself in the tunnel. As a train entered the station, he pressed himself against an indentation in the tunnel wall. Only a few inches separated him from the cars. As he held his breath, immobile, it seemed like an eternity until the train pulled out of the station. He let another train go by, took a chance that he'd lost his pursuer, climbed back up to the platform, and took the next train to return to Vitry.

When Tarek didn't see Wen, he assumed that he'd managed to board the train. Either that, or he'd run into the tunnel, and Tarek was not prepared to follow him there.

The next day he drove back to the château. He stood at the doorway to Jacques' office, knocked, and cleared his throat. "*Monsieur.*"

"Not now, Tarek," snapped Jacques, busy reading emails on his Blackberry. *Fuck it*, now that he thought about it, he wasn't even sure that the man in the train station was one of the painters; he never did know their names. *Maybe the man was an illegal immigrant. That's why he ran away.* It didn't make a lot of sense… There was no need to bother Jacques.

That night Wen told Li what had happened. "I want to go home," he said. He'd put aside some money from his job at the supermarket, but it was not enough for his plane fare. Between Li and Xi, they loaned him the difference, and the next day, he bought a ticket to fly to Beijing. He would go back to his old job, turning out reproductions. Li regretted his friend's departure, but he now had the spare bedroom that served as a studio all to himself, and he returned to his painting with renewed energy.

He felt safe in Vitry and at the supermarket, unlikely places to cross paths with Tarek. But he would avoid Place des Fêtes.

Chapter 49

Paris

ALEX HAD MADE AN APPOINTMENT for a facial massage, a mid-winter treat. As she arrived, she could tell from the esthetician's flustered face that patience was in order. On a low marble table, part of the décor designed to vaguely suggest a boudoir, were the sorts of magazines one never wanted to be seen buying, but that one eagerly read in waiting rooms. Somehow a copy of *L'Express* had found its way among the escapades of Europe's nobility.

Alex leafed through it distractedly, not reading until an article caught her eye: "The Rape of French Churches." It was a story about the theft of artworks in French churches, most in the countryside, without the benefit of video surveillance. Chalices, sculptures, paintings, all had disappeared into the illegal underground market.

A name caught Alex's eye: Charles-François Daubigny. Curious, she continued reading: *Charles-François Daubigny was a nineteenth-century painter of the Barbizon School and an important influence on the Impressionist painters that came after him. He is known for his landscapes and river scenes, but a rare seascape —* Storm Over the Sea *— has recently disappeared from a small church near Roscoff. Due to its unusual subject* *matter, art experts say the painting could be worth as much as eight hundred and fifty thousand Euros if sold at auction.*

Inserted in the story was a photo of *Storm Over the Sea.*

Her heart beat a little faster as Alex realized that she'd seen this painting very recently.

#   #   #

Two nights later, Alex met Eugene in front of Salle Pleyel. She wore a navy blue pants suit, the satiny fabric bringing out the intense blue of her eyes. Many of the concertgoers were dressed down. People increasingly didn't seem to care what they wore; dressing up for an occasion seemed to have gone out of style. But Alex didn't care, going to the recital was a special occasion, and she would be appropriately attired according to her own lights. Eugene wore a tie and a rather shapeless jacket; she was sure that it was something he must have picked off the rack at a discount menswear store. He was broad-shouldered with no excess fat, and she realized once again that Eugene could be quite attractive if it were not for his love of garlic.

She sat in rapt attention from the first trills to the end; forgotten were Trubenne, the metallic-green Peugeot, Marie-Agnès, Jacques, and Eugene. It was over all too soon and at the end of the recital Eugene asked if she wouldn't like to have a bite to eat at a brasserie on Avenue Hoche.

Eugene ordered a bottle of Chablis, and over a *choucroute de poisons*, he asked Alex how things were going at *Artixia*. "Oh, fine, I guess. By the way, Mila is the widow of a man named Pavel Korsikov. I thought you might want to know."

He was pleased that Alex shared that information even if it was not news to him. But then she continued. "You had mentioned that there are companies that help to find stolen paintings. Well, what happens when they do find them?"

Eugene took a sip of wine. "It depends on the circumstances. They will try to negotiate the return of the artwork. Why do you ask? Have you found a stolen painting?"

Alex swallowed some of the *choucroute*; it was her turn to sip her wine before responding. She reached into her purse and pulled out a photocopy of the article from *l'Express*.

"Do you read French?" she asked.

"Yes, I spent a year in France when I was in high school," he said, perusing the article. He looked up at Alex. "And…"

"And it's a complicated story. A man who worked for Jacques, his name was Bruno, disappeared about a month ago. The other day, I heard Jacques and Mila talking. It looks like his body turned up in the river last week. He had left this painting in the château, where someone found it, and it is now in a safe place. I'd like to get a reward for the person who found it, and I was wondering how one would go about doing that."

"Shouldn't this person have given the painting to Jacques?"

"I don't think they were thinking clearly at the time; it was just a package. They didn't discover that it was a painting until later. And Jacques never asked them if they had seen it, so he probably doesn't know that Bruno had that painting."

"So this someone stole a painting from someone who is no longer alive to claim it?"

"I wouldn't look at it like that. This person found the painting that was left in the château's family dining room. They didn't steal anything."

"Yeah, I guess you have a point there. And I suppose you've seen the painting." It was a statement, not a question.

Alex looked straight at Eugene. "Yes." A short silence, and she continued, "So, do you think you could help me get a reward for the person who found the painting? For the moment, I can't tell you more about her, but she's very deserving."

She was not ready to explain more about Ella, even less so about Marie-Agnès. She was curious to see what he would come up with. That might tell her more about Eugene Spector.

"Well, Alex, when you're ready to tell me more, we'll see if there's anything to be done to help this person." He wondered out loud, "So, what made you come to France?"

She smiled. "I inherited a share in a decrepit château that's been in my family for a long time, and I wanted to reconnect with my relatives and visit the château."

"That sounds wonderful. And where is this château located?"

"In the south, in the Languedoc, in a hamlet called Trubenne. My mother's maiden name was Vesla de Trubenne." She recounted her visit over the Christmas holiday, describing Charlotte. Still no mention of Marie-Agnès, though. This time, she couldn't say it was because she was too tired to talk about the attack and the decision for her friend to spend some time at Trubenne, out of harm's way. No mention either of the deliverymen with flowers from an unnamed admirer. Or of the unfortunate incident at Montbard. None of that had anything to do with Eugene Spector.

The night was clear. A three-quarter moon hung in the black sky as she walked back to her apartment on Boulevard Malesherbes. Dinner with Eugene had been so pleasant; it was a pity that he was married. *If I were more French,* she reflected, *that wouldn't matter, but I'm not interested in a dead-end relationship. The momentary pleasure is just not worth it.*

Chapter 50

CHARLOTTE WAS MAKING A FRESH pot of coffee when Marie-Agnès returned from her morning run, her face pink from the effort, her hair an unkempt mess resembling a tangle of thistles.

"I've been thinking," she began.

"*Et alors?*" Charlotte turned slowly to face her.

"I want to go back to Paris. Please don't misunderstand. I love being here, being with you, and I feel like I'm a different person now. But I also feel that I'm in a cage. What I'm trying to say is that I need to have a choice, Paris or Trubenne or wherever. I need to feel free to move around. Alex called again while you were away in Nîmes.

"It looks like a lot of things have changed. Alex said that they found Bruno floating in the river, the painters have disappeared, and Jacques has cleaned out their rooms—if you can call them rooms—and he had Mila and Tarek pack up the studio. She promised to tell me everything when we see each other.

"So after all this time, I doubt that there's any reason for him to come after me. I mean, no one else has showed up with a bouquet of flowers, have they?"

"Vengeance is not always very logical. Why not wait a little longer?"

"No, I've given this a lot of thought, and I can't hide out here any longer, as wonderful as Trubenne is."

A few days later, Charlotte drove Marie-Agnès to the train station in Nîmes, where she took the TGV back to Paris and the apartment on rue d'Orchampt.

#   #   #

Rue d'Orchampt, Paris

Alex couldn't get over the change in Marie-Agnès. She had slimmed down; she had traded the grey pallor that was part of the Parisian lifestyle for a clear, rosy complexion. And most of all, she was, perhaps not so much happy as grounded. Solid.

"You look fabulous. How are you feeling?"

"I feel great. Full of energy. And how are things with you? How did you find out about what happened at Jacques' château? You promised to tell me when we saw each other."

"Lately my life seems to be a series of coincidences. Remember when I told you that I sat next to Jacques Mornnais on my flight over here? And that he told me to get in touch with him if I was looking for work as a translator? Well, I did, but he thinks my name is Nathalie Martin and that I live in the fifteenth on Avenue Emile Zola. It's quite exhilarating to live a double life! Anyhow, I thought it could be a way to find out what he's up to."

She paused. *I guess I'll have to tell Marie-Agnès about Eugene.*

"And you'll never guess who I ran into—literally—in Parc Monceau? Eugene Spector, the man who's renting my house in DC. We had a coffee, he invited me to lunch, and then I had dinner with him the other night. He's in Paris on some confidential work for the government, whatever that means. Actually, it was a concert *and* dinner. I told him that I was working for *Artixia,* and I feel like he's been picking my brain, trying to learn more about Jacques and Mila. He says it's to help him recover the money his aunt paid for a fake that he says the dealer got from Jacques. But I think there's something more, even though I don't know what."

189

"Are you going to help him?"

"It may be more like he's going to help me. Do you remember Ella, the maid?"

"Yes, of course, although I don't think I exchanged more than a few words with her."

"Well, I got to know her, you know, having coffee and cake in the kitchen when we were alone."

Alex recounted the story of Bruno's last evening at the château. "Ella found a painting that Bruno had left in the dining room, wrapped in brown paper, and an envelope with a kind of certification from an art dealer. By the way, did your cell phone have a pink and red design on the cover? Yes? I think Bruno had it, but we'll never know for sure as Ella threw it in the river. And I'm quite sure Jacques does not know that Bruno had this painting."

"Doesn't surprise me. Bruno was such an unsavory character. They *all* are. Have you ever seen a cat playing with a lizard? I felt like the little lizard when I met Bruno at the Hôtel Lutetia."

"I know. Anyhow, the painting is now in a safe place, and I'm trying to figure out what to do with it."

"What do you mean?"

"First, Jacques went ballistic when he learned that Bruno had disappeared. But not a word about a missing painting. Secondly, I had read an article in *l'Express* about artwork stolen from country churches, and guess what, there was a photo of this very painting! It's called *Storm Over the Sea,* and it's by Daubigny—yes—the artist that my street is named after. My guess is that Bruno was going to sell this painting without telling Jacques about it."

"Okay," interrupted Marie-Agnès, "but what do you mean, what you're going to do with it?"

"I'm thinking that since Ella found the painting, it belongs to her, at least temporarily, until it can be returned to the church. But I think she deserves a reward, considering everything she's had to go through, especially with Bruno. "

"I see where you're going with this, but it's a bit of a stretch, don't you think?"

"Maybe, but it's too late for Ella to walk into the living room and hand the painting to Jacques. So, while Eugene is digging — ever so charmingly, I might add — I'm using him to find out how to go about getting a reward for Ella."

"Aha," Marie-Agnès said with a grin. "Intrigue and perhaps romance. Are you interested in Eugene, aside from getting a reward for Ella?"

"Well, he's quite good-looking, and when he's not prying about Jacques and Mila, I enjoy being with him, but"—she hesitated—"he's married."

"And?"

"And I'm not looking to complicate my life any further."

"Whatever."

"Um, there's something else. I wanted to ask what happened with the flowers, and your, um, secret admirer. You and Charlotte didn't seem to want to talk about it on the phone."

Marie-Agnès gave a forced laugh. "Are you sure you want to know?"

"Of course I do."

"There was a man in the woods, you know, right in front of the house, and he had a gun. Charlotte and I think he was waiting for the right moment to kill me, maybe both of us. We think he was one of the men who attacked me in the Métro. And this man, he was attacked by a *sanglier* — the woods are full of them and in the winter they're particularly hungry. So they made a meal of him."

"You're joking."

"No, I'm not. We heard a shot, then screams. When all was quiet, Charlotte went out to see what had happened. The beasts had already eaten his face and parts of his body, and a few days later, they finished him up, clothing and all. Charlotte found his gun and threw it down the well."

"You're giving me the creeps."

"Actually, I think he had it coming. He didn't try to kill me once but twice. So, I'll save my tears."

"I know what you mean. Do you remember my telling you about the man in the Peugeot? My story is as unbelievable as yours."

Alex had tried to push the incident at Montbard to the farthest reaches of her mind, but now the horror resurfaced as she shared her tale with Marie-Agnès. "And now, I can't get him out of my mind. Do you think he was partners with the other man, the one in the woods?"

"Perhaps. It seems logical. But why would he be interested in you?"

"I was thinking, maybe they didn't want to leave any trace of the three of us."

"Could be, but now that Bruno's dead, we'll never know."

#   #   #

Tarek dropped Jacques and Merv off in front of an imposing *hôtel particulier* on rue Rembrandt, overlooking Parc Monceau. On the way over, while they were stuck in traffic, Merv took the opportunity to fill Jacques in on the history of the Schneider family.

Their gallery, specializing in eighteenth-century furniture and *objets d'art*, dated back to the start of the twentieth century when Renaud's great-great-grandfather, Victor, opened his antique shop on rue Saint-Honoré. He developed an international clientele of captains of industry, wealthy members of high society, and serious collectors. The family prospered, and after the end of the First World War, Victor's son, Alfred, bought the present property on rue Rembrandt. During the German occupation of Paris, the Schneiders, who were Jewish, fled to Switzerland. When they returned, their house was empty, and they were forced to rebuild their collection from scratch. It took them ten years to do so, but by the 1960s, they were again one of the leading antiques dealers in Paris. Renaud took over running the gallery in 2000, and for several years, business boomed as dot-com millionaires came knocking at the massive wooden door. But all good things must come to an end, and so they did in 2008. Renaud was looking for ways to revitalize the business and Merv thought that perhaps a spread in *Artixia* could help.

Jacques smiled and thanked Merv. Of course, he knew most of the story already, and Merv had only confirmed his suspicions as to the Schneider family's financial distress. But what pleased him most was to see Merv's eagerness to tell all.

On the building's façade, there was a simple brass plaque with the name *Schneider*. They pushed the buzzer, and the door opened automatically onto a stone corridor, running through the center of the building.

Renaud Schneider, clad in an impeccably tailored dark suit, appropriate attire for a man with millions of dollars' worth of inventory, was holding open a glass door on the right.

"Merv, how nice to see you."

"You, too, Renaud. I'd like to introduce you to my friend Jacques Mornnais. He publishes *Artixia*."

"I'm very pleased to meet you, Mr. Mornnais. Won't you come this way?"

They took an elevator to the top floor, strolled through the four stories displaying the gallery's extraordinary collection of furniture and *objets d'art*, Renaud pointing out some small commodes that could be of interest to Merv. No pressure, just a very soft sell.

The walls were in an eggshell tone, pleasing to the eye, and the lighting was perfect, each piece carefully placed to highlight its beauty, the light never too harsh. Jacques didn't say very much, just quietly complimented Renaud on the quality of the renovation.

At last, they were back on the ground floor, and Renaud led them down a stairway to the basement. Unlike the intimate viewing spaces in the upper levels, the basement consisted of a spacious gallery of contemporary art. Occasional pieces of antique furniture provided an interesting juxtaposition between old and new, and Merv stopped to admire a marble-topped Louis XVI-style commode with its gilt-bronze frame and trellis marquetry panels surrounding a pastoral still-life on the central door. It would be a lovely addition to his secret garden.

"And now here is my favorite place in this house," exclaimed Renaud as he led them out of the gallery. They faced a glass wall, and behind the wall, a swimming pool. He put a card into the lock; a glass panel slid open. Humidity and the smell of chlorine permeated the air-lock entry. The twenty-meter pool was long enough to swim lengths. There were beach chairs, low tables, and tropical plants; the only thing missing was the sun. A bar ran along one end; behind it, there was a refrigerator and a dumbwaiter.

"We built the pool when we were doing the renovation. We felt that we needed a place to relax at the end of the day, although as of late we're doing too much relaxing and not enough working," he ended up ruefully.

"I was thinking about installing an indoor pool at my château," said Jacques, "but it seemed quite complicated."

"You're right. There are so many things you have to take care of, and we had to be especially careful about controlling the humidity since we have our gallery right across the hall. You would not believe the complicated machinery in our equipment room; we have a technician come once a week to make sure everything is working properly. When I think about it, it does seem a bit extravagant to have your own indoor pool in Paris, but the truth is, I love it."

"I can see that you have to be very careful. Is there a company you would recommend?"

"We used an American company with offices in Paris — they are the best — called Top Pools."

Renaud saw them to the door. As they sat back in the car's comfortable leather seats, Merv's thoughts focused on whether he could afford one of the commodes, whereas Jacques was dreaming of swimming pools. He would let a few weeks go by and then call Renaud and ask to talk with him about a spread in *Artixia*.

Chapter 51

Hotel on avenue de Wagram, Paris

EUGENE LOOKED AGAIN THROUGH THE slim file on Jacques Mornnais that Vincent Reiner had just given him, studying the photos of Jacques, Mila, Bruno, and Tarek. Jacques Mornnais had sprung to life at the end of the last century. He lived in France, but he had no administrative presence there, and he traveled with a passport from Montenegro. *Who is Jacques Mornnais? He must have a past, even if we haven't yet unlocked it.* He stared at Jacques' photo; his head was turned away from the camera in a three-quarter view. There was a shadow across the side of his neck, and Eugene tried to figure out where the light source was coming from. He was sure that he had never seen the man, but his eyes kept coming back to the photo.

Other than their photos, there was no information on Bruno or Tarek. In any event, Bruno was no longer in the equation. Eugene would focus on Tarek. He continued to leaf through the file. Mornnais's wife, some sixteen years his senior, was the widow of a Russian industrialist. *Well, I already knew that.*

Jacques might have an interest in a Singaporean company called the White Lotus that owned the Château d'Hélène in the Morvan region and a house in the south of France, called Mélandère, near the town of Roquebrune-sur-Argens. Mornnais seemed to spend most of his time at the château, and when he was in Paris, he stayed in an apartment that he rented on rue Bonaparte. *Why does he have a house in the south of France if he doesn't spend any time there?*

A feeling that he ought to go to Mélandère took hold.

#   #   #

Roquebrune-sur-Argens

Tarek left the château before sunrise. The air was soft and almost balmy as he headed toward the A6 motorway. He always enjoyed the trip south, and he smiled as he glimpsed the empty seat next to him.

A tangle of thoughts settled in his mind. Bruno. His heavy drinking habit and his hangovers. The hate-filled man with the ugly car, what was his connection to Bruno? What else did Bruno do when he was running errands? Jacques never seemed to pay attention to Bruno's comings and goings. And falling into the river? What was he doing there anyway? It was difficult to believe that Bruno stumbled and fell in — maybe one of his whores pushed him, or perhaps he had been dealing on the side, and things had gone wrong?

Some ten hours later, he had reached the outskirts of Roquebrune-sur-Argens and drove up the bumpy path that led to Mélandère. A nineteenth-century Italianate summerhouse, it stood on a low hill, overlooking a sloping lawn. The grass was a dull green marred by bare yellowish spots. A dense forest, crisscrossed by hiking trails, surrounded the property. The mansion had belonged to a family rich in property but short on cash. The family — generations of lawyers and judges—had fled the city each summer to spend their holidays at Mélandère.

In 2008, an unfortunate bet on the markets had left the patriarch, Raymond du Clos-Duporte, in dire straits, and it was his friend, Jacques Mornnais, who arranged for a transfer of the property to the White Lotus, in return for obtaining forgiveness of Raymond's debt.

The exterior of the house had a lived-in, shabby look to it. Some of the large shutters had slats missing, and spidery thin cracks marred the clean lines of the façade. Inside, there were egg tempura frescos in the three adjoining reception rooms whose ceilings were in need of a fresh coat of paint. Although German soldiers had bivouacked in the house during the Occupation, burning the furniture to keep themselves warm, they had left the library, crammed with law books, intact. Wasps had recently built a giant nest against one of the windows, but, like the rest of the house, this had been left untouched.

Upstairs there were eight bedrooms whose shutters were kept closed to protect the ancient wallpaper from the sun's rays. Most of the bedrooms had little round wood-burning iron stoves, but there was one bedroom with an adjoining bathroom where the wiring had been redone to provide some rudimentary twenty-first-century comforts. On the upper floor, the servants' quarters had been transformed into bedrooms and playrooms for the family's many children.

Tarek drove into a courtyard at the back of the house. He unlocked the door and brought his few personal items inside, leaving them in the long hallway that ran parallel to the reception rooms. Back outside, he descended a small flight of steps and opened the weather-beaten door leading to the basement. Here some improvements had been made: in front of him was a massive steel door that swung open silently when he punched in the combination. A smell of rarefied air, clean with just the right degree of humidity, surrounded him as he turned on the lights and entered a spacious vault, where paintings wrapped in bubble paper stood in wood frames. Quickly he went back to the van, removed the cargo, and carefully placed the paintings in the vault.

When he was done, he closed up, went back into the house, and took advantage of the renovated bathroom to enjoy a long, hot shower. Later he would take the path that ran through the farmland at the bottom of the access road and walk into the little town of Roquebrune-sur-Argens for a hot meal.

#   #   #

Eugene had arrived on the outskirts of Roquebrune and checked into a simple B and B. He would make discreet inquiries tomorrow, but for tonight, he walked into the town. Two restaurants were open at this time of the year, and he entered the one that was more crowded.

It was early in the evening, and he chose a table at the rear of the dining room, facing the street. For starters, he ordered a plate of raw vegetables with aioli. As he pushed a piece of bread in a circle to clear his plate of the remains of the sauce, he looked up and saw Tarek enter the restaurant.

Eugene focused on his plate, concentrating on chewing his bread slowly, and out of the corner of his eye, he saw that Tarek had been given a seat by the door, across the room. Slumped slightly in his chair, he looked tired, almost disconnected.

The waitress brought Eugene his main course: a slice of veal roast with new potatoes. He ate it more rapidly than he would have liked, made sure to pay promptly, and then lingered over his coffee while Tarek ate. He was ready to follow him as soon as Tarek left.

A mistral had cleared the sky, an almost full moon illuminating the path. Eugene hung back but he could see Tarek far ahead. When Tarek turned right onto the dirt road, he remained in the shadows, following him up to the house. Tarek walked around to the back of the building, then a door slammed. Eugene waited patiently until he saw a light in the upper windows go out. The dark woods hid him as he skirted the property, making out a van parked in the circle of bright moonlight. As he stood in the forest, contemplating his next step, a strong gust of wind rocked the nearby trees, and a large branch came crashing down, landing on the roof of the van with a loud thump.

Tarek tried to sleep, but the howling wind kept him awake and on edge. When he heard the snap of a branch, he got out of bed, walked across the hallway, opened the creaky shutters, and looked down. "Fuck, oh, fuck," he muttered when he saw the bough splayed across the van's roof. He pulled on his pants and a shirt and went down to the courtyard. While Tarek was wrestling with the branch, Eugene crept back through the forest to the dirt road. He would return tomorrow to have a closer look and try to see what Tarek was doing at Mélandère.

The branch removed, Tarek returned to the house and slid into his still-warm bed. But the howling wind continued to disturb him, and after a few restless hours, he decided to get on the road back to Paris. Eugene returned before dawn to keep watch on Tarek, but only the large bough remained in the courtyard. He tried the doors. Locked. He looked up and saw that last night's open shutter was now closed.

"Oh, shit."

Chapter 52

Paris

MARIE-AGNÈS HAD DECIDED THE surest way to keep the weight off was to get rid of the safety valve that her now-too-large clothes provided. As she stared at her half-empty closet, she realized the truth of something Alex had said earlier: despite the mountains of clothing, she always wore the same few pieces.

She felt light and free and decided to accept an invitation to a dinner party from one of her old friends. Since the incident in the Métro and everything that had followed, she hadn't been out at all. She wore a soft orange leather jacket over a white silk shirt, unbuttoned to show just a hint of cleavage. With her short dark hair, her firm, slender body, and healthy glow, her friends couldn't get over the change in Mag, her nickname from years ago.

The dinner party consisted of a buffet with tiny portions of shrimp, caviar, and other delicacies. It required so much work to balance the food and drink that there was no danger of overeating. Marie-Agnès remained vague about what she had been doing in the past months — taking a break and visiting family in the south of France. There were quite a few new faces, mostly lawyers, both male, and female.

Whereas in the past, Marie-Agnès would have felt inferior to the assembled jurists, with her newly found self-confidence, her primary emotion was one of boredom. Apart from the group, she sipped her champagne and stared at the patchwork of paintings decorating the walls — brightly colored abstracts, still lifes, and pastoral scenes.

A portly man, impeccably dressed, smiled at her. "They're so fucking boring, aren't they?"

"I assume you mean the artwork and not the guests."

"Lawyers can be pretty boring, but it's not what you know, but who you know that counts. I'm Merv Peters, and you're...?"

"Just call me Mag."

"Well, Mag, actually I was thinking about the so-called artwork. It's pretty awful."

"Yes, to you perhaps. But the owner obviously liked those paintings, and she likes to look at them, and isn't that what counts? Not what you or I think."

"Of course, but still, you have to wonder, what makes her like a painting? Sometimes, you need help to figure that out. For example, I've got a small private collection, for my eyes only, and I have someone who helps me to make the right purchase. You need to buy something that is coherent, something beautiful that will increase in value over time. Being a serious collector is time-consuming and expensive, but when I look at the junk on these walls and think about my collection, there's no comparison."

What a pompous, self-satisfied asshole. Now I remember why I avoid these dinner parties.

"How interesting. So you have a particular dealer who advises you?"

"Better than that. I've got a guy who publishes a fine arts magazine called *Artixia*. You may have heard of it. He knows the whole art market. He's gotten me some great deals."

Marie-Agnès felt a chill run up her spine, stiffening her shoulders, constricting her throat. She took another sip of champagne and tried to think of something to say.

"How wonderful. You're so fortunate. I'd love to know more, but I've got an early train tomorrow, so I'm afraid I'll have to say good-bye. It's been great meeting you."

Merv Peters was surprised. When he mentioned his private collection, it created an air of mystery, a point of attraction. But this woman, what was her name — Meg or Peg or something like that — expressed no interest. Probably didn't know anything about art. Not his type, even if she was attractive. And she slipped out of his mind as swiftly as she had left the party.

Chapter 53

ALEX WAS SAVORING A HOT white chocolate in Angelina's on rue de Rivoli. It was not really chocolate at all but velvety in texture, with a sinful unctuousness, and she sipped it slowly to make it last as long as possible. Beside her was her purchase, a *catalog raisonné* of the neo-impressionist painter Paul Signac.

She had just spent a delightful hour next door, in the Galignani bookstore, an elegant temple dedicated to beautiful books. The dark wooden bookshelves, the rolling ladders, the smell of the books, all harkened back to earlier and, indeed, simpler times. It was a much more satisfying experience than scrolling online, although admittedly not always as convenient. She overcame a momentary impulse to buy a lavish coffee table book for Richard. There was already too much clutter, and the book was too heavy to carry. On the other hand, the reference work on Signac was precisely what she was looking for.

Chapter 54

FRIDAY AFTERNOON AND ELLA HAD a rare weekend off. Tarek was driving her to the station in Dijon. Mila, making an effort to be pleasant, said, "Have a nice weekend, Ella, and don't forget that Tarek will pick you up on Sunday at six thirty, so don't miss your train."

Ella's friend Rosalinda lived in one of the tall towers at Porte de Choisy. Being away from Jacques and Mila felt like the sun breaking through on a cloudy day. She rose early on Saturday morning, eager to make the most of her few hours in Paris.

"I'll make lunch," she had said to Rosalinda. "We only eat French food at the château, and I miss our Filipino cooking." She walked the aisles of the huge supermarket, Wong Frères, buying tofu, meat, and vegetables. For dessert, they would have dragon fruit. Not seeing the vivid red fruit, she went up to a man unloading a crate of kumquats. Li recognized Ella at once while it took her a few seconds longer. But there was no doubt that it was Li.

"Li," she exclaimed, "how are you?"

"Ssssh, Ella, not so loud." He quickly emptied the carton of fruit. "Let's go next door and have a coffee."

There was an awkward moment as they first sat in the café, both remembering the events of the night Bruno had died. But then Ella smiled.

"I'm so glad to see you, and you must be so happy to be away from the château."

"Yes," he said, "things are much better for me but Wen is gone."

"Oh, what happened?"

"He was depressed by what happened and he returned home."

"I can understand how he felt."

"Yeah, I know. Anyhow, how much longer do you think you can put up with living at the château? Is it any better now that Bruno's gone?"

"I hate it there but I need the money. And not too much has changed, although there's a new woman to help Jacques — she's very nice, by the way — and they've closed the studio where you worked."

They talked for a few more minutes, and then Li had to return to the supermarket. On the back of the receipt for their coffee, he wrote his phone number. "Keep this to yourself but call me if I can ever help you."

Ella felt light-headed as she walked back to Rosalinda's. A big, heavyset man was walking toward her, and for a moment she thought he was Bruno. His drunken sneer, his bloodshot eyes, the smell of wine on his breath…they came back to her in a flash. She stopped in the middle of the sidewalk, put her bags down, and stood still. "Stop it," she said. "I'll get out of there, one way or the other.

#   #   #

On Monday Alex was back at the château. Jacques and Mila were both on the phone, and it was not until early the next morning that Ella told Alex about meeting Li.

"I don't want them to see us talking," she said as she brought her coffee and brioche into the office. Can you slip me Li's phone number before I leave? But watch how you do it."

Later that morning, Alex asked Mila, "Would you mind if Ella makes me a sandwich for the train ride back to Paris? The food on the TGV is so awful." Settled in the train, Alex dug into the food Ella had prepared for her. The sandwich — smoked salmon and creamy white cheese with fresh dill — was delicious. She unwrapped dessert — a hunk of pound cake. The icing on the cake was a grease-spattered receipt from a café.

Alex raised the footrest and closed her eyes. *My life is like a gigantic puzzle, a thousand pieces scattered randomly on a large table. If I try to match up all the pieces at the same time, I'll never get it done. But if I carefully assemble one part at a time, then pretty soon I'll complete the whole picture.*

#   #   #

Tarek, too, was back at the château, catching up on sleep after the long drive back from Mélandère. In the early afternoon, he was outside, raking leaves and placing them in grey plastic bin bags. He saw Jacques later in the day, informed him that the paintings were safely in the vault.

"We're going to Paris the day after tomorrow. Leaving early. I have a flight to catch in the afternoon. Mila will be staying on rue Bonaparte."

#   #   #

Tarek drove through Paris to drop Mila off at the apartment, left Jacques at terminal 2E at Charles de Gaulle, and returned to park in the garage on rue du Vieux Colombier. He unloaded the car and brought the luggage up to rue Bonaparte. The building's large oak doors opened when he keyed in the code, and he rode the elevator up to the duplex on the fourth floor. Mila was waiting for him. She had changed from her Chanel-inspired tweeds into a pair of black leggings and an oversized black mohair sweater. She was barefoot, the polish on her toes matched the deep red tones of the large Persian rug on the parquet floor, and her white-blond hair fell loosely over her shoulders.

She smiled at Tarek, stretched out her arms, and, placing her hands on his shoulders said, "So, how is my little driver? Tired? Perhaps you'd like to relax?"

Yes, I'd like to relax and get away from this horny bitch. Mila was not bad for her age, but still, about thirty years too old for his taste. Did Jacques know that he was fucking his wife? Probably. But he had control over her money, and that was what mattered. Tarek pushed her out of the living room, down the hallway into a bedroom, his thumbs pressing against her bony rib cage. *I'm like one of Bruno's whores, fucking for money.* The thought angered and excited him. He came quickly, but Mila didn't complain. It was the best she could get for the moment. She rested her head on his chest and, as usual, babbled on about Jacques…his latest project, the indoor swimming pool he was thinking of installing at the château. Tarek had fallen asleep, and when he started to snore, Mila realized that he was no longer listening.

Chapter 55

A CHOCOLATE ÉCLAIR, THE ICING a shiny dark brown, still in its white fluted baking case. Marie-Agnès stood staring at it on her kitchen counter. She'd been in a bad mood ever since her chat with Merv Peters the other night. What a pretentious, obnoxious man! He had money, but little else to recommend him.

The familiar twins — resentment and anger — had returned, swallowing up the happiness that she had brought back from Trubenne, and her craving for food had returned as well. She could smell the sweetness of the choux filling, could feel the chocolate icing melt in her mouth. *"No,"* she yelled and threw the pastry in the garbage.

She focused instead on a translation until it was time to leave. The cold weather had returned, and she was happy to leave winter behind her as she entered the Mosquée de Paris to spend some time in the hammam with Alex. Reclining on pillows, sipping mint tea, hidden from prying eyes, it was time to move forward, set goals, develop a strategy. A massage sloughed off dead skin, was wonderfully relaxing and yet stimulating. A last refreshing shower, and, bundled up against the cold, the women emerged from the moist cocoon and back into the real world.

Chapter 56

HER CHEEKS PINK, HER SKIN tingling from the massage, Alex walked from the Métro to Richard's apartment. There were never many people on the street — walking was not a preferred mobility mode in Neuilly — but with the cold, she was a solitary figure, her footsteps echoing on the empty sidewalk.

Richard, as always, was so glad to welcome her. Alex, seeking the smoothest way to ask for Richard's help.

"I might be receiving a sum of money—I'm still not sure of the amount—and I was wondering if there was some way I could receive it outside of France and the United States because I want to give it to someone else. I know that in the grand scheme of things, it's not that much, but still, I was wondering…" She let the question hang in the air.

"One can usually find a way to do things, but surely you're not selling drugs or guns?"

"Of course not! Ella, the maid — I think I've mentioned her to you. She's a very nice, deserving person. Anyhow, she found a painting — it's in the package that I left in your closet — that does not seem to belong to anyone at the château, and I want to help her get a reward by returning it to the rightful owners. The situation is a bit complicated, but that's it." *Please, let's not get into all the details. Just tell me if you can help me do it.*

"I'm sure we can work something out once you find out about the reward. Just be careful about Mr. Mornnais. I doubt that he'd be pleased to learn about your charitable instincts."

"Not to worry. I'm a model of discretion."

#   #   #

Sylvie Theytaud, bored and tired, went to the cafeteria in the basement of the American embassy for coffee and a pastry to get her through the morning. Fueled by a surge of caffeine and sugar, she returned to her office just in time to answer the phone. It was Eugene Spector, that handsome man who had come to see Vince almost two months ago.

"Hello, Vince."

"Gene, what's up?"

"I wanted to thank you for sending that photo; it could be helpful. And I wanted to ask if you could do me a favor."

"If I can, I will. What do you have in mind?"

Eugene outlined his request, and Vincent Reiner said he'd see what he could do.

#   #   #

Rue Legendre, Paris

It was noontime when Walter Helmann lit a cigarette and poured his first glass of white wine of the day. He inhaled deeply and stared out of the window, watching three East Asians conclude a drug deal in the entrance to the apartment building across the street. He had heard the neighbors complaining about drug trafficking, but apparently, the police couldn't be bothered to deal with such low-level players.

Walter was staying in the apartment of a fellow security consultant, a gentler and kinder way of describing his profession of mercenary. He scratched his two-day beard. He wasn't trying to be fashionable, he'd only been too lazy to shave. Vince Reiner had just called, asking if he'd be available to do a short assignment for them. He'd done work for both the French and the Americans. And while the French food was better, the Americans paid well, and he was at loose ends until he returned to Africa, so what the fuck, why not. It would keep him busy and get him out of the drab apartment.

He called the number Vince gave him, agreed to meet tomorrow, put on his blue anorak, left the apartment, and walked up rue Legendre to a café on Avenue de Clichy, where he'd eat lunch and have another glass of white wine.

Chapter 57

Champ de Mars, Paris

ALEX HAD ARRANGED TO MEET Eugene at a café near Ecole Militaire.
Mila was in Paris while Jacques was away, and she thought it best to avoid
the Café de la Fontaine, too close to rue Bonaparte. It was a grey, overcast
day, so typical of Paris in winter. Alex was bundled up against the damp,
cold air, only her nose visible under the bonnet and scarf. She was early and
decided to walk around the Champ de Mars, remembering school trips on
Wednesdays to see the puppet shows and to ride the merry-go-round.

A group of Asian tourists was taking pictures of the Eiffel Tower, its top
shrouded in clouds. *I hope they survive the scammers and the pickpockets.*
Paris is not the friendliest of cities. Her gaze followed the tourists as they
moved like a small herd toward the Eiffel Tower. It stopped when she saw
Eugene Spector and another man walking in the direction of Ecole Militaire.
Alex stepped behind a hedge although there didn't seem to be much danger
that Eugene would see her, as the men were too busy with their conversation.
Walking along a parallel path, she watched the two figures, both wearing
down parkas — Eugene's black, the other man's navy blue — continuing
on their way. When they reached the bottom of Champ de Mars, a tour bus

disgorged its passengers, and she lost sight of the men as they disappeared into the crowd.

Eugene, waiting for Alex, popped a chewing gum into his mouth, playing with his cell phone. Alex arrived at the café a few minutes later. "I'm so cold. I think I'll have a *chocolat chaud.*" Eugene tried to catch the eye of a waiter who was skilled in the art of treating customers as invisible. Alex turned to see if she would have better luck and caught sight of a navy blue down parka on the back of a chair, its owner scanning the pages of the *International Herald Tribune*.

Small talk about the weather. Coffee and hot chocolate served. Eugene's chewing gum, mixed with the sweet odor of the hot chocolate, masked the smell of garlic, and Alex leaned forward to talk.

"Have you thought about the reward?" she asked.

"Alex, I know you want to help…this person…but this may not be a good idea. The church will ask how you came to have the painting, and you risk getting caught in a web of lies, something you'd want to avoid if I'm not mistaken. You look disappointed. Can you let me think about this some more, see if there isn't some way to work things out?"

They were both silent for a moment, the air around them filled with voices and the sound of china cups clinking against saucers. Eugene took the leap. "And how are things going with your Mr. Mornnais?"

"It's a bit of a slog. Translating that bloody magazine isn't so bad, but his wife is so pretentious, and his driver gives me the creeps." Eugene had provided some pieces of the puzzle — he did seem willing to help her find a way to get a reward for Ella — and Alex felt the need to give him something in return for helping her. "And if you must know, I took the job only because they treated my friend Marie-Agnès very badly, and I wanted to find out what this Jacques Mornnais was up to. I'm pretty sure he's selling forgeries and stolen artwork. So he's probably behind the forged painting your aunt bought but I have no proof." She continued, "The person who found the painting I've asked you about is the maid, Ella. They treat her very badly as well — almost like a slave — and that's why I wanted to try to get a reward for her."

In a low voice, his eyes locking on to hers, Eugene asked, "What do you mean they treated Marie-Agnès badly?"

Alex wondered if she had gone too far, said too much, but the momentum kept her going and she recounted Marie-Agnès's misadventure, managing to laugh as she described their flight from the hospital.

"Well, that's certainly food for thought. It looks like it goes much deeper than my aunt's painting. Did you say that you could make out the paintings in her photos?"

"They looked a lot like paintings by Signac. I bought a catalogue raisonné, and I'm trying to find the precise painting, but it's slow going. I'm not an expert, at all."

"Hey, looking through the catalog is a great idea, Alex. You do that, and I'll see what I can figure out to get the reward for — what did you say her name was?"

"Ella."

"Yes, that's right, Ella. Let's stay in touch."

She got up. "Thanks for the chocolate, Eugene. Speak soon." As she walked out of the café, she forced herself not to look at the man with the navy blue parka. *Who is that man and what were they talking about on Champ de Mars? It makes me wonder just what is Eugene's job anyway?*

#   #   #

Rue Gagnée, Vitry-sur-Seine

Forty-five minutes by Métro and bus, going from the chic seventh arrondissement to rue Gagnée in the town of Vitry. A clean, orderly street, *sans histories* as the French would say, but light years from the center of Paris. Alex rang the bell at the concierge's small office. She picked up a parcel for Mme Georges — no need for her to use her own name — and left an envelope in its place. The package was not heavy, but it was bulky, and Alex called a taxi to take her back to Neuilly, where she felt more at home.

Chapter 58

Rue d'Orchampt, Paris

SITTING AT HER DESK, MARIE-AGNÈS played with Merv Peters's card. He had handed it to her, rather like a cowboy drawing his gun, the reflex of every lawyer on the make for business. You never knew who the person was, or whom they might know. No harm in trying.

She started to take the first steps of the scheme that she and Alex had laid out in the warm cocoon that was the hammam. It had started when Marie-Agnès told Alex about meeting Merv and learning that Jacques was his "art consultant." Some giggles. A scrub with black soap, followed by a massage. And a plan to use Merv Peters to introduce Eugene to Jacques Mornnais.

Opened a Hotmail account. Rehearsed her story until she was sure that it would roll off her tongue smoothly. Picked up her prepaid phone, to be used only when dealing with Merv. Called.

He answered on the fourth ring.

"Hi Merv, it's Mag. We met the other night at—"

"Yes, I remember," he interrupted. "How are you?" In fact, he didn't remember. Merv immediately wished that he hadn't interrupted her. But she continued to talk, so maybe he'd figure out who she was.

"I'm so sorry that I had to run off but I had to get up so early the next morning." *Oh, I remember now, that pretty woman with no money.* Ever the opportunist—*but of course, you never know.*

" Anyway, you know so much about the art scene, and I was wondering if you'd like to meet me at Druout. There's a viewing of Orientalist paintings, and I'd love to have your opinion."

Merv wasn't going to let his ignorance stand in the way of seeing Mag again. She was so clueless about art he was sure he could wing it. "I'm not an expert but I'd be glad to join you if I'm free. When were you thinking of going?"

"They're on display later in the week, so perhaps late one morning?"

They met a few days later.

"What kind of a name is Mag, anyway?"

Better to forget about Marie-Agnès. "Oh, it's short for Magda. I was named after my great-grandmother, and it's such an old-fashioned name that I shortened it to Mag. Been my name forever."

Merv hated his given name — Mervin — but felt that Merv had just the right sound to it.

They walked through the viewing room, Merv pontificating about colors and brush strokes and perspectives, Marie-Agnès nodding admiringly.

Afterwards, over a coffee, she thanked him for taking the time to help her. The paintings were out of her price range but at least she would have a better idea of what to look for in the future.

"When you're ready, I can introduce you to the man who helps me. He's really a genius at finding the right painting before they even make it to auction. Gives you all the documentation on provenance. He helps so many people you wouldn't believe it."

"That's good to know, Merv. I'm sure he's way above my pay grade but I have a friend who might need his help. I'll let you know."

Perfect, thought Merv, a *nother potential referral fee*. It had been evident that Mag had no money — and was therefore of no interest as a client — but he'd keep in touch to see if anything came of her friend. Too bad. She was quite attractive, and there was something mysterious about her. But he had to keep his standards.

Chapter 59

EARLY MORNING. MARIE-AGNÈS WAS waiting for Alex in a café on rue des Abbesses. Cigarette butts no longer littered the floor, but the place had an old-fashioned vibe: wine and beer were the drinks of choice for many of the patrons, whatever the hour. The café had not yet been overrun by tourists, the tables and chairs were worn, the walls stained by decades of grease and grime. Mag would have chosen someplace trendier, but this café was closest to her home. It reminded her of a pair of worn-out slippers, not fashionable but comfortable in a pinch.

"Thanks for coming to my neck of the woods. I've just started work on a big translation and I don't have a lot of time. What's up? You sounded so excited and mysterious when you called."

"Remember that I told you that I'd asked my *friend* Eugene to help me get a reward for Ella, you know, for the painting she found?"

"Yes, the one by Daubigny that was stolen from a church?"

"Yeah, well, Eugene said that first we had to be sure that it's a genuine Daubigny. He called me to say that he's going to ask the art dealer, the one that sold his aunt the fake Poussin, if he could confirm that it's a genuine Daubigny. Of course, we have the certificate of authenticity that the dealer had prepared for Bruno, but Eugene doesn't know that. I mean, I probably should have mentioned that, but I didn't."

"Why, don't you trust him?"

"Not entirely. He seems awfully curious about Jacques and Mila and I can't escape the feeling that he's using me to get closer to them. It's like he's got some other agenda that he's not prepared to share with me.

"Okay, so what happens now?"

"Assuming that it's not a fake, Eugene will try to get us a reward for returning the painting. He seems to know how to do this. But I don't feel comfortable turning that painting over to him. I mean, what if he disappears with it? I'm sure that stranger things have happened."

"Why don't you just take the painting to the church and give it back to them yourself?"

"Because they have no money. Eugene says there's a fund for these sorts of situations and I don't know how to handle that. But I think I have a solution."

"Oh?"

"Did I ever tell you that Ella ran into Li when she was visiting a friend in Chinatown in Paris? He's working in a supermarket and he gave her his phone number, which she gave to me. I called him and had him do a copy of *Storm Over the Sea* for me. And with your help, we're going to switch the paintings."

"What about the church? Isn't that cheating them?"

"Not really. They were quite careless with the painting, and I wouldn't be surprised if someone steals it again. I think that one person ought to profit from this situation, the person who has suffered the most, and that's Ella."

"I guess that's one way of looking at it. What do you want me to do?"

Alex motioned to the waiter, ordered two more espressos. "For starters, I'm going to drop the copy off at your place."

"And then what?"

"And then…" She laid out her plan to Marie-Agnès.

Chapter 60

TRAFFIC WAS LIGHT ON THE A6 motorway as Eugene drove to Fontainebleau. Swallowed his gum as he walked up the gravel path and rang the doorbell. A short, stocky woman — he thought she must be Portuguese — opened the door and led him into the now-familiar living room. Paintings covered most of the red brocaded walls, commodes crowded together on the floor space, several Tiffany lamps were scattered around the room.

Nicolas Pagès came into the room, arm extended. "How nice to see you again, Mr. Stokes."

"I wonder if I could look at the Poussin again. We're just not sure that we're crazy about a religious subject. Too bad that Russian didn't have any other Poussins in his collection."

Nicolas did his best to mask his annoyance as he went into a back room to retrieve the painting. Reeling in this big fish was becoming more difficult than he had anticipated. He placed the canvas on an easel. Stokes stared at it, his chin in his hand. "Oh yes, there was something I wanted to ask you. A friend of my wife's, not a good friend but someone we know, if you see what I mean, she has a painting that's been in her family for ages, and she may need to sell it. Short on cash. You know how it is."

"Yes, yes, I do understand."

219

Stokes went on as he continued to stare at the Poussin. "It's supposed to be a Daubigny, and as you're an expert on the Pre-Impressionists, I thought you'd be able to help us."

Nicolas Pagès felt a sharp pain in his abdomen at the mention of the painter's name. "I've rented a temporary office in Paris, Rond-Point des Champs-Elysées. I wonder if you could stop by and take a look, see what you think."

In fact, Nicolas wanted to have nothing further to do with any Daubigny but he could not think of a good excuse. They agreed to meet later in the week.

#   #   #

Neuilly-sur-Seine

Alex's cheeks were pink with excitement. Earlier in the week, she had bought a new purse at the Prada boutique on avenue Montaigne. Now, she removed her purchase from the shop's oversized shopping bag, and in its place she slipped the much more modest Lidl shopping bag containing Ella's painting.

She called Mag, "Are you ready? Do you remember what you have to do?"

"No problem, Alex, this is going to be fun!"

#   #   #

Rond-Point des Champs-Elysées

The sidewalk benches in front of the adjoining facades of high street stores were overflowing with shoppers, Asians, the Emiratis, north Europeans. Only France was not represented in the gathering of the world's shoppers. Marie-Agnès had managed to squeeze herself between two Japanese girls. She clutched a Lidl shopping bag to her breast as she waited for Alex.

At first, she did not recognize Alex when she walked past her. She was wearing a wig — dark hair cut into a strict bob. A black coat with a fur collar that Alex had found in one of Chloé's closets, red high heels, and a Louis Vuitton bag completed her ensemble. A large white shopping bag swayed against her leg. Marie-Agnès tried to suppress a grin, *that is so totally Not Alex,* as she followed her friend into the Regus office building on the Rond-Point des Champs-Elysées.

She stood next to Alex as they took the elevator to the fourth floor and followed her partway down the hallway and turned onto another corridor just before Alex reached the office Eugene had rented for the occasion. She sat on the small sofa in the hallway and opened a copy of *Les Echos,* hiding her face behind the newspaper. Eugene was waiting for Alex. They had agreed to meet fifteen minutes before Nicolas Pagès was scheduled to arrive. But Nicolas was late; it was as if he had a premonition that nothing good was to come from this encounter. Somehow that brute Bruno seemed to be following him from the grave and he walked as if in slow motion.

When Nicolas arrived, Eugene introduced Alex as his assistant. She reached into the Prada shopping bag, removed a Lidl bag containing the painting, and carefully unwrapped the package. As Nicolas looked at the seascape, he recognized it as the same one Bruno had brought to him almost two months earlier. He felt his heart pounding. He hoped they did not notice the vein pulsing in his neck. Had the mysterious out-of-cash woman asked Bruno for his help in selling the painting? He didn't believe Eugene's story. He wondered who the owner was….and who was Bruno's client? Hadn't they already seen the document Nicolas had prepared? It didn't make sense.

He turned to the business at hand. "Yes," he said, "this is most definitely a Daubigny, and a rare one."

"How much do you estimate it's worth?" Alex asked.

"Well, of course, there is the question of provenance, but assuming the chain of ownership is there, it might go for close to a million Euros. It all depends."

"Okay, can you do that research then? If all's good, then you can go ahead and sell the painting."

"May I ask who the current owner is?"

"All in good time, my friend. First things first. Can't be too careful.

She's a very sensitive lady."

Eugene's request had sent another searing pain through Nicolas's abdomen. He felt confused and frightened. What had that brute Bruno done? Bruno had not paid him, and here was the bloody painting showing up again. "In fact, I'm awfully busy right now. I'm not sure that I'd have the time to do this for you. I'm sorry."

"Ah, that's too bad, but of course I understand. We appreciate that you've come all the way to Paris to help us."

Although the room was not overly heated, Nicolas could feel rivulets of sweat running down his back. He put on his coat, shook hands, and tried to walk calmly out of the office.

After Nicolas left, Alex wrapped the painting and placed it in the Lidl shopping bag. "I saw a coffee machine in the hallway. I could use some, what about you?"

As they lingered over coffee, it took Marie-Agnès only two minutes to go into the empty office, grab the Lidl shopping bag on the desk, and replace it with the Lidl shopping bag she had been carrying.

Back in the office, Eugene picked up the Lidl bag on the desk. "I think it's time to go to the church and collect the reward for your friend. So I'll need to take this now."

Alex looked troubled. "Why can't I keep the painting and come with you?"

"And how should we explain your presence? I intend to say that I came across the painting as part of my work for the government. So, please trust me."

"Whatever you say. I don't have much choice, do I?"

As they walked out of the office, Alex did her best to keep a glum look on her face. Marie-Agnès left the Regus offices five minutes later. They met back at the apartment on Boulevard Malesherbes,

"Here it is!" laughed Mag, as she set the Lidl shopping bag and its precious contents on the table.

Alex had a small bottle of champagne in the fridge, and they toasted the success of the first step of their venture.

Chapter 61

March 2010, Château d'Hélène

TWO TRAINS OF THOUGHT WERE vying for attention in Jacques' mind, swimming pool construction and Paul Signac.

He had spent an afternoon with a salesman from Top Pools. They had explored the vast wine cellars in the château's foundations, a repository of several centuries' junk. Studied the documents now spread out on Jacques' desk, discussed the importance of dehumidification and environment control. Top Pools offered a state-of-the-art technical control room — really a walk-in closet — like the one at Renaud Schneider's home and gallery. Would he ever use the pool, he wondered. Jacques' daily exercise consisted principally of walking to and from his chauffeur-driven car. He had never bothered to get a driver's license — what was the point since he had always had someone like Tarek? Perhaps he could try swimming. Mila would love having the kind of pool he envisioned. Just as well, as he intended for her to pay for it. Of course, he had the means to pay for the pool himself, but what was the point of having access to Mila's money if he didn't take advantage of the situation?

Maybe it would make more sense to build the pool at Mélandère, his house in the south of France. But no matter its location, he would need to fully understand all the details of the installation.

As he thought about Mélandère, his attention shifted to the paintings he stored there, and to the two Signacs. He would need to start lining up buyers.

Chapter 62

Boulevard Malesherbes

ALEX HAD CLEARED THE SURFACE of the piece of furniture that she used as a dining table, desk, and repository of whatever she happened to have in her hand, to make room for the catalogue raisonné she had just purchased.

She opened the hefty volume. There was a long biography and many color plates of what she assumed were some of the Signac's best-known works. At the back, in chronological order, were hundreds of small black-and-white photos of the painter's oeuvre. The author had provided a history of each work. For some, there was much detail; for others, the history was scant, the current location unknown. So many ports and harbors, so many tall ships. Alex realized the impossibility of matching Marie-Agnès's photo to one of those images. While the painting in the photograph could be a copy of a Signac—she thought she recognized the tiny touches of color—the model could just as easily have been a painting by some other lesser-known artist.

Alex closed the book and slipped it under her bed. There was no point in cluttering her small space with a beautiful but useless tome.

Chapter 63

ALEX HAD ARRIVED EARLY FOR lunch at La Maison Neuve. It was one of Jacques' preferred restaurants, and it had become one of her favorites as well. She sipped her Perrier — sticking to her no alcohol rule while working — and observed the other diners. Tourists — American, Asian, and Russian — she could tell their nationalities by the way they dressed. Businesspeople, and she thought she recognized an MP surrounded by a group of fawning parliamentary assistants.

Jacques' client—a plump American woman with a mane of blond hair, too much hair for her age—was shown to the table. A clutch of bangles on one wrist, two watches on the other, rings stuck on her stubby fingers, she carried the ultimate badge of bling, a white Louis Vuitton Murakami Multicolor handbag.

Like Madonna, Blondell Royston spoke that kind of English affected by transplanted Americans—not quite American, nor English, but the words came out through a stiffening of the lips. She lived on Place des Vosges, had been married to a much older man, a wealthy investment banker who had profited handsomely from the market crash in '08, only to drop dead a year later. The walls of the apartment—it was over three hundred square meters—were depressingly empty; the grieving widow was thinking about starting an art collection, and the lawyer handling her affairs had referred her to Jacques. Although Blondell had lived in Paris on and off for five years, she couldn't be bothered to learn French. She felt that if she spoke slowly and clearly, people would understand her and respond in English. Since Jacques was not prepared to play that game, Alex's presence was required.

A *baise-main* for Blondell, a nod to Alex, and Jacques was seated.

The woman sitting opposite him was the ideal client for Jacques— wealthy, insecure, and interested in art as an investment, but above all, to impress. When the time was right, he would guide her into making the appropriate decision. Jacques explained that, through his network, he could have access to artwork before it came on the market and would help Blondell to acquire a coherent ensemble of paintings, with impeccable provenance. He put forward the idea that Neo-Impressionist painters might be an excellent focal point to start her collection. What did she think about that?

"You might want to consider a painter like Paul Signac—I have a colleague who has indicated that one of his later works might be coming available. I could investigate and let you know."

He kept the conversation going, cited painters, historical references. She nodded, thrilled. Her private advisor, someone to do all the legwork. All she would have to do was pay, and she had plenty of money to do that.

Later that evening, when Blondell met Merv for a drink, she thanked him for introducing her to Jacques Mornnais.

#   #   #

Boulevard Malesherbes, Paris

While Blondell and Merv were having a drink, Alex was settled into her bed. She'd plumped up the pillows and balanced the catalogue raisonné against her knees. Yesterday's gloom was gone. She was sure that she'd been right about Paul Signac. Now, she wanted to learn more about the painter, and she spent the evening reading the biography and carefully studying the color reproductions.

She'd watched Jacques at lunch. He lacked flamboyance, his suits were off the rack, his ties nondescript, and that made it easy for the people he dealt with to feel superior to him and, more important, to trust him. Blondell certainly seemed to.

The purchase of a work of art—whether for love or expected profit—was an emotionally charged transaction. Jacques knew that Blondell would feel a need to talk, to explain her feelings, and he had encouraged her to do so.

A spider spinning its web, a fisherman reeling in his catch, all clichés, but how apt. Alex was sure there would be another meeting and she would pay close attention to learn more about the Signac, and about Jacques Mornnais.

Chapter 64

EUGENE HAD CALLED ALEX. "I'VE got some news for you."

She suggested that they meet at the Café Carré, a brisk twenty-minute walk from her apartment on Boulevard Malesherbes.

Alex was tired of the understated, drab look she had adopted for her work with Jacques, so she donned her blue pleated ensemble for her rendezvous with Eugene. Felt instantly empowered, thinking what a difference the right clothes made.

Eugene was already there, and this time he dispensed with small talk.

As soon as the waiter took their order — two espressos — he said, "I've been able to get you a reward of ten thousand dollars, no questions asked, which I think is pretty damn good, don't you?"

"I was hoping for more—it's to help Ella buy a house in the Philippines—but thank you for your help. How do we go about returning the painting now?"

"Oh, you needn't worry about that. I'll take care of it."

The waiter had brought their espressos. Alex lifted the cup, took a small sip, put the cup down, and stared at Eugene, her eyes an intense blue, reflecting the color of her top. She forced herself to remain calm as an old saying ran through her head...*if you're right, you can afford to keep your*

229

temper, and if you're wrong, you cannot afford to lose it.

She smiled at him. "Oh, you've taken care of it. Just like that." Still smiling, she said, "So please tell me, who are you and what are you doing?"

"My name really is Eugene Spector, even if I told that Pagès guy that it's Eugene Stokes. While I'm over here on government business, I'm also trying to get the culprits who cheated my aunt, as I told you. Now it's true that my government work was helpful in getting you the reward — by the way, where do you want the money sent—but I can't tell you more than I already have. Believe me, I want to help you and your friend Ella."

"And I want to believe you, but I feel like I'm leaping into the dark." Alex removed a white index card from her purse. "You can wire the funds to this account. When I see that the money is there, I'll call you. You want to meet Jacques, don't you? Well, I'm trying to figure out how to do it."

Chapter 65

MERV STUCK TO BLONDELL LIKE a blood-sucking leech, calling her whenever her legal affairs provided a pretext, yet he was at pains to avoid becoming overfamiliar. He adopted a paternalistic approach. Blondell didn't know many French women, and this was a shame since she lived in Paris. He quite understood that she had no time to learn French, so he offered to introduce her to a delightful French woman who spoke excellent English.

Marie-Agnès heard a phone ring. She and Alex each had several cell phones for their different projects. This phone had a monster's head pasted on the back, so she knew it was Merv calling. He wanted to introduce her to a charming American woman and suggested that they meet for lunch at a restaurant on Avenue Malakoff, not too far from his office.

Merv and Blondell were already seated when Marie-Agnès arrived. He introduced Mag to Blondell, who was wearing a camel-colored cashmere coat that matched the color of her hair. She had kept her bangles and her watches; however, her fingers were bare, and she had opted for the classic Louis Vuitton brown and mustard monogram tote bag. Both women were dressed entirely in black, the French fashionista uniform. Blondell was relieved that Marie-Agnès spoke perfect English so she would not have to concentrate while she was enjoying her lunch. Marie-Agnès was curious as to why Merv wanted her to meet this American woman. She was sure there was a reason other than his stated desire to introduce two interesting women to each other.

"So, tell me what you are doing in France," asked Marie-Agnès.

Blondell related the story of her marriage, the apartment on Place des Vosges, her husband's financial success and untimely death. Once she had started to speak, she continued unabated and came to the topic that interested her — the creation of her art collection, aided by the art consultant who Merv had introduced her to, Jack Morner.

"Excuse me?" said Marie-Agnès.

Merv interrupted, "His name is Jacques Mornnais, the man I mentioned the other day when we met."

"Yes, we're going to start with the Impressionists. Mag, I'm so excited. He may be able to get me a painting by Paul Synak."

Lunch continued for a painfully long time. Marie-Agnès was still not sure why Merv had brought the two women together, but she took Blondell's card and promised to call her and to meet again. She could hardly wait to tell Alex about lunch.

#   #   #

"You're not going to believe this."

"Oh, okay, try me."

"Remember Merv Peters, the lawyer who buys his paintings from Jacques, you know, the one I'm cultivating, as we agreed?"

"Yes, and…?"

"Merv invited me to lunch to meet one of his clients, an American woman named Blondell Royston. And guess who her art consultant is?"

"Yes, I know. Jacques Mornnais."

"How do you know that?"

"Jacques took her to lunch to soften her up."

"Well, he did a good job. She didn't stop babbling about collecting art, buying a painting by a guy named Paul Synak. That's our friend Signac, by the way. She just went on and on. It gave me a chance to enjoy my meal."

"Why do you suppose Merv invited you both to lunch?"

"He said he wanted to introduce two interesting women to each other, but she seems lonely and I think he's set me up to be her friend."

"Now we'll both be able to keep tabs on Jacques' newest pigeon. It should be fun."

Chapter 66

MID-MARCH, THE TREES STILL LEAFLESS, but the light had changed, and the air had a softness to it. The piles of dirty snow had long since melted, and Alex walked briskly up Avenue de Villiers toward Neuilly, carrying the Lidl shopping bag.

"Been shopping again?" asked Richard.

"Not exactly." Alex smiled. "Want to have a peek?" and she removed the parcel, undid the wrapping, and placed *Storm Over the Sea* on the dining room table.

It was Richard's turn to smile. "I suppose you're going to tell me what this is all about?"

While Alex carefully replaced the wrapping, she recounted the meeting with Eugene and Nicolas Pagès, and how she and Marie-Agnès had switched the paintings. "The original painting had been found by the maid. It had been left in the château by a perfectly dreadful man, named Bruno. He's the one who tried to have Marie-Agnès killed. Then, he tried to rape Ella, but he had a stroke or something and then he died. Ella and Jacques' painters threw him in the river that runs behind Jacques' property."

"My goodness, how resourceful!"

Richard's cheeks were rosy, he seemed to be enjoying Alex's story. "Go on, then what happened?"

"I enlisted the help of a man I know—in fact, he's renting my house in Washington, but he's over here on government business—to get a reward for Ella. He said that he would return the painting to the church from where it had been stolen, but I didn't entirely trust him, so Marie-Agnès and I thought it wiser to give him a copy of the painting. Ella had run into one of Jacques' painters in Paris, he gave her his number, I called him, and he did the copy for me. So, the painting I gave Eugene—that's his name—is the copy, and I kept the original. I rather like it, and I think I'd like to hang it at Trubenne, what do you think?"

"It sounds like you took a lot of risks for this Ella woman. But I'm thinking, what about your friend, Mr. Mornnais?"

"Jacques apparently doesn't know that this painting exists. So it seemed only right to let Ella benefit. Her life hasn't exactly been a bed of roses."

"Here, let me help you," said Richard. He took the shopping bag from Alex and placed it in one of the suitcases that stood in a large carved wooden armoire in his office.

Richard has been surprisingly enthusiastic. Indeed, Alex's arrival had disrupted his life's dull routine, and Richard liked the idea of helping the women carry their plan forward.

"Then I have some good news for you. The transfer you were expecting has arrived," Richard informed her.

"Ah, very good. Now on to next steps."

Marie-Agnès came by a few minutes later. They talked about Blondell Royston, what to do, how to make the most of the situation.

"I feel sorry for Blondell Royston," said Marie-Agnès. "She may have a lot of money, but she's so adrift, so purposeless."

"Royston, did you say?" The man's face was just beyond reach. Richard's memory did that to him sometimes. "I recall someone named John Royston, I may have even met him on one occasion, although I can't be certain about that. Some people did very well when the market crashed in 2008. If Royston had been one of them, his widow is definitely sitting on a sizeable pile of money."

"This Merv Peters sounds like a real creep. You should probably avoid him as he's close to Jacques. On the other hand, why not make friends with Blondell? We can track her progress in becoming an art collector," said Alex.

"Yes, I'll call her and suggest a drink, just for girls."

"My lease on Avenue Emile Zola is up mid-April, which is when I will leave Jacques, so we have a lot to do between now and then."

"My dear Alexia, what are you up to now?" Richard sounded concerned. His earlier enthusiasm had disappeared.

"We're using Merv Peters to set up a meeting between Alex's friend Eugene and Jacques. It's not that difficult. Merv is so greedy." Marie-Agnès giggled. "It will be up to Eugene to squeeze the money his aunt paid out of Jacques. That's not our problem."

"And I want to find proof that Jacques is selling a fake painting to Blondell. He acts as though the rules don't apply to him and I want him to learn that he is mistaken."

#   #   #

Mélandère, Roquebrune-sur-Argens

Tarek, driving south again. He had gotten off to a late start and stopped outside of Lyon for the night. The next morning, he was up early, and it was midday when he arrived at Mélandère.

A group of backpackers was following the hiking trail that ran through the woods surrounding the house, and they were sprawled along the path eating lunch. Tarek had intended to pick up the two Signacs and turn around and drive back north. But as the backpackers sat, staring at the house and watching his every move, he changed his plans. He parked the van, avoiding the fallen branch, and went inside the house to wait.

Unseen by Tarek, a man in a navy blue parka ambled up the path and sat near the group. When they got up to continue their hike, he followed them for a short distance and then circled back through the woods and positioned himself behind some of the thick forest shrubberies.

Tarek found an unopened package of Wasa crackers; he unwrapped one of the packets and washed down the biscuits with a can of lukewarm Coke.

Looking out the kitchen window that framed the Rocher de Roquebrune-sur-Argens, he saw that the hikers were gone. He put the package of crackers in the van — something to nibble on the way back — and threw the empty Coke can into the garbage bin outside the door. It didn't take long to load the two paintings into the van, and then he was on the road back to the château.

Walter Helmann had taken a camera out of his backpack and photographed the transfer of the paintings. After Tarek had driven down the dirt road, he removed the Coke can from the garbage bin, put it into a plastic bag, and returned it and the camera to his backpack. It was a beautiful day and he enjoyed the walk back to the town where he had parked his car.

#   #   #

"Well done," said Eugene to Walter.

"Thanks for letting me know at the last minute. I almost didn't make it on time."

"My contact couldn't call me any sooner. Lucky for us Tarek didn't leave immediately." Eugene pointed to the can in the plastic bag. "I'll send this through right away."

Chapter 67

ALEX WAS IN THE OFFICE on rue de Prony, translating copy for *Artixia*. It had been raining intermittently for days, typical March weather. Although the heat was on, the damp air chilled her to the bone. It was the time of year when Parisians doubted that winter would ever end. She wrapped her scarf more tightly around her neck and tried to concentrate on her work. Ella was on her mind. Alex had been unable to talk with her the last few times she had been at the château. But now that the other three inhabitants were in Paris, it would be safe to call her.

At lunchtime, she found a table at the café on Boulevard de Courcelles, where she had gone for a coffee with Eugene after their chance meeting in Parc Monceau. By the time she was done eating, the place had emptied out, and she didn't have to shout over the midday noise.

"How are you, Ella? Everything okay?"

"Yes, Nathalie, it's okay."

"When are you coming to Paris to visit your friend Roslinda? I'd like us to meet."

"It will be next Friday, I think."

"Are you sure?"

"Yes."

"What time does your train get in?"

"Six o'clock."

"Okay, give me the address where you'll be staying. I'll meet you in front of the building at seven thirty p.m., and we'll grab a bite to eat in the neighborhood."

Back to the office in the thick drizzle. Mila approached her as she was hanging up her coat. "We'll need you the day after tomorrow at the château, Nathalie. The woman named Blondell Royston will be coming out to view the Signac. You can interpret and work on the *Artixia* copy — you'll be able to go up and back the same day. And Tarek saw you a few weeks ago near place Saint-Sulpice. Small world, isn't it?"

"Oh, did he? It's possible. I have some friends in that neighborhood."

Shit, that was the time I had forgotten that they live on rue Bonaparte. Good thing I'm more careful now. "I'll reserve my train tickets right away."

#   #   #

Château d'Hélène

Alex took an early train from Gare de Lyon. She wondered if Blondell would be on the same train—of course, Alex was traveling in second class, and she was sure Blondell would be in a first-class car—and already dreaded having to make conversation with her on the ride back to the château.

Alex need not have worried, as Blondell was not a morning person. She was slow to emerge from bed—she felt so comfortable—and for a moment, considered canceling the meeting with Jacques. But she imagined herself as an art collector, and with great effort, she managed to make the noon train to Dijon.

Tarek was pissed at having to make two trips to the train station. It was difficult to admit, but he missed Bruno. Not in an affectionate way, but with Bruno he had someone to criticize, someone to put down, a foil on whom to vent his ill humor.

Mila, putting on a charm offensive, said, "So, Madame Royston, did you have a good trip? Isn't the TGV wonderful?"

Blondell slumped down into the armchair. She was wearing her usual complement of jewelry and crossed her ankles so that the red soles of her Louboutin pumps were visible to all. "Oh, it was okay, thank you. Do you mind?" She pulled a Virginia Slim cigarette out of a pack in her Vuitton Murakami. Although she had asked, *Do you mind?* what she meant was *I'm going to smoke, and because I'm so rich, no one will dare say anything to me.* And she was right.

Having set the tone, she followed Jacques through to another part of the living room, where the Signac stood on a pedestal. Mila placed an ashtray on an occasional table.

"If I may tell you a bit about Paul Signac first," Jacques began, and he described Signac's childhood and adolescence, his friendship with Georges Seurat, the influence of Charles Henry on his use of color, his travels in France and in Europe.

Blondell stared at Alex as she translated. Mila watched as the ash on her cigarette grew longer, and at the last moment, Blondell flicked it into the waiting ashtray.

Her gaze was so empty of emotion, it was as though she was asleep with her eyes open. "And now," he said, moving closer to the pedestal, "allow me to share a very rare find with you. This painting, *The Marina at Saint-Malo*, has been lost for some eighty years. It was in a private collection in Switzerland and has only recently come on to the market. You'll notice the artist's masterful use of the pointillist technique, the asymmetry of the composition with the tall ships in the foreground, the eye being drawn to the tower in the background and up to the clouds driven across a windy sky."

Blondell stared at the canvas as Jacques spoke, trying to shut out the sound of his voice. She liked the colors, tried to imagine the painting hanging in the living room, or perhaps the dining room? "Very interesting," she said. "I'll have to think about it," her mind now focused on going to the Starbucks near her home. She stood up. "I guess I'd better be back off to Paris."

As the car pulled onto the road, "Do you mind?" said Blondell as she put a Virginia Slim into her mouth and felt around in her purse for her lighter. Alex, making clear eye contact, said, "Actually, I do. Cigarette smoke in cars makes me nauseous, so I hope you can wait until we reach the station.

It won't be long."

"Of course, I'm sorry."

"No problem, I'm a reformed smoker, and we're the worst."

Mindless chatter until they reached Dijon, left Tarek, and entered the station. Alex, now anxious to get away to the solitude of her second-class seat, leaned her cheek forward. "*Au revoir*, Blondell, so nice to have seen you again."

"Oh, Alex, you must come and sit with me."

"I'm afraid I'm traveling in second class."

"That's okay, let's go and change our tickets, I'll pay for it."

#   #   #

Tickets in hand, Blondell asked, "How about a drink in the bar car?"

I wonder if she's got something on her mind, thought Alex. "Sure, good idea."

"I didn't want to talk in front of Jacques' driver. There's something so unpleasant about him."

"Yes, he's rather surly, isn't he?"

"Anyhow, now, between us, what can you tell me about Jacques? I mean, Merv spoke very highly of him, but I need to be sure that I can trust him. He's asking me to come up with ten million dollars after all."

"Sorry, I cannot help you there. I just do translations for his magazine and act as his interpreter from time to time, as I do with you."

"Yes, of course, Nathalie, I understand. But you need to know that I really do not like the French very much. They're polite to me because I've inherited all this money, but they are so cold and, well, so closed. I have no friends here. The nicest person I've met is a French girl who does the same thing as you, she's a translator. Maybe you know her, her name is Mag?"

"Can't say that I do, but I'm glad that you have at least one person you can turn to. Why don't you learn French? That might help you to, you know, get along better."

"I tried when we first arrived. But I'm not good at memorizing verbs and learning grammar. It was hard for me, and whenever I tried to say something

241

in French, people just answered in English, like they had no time to waste listening to me try to express myself in French, so I said fuck that, I'll speak English. And that's what I do, and it works for me."

"Well, yes, whatever works."

Blondell was just warming up. "And this Jacques Mornnais, I liked him when Merv first introduced me, but today I found him, well, condescending, treating me like all the other French do. So I need to think about things, and look into things, and see where the linkages are."

Whatever is she going on about? thought Alex. *Well, Marie-Agnès can find that out.*

They went back to their seats. Blondell watched the countryside speed by, the first early signs of spring in a blur of green foliage along the tracks and mud puddles in the fields. She might have been arm candy for John Royston, but contrary to appearances, she was not an airhead. She couldn't shake the thought that, although she had never met them, there was something familiar about Jacques and Mila, and she intended to follow up on that thought.

Alex leaned back and closed her eyes. It had been a long but not unproductive day.

Chapter 68

Brittany

JEAN-MARC SAT AT THE DINING room table, staring at the glass of dark golden liquid. He savored the taste and aroma of the Calvados Hors d'Age, but his mind was restless. He'd received his commission on the sale of the chalices—an envelope left for him at a café in Roscoff—but what had happened with the Daubigny he had given to Bruno?

Word had gotten back to him that an American had come to the church a week ago, asking to see the priest, Father Jérôme. And had brought with him the Daubigny. Jean-Marc couldn't understand what had happened. Unable to reach Bruno, he had asked around. That was when he learned that Bruno had fallen into a river and drowned. It all sounded a bit strange, but perhaps he had had one too many, one time too often.

#   #   #

Galerie Ballastré, Quai Voltaire

François-Xavier Ballastré, third-generation owner, escorted the slightly built priest to the door. *Frail body but a strong mind*, thought François-Xavier.

Father Jérôme had described the American's surprise visit—the painting had been recovered from a group of art thieves, and an association the American worked with had traced the rightful ownership back to the Church of Sainte-Marie Près de la Mer.

"You must be more careful, Father," the American had said. "This is a valuable painting. You need to install an alarm system. I'm sure you'll be visited again."

They shook hands, and Eugene left Father Jérôme deep in thought. For the time being, he'd have to keep the painting locked in the church's vault. He had no money to install an alarm system; if he had, it already would have been done. But if the painting could not be displayed, perhaps inspiring the viewers by its beauty, what was the point of owning it? He looked up at the apse and along the nave, saw the water stains from leaks in the roof and the small fissures that had started to appear on the walls. The little church was desperately in need of repair. Perhaps the theft of the Daubigny and its return was God's way of telling him what needed to be done. Back in his tiny presbytery, he sifted through a pile of papers on his desk until he found the calling card for a man he had met at a retreat in Roscoff, François-Xavier Ballastré.

Father Jérôme brought the painting to the gallery. "A truly beautiful work, the colors are so rich and yet subtle. Are you sure you want to part with it?"

"We have no choice, I'm afraid. Sainte-Marie is in a terrible state of disrepair. How much do you think we can get for it?"

"I'll have to check, but I should think in the neighborhood of five hundred thousand Euros." François-Xavier was quite sure that that figure was on the low side, but there was his commission to think about. The church might be a charitable institution, but Galerie Ballastré was certainly not. *Storm Over the Sea,* the gift that would keep on giving.

Chapter 69

THE TABLE WAS SET FOR lunch for two. Michel de Clermont d'Auvergne arrived first. Jacques didn't like to be kept waiting, so he always came a few minutes late. Babs Tomason had retired to the kitchen to supervise the maid. A Perrier with a slice of lemon for Michel, a glass of freshly squeezed mango juice for Jacques.

Michel was glad Jacques had suggested meeting on rue Lalo. Jacques was a treasure trove of gossip—some outrageous, some extremely useful— but that did not mean that Michel wanted to be seen with him in his clubs. They were not at all in the same *milieu,* and as his grandmother used to say, *il ne faut pas confondre les torchons avec les serviettes* (don't mistake the dish towels for the napkins).

A starter of steamed green asparagus in hollandaise sauce, followed by *filet de sole à l'armoricaine,* Jacques sharing his latest tidbits, Michel wondering what Jacques wanted from him, knowing that there was no free lunch. Over cheese, Jacques began talking about a luncheon he was organizing, to take place in a month's time. The gathering would coincide with the publication of the latest edition of *Artixia.* He thought Michel might enjoy the company, and it would be great if Michel could bring his cousin, the MP Olivier de Clermont d'Auvergne. *Merde,* thought Michel. He would have to plead with Olivier to accompany him. In the end, he would give in, but then Michel would be obliged to do him a favor. It never ended. He wondered if he should not sell his apartment and move to the country and raise sheep. Life in Paris seemed less amusing with every passing day.

#   #   #

While Jacques and Michel were dining in the sixteenth arrondissement, Alex and Ella were eating copious bowls of Chinese soup in the Tricotin restaurant on Avenue de Choisy. Crowded and noisy, it was a place to have a great cheap meal and an intimate conversation.

"If you could do whatever you wanted, what would it be? For me, I think it would be to live in the south of France—and you?"

Ella smiled. "I would return to the Philippines and open a little restaurant with my family. I've saved some money, but not enough. So for now, I stay with Mr. Mornnais."

"How much do you need, Ella?"

"We each have to put in one million pesos."

"What would you say if I told you that your reward for finding the painting was five hundred thousand pesos? That's the amount that I got for returning it."

Ella looked down, put her spoon into the bowl, and lifted her chin. Her eyes were like two shiny black marbles. "How can that be?"

"It's a long, complicated story. But I was able to get a reward for the painting you found, and God knows you've paid for it with all you've put up with, so let's look to the future. I think the best thing would be if they fired you. You need to pretend that you're not feeling well, cannot do all the work. You know, keep sitting down at the kitchen table, and do your work slowly and not as well as you should. Come down later in the morning. Mila will look to get rid of you so fast, I promise. Can you do that?"

"Yes. When should I begin?"

"As soon as you get back to the château."

Alex slurped the last of her soup. "Where will you stay after you leave the château and before departing for the Philippines?"

"Maybe with Rosalinda as I am now. Or someone else. I'm not like Jacques and Mila. They have money but no friends. I have friends, and now I will have money."

\#   \#   \#

Château d'Hélène

Jacques returned to the château later that evening, and Alex came out the next day to finish going over the proofs for *Artixia*.

Mila, always cheap and lacking respect. Alex's invoices had not been paid, but instead of being upset, Alex saw this as an opportunity. She counted on Mila's bad behavior to provide the pretext to leave once Ella was gone. Did they pay Tarek on time? Probably, he was indispensable, and he knew too much about Jacques' dealings. And of course, he was a male. A random thought made Alex smile, as she imagined Tarek with Mila. *Beauty and the beast. You never know*.

In the kitchen, Ella was seated at the table, slowly peeling potatoes and carrots. Alex was in the office, proofreading, keeping to herself. All quiet. Alex looked out the window at the Mercedes parked on the circular drive. She went into the kitchen. "Have you seen them?" Ella looked up and pointed at the kitchen door.

"They're at the atelier?"

"Yes, I think so."

After lunch, Tarek would be driving the couple into Dijon. While Mila got her manicure and pedicure, Jacques would spend some time in the Musée des Beaux-Arts; for once, his interest in the collection from the Middle Ages was of personal, not professional, interest.

\#   \#   \#

Alex went through the motions of working, listening as the sound of the car faded and disappeared. Outside, she looked up the quiet, empty road, turned, and walked toward the atelier. She tried to open the door, but it was locked. Dark curtains covered the windows. At the side of the building, there was a slit where the curtains were not completely closed, and through the gap, she saw two paintings leaning against the back wall. They looked the same, perhaps two copies of Blondell's Signac, she couldn't be sure.

#   #   #

In the gentle sunlight, the warmth of an early-spring afternoon matched the introductory notes of Vivaldi's *Four Seasons*. As the car sped along, Mila said suddenly, "Stop, Tarek. We need to turn around. I forgot my nail polish." Only the limited edition of deep red Naughty Nostalgia would do.

Standing outside the atelier, Alex heard a noise, like a car door slamming shut. How could they be back so soon? They had only left a short while ago. She took a deep breath to quiet the beating of her heart, stepped back onto the path, and slowly walked farther along, past the atelier. She paid no attention to Tarek's rapid footsteps until he was almost upon her and turned to smile at him.

"Why, hello, Tarek."

He grabbed her by the arm. "What are you doing here?"

Alex, eye-level with Tarek, stared straight at him. "Get your fucking hand off me immediately. And what the fuck does it look like I'm doing, you idiot? I'm walking on the path."

Tarek let go.

"As you've spoiled my walk, I have no choice but to go back inside on this beautiful day and finish my work."

Tarek turned and strode swiftly back to the house, where Mila was waiting by the car.

"What is it, Tarek?"

"I saw Nathalie walking out by the atelier. Probably nothing," he mumbled. He got in the car and started the engine.

"Not again," said Mila.

"She wasn't actually at the atelier, only walking past it."

Jacques, looking at Mila, said, "Still, you need to keep an eye on her."

"Perhaps we should let her go, once the *Artixia* proofs are done."

"Good idea."

Chapter 70

Place des Vosges, Paris

BLONDELL, FAST ASLEEP AS SUNLIGHT streamed into the bedroom through the tall windows, her sleep mask matching her pink silk nightgown. But the mask could not filter out the noise from the pneumatic drills breaking up the pavement outside her building. No sooner had one set of pipes or cables been laid than drilling started to replace them, or so it seemed. She buried her head under the pillows but to no avail. There was no choice but to get up and start the day. She slinked into the living room, toes curling over the Persian rug laid out on top of thick wall-to-wall beige carpet. At the far end of the living room, to one side of the fireplace, a portrait rested on a wooden stand. The likeness of John Royston was the only work of art in the room, and it called attention to the emptiness of the ecru-colored walls.

The painter had done a flattering portrait. Absent was the web of fine red lines on his subject's nose and cheeks. Gone, too, were the bloated bags under his eyes. He had nonetheless captured the sharp intelligence in Royston's face, the sensuous mouth set in a tight smile. Every time Blondell passed the portrait, images of the five years they had spent together passed through her mind, like so many pinpricks of memory. Being arm candy had not always been easy. She thought of the swingers' club on the Canal Saint-Martin, the older men with sagging hairy bellies and fat-fingered hands. Remembered, too, the boring sex, how long it took him to come, like driving a car on a very long trip. But she also remembered how Royston would encourage people to talk. He was a good listener, uttering only a few words of encouragement at the right moment. It was so easy to get people to reveal their innermost thoughts. "You've got to learn to listen, Blondie," he liked to repeat. "When you've got money, you'll always have leeches sucking around, so pay attention."

Blondell thought about the train ride back to Paris the other day. Nathalie had answered her questions, but if you thought about it, she hadn't said very much. As for Merv and Jacques, she would need to become a better listener.

Then she remembered Mag, the woman Merv had introduced her to. She had seemed so pleasant. It was too bad she hadn't thought to ask for her phone number. She called Merv's office, but he was in a meeting. Well, perhaps a stroll along rue des Francs-Bourgeois would be the best way to start her day.

#   #   #

Le Marais, Paris

Marie-Agnès had taken an early-morning run up rue Lepic and around Sacré-Coeur. She'd worked on a translation and happily discovered a check from a client when she picked up her mail. In the past, she had indulged her twin cravings for food and fashion, but now that she had lost weight, only fashion was permissible. Okay, she'd picked up the old pastry crutch a few weeks ago, but that was then. She needed to take a break from her translation. What could be better than a fashion crawl through the Marais? Just looking, of course.

Starting at the imposing Saint Paul Church on rue Saint-Antoine, she strolled up the narrow cobblestone streets, reaching the shopping mecca that was rue des Francs-Bourgeois. It was a day without grey skies and the brilliant sun had brought out throngs of tourists that overflowed from the sidewalks onto the street. Marie-Agnès felt a slight irritation. The visitors had adopted the annoying Parisian habit of treating everyone around them as invisible, walking straight ahead and into whoever was in their way. Tourism was certainly a boon to the city—it was its number one industry—but the hordes of visitors made Paris seem more like a museum, focused on its glorious past, rather than looking to the future.

"Hey, Mag," a voice interrupted her funk.

As Marie-Agnès turned around, first she saw the hair, then the Murakami bag, and then Blondell.

"Ah, Blondell, what a nice surprise. I thought I'd look around the shops, but there are just too many people. It's not fun."

"I know what you mean. Why don't we go for lunch, my treat?"

A few minutes later, they found a table at a restaurant on rue de Turenne. With its old-fashioned décor, it was a favorite with American tourists and French bourgeois bohemian *bobos*. Crowded and noisy, but the food was good.

Blondell tried to read the daily specials that were written on a chalkboard and, as she would in New York City or Washington DC, embarked on a discussion in English with the waiter. Marie-Agnès, irritated by Blondell's assumption that because she spoke English, everyone else did as well, stared into space, placed her order, and while she was deciding whether to share her irritation with her companion, Blondell started to talk.

"I'm so glad we ran into each other. That lawyer of mine, Merv—of course, how could you forget him—he made me feel uncomfortable when we had lunch. Always hovering like a mother hen. Not that he hasn't done a good job with the estate papers. But he keeps talking about my becoming an art collector and about that man Jacques, who I think must be a friend of his. Anyhow, now we're just two girls."

Blondell, so eager to have a sympathetic ear, kept talking. "People all think I married John for his money, but you know, I have money of my own. I really did fall in love with him, but, well, things took some turns I hadn't expected. Before he died, we had talked about starting an art collection. John thought it would be a good investment. Of course, I don't know anything about paintings. That's why I have to rely on Jacques Morner. The funny thing is, I had an uncle who was a well-known collector, at least in Fairfax. We visited him and his family on and off when I was a child. They had a big house, rooms filled with paintings, or so it seemed to me at the time. But I have no recollection of what any of them looked like, if you see what I mean. Anyhow, enough about me, tell me about yourself."

"There's much less to tell, I'm afraid. I'm just a simple French girl, doing translations. Your life sounds a lot more exciting than mine, that's for sure. I mean, it's amazing to me that you could really be considering buying a painting that costs millions of dollars. Maybe you're following in your uncle's footsteps…what did you say his name was?"

"Frederick Blondell Whittaker. He was my mother's brother. They weren't really that close, and it was only after he died two years ago that we learned that he had been ill for some time."

"And what happened to the collection?"

"I think it was put up for auction. But now my aunt's complaining that the auction house stole two paintings."

"How does she think they did that?"

"Don't know. They showed her a list of the paintings they received and a list of what was sold, and they matched. My aunt is getting old, and I think she's a bit confused."

The waiter cleared the table, bringing warm *tarte Tatin* with vanilla ice cream for Blondell. Marie-Agnès had seen a fluid, body-skimming dress in a boutique window that allowed no departures from her regimen. Coffee, and the women agreed to meet again. Marie-Agnès left the restaurant feeling happy. She had managed to skip dessert, and she had some news to share with Alex.

Chapter 71

ALEX HAD FINISHED EATING LUNCH in a café on avenue de Villiers: salad, a spinach and goat cheese tart, and a glass of rosé. On the chair next to her sat her market basket, full of delights from the *charcuterie*, each item carefully wrapped in pale-pink-patterned paper. She couldn't be bothered to cook in her tiny apartment when such wonderful prepared dishes were so readily available. As she sipped her espresso, musing on why it was that the coffee in most cafés was so bad, and further musing that that really didn't matter if you looked upon being in a Parisian café as an experience in and of itself, her phone rang, and Marie-Agnès related her lunch with Blondell.

It was midafternoon when Alex returned to her rooms on Boulevard Malesherbes, loading up the little refrigerator with her goodies. The morning sunshine had faded, leaving the sky a pale whitish grey, the default color for Parisian weather. But it was springtime, and there was a brightness to the light filtering through the windows.

She had typed *Frederick Blondell Whittaker* into Google and was sifting through the information the search engine had spit out. Blondell's uncle had been a successful surgeon, like his father before him. In his free time, he devoted himself to his twin passions: collecting art and breeding orchids. He was a well known and well liked figure in northern Virginia society, hence the many obituaries, all saying mostly the same thing. There were some photos of Dr. Whittaker in his home, paintings covering the walls, but no in-depth discussion of the man or his collection.

Then, on page three of the search results, she saw an announcement of an auction of the Frederick Blondell Whittaker collection. As the sale had already taken place, there was only a short paragraph listing some of the artists' names: Caillebotte, Daumier, Gauguin, Klimt, Pissarro, Sisley... Dr. Whittaker had apparently been a fan of the late nineteenth century.

An interesting wrinkle, but not particularly useful.

#   #   #

Early evening. The days were already appreciably longer, a welcome relief from the winter's gloom and darkness. Eugene sat on a banquette facing the front of Café Carré on Avenue MacMahon. Alex had chosen the spot. She enjoyed the twenty-minute walk from Boulevard Malesherbes to the café, just off Place de l'Etoile. And she was confident that it would be a highly unlikely place to find Jacques, Mila, or Tarek.

"Am I late?" asked Alex, arriving fifteen minutes late. She'd spent some time window-shopping on rue de Courcelles on her way over. "I'm sorry."

"No problem," replied Eugene. He held out a box of chewing gum tablets before popping one into his mouth. "Nice café. I prefer it to that place at Saint-Sulpice. I'm not crazy about Saint-Germain, too many smart people for a slob like myself."

If he didn't reek of garlic, he wouldn't be too bad, thought Alex, but reflected that saying nothing about that was the better option. "The coffee here is almost drinkable, and the food is much better. So yes, we can continue to meet here from now on. Anyhow, I have some news for you."

Eugene, sipping his beer, looked fixedly at Alex. Again, she noticed the tiny gold flecks in his light brown eyes. "Yes?"

"Jacques has brought some paintings back to the château. I think they must have been at his house in the south. Remember, I told you that he'd sent Tarek down to Mélandère? He showed one of the paintings to Blondell, the wealthy American widow I told you about. But I think that there are two paintings, supposedly by Signac."

"How do you know that there are two of them?"

"I got a glimpse of them in the atelier, all locked up, but I looked through a gap in the curtains."

Eugene remembered the photos Walter Helmann had taken when he had followed Tarek to Mélandère. The driver had removed two paintings from the house. They were covered with protective wrapping, but there was a good chance that they were the two Signac forgeries. He didn't think it was necessary to share that thought with Alex. Instead, he asked, "Is she ready to leap?"

"Not yet. She's thinking about it. He's asking for ten million dollars, enough to make anyone think twice. But I have some other news as well. I don't know it if means anything, but for what it's worth…"

Alex paused and then recounted the story of Blondell's uncle, his collection, the auction, and the missing paintings. "I don't know if Jacques has even heard of him, and even if he did, I doubt that he would realize that Blondell is his niece. His last name was Whittaker, and her maiden name was Jamison. But since it has to do with Blondell, I thought this could interest you."

"Perhaps. Thanks for the heads-up."

They parted company. Eugene sipped his beer and tried to decide if Alex's news meant anything at all.

#   #   #

The pale blue sky had turned dark grey. Despite the threat of rain, Alex decided to walk to Neuilly to pay a visit to Richard. Too much time had elapsed since she'd last seen him. Along the way, new leaves contrasted with the trees' dark branches, making her think of delicate green lace. Yellow and white daffodils lined the streets, their colors bright under the leaden sky. The sidewalk was empty, the only noise coming from the passing cars and the sound of Alex's footsteps.

Maria opened the door. "Ah, madame," she whispered, a finger placed on her lips. In the living room, Richard was seated on a sofa, his feet resting on the coffee table, his head bent back against the cushions, snoring gently, a thin stream of spittle at the corner of his mouth. As Alex entered, he sensed her presence. With a little start, he lifted his head and opened his eyes.

"My dear Alexia, what a pleasant surprise," he said as he took a handkerchief out of his pocket to wipe his chin. "I'm afraid I dozed off."

"I'm sorry that I woke you up, Uncle Richard," she replied, planting a gentle kiss on the top of his head.

"No, no, that's all right. I was feeling a bit tired, but it's much too early to go to bed."

Richard did indeed look tired, his face drawn and dark circles under his eyes. It suddenly occurred to Alex that as of late she had been devoting all her time to finding proof that Jacques Mornnais was selling fakes and that she'd dropped the project that was her real reason for coming to France. Over dinner, she brought the conversation around to the property at Trubenne. "When I came back from Trubenne in January, do you remember my telling you that Charlotte said she would be happy to participate in the development, as long as she could continue to live there? That seems reasonable, don't you think?"

Richard was thinking about many things, all at the same time. That time was flying by so quickly. That he was spending too much time looking back instead of forward. That he was worried about Alex's involvement with Jacques Mornnais. That he needed to see that the property at Trubenne was properly developed, the family heritage preserved.

"Oh, yes, Alex, very reasonable. I need to get some rest right now, but perhaps you could come over on Sunday to talk about plans for Trubenne?"

"I'd love to. Shall we say three o'clock?"

#   #   #

Mila had asked Alex to come to work at rue de Prony on Saturday. She would arrive early and say that she had personal matters to attend to in the afternoon. The stress of the past few months was starting to take its toll.

This was not exactly the new life she had envisioned: getting the reward for Ella, spying on Jacques, trying to help Eugene, pretending to be Nathalie Martin.

Tired, she crawled into her bed on Boulevard Malesherbes and fell asleep at once.

# # #

A brief evening drizzle, the street glistening from the rain. Tarek sat in the enclosed terrace of a café on Avenue Emile Zola, across the street from Nathalie's apartment. There was no reason for him to be there, he knew that. But there was something about Nathalie that intrigued him. In all the time she had spent working with Jacques and Mila, she never said anything about herself. She spent some time in the kitchen, drinking coffee, exchanging but a few words with the maid, Ella.

Two times. She'd only spoken to him twice. Once, when that asshole followed him, looking for Bruno. And when he followed her to the atelier. The bitch had snapped at him. He didn't like that. For Jacques and Mila, she was just another in a long line of translators, and he wondered how much longer she would last. Sitting in a corner of the terrace, he kept one eye on the front door and the other on his copy of *L'Equipe*. At midnight, the waiter started stacking the chairs and cleaning the tables. Perhaps she would come home later, or maybe she was out fucking someone, but it was time to go. As he walked down the street, a thought, unbidden but clear, arose and stayed fixed in his mind. He was fucking Nathalie, on top of her, behind her, his penis in her mouth. He felt an unwelcome erection and hastened to get into his car.

Chapter 72

SEATED IN MERV'S OFFICE, BLONDELL realized that she missed her husband. He had always taken care of financial matters, and her only obligation had been to be an attractive, pleasant companion. A law firm in the US was handling her affairs over there, and Merv looked after things in Paris. They were all very nice, but could she trust their advice? Shouldn't she be asking questions? But what questions?

Merv led her to a table in his office, sat next to her, and started to go through the papers her accountants in Paris had prepared. The smell of his cologne was overpowering, and she wished that he were not sitting quite so close to her. "You need to be careful not to spend more than six months in France this year, otherwise the fiscal authorities will slap you with an enormous tax bill. Let's see, perhaps you can plan on spending the summer in the US, maybe some time this spring and at Christmas? Or maybe you'd like to do some touring, visit some exotic places?"

"I do miss my family back home. Yes, I think I could make a trip this spring. I have an elderly aunt that I'd like to visit as well. Good idea, Merv."

"Do you want to make arrangements to purchase the Signac before you go?"

"Uh, Merv, we're talking about ten million dollars. I've been reading up on Signac. I admit he's interesting, but I need to be sure that this is the artist to be the first in my collection. And, again, ten million is a lot of money. So, I'm not ready yet."

"Are you sure about that? I think Jacques has negotiated a very good price."

"Yes, I'm sure." She lifted her head from the papers on the table and looked at him. "I don't want to be rushed, okay?"

Fucking airhead bitch. With two billion to spend, this painting is small change for you. Merv saw his commission heading south.

"Of course, Blondell, whatever you say."

#   #   #

Back in her apartment, Blondell called Marie-Agnès. "I saw my lawyer today, and I need to spend time outside of France. I'm going to visit my family. I hate to travel alone. Would you like to come with me to the US for two weeks?"

#   #   #

Château d'Hélèné

Jacques had just settled back to take a power nap—he only slept five hours each night, and this was how he replenished his energy—when one of his Blackberrys rang. It was Merv.

"Yes, any news?"

"None yet, I'm afraid. She's still thinking about it. And she's going to the US for two weeks, so we'll have to be a little patient."

"What's the problem? I thought she was hot to start collecting. She seemed to like the painting when she came to the château. What happened?"

"Nothing. She said she wants to think about it. I can't push her."

"Okay. Keep me posted. Just remember where your interests lie."

The call had disturbed his ritual. He would need to explore other options in case the American woman got cold feet.

#   #   #

"Guess where I'm going."

Alex smiled. Marie-Agnès sometimes started sentences midway through the paragraph. It was part of her friend's charm. "I give up, where are you going?"

"America! Blondell invited me to come along when she visits her family. And she insists that I fly with her in business class. I'm so excited! I've always wanted to visit the States."

"Hey, that sounds great. If you visit her aunt, maybe you'll find out more about what happened to her uncle's painting collection."

"Maybe I will." Marie-Agnès rung off. She needed to start planning what she would wear. And this time, she felt that she could do it on her own.

Chapter 73

United States

BLONDELL'S BROTHERS AND SISTERS WERE spending a long weekend at the family compound, where each household had their own house, scattered among acres of rolling land near Lake Mahopac, about fifty miles north of New York City. The architecture varied—one house was a large stone structure, another modern, all concrete and glass, yet another was a simple white clapboard building dating from the nineteenth century. Winding paths led from one house to another, yet there was sufficient distance so that the inhabitants felt alone but not isolated. Two swimming pools, tennis courts, and an archery range gave the place the feeling of a summer camp. Blondell's grandfather, a builder, had bought the farm for a song in the 1940s. Today it was worth millions.

After France, everything seemed bigger than life-size to Marie-Agnès. There was so much room, so much space. Polished wood floors or deep pile carpet, kitchens equipped with huge refrigerators and every imaginable appliance. Blondell's family members were all well off, but not fabulously wealthy. So this was how the American upper middle class lived.

They spent the last days of the trip in Fairfax, Virginia, visiting Blondell's aunt. Milissa Whittaker could have been the prototype for older women of a particular class in the greater Washington DC area. Perfectly colored ash-blond hair pulled into a bun at the nape of her neck, a short, straight nose, she had had the good sense to insist that her plastic surgeon leave a few fine lines and some flexibility when he did her face-lift. A navy velvet headband matching her navy ensemble held a few wisps of hair in place.

After settling into guest bedrooms, it was late afternoon when Blondell and Marie-Agnès went downstairs to join Milissa in the living room. Large French doors opened onto a patio. Beyond was a lawn surrounded by colorful flowerbeds. The sun was still high in the sky, but its rays stopped at the patio, bathing the living room in a gentle glow.

"Would you girls like something to drink?"

"Maker's Mark for me," answered Blondell.

"And your friend?"

"A glass of red wine, please."

Milissa rang a small bell and a maid in a black dress came into the living room. Milissa asked her to bring their drinks, bourbon for her as well. She wanted to know all about Blondell's visit with her nieces and nephews and their children. Blondell described the visit in detail, as she knew that Milissa felt too tired to travel to Mahopac. She also noticed that her aunt seemed to have trouble remembering everyone's name. Well, they were a big family.

Marie-Agnès, in a well-made faux Armani black pants suit and white silk T-shirt, sipped her wine slowly as the conversation circled around her. She felt out of place, between Blondell, decked out in full bling, and her aunt, whose memory lapses — if that is what they were — detracted from her icy elegance. The litany of names, petty disputes, and family gossip was starting to wear her down. In her idealized world, an extensive collection of siblings and their progeny had seemed so much more exciting, so much more fun than her small family. But looking at Blondell's family, she was no longer so sure. It was time to move on to another topic of conversation.

She stood up and walked over to admire a large family portrait on the opposite wall. A man and woman sat in a garden, surrounded by three children, a dog at their feet. "What a lovely painting, madame. I assume that is you with your husband and children?"

Milissa looked at Marie-Agnès for several long seconds, her face empty of expression, then turned toward the painting. "Ah, yes, we had the portrait done when the children were young." Pointing, "There are some others in the hallway over there."

As Blondell picked up where she had left off, rambling on about a swimming meet, Marie-Agnès ambled to the hallway to admire the portraits. "They're all so lovely as well. I understood that your late husband had a marvelous collection—did you keep any of those paintings?"

A frown, another silence. "No, I did not. I put the whole lot up for auction. I didn't want them anymore. I was wife number two. The paintings came first. So when he died, it was normal that wife number one should disappear, don't you think?"

Milissa smiled, staring at the glass of bourbon she held in her hand. "In fact, I did quite well on the sale. But I'm certain that the auction house kept two small paintings."

Blondell interjected, "Aunt Milissa, how can you be sure?"

"They hung in his office here for a few years, and then he took them down and put them into his office closet. I don't know why. When the auctioneers came, they took them as well."

"But surely there must be records?"

"I gave everything to the auctioneer. I didn't want any of those papers cluttering up my home any longer."

Blondell remembered her Aunt Milissa when she was growing up. This woman was like a pale copy of her former self. She wondered if she could believe anything that Milissa said, and tried to reassure her aunt. "Why don't you call the auctioneers and tell them that I'd like to stop by and review the paperwork for the sale? I'm sure they would have no objection."

Listening to the exchange, it occurred to Marie-Agnès how much more self-assured Blondell was in the US than in France. But, she reasoned, it was only normal.

#   #   #

The colonial-era house—painted a cerulean blue with white trim—

housed the offices of Virginia Colonial Auctioneers. Its interior—hardwood floors overlaid with Persian carpets, antique colonial furniture—projected class and old money and hinted at some form of American aristocracy. A short, stocky man, with a shiny bald pate, greeted them. Allen George, one of the principals, was originally from Kansas, his midwestern twang softened by years spent in Virginia. Of course he remembered the auction of the Whittaker collection. All of the works had sold, and sold well above the reserve price.

Dr. Whittaker's attorney, David Steiner, had supervised the packing up of the paintings and had signed off on the inventory. "If you ladies will forgive my saying so, Ms. Whittaker is getting on in years, and perhaps her imagination is playing tricks on her. If you like, you could always talk to David Steiner. I'm sure he'll put your minds at ease. I've prepared a copy of our report along with the auction catalogue, which you can study at your leisure." He handed them a large white envelope. Allen George spoke softly and gently, but he made it clear that he could do nothing further to help them and that the meeting was over.

#   #   #

"Should we try to see that lawyer he mentioned?" asked Blondell as they were back on the sidewalk.

"I don't see any point. He'll just tell us what Allen George said. By the way, what did you think of him?"

"He tries to project old money, the right schools, the right family. But I think he's more of a new-money type. Like our friend, Merv," she added with a giggle.

#   #   #

One of Milissa's other children had joined them for dinner. Claudia lived in Bethesda and tried to stop by to see her mother whenever she could. They talked about the meeting with Allen George. Claudia was not impressed. "Sounds like a dead end to me," she said.

"The problem is, we don't know what the missing paintings look like, so it's impossible to know if they are, in fact, missing," pointed out Blondell.

"Whatever," sighed Claudia. The family had done so well on the sale of the collection that she didn't seem to care. "I'm still helping Mom sort through Dad's papers, and if I come across anything interesting, I'll let you know. But I wouldn't count on that," she said, turning her attention to scooping some tiramisu onto her plate.

The following day, Blondell and Mag rode out to Dulles Airport and caught the early-evening Air France flight back to Paris.

Chapter 74

A CAR MET THEM AT the airport, and Blondell had the driver drop Mag off on the way to her apartment. Marie-Agnès had a simple rule for dealing with jet lag — she would take a nap for one hour, no more, and remain active until bedtime. Within forty-eight hours, she slept normally and suffered only slight fatigue. When Alex called, she was already up and sorting through her mail.

"How was the trip?" asked Alex.

"Verrry interesting," chuckled Marie-Agnès.

"You'll have to tell me all about it. And there's something I have to talk to you about, so can we meet later today, if you're not too tired?"

"Yes, I'd like that," replied Marie-Agnès. "It helps if I'm out and about."

"Right, okay, come over around six. I'll pick up something to eat, and we can have an early dinner. Come through the rue Daubigny entrance. Not too hard to remember the name of the street, is it? I'll text you the door code."

On rue de Tocqueville, Alex stopped at the charcuterie for starters—avocados stuffed with shrimp—then went on to the butcher for a roast chicken and potatoes, finishing up with a baguette and two small strawberry tarts from the bakery next door. A bottle of wine from the shop on the corner, her errands were complete. *Oops, forgot about cheese.* She crossed the street and bought a hunk of Beaufort and a slice of runny Brie. Dinner, she was sure, would be both tasty and productive.

Alex heard the clank of the elevator gate, cracked her door open, and welcomed Marie-Agnès. She prepared two kirs and sliced some *saucisson sec*. Outside, black clouds had rolled in, darkening the sky and promising rain, but that did nothing to dampen the spirits of the two friends as they sipped their aperitifs.

Marie-Agnès described the compound at Lake Mahopac and then recounted the time spent with Milissa and the meeting at the offices of Virginia Colonial Auctioneers. "Her aunt is getting old. She sometimes has to force herself to pay attention, but she was adamant that there were two paintings stored in a closet that were unaccounted for. It also turns out that she was jealous that her husband devoted so much time to his collection. Blondell and I went to the auction house, but for them, all is in order. They gave us their catalogue and statement of what was sold. We can review it, but I'm sure that we won't find anything amiss."

"Hmm," said Alex, "sounds like a dead end."

"Yes, that's just what Milissa's daughter, Claudia, said."

Alex nibbled on a slice of *saucisson sec*, took another sip of her kir, and continued. "I've felt that we — or I, I should say — have been spinning our wheels. And I only have two weeks left in the apartment on Avenue Emile Zola, so I'll be leaving Jacques at that time. I'm hoping they'll let me go rather than my having to take the initiative."

She continued, "Jacques is such a slippery character. I've been in his offices for hours on end, and I've learned little that is useful. If this were a movie, I would have already caught Jacques red-handed.

"But I haven't. Okay, I did manage to get the reward money for Ella, not as much as I had hoped for but better than nothing, and that was good. But for the rest, I feel frustrated."

"You shouldn't be so hard on yourself, Alex. Getting the money for Ella was more than okay, it was brilliant, really." Marie-Agnès paused. "Oh, yes, there is something else. It looks like Blondell isn't going to buy the Signac, whether it's real or a fake."

Alex stared at her kir. She'd gone light on the *crème de cassis,* and the drink was a lovely pale rose color. She felt a tingle of excitement.

"Remember our plan to use Merv Peters to introduce Eugene to Jacques? We seem to have forgotten about that. But now might be the perfect opportunity. From what you've said, Jacques will be looking for another buyer. Another rich, not-too-bright American he can impress. So isn't it time to put Eugene forward in that role? You could introduce him to Merv Peters — you said Merv was asking if you knew potential buyers. Then Merv can introduce Eugene to Jacques, and Eugene can do whatever it is he does. He's been looking to meet Jacques, and we'll have put him squarely into the lion's den. What do you think?"

Marie-Agnès smiled. "I think that's another brilliant idea. We need to make Merv run after Eugene, have him play a little hard to get. If Blondell doesn't buy the painting, he's out a commission, so I'm sure he'll jump at the chance to meet another pigeon."

"And," added Alex, "we need to clean Eugene up a bit. Get him to stop eating garlic and chewing gum. He'd be an attractive man if he weren't such a slob. I'll have to take him shopping for the right clothes, have him grow a three-day beard, do something about his hair. But after all, re-looking is what I did in another life."

Activity whets the appetite, and dinner that evening was particularly enjoyable.

Chapter 75

April 2010, Château d'Hélène

AFTER SEVERAL DAYS OF WARM sunshine, the weather had changed, and a steady cold rain was falling, the drops beating against the roof of the atelier. Outside, the foliage was shining, polished by the downpour. Jacques was alone in the atelier, as Tarek had just left to deliver one of the Signacs to the south of France. The painting would be placed on the owner's yacht, on the way to its final destination. That left just one canvas to be disposed of. Jacques moved back and forth, admiring Li's brushwork. It was one of the most beautiful paintings that Signac could have done.

His mind called up an image of Blondell Royston, smoking her cigarette, followed by a wave of annoyance. He had expected to close the sale by now. If she was having second thoughts, then he had best find another buyer. All was not lost. He'd try to interest her in a less expensive work, bring her along slowly. Perhaps he had overreached a bit, proposing the Signac right off the bat, but that jerk Merv Peters had been so sure she would be easy pickings.

#   #   #

Blondell had been wide-awake until four a.m., reliving her trip, the farm at Lake Mahopac, her aunt's home in Fairfax. When she had complained about how hard she found it to live in Paris, how unforgiving the French were, Marie-Agnès had dismissed her grumbling. "Rich people's problems." *She may be right*, thought Blondell, *but I can't help feeling the way I do. Maybe I should sell this apartment and move back to the States.* But lurking in her semiconsciousness was the feeling that she liked to see the reactions when she casually mentioned that she lived on Place des Vosges, in the Marais.

The rainstorm had hit Paris as well. Behind her closed shutters, water ran off the sidewalks into the gutters, the rain washing the cobblestones that glimmered under the street lights. At last, she fell asleep, burying her head in the pillows, so that she did not hear her phone ring. Merv Peters left a message that he would call back later.

It was one p.m. when Blondell awoke. She opened the shutters and dropped back into her bed. It took too much effort to get up right now. Every day in Paris started the same way. She would stare at the ceiling, a feeling of dread tying knots in her stomach, sometimes moving upward to create a tightness in her throat as well. Then she would plan her day, force herself to take a shower, and wait for her anxiety to abate as she ate breakfast. Sometimes she felt better fairly quickly; other times the feeling stayed with her all day, until she took refuge in her bed at night. Today it was here to stay.

She found her cell phone, hidden in the pillows. Checked for messages and saw that Merv had called. Stared at the ceiling, her eyes bright with tears ready to spill down her cheeks. As she reached for a tissue, her phone rang. She saw it was Merv calling again. "What the fuck," she muttered, blowing her nose before answering.

"Hi, Blondell, Merv here. How was your trip?"

"Oh, hi. Trip was great, got back yesterday, terrible jet lag, just woke up."

"Yeah, you sound a little spacey." He tried to get a hook into the conversation. "How's your family?"

"Family is great, Merv." More tears welling up. "I miss them a lot. I dunno, maybe I'll move back to the States."

"Well, if you do, you could take your painting back with you, continue

270

collecting back home."

"My painting…oh, yes, of course."

Merv should have dropped it but pushed onward. "Would you like me to arrange a meeting with Jacques to move things ahead?"

"Not right now, I'll let you know. Thanks for asking but I need to think about things first."

"Of course, Blondell. Let's speak soon."

After they hung up, Merv was sure that Blondell would not buy the painting. But if she was serious about selling her apartment, he could refer her to some agents handling high-end properties who would pay him a finder's fee. He might make some preliminary inquiries, be ready should she follow through.

The next morning, he went upstairs to gaze at the paintings in his secret garden. It was a daily ritual, taking comfort in calling on old friends. But above all, on each visit he had a warm feeling in his midsection, an almost sexual pleasure, in the knowledge that all this belonged to him, as he calculated their worth on today's market. It was a pity that Blondell was going to disappoint him. He had counted on his commission to fund the purchase of the commode he had seen at Renaud Schneider's gallery. Well, perhaps something would turn up.

And it did. His phone rang as he descended the stairway.

#   #   #

It was Mag. One of her sister's friends was an American guy named Carl Weller. He lived in London and was frequently in Paris on business. He was a regular at auctions at Druout, on the lookout for an underpriced painting. Perhaps the man he had mentioned—she had forgotten his name—could help Carl. What did he think?

"Well, Mag, that might work. Of course, I'd have to meet him first, make sure that he has the right profile before I introduce him to Jacques."

Mag, enjoying the exchange, "You're quite right, and actually, I'd have to ask him if he's even interested, you know, he's so busy with his work. I'll let you know."

A few days went by, and when Merv didn't hear from Mag, he looked around for an excuse to contact her. He had been given two free tickets to a play at l'Odéon, and he called to see if she would like to join him. What a pity, but she wasn't free that night. He asked, in what he thought of as a casual manner, "And have you spoken to your sister's friend Carl?"

"Oh, yes, I was going to call you. He can meet you tomorrow at five thirty if you're free at that time."

Merv didn't want to be seen in public with Carl before he had a chance to size him up, so he suggested that they meet at his office. He would have his secretary move his appointments around to make time for them to get acquainted.

Chapter 76

TWO DAYS EARLIER, ALEX HAD met Eugene at Café Carré. This time she had arrived first and watched him as he entered, stopped for a moment to take in the large room, and then approached the banquette where Alex was seated.

She seemed excited, her voice losing some of the steely flatness that he had found unattractive. "We're arranging for you to meet Jacques Mornnais, and he's going to be anxious to make your acquaintance," she said.

Eugene leaned back in his chair and smiled. "And how have *we* arranged this?"

"Well," she began, "there's this poor little rich girl." She told him about Blondell and her reluctance to buy the Signac, and concluded, "Merv and Jacques would be on the lookout for another buyer. And *voilà,* that will be you, an American businessman living in London, who attends auctions at Druout."

Eugene, attentive, his eyes focused on a point beyond Alex's shoulders, said, "It might work."

"Yes, it will," she said. "We're going to make them wait, really want to meet you, so that when they do, they will already believe that you're the buyer they've been waiting for. First, you will meet Merv. He'll want to look you over, be sure you're the right stuff, and then he'll throw you into Jacques' arms. But Eugene…" She hesitated, then rushed on, "I hope you don't mind my saying this, but you've got to stop eating food with garlic. It just doesn't go with your persona. And we need to get you the right clothes, and a visit to the barber."

"Alex," he said very quietly, "I know all that, no need to worry. Let me take care of it."

"Yes, but…"

"I said, leave it to me."

That part of the conversation had come to an end. "All right," continued Alex, "when shall we tell Merv you're free?"

"No need to rush, let's say sometime next week. Not any sooner."

#   #   #

After Alex left, Eugene stood up and took her place; he felt more comfortable with his back against the wall, facing the comings and goings in the café. He ordered a beer, thinking about next moves. Had Alex been there, she would have noticed that his eyes were like two pools of pale mud. The golden flecks had disappeared.

Chapter 77

Merv Peters's office

"SHIT," MERV MUTTERED TO HIMSELF.

Mag had just called to say that they needed to postpone the meeting with her sister's friend, Carl Weller. He was still in London, his agenda clogged, and asked if the meeting could be put off until next week.

"Of course, Mag, whatever works for your friend. Can we say next Tuesday?"

"That sounds good, but I'll have to check and let you know, okay? Sorry, but you know how these things are."

Do I ever, thought Merv. He wondered if he should tell Jacques and decided not to say anything, just pretend things were going along as planned, that he was meeting a potential buyer. Jacques probably wouldn't ask him anyway. He wouldn't want to appear to be too eager. Yes, he knew how these things were, as she had put it. But that didn't stop him from being pissed. Why was it so difficult to sell the fucking Signac anyway?

#   #   #

A cloudless blue sky swept clean by a brisk northwest wind could not lift Alex's feeling of malaise. She had expected Eugene to smile, to say he was grateful, that she had done a good job, but instead, he said very little and seemed intense, withdrawn.

And to be honest, this was not the adventure she had had in mind when she left Washington. It was time to regain control over her life.

First, a glass of Crozes-Hermitage, then some decisions.

Nathalie Martin was returning from India in two weeks. Tonight Alex would move her few belongings out of the apartment on Avenue Emile Zola. Tomorrow she would pack her things and move out of Boulevard Malesherbes and stay with Richard in Neuilly. Alex was sure he would be happy to have her, and they could finally talk about Trubenne. She had paid the rent in advance on the apartment on Boulevard Malesherbes, but *tant pis,* it was time to cut ties.

#   #   #

Avenue Emile Zola, Paris

Alex trudged slowly up the steps at the Métro station Charles Michels. That third glass of Crozes-Hermitage had been too much of a good thing. *I need a quick espresso*, she thought and walked toward the café across the street from her apartment.

Tarek was sitting on the terrace, his attention focused on the building across the street. She saw him first, and fueled by the wine, she stood over him. "Why, Tarek, how curious to find you here. Aren't you far from home?"

Tarek was not without particular talents, but repartee was not part of his skill set. He managed to say, "*Bonsoir*, Nathalie," as he put some coins on the table and got up to leave, but Alex was blocking his passage. Her face inches from his, she hissed, "Tell me what you're doing here. Not spying on me, by any chance? Do you know that you're an asshole?" She turned and went to the counter, where she ordered her espresso. It was not necessary. She felt quite sober now.

Tarek felt a hot flush move up his neck to his ears. Furious at being

276

humiliated, he hurried out of the café. Alex, preoccupied with her encounter, didn't notice the man in the blue parka. He had been sitting at a table in the corner reading *Le Monde*, but he slipped out of his seat and followed Tarek as he left.

Chapter 78

ALEX HAD SLEPT FITFULLY. MARIE-AGNÈS'S image floated in the grey period between sleep and wakefulness. The obvious could no longer be avoided: a sincere if somewhat childish impulse to help her friend had turned into a tangle of false leads and dead ends. The man in the metallic-green Peugeot. And now, Tarek. At this moment, all Alex wanted was to be free of the whole mess. She would call Mag, tell her that she had decided that it would be best to drop everything.

#   #   #

Café Carré, Paris

An intense workout, followed by some time in the sauna. Eugene was feeling a flutter of excitement, a gentle buzz. Movement at last, things starting to come together.

Then his phone rang. It was Alex.

"Can we meet for a coffee?" she asked. "Usual place?"

"I guess so," he replied. "Is everything okay?"

"Yes, all good. I just wanted to go over a couple of things. Shall we say three o'clock?"

She arrived early again, spotted him the minute he passed through the door. He seemed to have dressed in anticipation of his meeting tomorrow, impeccable jeans, blazer, and crisp white shirt, no tie. A thought rippled through her mind, not for the first time—he was indeed an attractive man— but she chased it away, determined to follow through on her decision.

She stirred her coffee, noticed that the cloud of garlic fumes had disappeared, and found it harder than she thought to start, but she plunged in.

"You gave me ten thousand dollars without too much questioning, for a painting that was stolen from a church, not a rich owner. The more I think about it, the more it makes no sense. I just don't get it."

"The money came from a foundation," he said, still smiling.

"I don't believe you, but it doesn't matter. I've decided that I don't want to be part of this—what shall I call it—project anymore. Jacques Mornnais and his wife are very nasty people, that thug Tarek gives me the creeps, and I want out. And I never told you, but I think that one of Bruno's henchmen tried to follow me. Why, I'll never know." She rushed on, "So I'm going to have Marie-Agnès cancel the meeting with Merv Peters."

No more gold flecks, the eyes had turned a light muddy brown, and he had stopped smiling.

"Please, Alex, don't do that. Things have been a bit rough for you, but I need you to hang in just a bit longer. This meeting is the break I've been waiting for."

She got up to leave. "Well, okay, but after the meeting, I want nothing further to do with any of this."

Alex turned onto rue Tilsitt and then walked up Avenue Hoche to Parc Monceau. She looked for a bench away from the laughing, screaming children… she was not in the mood. Eugene was impossible to seize. He reminded her of her husband. Toward the end, it had been impossible to have a conversation that was not one-sided. She doing the talking, he sliding away. *Different man, same mistakes. Those who cannot remember the past are condemned to repeat it.*

#   #   #

Until today, he'd thought of her as tough and strong. He remembered how she had gone over last details when they had rented her house, her self-confidence, the impression she gave of being on top of it all. That was not the woman who sat across from him today. She'd been arguing with Tarek in a café on Avenue Emile Zola, Walter Helmann had said. He wondered if that had anything to do with her change of mood. And what was she doing there? The fifteenth arrondissement was not her usual stomping ground. *It's like she's got some other agenda that she's not prepared to share with me.* Once this was all over, he hoped there would be no more unanswered questions.

Chapter 79

MERV'S DESK, FILES STRAIGHTENED AND re-straightened, a crystal paperweight centered on a pile of papers, the impression that he sought to convey—busy but organized. Fidgeting in his leather executive desk chair, he got up, paced, sat down again.

Eugene arrived a few minutes late. Merv walked into the entry to greet him. "Ah, Mr. Weller, so pleased to meet you. Come this way, won't you?"

Eugene took in the plush green carpet, dark woodwork, the abstract paintings, the massive, well-ordered desk and smiled. *It could be a movie set, it's such a perfect office for a lawyer to the wealthy. Well, let's get on with the play.*

An exchange of cards, Eugene's announced that he is Carl Weller, CW Consultants.

His elbows on his desk, Merv made a pyramid with his hands. His forefingers rested on his lips, a thoughtful moment, before he clasped his hands and lowered them to the surface. "Mr. Weller, how can I help you?"

Eugene tried his best to appear tentative. "I want to add a painting to my collection. In my experience, these auction houses rob you blind, and my, um, friend Mag said you might be able to help me find the right artwork through other channels."

Merv hesitated before he said, "Perhaps I could be of assistance. But tell me a bit more about what you're looking for, Mr. Weller."

"It's my wife. She wants a painting by Georges Seurat, you know, the pointillist. So I was wondering if you might know someone who could find me one of his paintings, at the right price."

"And what is the right price for you? As I'm sure you know, a Seurat would have a hefty price tag, several million, I would think."

"Yes, that's what I imagined."

Merv sighed, tapped his fingers on the desk. "I may know someone who could help you. But I would need to check with him first. He's a busy man, always traveling someplace or other."

"I'd appreciate that," said Eugene. "You can reach me at the number on my card. I'm returning to London tonight, but I'm frequently in Paris, so I'm sure I could meet your contact if he thinks he could help me."

A handshake and Merv accompanied Eugene to the entry. "Thanks again for your time, Mr. Peters."

The door closed. In the silence of his office, fatigue crept up from the carpet, followed Merv as he slumped into his executive desk chair. Did he feel happy, or at least relieved that the meeting had gone well? Not really. He had merely checked off another box on the endless to-do list that governed his relationship with Jacques Mornnais. A thought crossed his mind, one that had been there for the last week: *do I really give a shit about that commode?* He would call Jacques, follow through as he had done in the past, but this would be the last time. His overwhelming desire was to get rid of the constant jabs of pain in his abdomen.

Chapter 80

Rue Bonaparte, Paris

MILA HAD SENT TAREK OUT to buy sushi for lunch. Jacques didn't want to pay the delivery person by credit card, so Tarek had to go to the shop to pay in cash. It wasn't up to Jacques' usual dining standards, but they had some issues to resolve.

"I think we'll have to let Ella go," said Mila. A frown spoiled the otherwise perfect symmetry of her features. "She's complaining that she's tired, and I don't have time for this shit. I have a household to run." She turned to Tarek. "Can you ask around and get me someone else, younger this time?"

"And Nathalie," she continued. "Didn't we say she'd worked for us long enough? There's no point in anyone becoming too familiar with our business, is there?" She didn't add that she'd caught Tarek staring at Nathalie when she wasn't looking, and while Nathalie barely spoke to Tarek, one could never be too careful.

Jacques swallowed a mouthful of rice. "Yes, call and say we have no further need for her right now, but that could change, and you'll let her know. Don't we owe her money?" he asked.

"I suppose we do." Mila frowned again.

"Well, pay her, for fuck's sake. Just get rid of her."

Jacques' face brightened, or more precisely, his eyes lit up. "Merv Peters called. It looks like he has another client—the guy asked about Seurat, so perhaps we can interest him in Signac. It's a shame we no longer have the painters—Li was a genius when it came to pointillism. Seurat, Signac, same difference, right?" Jacques cracked a smile. It was a sign of satisfaction.

"What about that rich widow," asked Mila, "have we lost her for good?"

"Ah, yes, the rich widow, Madame Royston. Did I tell you that I had some dealings with her late husband? No point in mentioning that to her. It would just muddy the waters, create unnecessary confusion. It looks like she's not going to buy the Signac. A pity. She could certainly afford it. But I'll have Merv talk to her, maybe try to sell her something less expensive."

Mila pushed away the plastic sushi plateau. A little vial containing soy sauce fell, leaving a small brown puddle on the table. She glanced at Tarek. He stood up and started to clear away the remains of the meal. Jacques was playing with his Blackberrys. Mila's mouth turned upward into the facsimile of a smile, and Tarek, his face expressionless, wiped the table clean and tied a grey garbage bag closed.

Chapter 81

IN THE EARLY AFTERNOON, ALEX ordered a taxi to pick her up on rue Daubigny. The concierge, whose *loge* was in the front of the building, was off doing housekeeping in other buildings in the neighborhood, but Alex didn't want to take any chances that she might see her moving out. Madame Da Silva, the *gardienne de l'immeuble,* was friendly enough. But Alex knew the well-earned reputation of the Parisian concierge— it had hit a high or low point, depending on your perspective, during the Nazi Occupation—keeping an eye peeled on the comings and goings of the building's residents, always willing to share information in exchange for a gratuity.

A half an hour later, the driver deposited her in front of Richard's apartment building.

Early the following morning, she went to the *Artixia* office on rue de Prony. Like Neuilly, there was the same mix of people on the street, the well-dressed Caucasians and the Asian and African maids accompanying children to school.

Mila was alone. She said that Jacques was at a meeting. *It's probably true,* thought Alex, *but now that he no longer needs me, it's as if I've ceased to exist.* Mila handed her an envelope and, in a crisp voice, thanked her for helping them.

"You know, your friend Ella has left us." The hint of a sneer formed around the words *your friend*.

"Really? I didn't know that," replied Alex.

"We already have a new girl, younger, that Tarek found."

"Oh, that's good." As Alex turned to leave, her eyes were drawn to a large book on the low table. The cover was the iconic portrait of Félix Fénéon, one hand clutching his hat, his other outstretched hand holding a flower. Brilliantly colored, it was an arresting tableau, all the more so because she recognized the cover of the catalogue raisonné that she had been perusing not so long ago.

In a smooth movement, Mila placed a nearby copy of *Le Figaro* atop the book, walked to the door, and, hand extended, said, "Thanks again," signaling that it was time for Alex to leave.

"Nosy *little bitch,*" she muttered after the outer door slammed shut.

#   #   #

Avenue Emile Zola, Paris

Now that Nathalie no longer worked for Jacques, Tarek saw her all the time. Every slender blond woman—and there were more than a few in Paris— conjured up the thought of Nathalie. When he was with Mila, he imagined that she was Nathalie. Mila said their sex had never been so good.

When he was not required to be at the château, Tarek would end his evenings at the café on Avenue Emile Zola, waiting for Nathalie to come home. Imagining what he would do once he found her in her apartment, he paid careful attention to avoid her surprising him the way she had the previous week. When she failed to appear, his sense of frustration and desire grew.

#   #   #

Rue d'Orchampt, Paris

Marie-Agnès, hunched over her laptop, had been working steadily since

286

early that morning. The translation, a lengthy contract, was intrinsically dull, so she erected a digital wall — no email, no surfing the web — until she reached a stopping point. At the end of the day, she attacked her inbox — a jumble of useless emails on self-improvement, fashion, travel, diet, news — and worked at filling up the trash bin. In her haste to clear some space, she almost overlooked a message from Claudia, Blondell's cousin.

Dear Mag, I sent this email to Blondell, but it bounced back to me, so I guess I don't have the right address. So I'm forwarding the message on to you, I hope you will receive it and share it with her. See below. Thanks and warm greetings, Claudia.

Dear Blondell, I'm helping Mom to sort through Dad's papers. There's a lot of junk that we've thrown out, but we came across two photos: one that looks like a drawing, the other is a painting. Mom says they look familiar, so perhaps they are the famous "missing" paintings she talks about. They were not among the works sold at the auction. Maybe Dad was only thinking about buying them? I guess this opens more doors than it closes, but for what it's worth, I've scanned the photos and am attaching them. I hope you'll be back for a longer visit soon. Love, Claudia

As she read Claudia's email and recalled the trip to the US, the familiar feeling of lack of money washed over her, like a tepid shower in winter. Not quite a shiver but a sense of discomfort.

Blondell had been generous—she had paid for the airplane tickets—but traveling with her had been a black hole for money. They had gone out, tried restaurants Blondell had read about, had chats over coffee or drinks. It was all so expensive, and Marie-Agnès couldn't let Blondell pay for everything. She turned back to her translation. Finishing it and getting paid trumped the mystery of the missing paintings, if there were any.

#   #   #

Like a dog with a bone, Merv didn't want to give up on Blondell. His worldview was simple: things were fair or unfair. And a wealthy woman's refusal to buy an expensive painting, meaning that he lost a juicy commission, was unfair. But he couldn't just call Blondell. He was, after all, her lawyer, and lawyers didn't pressure their clients, at least not outright. He was spared further contemplation of his dilemma when the phone rang.

"Merv, it's Blondell."

He smiled. "Blondell, nice to hear your voice." It was difficult, but he managed to sound detached.

"I have a question for you."

"Yes?" Perhaps she would ask about the painting.

"Your friend, Jacques Mornnais, what does he do besides be an art consultant?"

Not going in the right direction, he thought.

"I'm not sure. Why do you ask?"

"Oh, nothing. I was thinking about something else, and his face just popped into my mind." She gave a nervous laugh. "Really quite strange, don't you think?"

Not only did he think it strange, it was decidedly unhelpful. A hesitation, and then, pulled along by his overweening greed, he said, "And that beautiful Signac, are you thinking about that?"

"No, Merv," she sighed. "I thought I already told you. I'm no longer interested. But I might want to look at something a bit more modest. I'll let you know. You needn't worry." The door was firmly shut.

#   #   #

Place des Vosges, Paris

Blondell rummaged through the drawers of the extra-large refrigerator, looking for the right combination of frozen meals: appetizer, main course, dessert. Picard frozen food was one of her favorite things about France. Dinner organized, she opened a split of rosé champagne and took her glass into the room that she used as her office.

She examined the built-in wood bookcases, their shelves lined with rare first editions, the leather bindings giving off an aura of peace and solidity. A thought flitted through her head—*I ought to open these books one of these days*— but it did not stay for long. On a lower shelf, she found what she was looking for: two albums of photos taken at dinners she and John had attended in Paris, assembled by one of his firm's PAs.

Older men in tuxedos or in dark business suits. Much younger women, occasionally in long gowns, usually in cocktail dresses. Perfect hair, unbearably white teeth. When her glass was still half-full, she found what she had been looking for. They were seated at a round table, four couples and an austere-looking old man with an aquiline nose and piercing eyes. He was one of her husband's business associates. Farther back in the ballroom, another table: ten people, five men and five women. One couple was turned away partially from the camera, but there was something about the turn of his head and the perfect profile and white-blond hair of his companion. She was confident that she was looking at Jacques Mornnais and his wife.

So I did see him someplace else, she thought. She went into the kitchen to refill her glass. Then she remembered the aristocratic-looking old man. He had stopped by one evening for a drink before he and John went out to a meeting. Her husband had teased him that they both had towns named after their families. "Although yours, Richard, is of course much older."

"Yes," he had replied, "but much smaller and poorer."

"True," said her husband, "but you've got a coat of arms—why don't you show your visiting card to Blondell?"

Champagne in hand, Blondell rummaged through the desk, and by the time the glass was empty, she found the card with the Vesla de Trubenne coat of arms, in red, black, and gold, with its horse heads, arrows, and laurel wreath.

"Yesss," she said out loud: Richard Vesla de Trubenne. *It's too late to call him tonight, but I'll do it first thing in the morning.* The next day Blondell did not linger in bed, but showered, dressed, and had breakfast before nine a.m.

Chapter 82

Avenue Emile Zola, Paris

NATHALIE MARTIN RETURNED FROM HER three months in India early in the morning. Exhausted but surfing on a burst of energy, she had unpacked her suitcases and put the first load of laundry up to wash. Alex had left the keys atop a pile of mail on the table, slamming the door shut behind her. Once she had packed up her belongings, she had left for good. Other than a thin layer of dust—an inevitable consequence of Paris's polluted air—the apartment was in perfect condition. Not surprising, given the limited amount of time Alex had spent there.

The air felt light, the spring sun's rays warming the building's damp, cold walls. She went out to shop, stocking up on food to fill her empty refrigerator and kitchen shelves. After India, the market seemed so calm, almost empty, and so different from the piles of fruit and vegetables and the odor of spices that had been a part of her life these past months. By six p.m., she could no longer keep her eyes open and slept for fourteen hours straight. Over the next days, she managed to stay awake until eight p.m., and one night, when Tarek passed by to look for Alex, the apartment was dark.

He hated himself every time he sat in the café, staring at Nathalie Martin's building, waiting to see her come up the street. Once, he had managed to slip into the building behind an elderly couple and waited while they took the elevator. A list of tenants' names and apartment numbers hung on the wall; Nathalie Martin lived in apartment 3A. He climbed the stairs to the third floor and saw that apartment 3A faced the street. Now he knew exactly where she lived, and her absence only increased his sense of anger and frustration. Like a hamster on a running wheel, the thought circled endlessly in his mind, *Where is the bitch?* Another thought followed: *I'll teach her a lesson.*

By the end of the week, Nathalie's sleeping patterns had changed. Now, she was wide-awake at midnight, answering emails, checking Facebook, catching up with friends.

Jacques and Mila were in Paris that week. On Friday, Tarek took them home after dinner, and although it was after eleven, he could not resist returning to Avenue Emile Zola. He arrived just in time to see the café tables rolled inside and the chairs stacked one on the other. But his breath came in short spurts when saw the light on in Nathalie's apartment. He counted the floors. Yes, it was her apartment. She had returned. She'd been traveling, maybe out fucking? It didn't matter. She was back, and he wasn't going to let her get away again. But this was Paris, and there was no place to park, not even on the pedestrian crosswalks. He would have to come back another day, earlier, or he could always take the Métro.

Walter was puzzled. Tarek was on the lookout for someone, but whom? He had seen him enter the building at Number 133 bis, and he'd let himself in after Tarek had left and taken a photo of the list of tenants. The names meant nothing to him, but perhaps Eugene would be more inspired.

Chapter 83

Neuilly-sur-Seine

WHEN HE FIRST TOOK THE call, Richard's mind went blank. A woman was speaking to him in English, with an accent that he couldn't place. Her husband, a dinner, his coat of arms. Who was she and what was she talking about? Words tumbled one after the other along a sinuous path. He said yes at appropriate intervals, waiting for the fog to clear. As she started to run out of words, he remembered her: Blondell Royston, widow of his occasional business partner, John Royston. An American woman best described by the difficult-to-translate French word: *une originale*—perhaps not quite eccentric, but somehow a bit divergent from the norm, walking to the beat of a different drummer, one would have said decades earlier.

"Ah, yes, madame, of course I remember you. I trust you are well?"

The rush of words resumed. "It's something to do with my late husband's estate. There's a question I have, and I thought you might be able to help. Is there someplace we could meet, or would you like to come to my apartment on Place des Vosges? There is something I'd like to show you. I'm sure it would not take too long."

As she talked, Richard weighed his options. He could invite her to his apartment, but what if Alex or even Marie-Agnès stopped by? He'd have to explain how he knew Blondell and that would just lead to questions about things that were in the past, and he'd like to keep those doors closed. She said she wanted to show him something, so perhaps the privacy of her apartment would be a better idea.

They agreed he would stop by her apartment tomorrow afternoon.

#   #   #

Place des Vosges, Paris

Richard exited the Métro at the Saint-Paul station. Rue Saint-Antoine was, as usual, thronged with shoppers. He was early for the meeting with Blondell, so he took his time as he walked up rue de Turenne. The weather was mild. He bought a copy of *Le Monde* and read it while sitting on a bench in Place des Vosges.

At five minutes past the appointed hour, he got up, walked across the square, and pushed the buzzer marked *Royston*. Blondell, intuiting that in this instance less would be more, was dressed in black, *sans* bangles and rings, wearing a single wristwatch. A pot of green tea, the gentle clink of cups on saucers.

"Thank you so much for visiting me, Mr. de Trubenne. I am truly appreciative."

"It's my pleasure, madame. Your late husband and I worked on some projects together, and I am happy to help you, in any way I can."

Blondell, sitting next to Richard on the sofa, picked up the photo album on the coffee table in front of them. She opened it to a page with a yellow Post-it.

"I went to so many functions with my husband," she said. "I met so many people I can hardly remember them. And I'm sure that they don't remember me, either. Not worlds in collision, just worlds on parallel tracks, never meeting. Anyway, you know how there's always a photographer hovering about, taking pictures? So one of John's assistants collected them into albums. And I wanted to ask you about this photo."

Richard, neutral, uncertain where the conversation was going, said, "I think I remember that dinner. Can you see the logo GEPPAD? The Greater European Project for Peace and Development. It was a vehicle for investing in factories in Eastern Europe. Why do you ask?"

Blondell pointed a perfectly manicured red nail at a man with his face turned away from the camera. "I wonder if you know who that man is, and the woman sitting next to him."

"I'm sorry, but I don't think I can help you. There are so many people involved in these kinds of projects, and one never knows who most of them are. But I am curious, madame, as I said before, why do you ask?"

"To tell the truth, I don't know myself. But let me explain. Maybe this will make some sense to you. The lawyer handling my affairs here introduced me to an art consultant, someone to help me start a collection. For a while, I thought I'd like to do that. The name of the consultant is Jacques Mornnais. And I have the feeling that he is the man in the photo. Do you see the woman sitting next to him? I'm sure that that is his wife, Mila." Jacques, so careful of his image; Mila, not so camera-shy. "And it just struck me as curious to think that Mr. Mornnais was having business dealings with my late husband. It just all seems so...random."

Richard tried to approximate a thoughtful frown, looking pensive. "I'm afraid I've never heard of a Monsieur...did you say his name was Mornnais?"

Blondell gave a wan smile. "Well, it's not that important. I'm sorry I wasted your time on such a silly thing."

He stood up, now anxious to leave. He had recognized the couple in the photo, but at the time it had been taken, he ignored that the man was calling himself Jacques Mornnais. However, Richard was not ignorant of the role he had played in the project—one of the several intermediaries facilitating payment of the "transaction tax"—a euphemism for a bribe—to make sure the GEPPAD investment deal went through.

Chapter 84

Hotel on Avenue de Wagram, Paris

EUGENE HAD STUDIED THE NAMES Walter had sent him. There were only eleven apartments in the building at 133 bis Avenue Emile Zola, and he focused on the single women — Nathalie Martin on the third floor and Laetitia Spitzer on the fourth floor. On the ground floor, the concierge's lodge was now a studio, inhabited by Pierre Roule, a retired construction worker. Perhaps he'd be worth talking to.

A short time ago, Eugene had received a text message.

Tarek Abdelhamid, born 1972, Carthage, Tunis, Tunisia

Last known address: 21, rue de Crimée, Paris 19

Employment: driver for Artixia publishing house

Languages: French, Arabic, English

Multiple convictions in Tunisia for assault, accused of rape, but victim refused to testify

Charged with assault in France, given a suspended sentence

Suspected of raping prostitute, insufficient evidence

\#   \#   \#

A FORGERY IN PARIS

Place des Vosges, Paris

Blondell looked out the window at the rain, a steady stream of droplets, like a thin curtain hanging over the streets, the sky a grey dome. *I hate this weather, but if I don't get out of this apartment, I'm going to lose it.* She put on her leggings, her sports bra, her warm-up pants, and jacket and prepared to go out into the sad, dark day.

Before she left, she checked her email. Marie-Agnès had forwarded Claudia's message to her. Yes, the photos only raised more questions than they answered. Before she met Merv, she had never given much thought to paintings. To be sure, she enjoyed visiting museums, but she couldn't say that art was one of her passions. But now, what with Merv's nagging and her aunt's complaints, it had become a source of unease.

As she walked out the door, her phone rang. It was Merv's office, asking if she could stop by to sign some papers. "I'll have to call you back," she said, "I'm on my way to the gym."

She did two exercise classes, worked on the machines, and after three hours, she had managed to tamp down her anxious thoughts. But when she returned home and called Merv's office to make an appointment, the hard, round knot in her diaphragm returned.

When her phone rang, she was tempted not to answer, until she saw the caller ID—it was Mag. "Hello, Blondell, just calling to see how you're doing. We haven't spoken in a while."

Tears welled up. "Oh, I guess I'm okay."

"You don't sound okay. Why don't we meet for a drink?"

Two hours and two kirs later. Mag didn't say very much, she just listened to Blondell's litany of familiar complaints, punctuated by tears and sniffles.

"My life is so empty. The only worthwhile thing I do is teach English to immigrant kids twice a week."

"But I think that's wonderful. Helping others, not enough people do that. You should be proud of yourself."

"Do you really think so?"

"Oh, absolutely."

Despite the relentless rain, the day ended better than it had begun.

#   #   #

Merv Peters's office, Paris

The rain had stopped, an occasional shaft of sunlight escaping the thick layer of pale grey clouds. Blondell wanted to get the meeting with Merv over and done with. She had agreed to an early-morning appointment—ten a.m. was early for her—and now she hurried to arrive on time, having spent too much time in bed, staring at the ceiling.

Merv had returned a few minutes earlier from a breakfast meeting at La Belle Fermière. Jacques had stopped by the restaurant. "I was hoping you'd have some news for me," he had said in the quiet, almost menacing voice that always made Merv feel unsettled. Irritation joined uneasiness: Jacques seemed to have already forgotten the introduction to Renaud Schneider. A line of maybes marched through Merv's mind: *maybe Blondell will buy a cheaper painting. Maybe I can arrange a meeting with that guy Weller. But then I'm done.*

The receptionist showed Blondell into the conference room, where files from her affairs were stacked on the table. "The notaire sent over the documents that transferred ownership of the apartment on Place des Vosges," he said, "and I've prepared copies for you."

He leaned back to look at her and thought, not for the first time, *She is truly the queen of bling. It's a miracle no one has mugged her or at least grabbed that ugly expensive bag.* He had tried to talk to her once about the danger of attracting predators, but she had brushed him off. "Oh, I'm quite careful. You don't have to worry about me. But thanks anyway."

"I don't know if your lawyers in Washington have mentioned this to you, but I was wondering if you have a Will. Seeing as you've come into a great deal of money and property, this is something you ought to be thinking about."

"A Will." She took a sip of coffee. "Do you think you could ask your secretary to bring me another cup? This has gone cold."

"Of course." He reached over to the phone.

She continued, "A Will, no. I don't think so, but I guess I should have one, shouldn't I?"

"I could draw it up for you, but seeing as how your lawyers in the US have all the financial files, I think it would make more sense for them to do it."

For once he's not trying to squeeze money out of me. How refreshing

A fresh cup of coffee appeared. "Do you mind?" she asked as she lit one of her extra-thin cigarettes. "I see there's an ashtray on the table, so I guess I'm not your only client who smokes."

She stood up and walked over to the window. "This weather. I can't stand the rain and the constant grey. I don't know how you put up with it."

"I find that when I concentrate on my work and my projects, I don't really notice the weather. And Paris is one of the most beautiful cities in the world, rain or shine."

"Yes, of course. Well, I feel that I need to get away."

Merv watched as she paced the room, cigarette in hand, hoping that she would not drop ashes on his carpet. "You said I needed a Will. I think I'll go back to Washington for a few days and see my lawyers."

"That's a good idea, Blondell." And before he could stop himself, added, "When you return, perhaps you'd like to see my collection? I only show it to a very few people."

"Merv, are you hitting on me or what?" She smiled, stubbed out her cigarette.

He had the grace to look embarrassed. "I only thought you might see how much joy one can get from collecting beautiful things—it takes your mind off the weather, I assure you."

"Sure, why not." She gathered her coat and bag and left to make her plane reservations.

Chapter 85

Café Carré, Paris

BEFORE THEY STARTED TALKING, ALEX focused on spearing an olive. It was much easier when the olive was already pitted, but here, the toothpick kept sliding over the smooth pale green surface. It was as though the pit was pushing her fingers away. In fact, she didn't even care for these bistro olives. They were too salty for her taste—that was how bistros encouraged you to drink more. Trying to spear the olive gave her something to do with her hands. She didn't want to show how on edge she was to learn how his meeting with Merv had gone.

"All good," said Eugene. "Everything went according to plan. I'm in London right now and will let him know when my activities bring me back to Paris. Then I'll move on to meeting your friend Mr. Mornnais."

"My friend indeed." Alex wanted to laugh, but the chuckle froze in her throat and sounded more like a croak. "You can't imagine how happy I am to be out of that toxic atmosphere. I was so stressed, trying to remember who I was…" She let the sentence fade out, realizing that she'd never told Eugene about her stint as Nathalie Martin. Oh, well, what did that matter now?

He smiled, gold flecks lighting his brown eyes. "Trying to remember who you were? Was that some existential dilemma?"

"Not at all. It's a bit of a shaggy-dog story. And frankly, when I think back on it, I'm sorry I ever got involved. Of course, I'm glad if I've been of some help to you."

Eugene, still smiling, but perhaps a bit more tentative, said, "I'd love to hear your shaggy-dog story, Alex."

Too late to rewind, she realized that she'd have to dump the whole story in Eugene's lap. She was afraid he wouldn't be happy about that, but he asked.

"Well, the real reason I got involved with Jacques Mornnais was because of my friend Marie-Agnès. She's the one called Mag." As she told him about Marie-Agnès, he began to fill in some of the blank spaces in his mental file. She noticed that the flecks in his eyes had dulled, or was it her imagination, as she described the photos Marie-Agnès took of the paintings and the painters. There was no point in saying anything further about Li, she decided. It was really beside the point.

"So, in a fit of anger, I decided that I would take Jacques up on his offer of a job and just see what happened. In retrospect, that was not too clever, but anyway, that's what I did. And because I knew that these were dangerous people who could be violent, I felt that it would be best to hide my identity. It was quite easy, as Jacques never asked me for my name when I met him on the flight to Paris."

"You say you changed your identity. How'd you do that? I can hardly imagine you buying a fake passport at Barbès."

Alex smiled. She was getting to the part of the story that she enjoyed the most.

"It was really quite simple. I found a girl who was subletting her apartment for a few months, and I became her. I paid the phone bill for her landline even though I never used it. I paid the gas and electricity. I had her name and her address, and as Jacques paid me in cash, I never had to show an ID or provide bank information. He's slipped over the line of what's legal, and that worked to my advantage."

She paused and then continued, "But it's not easy being someone else. I had to be careful all the time not to slip up, and once we worked out the plan to introduce you to Merv Peters, I wanted to get out of there as fast as I could. After Tarek saw me near the atelier, I think they decided to get rid of me—hopefully not like Marie-Agnès. They are such unpleasant people, Jacques and Mila, and I felt more and more uncomfortable about Tarek. He would stare at me when he thought I wasn't looking, and to tell the truth, he frightened me."

"Fascinating. And what was your name?"

"Oh, the most banal French name you can imagine. Nathalie Martin."

Still no gold flecks, just two muddy-brown eyes stared at Alex. "Sorry, Alex," he said, "I need to make a phone call."

Alex, not understanding why Eugene suddenly looked so...grim—yes, that was the word—picked at an olive.

"Listen," she heard his voice, low and intense, "Nathalie Martin is the girl he's been watching for. But he thinks that Alex Thornhill is Nathalie Martin. It's a long story. Hold on a minute." Eugene looked at Alex. "Do you know if Nathalie Martin is back? I don't suppose you've spoken to her?"

"I think she was due back last week. I've meant to call, but you know, with one thing and another..."

Eugene returned to his call. "This girl, Nathalie Martin, sublet her apartment to Alex for a few months, but she may have returned last week, so you'd better get over there. I'll call you back in a little while.

"Alex," he said, "I do wish you had let me in on your decision to become someone else. You're playing a dangerous game, and while I don't think you did it intentionally, you've put an innocent woman in danger."

A warm red flush crept up her neck. "What do you mean, I've put someone in danger? And who are you to tell me what I should and shouldn't do? I think I've been quite helpful to you. And do you mind telling me who you're talking to about *my* business?"

He took a deep breath and said in a quiet voice, "Look, Alex, let's not argue, okay? Your friend Tarek, his name is Tarek Abdulhamid, by the way, and he's a violent petty criminal. He's been hanging around across the street from Nathalie Martin's apartment, and I think he's waiting for you. You frightened him away the other night, but I'm sure he'll be back."

"What do you mean, I frightened him away?" Alex hissed.

"Alex, we saw you yelling at him but at the time couldn't figure out why. Now it's a bit clearer."

"*We?* Just who is *we?* So, you've been following me. I can't believe it."

"No, in fact, following Tarek. You just happened to show up."

Alex had managed to spear an olive. She held up the shiny pale green orb, popped it into her mouth, chewed it slowly, sucking on the salty juice.

"You still haven't answered my question: who is *we?*"

"A man who works for me. His name wouldn't mean anything to you."

"And what do you *do*, Eugene? Please don't tell me you're here because of your sister's painting."

"I'm sorry, but that's the truth, Alex. But I'm also here on government business."

"I don't believe you. But never mind that. Can you at least tell me *why* I've put Nathalie in danger?"

"Because Tarek is stalking you. He thinks you are Nathalie Martin, right? He's been accused of raping several women, so that puts the real Nathalie Martin in a rather dangerous situation, wouldn't you say so?"

Alex was gripped by anger and fear. Anger at Eugene. Why didn't he share his information with her? She had told him how uneasy Tarek made her feel. But especially, anger at herself. How could she have thought that assuming someone's identity was without risk? A cold wave of fear crashed down on her anger: what would Tarek *do* when he discovered who the real Nathalie Martin was? She had to make things right.

Alex removed the olive pit from her mouth, gently placed it in the ashtray, and stood up.

"Well, if Tarek's looking for me, then it's best that he find *me*, isn't it?" And she walked out of the café. Eugene threw a twenty-Euro bill on the table, but by the time he was on the sidewalk, Alex had disappeared.

Chapter 86

Avenue Emile Zola, Paris

ALEX RAN INTO THE MÉTRO at Etoile. She sat on a bench on the platform of Line Six, found Nathalie Martin's phone number in her iPhone. Called her. After five rings, Nathalie picked up.

"Nathalie, hi, it's Alex. Your renter. I guess you're back. I just wanted to be sure everything is in order. And how was your trip?" she added.

"Oh, Alex, hi. Yes, my trip was great. I'm just about over my jet lag. Did you enjoy your stay chez moi?"

"Yes, it was wonderful. I was wondering if I could stop by tonight. I had wanted to leave something for you, but in the rush to move out, I forgot. I won't stay long."

"Oh, how sweet. I'm out now, but I'll be back around eight. Is that good for you?"

"Perfect. See you then."

It was rush hour, and every two minutes a train came through the station. As Alex watched the clumsy ballet of voyagers exiting and entering the cars, she wiped her sweaty palms on her jeans. *When was the last time I felt like this?* She couldn't remember. Fear was not an emotion she encountered very often. *What if,* she thought, *what if Tarek already found Nathalie? What if he was there right now? Wait, Nathalie said she was out, be back at eight. He doesn't know what she looks like, does he? It's me that he's looking for. I'd better get there early, just in case. Just in case what? I run into Tarek? Oh, fuck.*

No sound reached her ears. Not the noise of the trains, one following the other, not the teenagers' shrieks, not the passengers' hurried conversations. Alex heard nothing but the beating of her heart and the air whistling through her nostrils.

She wiped her palms on her jeans again. Nausea rippled up from her stomach, tensing her throat. *Am I going to vomit right here in the Métro? Stand up and take a deep breath.* Legs quaking, she went over to a vending machine, bought a can of soda to settle her stomach, and sat down to drink it. *Get a hold of yourself, Alexia.* Another wave of anxiety, but smaller this time. *Cut this shit out,* she whispered to herself. *No one's looking at me. People in the Métro talk to themselves all the time.* She cracked a timid smile. *I can handle whatever comes my way.*

Alex relaxed for a moment, remembered seeing someone selling flowers at the entrance to the Métro. Of course, she ought to have thought about a more original gift for Nathalie, but that would have to do for now. She took the escalator up to the surface, bought the biggest bouquet on sale, more substantial than beautiful, took the escalator back down, looking at the faces around her, thinking *if they only knew.*

Surrounded by the stale smell of metal, dirt, and body odors, she stood in the crowded Métro car, clutching the bouquet to her chest, examining her different emotions, trying to figure out her next steps. *I feel guilty if I've endangered Nathalie, I feel afraid of what Tarek might do, and I feel guilty as well that I've disappointed Eugene. I need to make it all right.* Her thoughts looped around in her mind as she exited the Métro at Charles Michels and walked up Avenue Emile Zola.

When she entered the apartment, it was clear that Nathalie had been to India. Sticks of incense gave off a pungent aroma, she had draped brightly embroidered cloths over the sofa and chairs, and a print of the four-armed Vishnu hung on the living room wall. Kiss-kiss between two women who had met on one occasion, flowers presented, many thanks as Nathalie put them into a large glass vase that she placed on the coffee table, loaded with books on India.

Alex, worried that Tarek could show up at any time, stretched out her arms and put her hands on Nathalie's shoulders. "Look, Nathalie, there's this man from work who's obsessed with me, and I'm afraid he's stalking me, and he may be coming here. So you need to be careful. I will stay here for a while…"

"Someone that you work with is stalking you?"

"I don't exactly work with him. He's my employers' driver. Actually, I don't work for them anymore. But that may not matter."

"But are you sure? I mean, has anything *happened*?"

"Not yet, but I ran into him in the café across the street just before I moved out. And I'm worried that he may be coming back."

"So nothing has happened yet?"

"No, but…" Alex was preparing to tell Nathalie how she'd assumed her identity, when Nathalie interrupted.

"No negativity, Alex. Here, join me for a short meditation." She sat crossed-legged on the floor, closed her eyes, and took deep, slow breaths.

"Ummm, I'm afraid that's not for me. Anyway, I'm much too stiff to sit like that," mumbled Alex. "I can see you've brought your Indian experience back to Paris. Okay, I'll give it a try." She sat on the sofa, too nervous to keep her eyes closed for more than a few seconds, and tried to slow her breathing, following Nathalie's rhythm.

Alex heard the elevator door open and clank shut. Then silence, followed by the creaking of footsteps on the wooden hallway floor. The doorbell rang.

Nathalie opened her eyes as Alex tiptoed to the door, looked through the peephole. "Yes," she said, "who is it?" at the same time seeing Eugene and a man in a blue anorak.

"Alex, is that you?" asked Eugene. "Please open up."

Nathalie grabbed Alex by the arm and whispered, "Who is it? Is it that man?"

"No, it's okay, it's my um, partner, we're working on a project."

"How nice to see you here, Alex." Eugene smiled.

"Yes, of course," she replied, trying to affect an air of calm that she did not feel. Before Eugene could say anything further, she continued, "Nathalie, I didn't get a chance to finish. The stalker, he thinks my name is Nathalie Martin. It's a long story."

"Yes," Eugene jumped in. "So it's important not to open your door to anyone who you don't know. You had best be careful until we're able to deal with him. He thinks Alex is Nathalie Martin. He won't bother you on the street. He doesn't know who you are."

At first, Nathalie was confused, speechless. Was it lingering jet lag? A remnant of the Zen bubble that had popped when Eugene knocked on the door? *There's a man who thinks that Alex is Nathalie Martin. That she's me. This didn't just happen on its own.* Nathalie looked at Alex, saw the strong, chiseled profile, remembered now how self-confident Alex had been when they'd negotiated the rental of her apartment . *"I'll go to the post office and pay the utility bills, and forward your mail." She'd planned it all from the very beginning.*

Nathalie glared at Alex. More clarity now. She made a last effort to control her breathing before anger took over.

"You bitch," she said. "I sublet my apartment, you come in with your fucking snob vibration, and you steal my identity. Not cool at all."

Taken aback, Alex started to speak, "Nathalie, I am truly sorry. I didn't think this could cause you pain."

Nathalie's voice rose. "What's going to happen? I mean, who is this man? Why do I have to be careful when I haven't done anything wrong? You need to tell him that you're *you* and not *me.*"

"That's why I came here. To tell him when he shows up."

"When he shows up? You mean, he's coming here? How could you do this?"

Eugene cut in. "Look, what's done is done, no point in further discussion."

All this time, Walter Helmann walked around the living room, poked around the kitchen and the bedroom. He spoke for the first time. "It's good that you have no balconies, but keep your windows shut anyway." He turned to Nathalie. "I"ll be in the café across the street trying to keep an eye out for our friend." Looking now at Eugene, he said, "Let's get going." And they were gone.

306

#   #   #

Jacques had given Tarek the rest of the day off. He appreciated the man's many skills, but sometimes he found his presence oppressive. He preferred it when Tarek was either driving or running errands.

Tarek had met a girl in a club in the nineteenth arrondissement, where he lived. Not much to look at, but a lot less demanding in bed than Mila. But neither the girl nor Mila could take his mind off Nathalie Martin. The cup of coffee before him on the table grew cold. The curtain behind the third-floor window moved slightly, and he tried to see if he could glimpse her. No luck.

He saw the same elderly couple as before, coming home from shopping. He crossed the street and followed them into the building, let them enter the elevator. A whiff of damp, cold air irritated his nostrils. The basement door was ajar. Someone had been down there and had forgotten to close it. Never one to miss an opportunity, Tarek switched on the light and walked down the stairway. Perhaps the same person had forgotten to lock their storage room? He methodically examined each room, looking through the slatted wooden doors. The occupant of number eight was using his storage room as a *cave à vin*. There must have been as many as one hundred bottles of wine neatly lined up. Maybe he'd come back and take a closer look. The padlock on the door would pose no problem. And there would be no need to bother Jacques. He and a friend could handle this by themselves…

Tarek didn't hear Eugene and Walter as they exited the building and settled themselves across the street, hoping that Tarek would appear sooner rather than later.

Nathalie, feeling drained by the evening's events, had changed into a bathrobe. She wished that Alex would take the hint and leave; otherwise she'd have to tell her that she needed some time alone. She was too tired even to feel pissed or nervous. She just wanted to curl up in bed and go to sleep.

When the doorbell rang, Alex thought it must be Eugene, telling them that they had apprehended Tarek. "Back already?" she said as she opened the door.

Chapter 87

Place des Vosges, Paris

SANTA CLAUS IS COMIN TO town. Christmas was long gone, but Blondell couldn't get the jingle out of her head as she thought about disposing of her fortune. Sisters, nieces, nephews, cousins: who was naughty, who was nice? Made her list. Checked it twice.

In the background, CNN International, her default auditory environment. Talking heads yammering about the eruption of a volcano in Iceland, spewing ash across Europe's skies. Blondell didn't care. She found the noise soothing.

Chapter 88

Avenue Emile Zola

TAREK SHOVED HIS WAY INTO the room, slamming the door shut and locking it. Looked at Alex, then at Nathalie in her bathrobe. It didn't compute. Then it did. Nathalie was gay. That was why she ignored him.

"Tarek, you need to leave right now," Alex said.

"What, you're not going to invite me to your little party? I could liven things up for you girls."

Alex edged toward the window. She hoped Eugene or the man in the blue anorak would look upward. "Get out, Tarek. You're not welcome here," this time raising her voice. "If you don't leave, I'm going to call the police." *Where is my phone? Oh, shit, it's in my bag. Nathalie, do something!*

While Tarek was looking at Alex, Nathalie edged toward the door. *"Au secours,"* the cry stuck in her throat as Tarek grabbed her and slammed her against the door, his hand around her neck. "Don't get any ideas," he snarled. "I said we're going to have a party." As she struggled to free herself, he slapped her face, and she crumpled to the floor.

Alex was at the window when Tarek grabbed her and threw her on the musty carpet. She had been grasping at the curtain, trying to open it, and

309

it came tumbling down along with the curtain rod. He pulled a knife from his pocket and held it to her throat. "Stay still. You're going to enjoy this, much better than what you get from your girlfriend here." Tears welled up in Alex's eyes as she looked at the ceiling trying to figure out how to get out from under Tarek's body, heavy with the smell of sweat. He put the knife down, just beyond Alex's reach, as one hand gripped the base of her neck, the other working on pulling down her jeans.

"You fucker," Alex screamed, her arms flailing. Fear. Again, the fear, this time more intense. Sweat poured off her scalp. Her heart beat so rapidly she thought her chest would explode. Tarek tightened his grip around her. *He's going to choke me to death.*

Nathalie slowly sat up, leaning against the wall, her head aching, her vision coming back into focus, her face already red and swollen. She saw that Alex's jeans were around her knees, Tarek grabbing at her underwear. On all fours, she crawled to the coffee table and managed to stand. Picked up the vase of flowers and tried to bring it down on Tarek's skull. It grazed the side of his head, the full force landing on his shoulder. He grunted as he rolled off Alex. Nathalie couldn't grab the vase, but she managed to push the flowers into his face. He struggled to wipe his face free, his shoulder aching from the blow.

"You bitch," he screamed, "I'll fix you both." Alex had grabbed the knife, and without hesitation, she plunged it into his back, ripping through the thick fabric of his jacket. He turned as a small red spot stained his jacket, bellowing as his arms reached out to Alex. She jumped back, and, seizing the curtain, threw it over his head.

"Quick, help me," she screamed at Nathalie. As Tarek struggled, they managed to wrap the curtain around his arms, the knife clattering to the floor.

A loud knock on the door. "Quick, see who it is."

Nathalie jumped up, looked through the peephole, saw the two men from earlier, and opened the door.

"What the fuck!" exclaimed Eugene. Tarek, lying still now. "What the hell happened?"

"The fucker came to rape me," exclaimed Alex.

"Well, you seem to have defended yourself."

310

"No thanks to you. It was Nathalie who knocked him on the head."

Eugene nudged Tarek with his foot. He groaned but did not move. Walter unwound the curtain and saw the blood escaping from the wound in his back.

"How did this happen?"

Alex managed a tight smile. "Oh, he threatened me, but it looks like things didn't work out the way he intended, the fucker. Yes, I managed to stick that knife in his back, and I'd like to do it again."

Walter had picked up the knife. He cut Tarek's jacket and shirt away, made strips from the curtain, and bound the wound. "We need to get him to a hospital."

"Let's drop him on the street in Saint-Denis. They'll call the police, just another settling of accounts. He won't say anything," said Eugene.

Alex looked over at Nathalie. The woman was sitting on the sofa, arms curled around her chest, rocking slowly back and forth. "Nathalie, if you want, I'll help you clean up, stay here tonight," offered Alex.

Nathalie, fingering her swollen cheek, sighed. "I guess, why not."

"I'm so sorry about this. I'll try to make it up to you somehow." But for now, she needed to do something about the tremors in her legs. She sat down heavily in the easy chair, waiting for the tingling to cease and for her breathing to return to normal.

The two men hoisted Tarek up, pulled him into the elevator. The building was quiet as they dragged him out to the street, into Walter's car. He removed the license plates, pulled two other plates out of the trunk, and affixed them to the car. They drove to Saint-Denis, found a quiet street with no CCTV cameras, and rolled Tarek out of the car and onto the sidewalk.

The following day, Tarek called Jacques from the hospital, said he'd gotten into a bar fight, would be back to work in a day or two. When he returned to his apartment, he found a note on the table. *Stay away from her. Next time you won't be as lucky.*

Chapter 89

ALEX RETURNED TO RICHARD'S APARTMENT the following day. She had hardly slept at all. Images of Tarek, thoughts of what-if passed in an unending loop. What if he had managed to rape her and Nathalie? What if he had beaten them to death? What if the knife wound had proved fatal? What if Eugene and Walter had not come in time? What if the police had come to investigate?

Her mind out of control, she tried taking slow, deep breaths. That didn't help much. *Shit, I should have been practicing meditation all these years.* Now images of Eugene occupied the loop. Alex remembered his reaction when she told him about posing as Nathalie Martin. She replayed her outburst, saying she'd like to stick the knife in Tarek's back again. She hoped Eugene did not think too badly about her, and then she felt troubled that she even cared what Eugene thought.

#   #   #

Blondell had returned a few days ago from her trip to the US. Her Will was taken care of, although she was sure that it would go through many changes over the years to come. But for now, all was in order.

At this moment, she was following Merv up the stairway in his penthouse. Worn down by his insistence, she had agreed to visit his collection. Merv made such a big deal about it, she was curious to see it. He unlocked the door and she cringed inwardly as he took her elbow and ushered her into the room.

Paintings and drawings covered two of the walls. Still empty was the wall space surrounding the door and part of a third wall. The works seemed to be arranged in a vaguely chronological order, starting with representational pastorals and still lifes and moving to Impressionist and then abstract styles.

She stared at the paintings, took a step back, then forward. Blondell found it challenging to take it all in. The array of works reminded her of the enormous Club Med buffets, so much beautifully presented food, so many different dishes, all crammed together. Here, dead birds and fruit, there, black and white squares with touches of red.

"Well, what do you think?" She could hear the excitement in his voice and saw the look of pride on his face.

"It's…overwhelming. Do you love them all equally, the way parents are supposed to do?"

"It depends on my mood. Some days I feel like I need something abstract, a little crazy, to pick me up. Other days, I'm happy to contemplate trees and rivers." Then Merv pushed a little. "You could do the same thing, only better, if you wanted to."

The charmed moment passed. The small bubble of possibility had expanded briefly and then burst. "Yes, if I wanted to," she replied.

Merv led the way out, Blondell teetering on her stilettos as she negotiated the spiral staircase. "Thanks, Merv, for sharing your jewels with me." She extended a gloved hand and started to pivot on her heels.

"Shall I call you a cab?" he asked.

"No, thanks, that's okay, I think I'll walk a bit."

Something was off, not quite right. The familiar feeling of being anxious for no reason hovered over her. Her pace slowed, as she realized that her shoes were not made for walking more than a few feet, at least not on pavement. They were more for sitting with legs crossed, flashing an expanse of thigh. A small ache started in the arch of each foot, moved to the heel, through the ankle, and up her calf. At Avenue Foch, she hailed a cab, removed her shoes as soon as she was seated. When she arrived at her building, she didn't bother to put her shoes back on but walked into the building in her stocking feet.

France had been late to accept the need for schoolchildren to learn English, but pragmatism had, at last, prevailed over pride, and so it was that every Wednesday and Friday afternoon, Blondell went to a community center near the Place de Stalingrad, where she tutored children in English. She understood so well how difficult it could be to learn another language, and she had unlimited resources of patience. No one here made her feel uncomfortable or inadequate, and it was always the most enjoyable part of her day. She changed into comfortable, unfashionable clothing and snuggled her aching feet into her Uggs.

#   #   #

When Blondell returned home in the early evening, as always, she felt lighter, her anxiety gone. She made herself a kir and sat down to clean out her inbox. Rereading Claudia's email that Marie-Agnès had forwarded, she remembered that she had downloaded the attachments. When she looked at them again on her desktop, she could feel her heart thumping, her mouth dry, her breath short. She knew where the feeling of something not being right had come from.

She thought back to her childhood visits to her aunt and uncle. Sometimes Aunt Milissa would ask her to bring a plate of cookies to her uncle when he was doing paperwork in his office. She remembered placing the butterscotch cookies on his desk and looking up at the painting that hung on the wall behind him. As a child, it frightened her, a broken doll that had not been put back together correctly. Her uncle had smiled. "Why are you frowning, blondie? Don't you like that painting?"

"No, it's a little scary."

He laughed. "Maybe that's because cubism is more for grown-ups than for kids. Don't worry, you'll get to like it when you're older."

She recalled the small painting by Picasso that Merv had pointed out to her. "It's an excellent example of his work, if I may say so," he preened.

Blondell was now a grown-up. She loved the paintings from Picasso's blue period, but she still didn't much care for his discombobulated images, eyes and breasts and arms all rearranged. She didn't understand why someone with so much talent could create such monstrosities. But as she looked at the photo Claudia had sent, it reminded her of the painting in her uncle's office, and she thought it also looked a lot like Merv's Picasso. But was it the same one?

She rummaged in the refrigerator and found the remains of a veal roast, heated up some frozen vegetables, took out a partly finished container of raspberry sorbet. Ate dinner at her desk, looking at the photo. As she stuck her spoon into the softened sorbet, she called Merv, left a message asking if she could see his collection again. The visit had inspired her.

He called back the next morning. His collection was his secret garden, but if he could help her to experience the same joy, he'd make an exception.

\#   \#   \#

This time she wore jeans and a blazer, comfortable flats. The climb up the spiral stairway was much easier. Looking at the paintings, she fingered the bangles on her wrist. "Oh, Merv, I think one of my bangles dropped when we were walking up here. Do you mind having a look?"

"No problem, Blondell."

He began to descend the stairway, giving her enough time to take out her cell phone and photograph the Picasso. Merv returned. "No luck, I'm afraid. Are you sure you lost it here?"

"Oh, never mind, maybe I'm mistaken. Tell me, did Jacques Mornnais help you to purchase all of these paintings?"

"Yes, he did. Can you imagine what he could do for you?"

"That's what I'm trying to do," she answered.

\#   \#   \#

Blondell went to a print shop, had them print out the photo from Claudia and the one she had taken at Merv's. Placed side by side, if there was a difference, she couldn't see it.

She called Merv's office and made an appointment to see him. *What now* he thought. Blondell was beginning to get on his nerves. Her hair, her bling, her voice, they combined to put him on edge. He hoped she was coming to ask him about Jacques Mornnais. If not, he wasn't going to waste any more time with her.

Merv's receptionist showed Blondell into his office. She was wearing a faux leopard coat and matching hat, her hair spilling out over her shoulders, caramel-colored Uggs on her feet. "Thanks for seeing me," she said. "I know how busy you are, but I have something important to tell you."

At last, he thought. She's finally coming round.

"Your Picasso struck a chord," she started to say.

"Yes," he interrupted her, "it's one of my favorites."

"Is it?" she asked. "Funny, my uncle—he was a collector like you—my uncle shared your view. On the other hand, his wife—my aunt—and I really can't stand the way he decomposes bodies. A question of taste, I guess."

A prickly feeling in his gut, Merv sensed that this conversation was not going as anticipated. "Oh, I thought you rather liked that painting."

"I was attracted to it. But not for the reason you think. Have a look at these." She opened her purse and placed the two photos on his desk. "They look alike, don't they? One is yours, and one is from my uncle's home, and that painting disappeared after he died. No one knows what happened to it. A mystery. Now, I'm not saying that you have his painting. I don't know when you bought it. And perhaps my uncle's was a copy, or perhaps yours is a copy. Again, a total mystery, wouldn't you say?"

Merv's cheeks were pink, but he said in a calm voice, "Now, Blondell, I hope you're not suggesting that I have a stolen painting in my possession. I can assure you that every work I buy comes accompanied by an impeccable provenance. I cannot speak to your uncle's painting. All you have is a photo — perhaps it is indeed a copy, or perhaps it is a very similar painting. You may not know it, but Picasso did many."

"Yes, that's just it. I wonder what the provenance of your painting is. You see, I remember seeing that painting on the wall in my uncle's office when I was a child, so he possessed it long before you did. So I'm wondering about the chain of ownership."

"I'm sorry, Blondell, but I do think you've pushed the envelope a bit too far here. I've been very kind to you, tried to be a friend to you. And you reward me by sneaking a photo of my painting—a lost bangle, did you say? And then practically accusing me of having stolen your uncle's painting. Your uncle had a similar painting or a copy of mine, I don't know. And neither do you. So be careful about what you say. I will not have you call my honesty into question. And I think under the circumstances that you may want to shop around for another lawyer."

Merv stood up. "And now, if you don't mind, I have work to do." Before he could stop, he added, "Some of us have to work for a living."

Blondell rose from her seat. "When I walked into this office, I was unsure. But I am no longer. I'll leave these with you," pointing to the two photos. "You and your art consultant may want to think about this situation." She closed the door quietly as she left. There was no need to slam it. She'd made her point.

Merv waited five minutes until his heart stopped thumping, until he felt that his voice had returned to normal. He called Jacques and asked if they could meet tomorrow morning at La Belle Fermière.

#   #   #

La Belle Fermière, Paris

The eggs were, as always, done to perfection, but Merv played with his food, rather than eating it. He had no appetite since his meeting with Blondell yesterday. Jacques arrived in a taxi, forced by Tarek's absence to forego his usual chauffeured ride.

A glass of mango juice in hand, he smiled his bland, lips-only smile. "You wanted us to meet, so here I am."

Merv pushed his plate to one side. He'd given up on the eggs altogether. "Do you remember that small Picasso I bought from that Swiss trust last year? Well, that bitch, Blondell, came to my office yesterday insinuating that it had been stolen from her uncle. Can you believe that?"

He related their conversation. "Then, she asked about the provenance, but I didn't get involved, didn't think it was any of her business. I checked my file. It belonged to a trust for some guy in Switzerland. That's right, isn't it?"

"You need not worry, my friend. Your tableau was certified as an original Picasso, and the chain of ownership is clear and definitive. I wouldn't pay any attention to that woman's ramblings. I remember thinking that she was a bit, shall we say, fragile, when I met her."

"Yes, but…" Merv was still not completely reassured. "What if she goes around spreading these nasty untruths? You never know what's going to come out of her mouth. I mean, I'm her lawyer, for Chrissake. How does that make me look?"

"Would you like me to call her, set things straight?" he asked.

"Do you think you can? My reputation is at stake here." He didn't need to mention that it was Jacques who had arranged the sale of the painting.

"Don't worry. I'll take care of it. I'm sure she'll understand. Can you remind me of her phone number and address?"

Merv's appetite returned. It was a pity that the eggs were stone cold. He signaled the waiter and placed another order

Chapter 90

MARIE-AGNÈS WAS ENJOYING A stroll along the Coulée Verte, a walkway built atop an abandoned elevated railway line. People were always criticizing the government, but this promenade, thick with plants and shrubs and bright yellow forsythia, was a successful venture. And where but in Paris, she wondered, could you find a police station with copies of a Michelangelo sculpture on the roof overlooking the walkway? Birds chirped, water glistened in little ponds, the air was fresh, and she felt complete and at peace.

Her cell phone rang, breaking the spell. She saw Blondell's name on the caller ID, hesitated for a moment, and then answered. Blondell, despite her wealth—or perhaps because of it—seemed so lonely, so isolated. If only she had had to plunge into life, sharpen her elbows and earn her living, she might have been happier. So thought Marie-Agnès as she said, "Blondell, hello, how are you?"

"Oh, Marie-Agnès, okay, I guess." Her voice said she was something less than okay.

"Are you sure?" asked Marie-Agnès. "Is something wrong?"

"Well, it's about Claudia's email, you know, with the photos? But I don't want to talk about it on the phone. Do you think we could meet for a coffee? Or perhaps you'd like to come over to my place?"

"Sure, how about Friday, can it wait until then?"

"Yeah, I teach that afternoon but come over for dinner. We can order sushi if you like."

"I'd love that, Blondell. See you on Friday then."

#   #   #

Neuilly-sur-Seine

Alex and Richard were seated at the dining room table, poring over his collection of old photos and maps. "This is your family, Alexia," he said, fingering the photos, some yellowed with age, as he attached names to faces. "We should renovate the old château—I know Charlotte is happy there, but the whole house needs redoing—build a proper winery, bring in an expert to upgrade the vineyard." Richard's cheeks were pink with excitement.

Alex, too, was excited. The reason she had come to France in the first place was to reconnect with Richard and to explore her roots.

"This is wonderful, Uncle Richard. Maybe we should plan a trip to Trubenne, visit with Charlotte." She continued, "I'm so glad to be done with Jacques Mornnais. It was such a distraction. I wanted to help Marie-Agnès but all I did was waste my time with some very unpleasant people. At least we got some money for his housekeeper. I need to talk to her about where to send the funds."

It was a short leap from Jacques Mornnais to Eugene Spector—an attractive man, when garlic free. She wondered if he had told Merv when he would be available to meet Jacques. As far as she was concerned, that was the last piece to put in place in this sorry puzzle. Or was this also an excuse to see Eugene again? She felt that she wanted to explain further why she'd stolen Nathalie's identity—it had been for a good cause.

She called him, said she would be leaving Paris shortly and perhaps they could meet to touch base one last time?

"Sure, Alex, why not?" He sounded subdued, noncommittal. "Friday afternoon? I plan on seeing Mornnais next week."

#   #   #

Rue de Turenne, Paris

Antoine Tipette spent his days as a management consultant and his nights clubbing, fueled by appropriate quantities of booze and drugs. He had returned home a day early from a business trip. That evening he celebrated a successful closing and slept in until midafternoon, when a whining sound, like a creaky gate, pierced his consciousness and woke him up. It was his dog, Ollie Blue, reminding Antoine that he was long overdue to be taken out to do his business. A management decision was made. It would be better to take Ollie Blue out for a walk than for him to get into the habit of making a mess in the kitchen. He dressed quickly and raced down the stairs, the dog pulling on his leash. They walked up rue de Turenne, Ollie Blue stopping to spray lampposts and the tires of an illegally parked car. As he deposited a pile of turds, Antoine reached into his jacket pocket for a plastic bag. "Oh, shit," he muttered. He had forgotten to replenish his supply of poop bags. Well, just this once, no great harm done. It had started to rain, and he was anxious to return to the warm comfort of his bed and go back to sleeping off the previous night.

#   #   #

Blondell left her apartment in the afternoon, a little earlier than usual. There was a Métro strike, nothing unusual in Paris, but always inconvenient. She mused on how Parisians, forever down at the mouth and complaining about something, nevertheless put up with endless labor stoppages, blocked streets and highways, turmoil at airports. *I have to be like them and just suck it up and get on with it.* She was wearing her teaching uniform: a loose mini-dress, leggings, boots, and her fake leopard coat and hat.

A steady stream of rain was falling as she walked along rue de Turenne, her thoughts focused on how long she would need to wait for a train. Usually, the strikers intensified their stoppage when people needed the Métro the most — going to work and coming home. The wind picked up, and she held on to her umbrella more tightly, lowered her head to avoid the rain blowing into her face.

A scooter rumbled up the deserted street from behind her. The sidewalk was empty of people as the motorbike slowed slightly. The rider on the back seat reached out and grabbed her Murakami bag. At the same time a gust of wind lifted the umbrella, and as she struggled to regain her balance, the soles of her boots slid over some dog shit that the rain had melted, her legs slipping out from under her. She fell backward, her head slamming the pavement.

The motorbike accelerated, turned left onto rue Saint-Antoine, and headed back to the nearby suburb of Saint-Denis. It was a profitable haul. A purse for a girlfriend, a fancy cell phone, a wallet with cash and credit cards, a checkbook, and house keys.

Blondell lay motionless on the sidewalk, the rain soaking her inert body, her arm at a strange angle. Minutes later, a passerby called the fire department. They came quickly and took her to the hospital.

#   #   #

Place des Vosges, Paris

Marie-Agnès arrived at Blondell's a few minutes past eight p.m. Rang the bell, no answer. Perhaps she had been held up by the Métro strike. Tried her cell phone, but the call went to voicemail. She walked outside the building, thinking to wait for Blondell to return. She tried calling again, still no answer. Could Blondell have forgotten their dinner? Doubtful, as it was she who had invited Marie-Agnès over. By ten p.m., she called Alex, but she was on voicemail as well, and Marie-Agnès decided to call the police and report Blondell missing.

Chapter 91

THE NEXT MORNING, STILL NO sign of Blondell. Marie-Agnès, Alex, and Richard were sitting in his living room, drinking coffee, talking about Blondell's disappearance.

"The last time we spoke, she sounded off, like she was definitely not okay. It had to do with an email we received from her cousin Claudia. Something about her uncle's missing paintings."

"Did she say anything else?" asked Alex.

"No, she said she'd explain when we met for dinner. Something bad has happened, I just know it," said Marie-Agnès.

"I think so, too," agreed Alex.

Tears welled up in Marie-Agnès's eyes. "I mean, what can she have been up to? I called the association where she gave classes, and they said she never turned up. I just don't get it. I'm very worried."

"Yes, there is a reason to be concerned," added Richard. He had not told Alex about his meeting with Blondell, no need to further complicate matters, but Blondell's going missing worried him, too. He didn't know anything about her uncle's paintings, but Blondell had been interested in Jacques Mornnais.

"I should call that creepy lawyer, Merv. What do you think?" asked

Marie-Agnès as she blew her nose.

"Yes, why not," replied Alex. "It can't hurt, and maybe he can find out more than we can."

Marie-Agnès fished around in her bag and found the cell phone she used to talk with Merv, called him, and left a message for him to call her back. She returned to her apartment, as she had translations to complete, and Alex readied herself for her meeting with Eugene. As she applied her mascara, she wondered whether he could help them to find Blondell. Richard leaned back, closed his eyes, and took a catnap.

#   #   #

Merv felt nauseous, his mouth dry, his breath shallow.

He had been in a meeting when Mag called, and then off to a delightful seafood lunch. But after he called Mag back, the meal seemed to be moving up rather than down his digestive tract. Blondell had gone missing. He remembered Jacques' words, *Don't worry, I'll take care of it.* What did that mean? Could Jacques be involved in her disappearance? And where did that leave him?

Perhaps he ought to get rid of the Picasso, put it away someplace safe. But was that necessary? After all, he had a perfectly good provenance— or did he? Doubts—buried under layers of denial and willful ignorance— surfaced. His paintings came from trusts or unnamed private collectors. In other words, he had no idea who had owned them. Of course, Jacques had explained that the owners did not want the sales to be public knowledge, hence the discounted price. And yet.

He came face-to-face with the chilling reality that he had no control over the situation. It was time to try to minimize his losses. After his secretary had left for the day, he put his provenance documents in an envelope addressed to his sister, who had remained in Fresh Meadows. The following morning, he went to the DHL office on Avenue d'Iéna and sent the package to his sister, with a note to keep the envelope in a safe place.

As for Blondell, he was conflicted. On the one hand, daring to hope that she had vanished for good, and on the other, wondering how he could feel that way. It was too late now, but how he wished she had never been his client.

#　　#　　#

Alex had a light lunch. She was nervous about meeting Eugene—what did he think about the way she had acted—then was annoyed once again for caring what he thought at all. She chose clothes she was comfortable in: black jeans, a red turtleneck sweater, black leather jacket, her Prada bowler bag. The images of the time she had spent with Blondell—at Jacques' château and then in the train—crossed her mind repeatedly although they had only met those two times. Alex had had the impression that, under Blondell's irritating persona, there lurked an unhappy woman. Parisians could be so cruel sometimes, and it had been Blondell's misfortune to encounter more than her fair share of petty, mean-spirited specimens.

Like two old friends, Alex and Eugene exchanged air kisses. Sencha green tea for her, a Heineken for him.

"How are you? Have you recovered from the other night?" he asked.

She stirred her tea, eyes cast downward, looking for the right words.

"I'd like to say that I have, but in fact, I'm not so sure. I think I've handled things pretty badly. You were right, I should never have pretended to be Nathalie. I was just thinking about myself. But I never thought that I was putting her in harm's way.

"Perhaps I have helped Ella—thanks to you—but I never did get to find proof that Bruno and Jacques were behind the attack on Marie-Agnès. And then there's that asshole Tarek. The events at Nathalie's keep running through my mind, like the television news coverage of a disaster. The same images, over and over again. I keep thinking what if, what if you and your man hadn't shown up, what if he had raped us both, or even worse? And what if I had stuck the knife in a more lethal place? What if I had killed him? What's worst of all, I'm afraid I haven't seen the end of him."

Another long silence, only partly filled by the café's background noise. Little smile lines formed around Eugene's golden-brown eyes as he said in a soft voice, "Don't be too hard on yourself, Alex. I know you were doing what you thought was right, trying to help your friend. And you have gotten me closer to Mornnais. As for Tarek, try not to think about what might have happened. It's in the past, over and done with. And guys like that usually get what's coming to them, sooner or later."

"I guess," she said. Starting to feel released from the months of tension, she fought the urge to tear up. Not in front of Eugene.

"There's one thing I'm worried about," she said. "Blondell has been missing since Friday night, and we're afraid she's had an accident, or worse."

"Blondell?" he asked.

"Yes, you remember, that rich widow whom Jacques was trying to sell a painting to. She was having serious second thoughts, and now she's gone missing. Marie-Agnès notified the police, we've been calling hospitals, but so far no news. I'm wondering if I shouldn't contact the Institut médico-légal here in Paris."

"You need to give it a few more days. I'm sure she'll turn up before long." He didn't think there was anything more to say about Blondell, so he moved on.

"Do you have any plans?" he asked. "What are you going to do now that you're free again?"

"I think I mentioned that my uncle and my cousin and I are joint owners of an old, run-down château. I inherited my share from my mother. We want to upgrade the vineyards and renovate and develop the house, which is in a great state of disrepair. Did I ever tell you that I was born in Paris and grew up here? After living for years in Washington, I realized that I wanted to come back to France, find some roots, reconnect with my family, you know, that sort of thing. But first I have a few things to take care of. If I recall correctly, your lease is up in two weeks…"

Eugene interrupted her, "Yes, it was a great house. Sorry I didn't spend more time there. But my wife enjoyed her stay. She's already moved our things into our new apartment. I think your real estate agent must hav the keys."

I should tell her about Kate, but it's not the right moment. Right now I need to concentrate on finishing up this business with Mornnais. Plenty of time after that.

"I didn't know that. Well, anyway, I'm going back to DC to settle my affairs and put the house on the market. Then I'll be returning to France. I regret having gotten so side-tracked, but that's all over now." *He looks distracted. Is he even listening to what I'm saying?* An image of their first meeting popped into her mind, the three of them drinking champagne in her dining room, and she asked, "Perhaps you'll both join me for another glass of champagne if you're in DC?"

"Yes, good idea." He finished his beer. "I'd better get a move on, have to do some prep for my meeting." He gestured to the waiter, paid, stood up, and this time, shook Alex's hand. "See you in DC," he said as he hurried off. It seemed to Alex that, in less than a minute, Eugene, like Elvis, had left the building. They headed in opposite directions, each wondering if they would ever see the other again.

Chapter 92

WHEN HER PHONE RANG PAST midnight, Marie-Agnès felt it had to be the police. With a sense of foreboding, she answered and learned that a woman who matched Blondell's description had been brought to Hôpital Lariboisière. Marie-Agnès tried to calm her throbbing body. Was it too late to call Alex?

#   #   #

Alex, wide-awake in her bed, sleep just would not come. *I fucked up the meeting with Eugene. He just wasn't interested in what I was saying. Why did I bother?*

Her ruminating was cut short when her phone rang. No, it was not Eugene, but Marie-Agnès calling. They agreed to go to the hospital early in the morning.

#   #   #

The unrelieved grey sky hung like a damp blanket over Paris. In the misty morning, a slow-moving ballet of the homeless, addicts, dealers, and panhandlers glided between the hospital and nearby Gare du Nord. *Could there be a more depressing moment than this* wondered Marie-Agnès.

Inspector Boris, with the prematurely lined face of the inveterate smoker, was waiting for them at the hospital entrance. He put out his cigarette as they approached. The hospital was laid out around a large grassy quadrangle. It reminded Alex of an American university campus. They sat on a bench in the moist morning air, as Inspector Boris explained that a passerby had found the woman on rue de Turenne. It appeared that she had slipped in some dog shit that had been melted by the rain. So much for civil behavior in hip neighborhoods. Her shoulder was dislocated, and the police hypothesized that she had been the victim of a purse snatcher, and that had caused her to slide and hit her head on the sidewalk when she fell, although it was also possible that she had just slipped and fallen and a thief had taken her purse.

Marie-Agnès shook her head. "All that bling. I should have said something."

"We don't even know if it's her," said Alex with a sinking heart.

They followed the inspector through a labyrinth of hallways, up and down stairs, until they reached a room where the woman lay, unconscious, colorless skin stretched tight across her face. Nurses and doctors rushed past, attendants pushed gurneys, the place illuminated by harsh fluorescent lights, the smell of disinfectant hanging in the air. It was a continuation of the depressing exterior surroundings.

"So, do you confirm that this is your friend?" he asked.

"Yes," said Marie-Agnès, and she started to cry.

If needed, there was further proof in the faux leopard coat that hung in the closet. Alex thought back to her escapade with Marie-Agnès — it seemed so very long ago. There would be no whisking Blondell out of the hospital to the comfort of her apartment. Then she realized that whoever had Blondell's purse had her keys, cell phone, credit cards, and knew her address.

She turned to Marie-Agnès, who had been holding Blondell's free hand, sniffing back tears. "You'd better call her lawyer again, ask him to have the locks changed on her apartment and her credit cards blocked. Can you do that?"

Marie-Agnès fished a tissue out of her pocket, wiped her nose. "Yes, of course, I'll do that right now."

A nurse, square-shouldered and unsmiling, stepped into the room. "Good morning," was not a phrase that came easily to her. "Are you done?" she addressed Inspector Boris. "You should not be disturbing the patient."

Alex didn't think that Blondell was in any way disturbed, but sidestepping an argument, she asked, "When can we see her doctor to find out about her condition?"

"Who are you? We can only give that information to family members."

"Her family is in the United States but…" Alex tried to continue, "we're her close friends." The nurse interrupted, talking over her, "Then I'm afraid you'll have to leave now." She stood in the doorway, willing them to leave, which they did.

Marie-Agnès felt crushed. Blondell already looked like a corpse. Mag wanted so much to be reassured that her friend would pull through.

Alex was angry. "When you call Merv, ask him to find out about her condition. He's her lawyer, after all. And I think you'd better contact her cousin Claudia."

#   #   #

Merv did what he could. Had the locks changed. There was an alarm system as well, so no one had gained access to the apartment. Managed to speak to the neurologist who was treating Blondell. She had suffered a traumatic brain injury as a result of the freak fall, and they would have to wait and see. Shared the news with Mag. She said almost nothing, just thanked him for calling. He would have preferred it if she had been more emotional, but Mag was numb with grief.

He knew that Jacques was not grieving over Blondell, but, like Mag, Jacques said almost nothing. "Oh, really?" was his response.

"It doesn't look good," said Merv. "She could die, you know."

"That would be a pity, my friend, but that's life. *On est bien peu de chose, we're so insignificant.* Anyway, I'm looking forward to meeting your collector. I'm sure it will be an interesting encounter."

Jacques had seemed so detached, so unconcerned about Blondell. Had he had a hand in the "accident"? There was no telling. But Merv had a strong feeling that it would be best to remove the Picasso from his Paris apartment. He thought a weekend outside of Paris would do him some good. Why not kill two birds with one stone and take the painting up to his country house?

#   #   #

Merv enjoyed the drive to Saint-Germer-de-Fly, once he got past the ugly suburbs north of Paris. The town was noteworthy for the remains of a late-Romanesque, early-Gothic church, but that was of little interest to him. Instead, he had renovated an old farmhouse and its outbuildings, creating a comfortable nest in the peaceful countryside. A dirt road led to his house and he parked at the end of the track, unloaded the car, and unlocked the front door. The air smelled cold and damp. He turned on the heating system and was relieved that it still worked. An ancient nail protruded from one of the exposed stone walls and he hung the Picasso from it.

Free to relax at last, he poured a glass of Calvados. The neighboring farmer's brother was a producer who kept him supplied with the best Hors d'Age Calvados. He was happy to be completely alone. No one other than his sister knew about this place. The people he spent his life sucking up to would not be impressed, but that was fine with him.

He had fallen asleep and awoke with a start. He looked at his watch—it was two a.m.—and at the Picasso. He was bleary-eyed, and for a moment, the painting's elements seemed to move. He blinked to focus. The movement stopped, but his anxiety had returned. With a sigh of regret, he took the painting down and wrapped it in some bubble paper he found behind the sofa. A pair of rubber boots lay on the floor. He pulled them on and went outside. He carried the painting across the lawn, his feet making a squelching sound on the wet, overgrown grass.

One of the outbuildings was an old barn, where he kept a lawn mower, gardening implements, and tools he never used. The barn had sliding doors, and with great difficulty, he pushed them open along the rusted track. Once inside, he stood still to catch his breath. With trembling legs, he climbed up to a cluttered loft and slipped the painting behind some junk.

Back in the warmth of his house, Merv poured himself another glass of the dark golden liquid. Savored the aroma as the nectar trickled smoothly down his throat. Once again at peace, he went into the bedroom. *I'll have to get that damn barn door fixed*, he thought as he curled up under the down comforter and went to sleep.

Chapter 93

Fontainebleau

NICOLAS WALKED TO THE WINDOW when he heard the sound of tires on the gravel driveway. He saw Stokes get out of his car, carrying a large shopping bag from the BHV department store.

"Hi, Nick, up to your old tricks?" Stokes smiled as he shook the art dealer's outstretched hand.

"I'm afraid I don't understand, Mr. Stokes."

"Oh, nothing, just joking. I'm in a bit of a rush, so let's get down to business. Can you get the *Baby Moses*, please?"

Nicolas had a queasy feeling as he placed the painting on a stand. He didn't know why, but he felt that something wasn't right.

Stokes stepped up close to the painting. "It's a lovely picture, Baby Moses floating in the reeds. Poussin must have really liked that image to have painted it more than once."

Nicolas, relieved when he heard Stokes say it was a lovely picture, replied, "Yes, indeed, he did do other works inspired by the Biblical legend."

Stokes wasn't smiling, but he didn't look upset, either, as he locked onto Nicolas's eyes. "What I don't get, though, is that he would do the same

333

painting at least twice."

The queasy feeling returned, churning Nicolas's bowels. "I'm afraid I don't understand," his default reply to Stokes's verbal jabs.

"Here, Nick, let me show you." Eugene removed his aunt's painting from the BHV shopping bag, held it next to the painting on the pedestal. "Same painting, same provenance. You sold this one to a lady named Madeleine Connor. Does that ring a bell? How many of these did you get from Pavel Korsikov's widow? I'm curious to hear what you have to say."

Nicolas felt a hot flush start in his abdomen and rise to his neck. He was silent for a few moments, his heart beating so rapidly that he felt as if his chest were about to explode. "Now, Mr. Stokes, these are a rare pair..."

Stokes cut him off. "Cut the crap, Nick. A laboratory analyzed this painting, and they confirmed that it's a fake."

Nicolas felt as if he were drowning, tried to reach for a lifesaver. "I don't know that your laboratory is correct, but if you provide proof of ownership, I'll ask Madame Korsikov to refund Madame Connor."

"Good idea, Nick," said Eugene as he put his aunt's painting back into the BHV bag and swiftly removed the *Baby Moses* from the pedestal. Nicolas tried to stop him, but Stokes pushed him aside. "Here's what's going to happen. I'm taking this painting, and I will give you forty-eight hours to obtain the refund from Mme Korsikov, at which time I'll return both paintings to you. If you're not happy, we can call the police and explain the situation to them. And I'm sure that the *Canard Enchaîné* would love a story like this. They'll probably snoop around to find out more about Mme Korsikov and this Pavel fellow, and who knows what they might turn up."

Nicolas watched as Stokes walked out of the house, carrying the two paintings. He wanted to run after him, but he stood stone still, listening to the car pull out of the driveway and onto the street. He went into the kitchen, poured a glass of water, sat down, and tried to gather his wits together before he called Jacques.

#   #   #

Jacques listened as Nicolas, his voice getting shriller, cracking at times, recounted the meeting with Stokes. "I can't believe how you fucked this up, Nicolas. So, your Mr. Stokes is coming back in forty-eight hours? Let me figure things out. Just stay where you are, and I'll get back to you."

Even before he had ended the call, Jacques knew what needed to be done. He made a phone call, admonished the listener. "And no fuckups," and turned his attention to his upcoming meeting with Carl Weller.

#   #   #

Two whiskeys later, Nicolas' nerves began to settle. Jacques had told him to stay put, but he had a better idea. He would pack up all the records of the paintings he had received from Jacques, take a few days off to drive to Switzerland, and store the files in a safe place.

He sent his daughter a text message: *Going to Switzerland for a few days. Will call when I return. Bisous, Papa.*

His housekeeper had left for the day, and in the stillness of the workroom, he concentrated on filling several boxes with the blue files. *As for that shit, Stokes, I'll let Jacques take care of him.* No sooner had the thought crystallized than the bell at the rear door rang. He stood up with a start and glimpsed Jacques through the door's windowpanes.

A wave of relief passed through him. Jacques would tell him what he planned to do.

"Hello, Jacques, I was just thinking about that *salaud,* Stokes. Have you figured something out?"

"Not to worry, my friend. Yes, I've worked things out." Jacques' gaze fell upon the boxes filled with blue folders. "Ah, I see you've been getting organized."

"Yes," replied Nicolas. "I plan to drive to Switzerland and store these in a safe place until we're sure Stokes won't cause any trouble."

"Excellent idea."

Jacques had said he'd worked things out, and that was enough for Nicolas. *The less I know, the better,* he thought, and turned to finish loading up the last box. At that moment, Jacques stepped back to open the door. Two men slipped in, and Nicolas suddenly felt strong hands around his neck, squeezing until he blacked out.

"Find his car keys, finish packing up those files, and put them in his car." Nicolas' Mini Clubman was in the garage at the rear of the house. A high hedge surrounded the property, hiding the garage from view. Henri, the taller of the two men, fished around in Nicolas's pockets. "They're not here."

"Well, find them, for fuck's sake," snapped Jacques. Then Stéphane, the second man, walked out to the garage and came back holding the keys. "Found them in the ignition. Trusting fellow, isn't he?"

Jacques handed Nicolas' laptop to one of the men. "Take this as well." They carried Nicolas out to his car, laid the body across the back seat. Jacques, sitting in the passenger seat, Stéphane in the back, Henri at the wheel. They drove up the street, where Tarek was waiting. Jacques got into the Mercedes, Stéphane got behind the wheel of a dirty black van. The three vehicles drove slowly into the Fontainebleau Forest, stopped one hundred meters up a dirt road. In the gentle light of dusk, they transferred the boxes, the laptop, and the still unconscious Nicolas into the van.

Henri drove the Mini Clubman to an automobile scrap yard where he had done previous business with the owner. The car would be stripped for parts and then put into the compactor.

Tarek continued along the dirt track until it crossed a small paved road. He followed that road to an abandoned farm. Stéphane brought up the rear. At the farm, Jacques stood to one side, watching the two men dig a shallow grave.

A sound came from inside the van. Not exactly a sigh, not a cough, either. Nicolas was still alive.

"I said no fuckups." Jacques glared at Stéphane.

"I'll take care of it," said Tarek, holding a knife at his side. He had hated the condescending little man, and he relished the opportunity for revenge.

They removed the body from the van. Henri spotted the Rolex on Nicolas's wrist. "A shame to bury this with him, don't you think?"

Jacques smiled. "It's all yours, my friend."

Once Nicolas was buried, they continued to drive into the empty countryside, stopping in a patch of gravel several kilometers farther, where they set fire to the van and its contents. Henri got into the Mercedes, they picked up Stéphane on the road near the scrap yard, and Tarek dropped the two men near the train station in Nemours before driving back to Château d'Hélène.

Jacques leaned back in the comfortable leather seat, a tight smile on his face as he imagined Nicolas' Mr. Stokes showing up at the antique dealer's gallery. *Let him do whatever he wants*, he thought. *There's no connection to me.*

#   #   #

Under the clear night, starlit with a crescent moon, a black sedan drove slowly up the

dirt road that led to Mélandère and parked at the back of the house. Two men alighted. Each carried a small suitcase. They descended the stairs that led to the vault.

After twenty minutes, they had disabled the alarm system and opened the door to the vault. Once inside, they removed the protective covering from each painting, photographed and rewrapped it. One of the men, who had a more developed esthetic sensibility, took a long-exposure photograph from inside the vault, pointing the camera to the open door and capturing the star-filled sky.

Their work completed, the men sent the photos to Eugene Spector and drove to Saint-Raphael, where they spent the remainder of the night. The following day, they drove back to Paris and submitted their expense report to Vince Reiner.

Chapter 94

HE HAD BEEN DREADING THE phone call, and when it came, for about a minute, which could be a very long time, his mind when blank. He didn't know what to do. Then he called Mag. Let her take care of it.

Mag waited until early afternoon before calling Claudia to tell her about Blondell's passing. It would be morning in Virginia. "Oh, how awful," Claudia exclaimed. "We had been expecting her to wake up and recover." A pause and she switched to practical mode. Took down Merv's details, made a note to contact Blondell's lawyers in New York, said she would be coming to France and would let Marie-Agnès know once her plans were set.

Marie-Agnès looked out her window at rue d'Orchampt, bathed in the afternoon sunlight. No more tears. She felt numb, felt as though a tennis ball was lodged in her throat. Neither Merv nor Claudia seemed *concerned* by Blondell's death. It was more like an inconvenience than a source of grief. She thought about Blondell's life here in Paris. Perhaps tutoring the kids had given it some meaning. She would find out the exact address of the association and go over there herself and let them know.

Lastly, she called Alex and left a message.

Chapter 95

THEY MET FOR LUNCH AT La Maison Neuve. Jacques had been playing with his Blackberry. He looked up as a man walked toward his table and realized that something was out of focus. It was like when he first awoke in the morning, the world was all blurry until the fog lifted and he could see clearly. He blinked his eyes rapidly as the man approached. The mist disappeared.

Jacques regretted having let Nathalie go. He could have used her for this lunch. Well, he'd just have to make an effort, let this Mr. Weller do most of the talking.

Eugene took Jacques' outstretched hand. "Mr. Mornnais? Carl Weller. Pleased to meet you."

"The pleasure is mine." Jacques pursed his lips in a mirthless smile. He stared fixedly at Eugene. "Haven't we met before?"

"I was thinking the same thing," said Eugene. "You know, I spent a year in France when I was in high school. My family, they're a bunch of snobs, wanted to give me some culture with a capital C. And you remind me of a boy in my class. Very bright little fellow. Was bullied by some of the other boys. I remember I got into a fight once when they were pushing him around. I've got a little scar on my hand to prove it. Those were the days, weren't they, Jean-Charles?"

"Excuse me. I think you must be mistaken."

"No chance of that, my friend. I don't want to be rude, but if I leaned over and ripped your shirt away from your neck, I'd find a red birthmark there, wouldn't I?"

At that moment, the waiter brought the menus. Eugene took his time, as if making his selection was uppermost in his mind.

Jacques' face was pale, his eyes two black holes, as he continued to stare at Eugene. "Ah, yes, Eugene Spector. A big, dumb American."

"Who saved your skinny ass," interrupted Eugene.

"But you're calling yourself Carl Weller these days." A thought raced through his mind. *That asshole, Merv Peters. What's he playing at?*

"I take it you're a regular here. What do you suggest?"

"Look, why don't you just order whatever you like — everything is good here — and let's get on with it. I can hardly imagine that you're here to purchase a painting, so tell me what it is that you want."

They skipped a starter and each ordered *filet de sole meuniere.* The conversation had cut their appetites.

"Well, Jean-Charles, I'm here on a personal matter. Remember when we were in school together? It was my aunt Madeleine—I loved her dearly, she died a few years ago—that insisted that I spend a year in Paris. Very nice lady, very cultivated, very well-off. And your pal, Nicolas Pagès, sold her a phony Poussin. So I thought that I'd look into the transaction.

"When I stopped by his gallery, asking to buy a Poussin, he offered to sell me the same painting that my aunt had bought. Hard to believe, but there you have it: two identical copies. When I confronted him, he offered to refund the purchase price, and then, you know what? He disappeared. Now, he came up with identical certificates that state that the paintings came from the estate of Pavel Korsikov. That's the late husband of your wife, isn't he? So that would be Mila Korsikova who needs to refund me, wouldn't you say? Here's the situation, Jean-Charles. I now have both paintings—he let me keep the second one free of charge—and it seems only fair that someone refund the money my aunt paid."

"Ah, Pavel Korsikov, a shrink-wrap titan. It's unlikely that he was a collector. I deal with many galleries, including Mr. Pagès. But he's hardly my pal. I'm sorry about your aunt, but if Nicolas is making up stories, then you'll have to take it up with him. It sounds to me like he has a most active imagination." He paused to eat some fish, moist, perfectly cooked.

"Let me tell you what I'm imagining: all your fancy friends learning that you started life as Jean-Charles Molina, the son of a concierge and a construction worker. Not that there's anything wrong with that, but can you imagine what people in your orbit might think? Or what would they think when they learn about my two forged Poussins? I imagine they'll say, *Where there's smoke there's fire,* or something like that."

Jacques looked up from his plate. Perhaps it was just as well that no one else was present. He would not—could not—let Eugene see the anger boiling up inside him. A thin smile. "Dear friend, it's all a question of perspective. I could be a parvenu, or I could be a success story—you Americans love that, don't you? I could be a forger, or I could be someone who's been horribly taken advantage of by an unscrupulous art dealer."

"An art dealer who has disappeared."

"Why don't you look for him, Eugene? "

"Yes, who knows what I'll find?"

The waiter brought the dessert menu, but both men ordered only coffee. Each had his reasons to put a quick end to their encounter. Jacques insisted on paying for lunch. He had, after all, chosen the restaurant and he wouldn't lower himself to quibble over the bill.

#   #   #

Café, near Ecole Militaire

Walter Helmann nursed his beer and peered at *L'Equipe*, spread open on the café table. His face had a greyish pallor, despite his permanent suntan. There was no rosy glow, just the crackled, lined skin of those who work permanently under the sun's harsh rays. He felt a craving for nicotine, but he needed to go outside to smoke. *Fucking French, too many rules.* As he stood up and reached for his cigarettes, Eugene walked up to him.

341

"How did it go?"

"Pretty well, just as I thought it would. But I'm concerned about our friend Nicolas."

"Yeah, well, I wanted to tell you about that. When I got near his house, I thought I saw him driving away. By the time I got back into my car, he had disappeared."

"Really? I have the feeling we'll not see Nicolas anytime soon."

As they walked out of the café, Walter already had a cigarette between his lips. The hand holding his lighter was shaking.

Weird guy, thought Eugene. *He's a bundle of nerves now that that little job is over. Go figure.*

#   #   #

Paris was, as usual, choked with late-afternoon traffic. It took forty-five minutes to go from the center of the city to the ring road, another forty-five minutes to get to the A6 motorway, and another twenty-five minutes before the southbound traffic thinned out. During that time Jacques tried to take his mind off the meeting with Eugene by going through the newspapers Tarek had bought that morning, *Les Echos* and *Le Figaro*. But the words were an incomprehensible blur, as he read without anything registering.

He felt anger—of course with Eugene, but also with himself, for having let the situation get out of control. He called Mila and shouted at her, then told Tarek to play Beethoven's Third, and the strains of the Second Movement's "Funeral March" momentarily calmed him. His anger boiled up again, and he sat in stony silence, trying to decide how to deal with Eugene, who had the two forged Poussins, with their identical phony provenance. Although Nicolas was no longer in the picture, there was now his old school chum. He would need to get those paintings back, of course, without paying for them.

He plotted his next steps, he got back on center, and by the time Tarek pulled into the circular gravel drive, his breathing was back to normal, and he even pecked Mila on the cheek when she came to the door to greet him.

Chapter 96

Rue Legendre, Paris

WALTER LEANED BACK AGAINST THE pillows propped up on his bed. He had lowered the volume on the television to a low murmur, just something to fill the silence in his bleak apartment, with its harsh yellow light and faded flocked wallpaper. Again and again, he made the same calculation: one more gig, and he'd be free to quit this business and move to Thailand, with its pristine beaches, summer-like weather all year round, and a limitless supply of girls and boys.

He stared at the screen. It was a rerun of *Columbo*. He watched Peter Falk, raincoat flapping, eyes squinting, trap the culprit. Not that that had anything to do with real life, but it was fun to watch.

The phone on the bed vibrated, *JM* on the caller ID, and although it was late, he answered.

"Yes?"

Walter smiled as he listened to Jacques explain what he wanted.

"I know all about Eugene Spector and the paintings. And I saw your buddy Nicolas Pagès with you and your friends the other night."

"What are you talking about, Walter?"

343

"Cut the bullshit, Jacques. I was across the street and followed your little motorcade. Need I say more? "

"Does Spector know?"

"Not yet, but I'm sure he'd pay for this additional information."

The negotiation commenced, Jacques pretended to bargain, and it ended when he agreed to pay four times Walter's usual rate for the assignment he had in mind.

"You'll have to do it tonight. Tarek is in Paris. He'll wait for you after you've done the job. And Walter, this is important, no fuckups."

Walter lit a cigarette. As he packed his toolkit, he focused on the image of white sand and blue water and tried not to think about Eugene.

#   #   #

Hotel room, Avenue de Wagram

Eugene walked up a narrow street, carrying a *Baby Moses* painting under each arm. An old building was under renovation, and the scaffolding began to tilt dangerously. As he quickened his pace to avoid a collapse, the asphalt peeled back, revealing the cobblestones that started to separate, forming a hole with a stairway leading downward. He descended the stairs but stopped when he saw Jacques standing at the bottom, smiling. He turned to climb out of the hole.

He awoke with a start, his heart pounding. Someone was tinkering with the door lock. He stood up and grabbed the flashlight by the bedside as the intruder entered the room. Eugene recognized Walter in the flash of light and lunged toward him. Walter sidestepped the blow aimed for his head that landed on his shoulder. As the two men grappled, Walter gave Eugene a hard punch to his midsection. Eugene fell to the floor and hit his head on the chest of drawers. Crouching on all fours, his head throbbing, Eugene tried to catch his breath as he struggled to stand up. Walter was opening the closet, looking for the paintings, when Eugene hooked one arm around his neck and pulled Walter's right arm behind his back until he heard a snap. Walter screamed in pain, Eugene punched him in the face, and Walter fell

344

with a thud on the carpet.

"What the fuck are you doing, Walter?" hissed Eugene. "Looking for the paintings, by any chance? Did you really think I'd keep them here?"

He hoisted Walter up, shoved him against the wall. "Tell me who you're working for. You're too dumb to do this on your own. Mornnais, perhaps? Tell me before I break your other arm."

Walter leveraged himself against the wall, landed a vicious kick on Eugene's shins. Eugene fell. Walter ran out of the room and down to the street. He saw Tarek's van parked in a delivery zone at the end of the block and walked to the van, his broken right arm hanging loosely at his side. Tarek looked up.

"Open the fucking door," screamed Walter. "He broke my fucking arm, the fucker."

Tarek got out, walked around the van, and slid the door open. "Not so loud," he said. "You'll wake the neighborhood." The sun had not yet fully risen, and a thick grey fog hung over Paris, blotting out noise and color.

"My fuckin' arm is killing me," whined Walter. "I need to get to a doctor."

"Yes," said Tarek, concentrating on driving. "Stop complaining. Looks like you fucked up big-time."

"It's not my fault if he didn't have the paintings in his room."

"Yes, but it doesn't sound like you took care of him, either. So as I say, you've fucked up big-time, Mr. Mornnais' not going to be happy."

"I'll deal with him after I get my arm taken care of. Pull over. I'm getting out."

"All in good time."

"No, now," yelled Walter and he reached for the steering wheel with his left hand, the pain shooting up through the right side of his body. It had occurred to him that his beach holiday would have to be postponed.

#   #   #

In the city of Levallois, just outside of Paris, Hans Renard had been spending the evening with friends, drinking wine and enjoying a sampling of drugs. Most of the partygoers had passed out, and Hans, overcome by an irresistible urge to ride his motorcycle, left the gathering.

He drove across the bridge spanning the ring road and accelerated into the soft grey foggy cocoon hanging over Avenue de Wagram.

At that moment, Walter was pulling the steering wheel to the right and Tarek, with a better grip, pulled it too hard to the left. The van skidded across the road and came to a rest perpendicular to the oncoming traffic. Hans hit the side of the vehicle with such force that he and the bike were thrown into the air. He landed on the road, and the motorcycle crashed into the windshield. Help arrived some twenty minutes later, too late for the motorcyclist or the van's occupants.

#   #   #

Eugene had showered, straightened out the room, and headed to a brasserie on Place des Ternes for breakfast. When he heard the sirens and saw the police and fire vehicles, he continued up Avenue de Wagram. He saw an inert body on the pavement and the rear tire of a motorcycle protruding from the windshield of a white van. As he walked by the wreck, he remembered the white van he had seen Tarek driving at Mélandère. He would have liked to get a closer look, but a police car was already at the scene. *What if it's Tarek's van? Is it just a coincidence that he was driving in the neighborhood of my hotel?*

The ambulances took the three bodies to the morgue. The fire department removed the carcasses of the van and the bike, and the police cordoned off the road. By now the early-morning rush hour had started, and vehicles inched around the site of the accident. As the fog dissipated, it started to rain, bringing the traffic to a standstill.

Later in the day, Eugene called Kenneth Petit and learned that the bodies in the van were those of Jacques Mornnais' driver and a mercenary by the name of Walter Helmann.

Chapter 97

Pizza restaurant, rue Madame, Paris

THE DISH, BAKED MOZZARELLA SURROUNDED by tomato sauce and arugula, made him think of Christmas and the time that the four of them—Tarek, Bruno, Mila, and himself—had eaten dinner together in Hong Kong. When he mentioned that to Mila, she nodded and concentrated on chewing her marinated baby artichoke. He was dipping a piece of bread into the gooey cheese when his phone started to vibrate. He answered when he saw that the call was from the Interior Ministry.

"Yes," he said, "I see." Mila watched as a flush rose from his neck to his cheeks. "I was expecting them to pick up some merchandise. Can you be sure that no one touches the van? Oh, nothing, I see. Yes, I'll be over tomorrow. Thanks for letting me know."

"Is something the matter?" she asked.

"There's been an accident."

"An accident? Who?"

"Tarek and some guy you don't know."

Now she was the one to turn rosy from fear, and she couldn't stop herself from asking, "And is he okay?"

He curled his lip. "I assume you mean Tarek and not the other guy."

"Fuck you, Jacques," she hissed.

"Fatal accident, I'm afraid."

Mila dabbed at the corners of her mouth. Her red lipstick stained the white napkin. She stood up and hurried out of the restaurant.

Jacques stared at the melted cheese. It had cooled to the consistency of glue. His appetite now gone, he, too, stood up, threw a one-hundred-Euro note on the table, and left. He didn't want Mila going batshit crazy. Things were bad enough already and he had to think through the situation and find a solution before it got any worse.

# # #

The restaurant was on rue Madame, only a few minutes' walk to their apartment on rue Bonaparte. The elevator took forever to reach the fourth floor. Mila stormed into the apartment, threw her coat on the floor, and headed to her bedroom.

The maid picked up her coat and followed her down the corridor. "Madame, there's some—"

"Not now, Virginia," she snapped, slammed the bedroom door shut, and locked it behind her.

At last she was free to cry and pound the pillows. *Jacques didn't have to be so nasty. After all, it's not like he wants to sleep with me. He's only interested in the money I got from Pavel, and when I ask to see how he's been handling my funds, he just puts me off. When was the last time he showed me my accounts? How many times have I asked him to go over things? This time, I won't take no for an answer until I see what he's been up to.*

Mila looked at her reflection in the mirror. Her ivory skin was covered with red blotches, her eye makeup had run, her lipstick smeared around her mouth. *I need to clean myself up and calm down.* In the time that it took her to redo her makeup, Tarek's image had given way to thoughts about her offshore accounts. She took a Lexomil, closed her eyes, and tried to sleep.

# # #

Rather than going straight home, Jacques headed to the Luxembourg Garden. Perhaps a walk in the beautiful park would settle the tumult in his mind. But, instead, the bands of laughing children and the couples of all ages walking hand in hand irritated him, and he returned to his apartment more tightly wound than before.

"Monsieur," began Virginia as he crossed the threshold.

He cut her off. "Is Madame here?"

"Yes, Monsieur, but…"

"Well, what is it?" he snapped.

"But there's someone in your office. I tried to tell Madame, but she went to sleep."

Jacques felt a tightening in his chest. "What do you mean there's someone in my office?"

"A man, Monsieur. He came a while ago. He said he had an appointment and would wait in your office."

Jacques rushed down the hallway, not breaking his stride as he pushed open the door to his office. An arm hooked around his throat as a hand reached out to close the door and turn the key in the lock. Dazed, he thought of the last visit to Nicholas Pagès; the tables now turned, but who was playing the role of his henchmen?

He was having trouble breathing and tried to pull away from the arm that circled his neck but to no avail. "It's been quite a day, Jean-Charles," Eugene Spector chuckled. "I heard about Tarek and Walter. So sorry for your loss." *How did the American know about the accident? It had happened only a few hours ago.* Eugene continued, "Not very nice, sending Walter after me, but never mind. Now that this morning's excitement is over, we need to take care of our unfinished business."

Eugene propelled Jacques into the chair behind his desk. "Please have a seat, my friend." Jacques glimpsed the two *Baby Moses* paintings leaning against the wall as he did so. Eugene sat facing Jacques, and when he said nothing, Jacques snarled, spurred on by a mixture of anger and humiliation, "Let's get this over with. Why don't you tell me what you want?"

As though he hadn't heard him, or perhaps as though they were having a pleasant conversation, Eugene added, "I've been meaning to tell you, that's a charming house you have in the south of France. A bit run-down, but the vault in the basement, that's another story. It took us a little time to open it, but it was worth it."

Eugene reached into his pocket and slid the photo of the vault's entrance silhouetted against the sky.

"Stunning shot, isn't it? You've got some beautiful pictures down there. We photographed all of them. And I think you'd like to add these two to your collection, wouldn't you? So please, Jean-Charles, let's get on with the refund. I think you'd best do the transfer from your computer. I'll hold on to your phones." Jacques laid his Blackberry on the desk.

"I guess you didn't understand me, Jean-Charles. I said phones. Pluriel. More than one. It looks like I'm going to have to pat you down." Jacques stood up and tried to reach the door, but Eugene was quicker and blocked his escape. He found the other Blackberry and pushed Jacques back to the desk chair.

Jacques, furious, glared at Eugene, then reached beneath his desk and pointed a gun at him. "You're not as smart as you think. It's a lucky thing I caught you trying to rob me." He pulled the trigger—a tiny click. Eugene smiled, reached into his pocket, and held out five bullets.

"I think you'll find that your gun works better when loaded. Now, Jean-Charles, let's do it. I'm running out of patience, and I would hate it if something happened to your house and those fine paintings."

Jacques did a quick cost-benefit analysis and decided that it was cheaper to pay off Eugene Spector than to risk the greater loss in the long run. Besides, he would take the money from one of Mila's accounts. She did not need to know about that.

#   #   #

As Eugene walked down the corridor that led to the front door, Mila emerged from her bedroom. "Good afternoon, Madame." She nodded, smiled, and went into Jacques' office. It was time for a money talk.

"Who was that nice-looking man?"

"Oh, just someone I'm working on a deal with."

"I thought you sold those," she said, pointing to the paintings leaning against the wall.

"Yes, well, one of the owners has asked us to sell it for him, and we're finishing up the paperwork for the other one."

If Mila had been paying attention, she might have thought it curious that Jacques had shown his visitor the two identical copies—or perhaps she assumed that he was in on the scam.

"Jacques, I've been thinking. You haven't shown me my accounts in some time, and I'd like to see them."

It didn't take her long to get over Tarek, did it?

With Eugene Spector and the threat he represented gone, he had begun to plot his next steps. "Of course, Mila. There's a lot to go through. I was planning to go to Montenegro for a few weeks. Why don't you come with me, and I can show you everything."

"Montenegro? Why now?"

"I want to concentrate on my other businesses, stop selling tableaux for a while, and I've decided to ship the paintings at Mélandère to our place in Montenegro."

Chapter 98

NEVER ONE TO SUFFER IN silence for very long, Blondell had complained to her lawyers in New York about life in Paris, about Parisians, about her local lawyer, Merv Peters. Thus, when her will was admitted to probate, they contacted their own corresponding attorney to handle the France-based aspects of her estate, which included a small gift to the association where she had taught English and transferring the title to the apartment on Place des Vosges to Marie-Agnès Duvalois.

Chapter 99

Mélandère, south of France

BEFORE DAYBREAK, JACQUES MOVED FROM room to room, making sure the windows were securely closed and fastening the shutters. He had started on the top floor, working his way down. First the servants' quarters, then the bedrooms, until he reached the ground floor receptions and dining room. And room by room, a cold darkness took hold of the house, until only the kitchen was illuminated by the pale light of early dawn, a thin yellow-grey light that continued down the long hallway.

Jacques sat at the wooden table in the kitchen, and through the window, he could see the still dark silhouette of Mont Roquebrune. He finished his coffee as Mila washed the coffeepot and their cups and saucers, emptying the coffee grounds into a plastic bag. He was so nervous that he smoked a cigarette as he waited for his cell phone to ring.

The dog walker has arrived.

He smiled and crushed the cigarette in the ashtray. The paintings in the vault were on their way to safety in Montenegro, far beyond the reach of Eugene Spector. Too bad about Tarek. He was certain Mila missed him more than she let on. As for Walter, another loose end nicely tied up. No one was sure what the two men were doing together, and he'd seen to it that no questions would be asked.

Jacques closed the shutters to the kitchen window and then fastened those on the outside door before locking it. "Start the car," he said to Mila. How convenient that she liked to drive. He could tell that she was still preoccupied, anxious to go over her accounts. She had married well the first time around, especially considering her origins, but she seemed to have forgotten that had it not been for him, she would have gotten nothing when her husband died. Still, he could imagine the scene if she learned about the refund for the *Baby Moses*.

Mila walked across the gravel yard to the car. She did not look back at the house, for in her mind, she was already on the beach in Montenegro, where warm sun and white sand awaited her. As she turned the key in the ignition, these were her last thoughts as a fireball engulfed the car.

Epilogue

May 2010

ELLA HAD A LAST ERRAND to run before taking the bus to the airport. She went to Wong Frères, hoping that Li was still working at the store. She found him unloading crates of cabbage. "Li," she murmured. He heard her and looked up. "I'm going back to the Philippines," she said, "and I wanted to say goodbye and thank you once more, as I don't think we'll be seeing each other again."

"Good luck to you, Ella," he said. "I hope you will find happiness."

"Same to you, Li." They embraced. She swallowed and walked quickly out of the store and onto the crowded street.

#   #   #

Air France ground personnel at Charles de Gaulle airport had announced that there would be a two-hour strike. *If I'm going to live in France, I'd better get used to this,* Alex thought. Eventually her flight took off, she exchanged few words—*bonjour* and *au revoir*—with the man sitting next to her, and as she stood outside her house in Georgetown, unlocking the front door, she found it difficult to believe that she'd been away for only six months.

Inside, the air was stale, but the house was immaculate. She dragged her suitcase upstairs (she had left her other bag at Richard's apartment), and went into her bedroom. There was a single man's cufflink on the night table. The housekeeping service must have found it when they cleaned. Was it her ex- husband's, or had Eugene left it there? And did it matter?

She called the real estate agent to say it looked like Mr. Spector had left a cufflink in the house. Did he have a number where she could reach him? The agent gave her the number he had on file. She called. Disconnected.

The mysterious Mr Spector. Okay, that's it, she said to herself. And she set upon the task of closing out her life in Washington, DC.

#   #   #

Véronique Pagès, Nicolas's daughter, filed a missing person report with the local gendarmerie. Véronique had not been close to her father, but she remembered that he had gotten her out of some nasty situations. Worried and ill at ease, she felt that she had to do something. She moved into the house, hoping that she'd discover some clue as to what might have happened. A search of his office turned up nothing, but on the night table by his bed, she found Jacques Mornnais's card. The name was familiar to her. She recalled her father saying that Mr. Mornnais had been there when they needed help. It seemed like a good place to start and she called him several times, but he was always on voicemail.

#   #   #

The law firm in Paris that had been retained by Blondell's estate settled Merv Peters's outstanding bill for services rendered. The amount was on the high side, but it had not been worth their time to quibble. They sent a messenger to his office to pick up her files. For a moment, he saw Blondell again, sitting in his office, smoking her Virginia Slim, heard her monotonous whining about how tough life in Paris was, like a steady drip of tepid water. He did not particularly regret her passing, but he did have his regrets. No more fees for handling Blondell's affairs, no hope of a commission on her purchase of a painting. Then, in place of Blondell's image, he saw that of Carl Weller. Curious to know how the meeting had gone, he called Jacques and left a message. Perhaps Mag had heard back from Weller. He called her, but she, too, was on voicemail. He perked up when his secretary rang, announcing that a new client had arrived for her appointment. She might not be another Blondell Royston, but he'd make the best of the situation.

#   #   #

Rue d'Orchampt, Paris

Marie-Agnès stared at the ceiling, listening to the noise of the water running through the pipes as her neighbor took his shower. Six months ago, she was worried about making it to the end of the month, and now she owned an apartment on Place des Vosges. Instead of elation, or at least relief, she felt the heavy weight of guilt, remorseful that she had not done more to discourage Blondell from parading her bag that was like a beacon flashing *steal me, steal me*.

She showered and dressed, made herself a cup of coffee, and set to work on a translation. It occupied her mind temporarily, but by noontime, the waves of negativity started to wash over her again. Another cup of coffee. Her appetite had left her since Blondell had gone missing. "I've got to get out for a while," she said out loud. Walked over to Parc de la Turlure and sat for a while, looking at the silhouette of Sacré Coeur. Thinking about the apartment again, she realized that she could not bear to live there, surrounded by the memory of Blondell, sleeping in her bed, eating off her dishes.

When she returned to her flat, she called the lawyers and told them her decision—she would put the apartment up for sale, sell or give away the clothes and furnishings, and put the books and papers into storage. With the funds from the sale, she could buy a three-room apartment, more than enough for her needs, and invest the remainder.

"Perhaps that's not such a bad idea," said the lawyer. "Your apartment is probably worth three to four million Euros. And," he continued, never one to miss an opportunity "where were you thinking of moving to? Right bank or Left? I know someone who could help you find what you're looking for."

"Lyon," she said. "I'm going to move to Lyon."

THE END

PLEASE ENJOY THIS SNEAK PREVIEW
OF BOOK TWO IN THE SERIES

A FRENCH DECEPTION THRILLER

JANICE NAGOURNEY

Prologue

January 2010

HE HEARD VOICES—NOT WORDS, only muted sounds. He felt his heels dragging through the gravel, heard that sound too. He tried to open his mouth, tried to scream, to tell them to stop, to put him down, but his face, like his body, was frozen, immobile. Then he felt the cold water holding his body in its icy grasp. He spun down into a dark vortex, pulled along by the current until his body rose to the surface, and he gasped for air. On his back now, he opened his eyes, looking up at the starlit sky.

He floated downstream until his head struck some reeds at the river's edge. The water was shallow there, and he managed to crawl up the muddy riverbank. He was shivering; the noise of his teeth chattering reverberated in his head. He squeezed his eyes closed, and when he opened them again, he saw a stone cottage. On all fours, he slithered through the mud up to the cottage door. He did not recall seeing the cottage before. Yet, weak and exhausted, he moved his hand over the base of the building, found a chink in the mortar, and extracted a key. He shook violently, but after much effort, he was able to insert the key in the padlock that held the door shut.

He collapsed on the floor and removed his wet clothing with trembling fingers. There were tools and gardening implements laid out against one of the cottage walls. In the center was an old wooden table with two chairs. An armoire stood against the wall behind the table, its doors open. Some old clothing hung from metal hangers, and on the armoire's floor was a pair of worn boots. On the other side of the armoire, there were three glasses, two mugs, some flatware, a few chipped plates, and a small gas camping stove. A bed was pushed up against the third wall; on it was a sleeping bag, covered by a moth-eaten woolen blanket. Naked and shaking with the cold, he crawled into the sleeping bag and fell asleep.

It was dark when he awoke. In the moonlight that filtered in through the dirty windows, he saw a small kerosene heater. He wrapped himself in the blanket and fished around in the armoire until he found a box of matches. He then adjusted the wick, lit the heater, and got back into the sleeping bag. He fell asleep again.

The next morning, the room was warmer, but the garments he had worn were still damp. He picked them up and draped them over one of the chairs to dry. Next, he turned his attention to the clothing hanging in the armoire, pulled a shirt and jeans off the hangers, and tried them on. They fit. He found the old pair of work boots at the back of the armoire—they were his size as well. He continued to look through the armoire and found two bottles of water and some food—instant soup and instant noodles. Using the small gas camping stove, he made himself a meal.

He stepped outside the cottage. To his left, some distance away stood a large house, but it was as unfamiliar to him as the cottage. His stomach grumbled; still hungry, he went back inside, made the remaining container of instant noodles, and finished drinking the bottle of water. There was an open bottle of red wine on the kitchen table. He removed the cork and poured a small glass, but the odor of the wine made him nauseous as he brought the glass to his mouth, and he stepped outside to empty it. Looking towards the big house, he thought he saw a woman standing in a doorway, but she meant nothing to him.

It was too cold to remain outdoors for very long. He went back into the cottage, slipped into the sleeping bag, and again fell asleep. Previously his sleep had been dreamless, but this time there were vivid images.

361

He was walking along a river until he turned to cross a long bridge. He saw two rivers converging and looked up at the pastel facades lining the rivers' quays. He strolled down an endless road filled with fruit and vegetables of every type and color. Yellow and white cheeses shone their lights on him. He collided with bloody sides of beef and heard the crackle of chickens roasting on a spit. Then he was falling down a funnel into darkness.

He awoke with a shudder.

The clothes on the chair were now dry. He changed back into them and put on an old coat that was hanging in the armoire. He put the remaining bottle of water in his coat pocket, turned off the heater, and locked the cottage door, returning the key to its hiding place. He turned to the right, walking away from the big house and following the riverbank until he came to a small road that led to the highway.

Although he had been living rough for the past days, he still found a trucker willing to pick him up and take him as far as the train station in Mâcon. He scavenged food from restaurant bins in the train station and hopped on a TGV to Lyon. It was a short ride, and no one came to check his ticket. As always, Gare de Part-Dieu was packed with commuters and long-distance travelers. In the crush of moving bodies, he managed to lift a wallet from a woman's open backpack. He went to the men's room, locked himself in a stall, pocketed 350 euros, and threw the wallet into a trashcan.

Place des Terreaux . . . Place des Terreaux. The words looped through his mind. He got into a taxi at the front of the station. "Place des Terreaux," he told the driver, although he didn't know what that meant. But when the driver dropped him off, he recognized the Hôtel de Ville de Lyon on the east side of the square. He sat on a bench, searching for another familiar feeling. When it came, he stood up, walked to the north side of the square, wended his way to Montée de la Grande-Côte, and started to climb the steep hill.

Midway, he stopped to catch his breath, looking down the street at the panoramic view of Old Lyon and the Fourvière Basilica bathed in the gentle light of the evening sun. Turning to plod on, he stopped in front of number 102, climbed to the third floor, and rang the bell. He heard footsteps, and then a woman opened the door. "Bruno!" she exclaimed. "Is that really you?" She wrapped her arms around him. "Come in, come in." He stood in the entryway, searching for her face in his memory.

"Bruno," he said. "Is my name Bruno?"

Chapter 1

June 2010
Croix-Rousse, Lyon

THE *CLICK-CLACK* FROM MADAME de Prie-Louvois's stiletto heels echoed as she walked through the apartment's empty rooms. She waved her arm in a wide arc. "This is what we call 'factory architecture,' *chère Madame*." The flat had been a silk factory in the nineteenth century. It had four-meter-high ceilings; the exposed beams had been used to steady the vibrations from the Jacquard looms. The worn floor tiles glowed in the sunlight that streamed through the windows.

The client, a slender woman, her face framed by a cloud of dark red hair, nodded. "Yes, I know. I've read about the *canuts* and their struggles."

"Ah yes, *les canuts*. Well, times have certainly changed; this is now a quite exclusive neighborhood."

Marie-Agnès Duvalois knew that was just so much commercial fluff. If she had wanted to live somewhere truly exclusive, she would have opted for the sixth arrondissement at the foot of the *Presqu'île*. Instead, the Croix-Rousse neighborhood was lively. It had the largest outdoor produce market in Lyon, and all of the bistros and restaurants made her think that here, people did not eat to live, but rather lived to eat. It would be a challenge to keep her newly slim figure—she was looking forward to it.

Her thoughts turned to her friend Blondell Royton and her death in a stupid mugging accident. She had inherited Blondell's apartment on Place des Vosges in Paris. With the proceeds from its sale, she had switched from living month-to-month to a much more comfortable lifestyle. Yet, she was still getting used to her freedom after years of financial stress.

She followed the real estate agent through the apartment, impressed by how easily the woman navigated the tiled floor in her impossibly high heels.

"Well, what do you think?" asked Madame de Prie-Louvois as they walked back into the large living room. Marie-Agnès liked the apartment very much; it was by far the nicest one she had seen. *But what would Alex say?* She thought.

"It's quite nice, but I need to think about it. The price is a bit high compared to other flats that I've visited."

Madame de Prie-Louvois smiled. "Yes, it is high, but this is a unique product. If you're truly interested, I could perhaps talk to the owner, to see if there's some flexibility."

It was Marie-Agnès's turn to smile. "Yes, please do."

One of her cell phones rang. She fished in her Vanessa Bruno tote bag and pulled out the phone she reserved for her conversations with Merv Peters. She let the phone ring and returned it to her bag.

#   #   #

Merv Peters's office, Paris

"Shit. Shit. Shit." Merv Peters stood at the window of his office. It was June. Paris should have been warm and sunny, but it was cold and overcast. Despite the early evening light, a thin grey curtain hung over the streets and buildings, depressing for even the hardiest of spirits.

Merv had arranged for Carl Weller, a wealthy American, to meet the art consultant Jacques Mornnais. That meeting had taken place at the end of April. Now it was June, and he'd had no word from Jacques, or from Mag—

the girl who had introduced Merv to Weller—or from Weller himself.

He'd heard that Jacques' wife had been killed in an automobile accident in the South of France—but for fuck's sake, had he buried his BlackBerrys with her? And that twit Mag,

Merv had tried to contact her through Blondell's new lawyers, but since they had paid his outstanding fees, they'd given him the cold shoulder. Was it because his bill was on the high side, he wondered. But what the fuck, he had to make a living. He'd tried to reach Weller as well, but the number just rang until it disconnected.

It wasn't even that he'd missed out on another commission. What pissed him off more than anything was that no one was answering his phone calls. Something was up, something was not right, but what?

Merv called Mag's number again and left a message. And although he knew it was pointless, he rang Jacques. Voicemail. All that remained was to continue to eat breakfast at La Belle Fermière: among the flow of people stopping by his table to trade gossip, perhaps someone would have news of Jacques Mornnais.

#   #   #

Rue de Prony, Paris

"Anne-Laure, bring me a coffee, would you please?" Jacques Mornnais didn't look up, what was the point? He knew that the young woman was in the office, he knew that she had blonde hair, not the almost white platinum of his deceased wife, Mila, but lighter than Nathalie Martin, the girl who had worked for him until Mila fired her last March. All blondes, did it mean anything he wondered? He didn't think so; they were just random facts, like individual beads strung together to make a bracelet. On the other hand, what did matter was that Anne-Laure was the daughter of Henri de Montcalm, one of the boys who had bullied him back when he was at the *lycée*, and it gave him a small pleasure to treat her no better than his maid Mercie. Of course, his classmates had known him when his name was Jean-Charles Molina.

Jacques published a bi-lingual art and lifestyle magazine—*Artixia.* He'd posted a position for an intern at one of the business schools here in Paris. It was an unpaid job, but students were eager for any kind of work that would fill out their resume. "Anne-Laure de Montcalm," he had read. When he confirmed that Anne-Laure's father was Henri de Montalm, he called her in for an interview, but he was already determined to hire her, as long as she was able to translate from French to English.

"*S'il vous plait, Monsieur.*" Anne-Laure placed the coffee on his desk— "*Merci,*" he grunted. For the first time that morning, Jacques raised his head and nailed her to the wall with a hostile stare. She gulped: "shall I continue to work on my translation?"

"Yes, I'd like that."

#   #   #

As Anne-Laure stared at the computer screen, her eyes filled with tears. She'd been so excited when she'd been offered an internship at *Artixia,* but the taste of metal had replaced her dream of working in the glamorous world of Culture. She had a constant lump in her stomach when Jacques was in the office. He was an ordinary-looking man, slight of build, but he frightened her: was it his eyes, blinking behind his rimless glasses, or the way he ordered her around, as though she was a maid and not a student from a prestigious *école de commerce?* All that she knew was that she could not continue to work here. She'd have to find another internship, but *tant pis.* The only problem was that she had to tell Jacques that she was leaving.

#   #   #

Jacques listened to the messages on his Blackberrys. The tiresome lawyer, Merv Peters, had called yet again, but Jacques was still too angry to talk to him. Merv had arranged for Jacques to meet a potential client, a man who called himself Carl Weller. But when they met, Jacuqes discovered that Carl Weller was in fact only a pseudonym for an American named Eugene Spector. Jacques and the art dealer Nicolas Pagès, had sold Spector's aunt a fake Poussin, and Spector had forced him to reimburse the sum paid. While

Jacques had managed to remove Nicolas Pagès from the equation, Eugene Spector had outsmarted him anyway.

The more Jacques thought about it, the more he realized that he was lucky that Eugene Spector didn't seem to care about the forgery, once he'd paid him. It had cost him, or more precisely, his deceased wife Mila, as he'd taken the funds from one of her accounts that he controlled. As long as he never crossed paths with the American again, he'd consider that chapter closed.

Jacques turned back to the fax he had been reading. The message was short: *"Dear Mr Mornnais, A mutual friend suggested that I get in touch with you to discuss a business proposition that I think you'll find interesting. I've tried to reach you by phone, but no success. I'd be grateful if you could call me at your earliest convenience. Yours, Thomas Smith.*

"Sir?"

"Yes, Anne-Laure, what is it?" Jacques' mind was on the fax.

"I, I think I've got a fever sir, I'm not feeling well and if you don't mind, I need to go home."

She stood in the middle of the room, her body tensed to pivot out the door. He noticed that she was wearing the jacket she'd come to work in, and her purse hung from her shoulder. "Well yes, if you're ill, then it's best that you get some rest. Let me know when you can come back, I'm counting on you to finish that translation for our next issue."

He had so much to do today: organize an upcoming luncheon, talk with his clients in Brezikstan, and find a buyer for a beautiful fake Signac. Thinking about the painting brought a smile to his lips and he did not hear the door close as Anne-Laure left the office.

#   #   #

Later that afternoon a message spilled out of the fax machine: *Dear Sir, I regret to inform you that my health does not permit me to continue working for Artixia. I am sorry for any inconvenience and thank you for the opportunity. Yours truly, Anne-Laure de Montcalm.*

How annoying, he thought. He'd have to contact the business school and post another job offer. As so often happened when he had to get involved in running the office, Jacques ruminated that this situation was something that Mila would have handled. Still, the trade-off—possession of her accounts and freedom from her nagging in exchange for handling administrative matters—was worth it. Love was not a variable in his calculations.

Jacques turned his attention back to the fax he'd received that morning. Who the fuck was Thomas Smith and what did he want?

FOR MORE ON THE WORLD AND CHARACTERS OF FRENCH DECEPTION, COME TO JANICENAGOURNEY.COM

CASTLE BRIDGE MEDIA RECOMMENDS...

If you liked *A FORGERY IN PARIS*, you might also enjoy reading the following titles from Castle Bridge Media available on Amazon or by order at your favorite book store:

Animal Charmer
By Rain Nox

Austinites
By In Churl Yo

Bloodsucker City
By Jim Towns

THE CASTLE OF HORROR
ANTHOLOGY SERIES
Volume 1
Volume 2: *Holiday Horrors*
Volume 3: *Scary Summer Stories*
Volume 4: *Women Running From Houses*
Volume 5: *Thinly Veiled: The 70s*
Volume 6: *Femme Fatales**
Volume 7: *Love Gone Wrong*
Volume 8: *Thinly Veiled: The 80s*
Volume 9: *Young Adult*
Edited By Jason Henderson
and In Churl Yo
*Edited By P.J. Hoover

Castle of Horror Podcast
Book of Great Horror:
Our Favorites, Top Tens
and Bizarre Pleasures
Edited By Jason Henderson

Dream State
By Martin Ott

FRENCH DECEPTION
A Forgery in Paris
By Janice Nagourney

FuturePast Sci-Fi Anthology
Edited by In Churl Yo

GLAZIER'S GAP
Ghosts of the Forbidden
By Leanna Renee Hieber

The Hermes Protocol
By Chris M. Arnone

Isonation
By In Churl Yo

MID-LIFE CRISIS THRILLERS
18 Miles From Town
By Jason Henderson
Lost Angel
By Sam Knight

Nightwalkers: Gothic Horror Movies
By Bruce Lanier Wright

THE PATH
The Blue-Spangled Blue
By David Bowles
The Deepest Green
By David Bowles

SURF MYSTIC
Night of the Book Man
By Peyton Douglas
Dark of the Curl
By Peyton Douglas

Yesterday's Tomorrows:
The Golden Age of
Science Fiction Movies
By Bruce Lanier Wright

Please remember to leave us your reviews on Amazon and Goodreads!

THANK YOU FOR SUPPORTING INDEPENDENT PUBLISHERS AND AUTHORS!

castlebridgemedia.com

CPSIA information can be obtained
at www.ICGtesting.com
Printed in the USA
BVHW032320140223
658501BV00004B/70